FIBONACCI TALES

FIBONACCI TALES

Knight Tales

eLBe

Fibonacci Tales by eLBe

This book is written to provide information and motivation to readers. Its purpose is not to render any type of psychological, legal, or professional advice of any kind. The content is the sole opinion and expression of the author, and not necessarily that of the publisher.

Copyright © 2018 by eLBe

Printed in the United States of America.

New Leaf Media, LLC
175 S. 3rd Street, Suite 200
Columbus, OH 43215
www.thenewleafmedia.com

CONTENTS

Funeral Guest

"Dad..., there's a bat in the living room."

Jacob shares a glance with Hester and asks, "Who brought a bat in the house?"

"Not the baseball bat, Dad, a bat, the kind that lives in caves and flies at night."

And drinks blood..., the thought rises unbidden as swift as the shadow that shot from the grave when the first shovel of dirt hit. Stepping to Hester Jacob whispers, "what do we do now?"

Hester draws back to meet his eyes and solemnly replies: "You know what must be done. I will keep the children busy while you do it."

"The girl should see...."

Three heartbeats pass, "Yes, she should see the death and the burning. Then she should forget. She won't understand why you will kill the bat and will ask you to let her keep it, to study it, she will say. She's in the basement finding the birdcage to help persuade you to let her keep it."

Jacob is silent a moment and murmurs: "That's a disturbing thought, isn't it?"

"Chilling..., enough to inspire you to capture, kill and burn it before the sun sets and he can shift again."

Jacob wilts under the weight of brother-love and those words, and she reaches to give strength for the choices made by ones loved without condition. Hester witnesses his surrender of the brother love that might check his arm and arrest the inevitable completion of the usual cycles of life.

Reconciled to what must come, Jacob nods a salute, the steps away to battle an ancient adversary now his own to heal and release.

The Best Within

He did not know. I must believe that. If not, *they* will not believe and he will be shunned, he will be unforgiven and become unforgivable. To be unloved is a life worse than death…, he is too young for such grave retribution…, too young to know what he did.

His birth – such a rending pain for so long I feared for him. I feared for me…. I fear for him now, for what he has done and for the dark sin of it. My unborn is still since then. I grieve for him, my child within who does not move; and for the one who lives but did not know.

I have seen him though before he strikes, seen the flash of evil that sparks golden in his eyes and lends force for the stiff-armed blow to the back, for the falling, for the cry, for the pain, for the golden eyes watching as though charting effects of an experiment with clinical curiosity.

He is a *child*! He is a child still, a year from his age of reason. He is *innocent* in the eyes of God….

But *my* weak eyes recognize the delight in his and in the sweet Cupid bow curve of his lips as he watches me writhing in pooling blood embracing my unborn against the pain…, against the pain…, against the pain of golden eyes watching.

To draw out the best within and to evoke the best possible outcome, see only that, for what you believe is what you see. I choose then, for I can choose.

My golden son did not know and my unborn child still lives.

Please, God make it so and let this bitter cup pass from me, oh God forgive me this *cup*….

The Burn Barrel

"Help me empty the burn barrel."

"There's a lot of room in it so we could put stuff on top to… burn a bat. *Why* are you burning the bat?"

Jacob gives a sad, lopsided grin, "we are about to perform an ancient ritual to release Spirit from this form" he raised the bat still pinned in his left thumb and fingers, "and the barrel needs to be empty."

"Have you done this ritual before?"

Jacob hears the challenge in the question and replies gently "once, years ago."

The girl grabs the rim of the drum, spins it over so it peals where it falls. With fierce determination, she upends the barrel, drums the bottom to release the residue, pushes the drum over, sets it upright, and wheels it back into position and ready for the next filling. "Why not since…?" Snatching a forked branch, she scatters the spill of ash, collects a handful of windfall and shoves it in the barrel to form air chambers for oxygen to feed the coming blaze. She does not meet his eyes.

One handed, Jacob follows her example, working silently awhile. "There was no need to release Spirit from form before now."

The girl glances up to see light glint off a tear as her father turns back to wood-gathering. Silently she honors his sorrow speculating on the cause and on his devoted grip on the bat. After a moment she notes "we have killed before and done no ritual."

"Yes, we have killed before; and we have done a ritual, but very different from the one we do today. Before we eat flesh once inhabited by Spirit we bless the food and give thanks to Spirit for living as the animal whose flesh will feed us. Common, we're not done yet, we need more wood in the barrel."

"If you worked with *both* hands we'd be done faster" she snaps. How much firewood *do* we need to burn one bat?"

Jacob's eyes close in the face of unfathomable truth "It is not the bat we purify in this ritual, child. We mean to transmute misuse of the powers of Spirit to inhabit, direct, and to feed on, the life force of another."

The girl falls back, pointing an accusing finger, "Are you saying someone controlled that bat?"

He meets her eyes a silent moment, and replies "When they threw the first shovel of dirt in Uncle's grave today, what did you see?"

She falls back again shaking her head in defiance, "dust…, I saw dust come up from the grave."

"You saw the dust fly up that looked like a bat, and followed it with your eyes until it dissolved…, I watched you."

She spins away hissing "there *should be* things that cannot be real and are never seen because *they do not exist!*"

"There should be, yes" Jacob agrees with quiet conviction. "Get the gasoline can for me will you, and make sure it's full. Hurry, it will be sunset soon and the ritual must be complete before dark."

Carefully dousing the wood and windfall with gasoline, Jacob mouths silent words of healing and release. Striking a match he summons the energy of purification while lighting a circle of twelve leaping flames, then reverently places the 2x4 stake used in the killing in the ring of fire. Experiencing the sorrow of endings, Jacob rejoices in the everlasting promise of renewal and the flames blaze high and roar through the stake until the whole of it glows red. Mouthing ancient words of release, Jacob reaches into the conflagration and reverently places the bat on the *baton rouge* and watches as first it sizzles, then grilles, then flames into a bright angry coal glaring from the ebbing flame. *Carbon to ash.…. This is the first transformation of substance.*

When the embers cool to ash Jacob says "bring the galvanized pail from the shop, and put the gasoline can back in its place." In uneasy silence the girl receives the can and turns to fetch the pail.

When she returns and places the pail where Jacob points, Jacob picks up the drum, carefully tilts the ashes into the pail, and holds it while the girl drums ashes from the barrel to the pail. Returning the drum to its place, Jacob takes up the pail, checks the progress of the sun to horizon, motions the girl to follow, and walks to the hydrant. Mouthing words of transformation, release, and renewal, Jacob opens the tap; carefully wetting the ash to rest, then fills the pail with water. *Ash to water, the second transformation of substance,* he exhales.

"Come," he invites taking up the pail and walking toward the copse of trees beyond the house.

When the girl enters the grove the silent sentience of the trees gives pause until she feels the welcome and invitation to enter. As always, she smiles as the trees encircle her as she follows her father to the abandoned well. Jacob slides the cover aside while humming words of release and assimilation, then tips the grey water into the well. *Water to earth…, the third substantial transformation.*

The cycle is complete, the path of separation is sealed, oneness is restored and the old is new again…, and newly indifferent to myths of the fall.

Hunting Lessons

"With enough bullets anyone can kill from a moving car. There is neither art nor smart to that contest. Tycoons with elephant guns killing buffalo hunts from slow trains advanced destruction of the life of plains Indians by thirty years." Jacob spoke as soft and keen as words can be shared while stalking game that hears the wordless counsel of the wind. "How would a hunting Indian find its game?"

Into the thoughtful silence that follows Jacob whispers "never brush the teeth of a cat."

Twin giggles erupt and are abruptly suppressed. "*What?*"

"What, you don't get the *connection?*" Jacob challenges with a lopsided grin. Both sons eye him askance "Nature has rights of its own and man infringes them at his risk. If I say don't brush the teeth of a cat, what natural rights come to mind?"

"The right of cats to have bad breath?" The eldest offers.

They pace three soft steps and second son counters "if you think about what a cat hunts and eats, you won't expect sweet breath."

"What can you tell about a cat from its prey?"

"They're sprinters, I can outrun a cat in four paces."

"Four?"

A soft chortle whistles over the field "*after* I catch up to it, of course, *then* I can outrun it in four paces."

"What does that tell you about the prey of a cat?"

"It has to be fast and small so one cat can take it; or big, and the pride hunts it together."

"What's a pride, second son?"

The boy grins, "It's a group of cats that lives and hunts together, and maybe share food and den space."

"Well done, my sons." Three paces later Jacob cautions "don't eat the slow moving mice."

Jacob feels their eyes, their startled curiosity, and the processes of thought that seek relationship and connection among disparate facts and beliefs. A whisper announces "slow moving mice are old or sick."

"Or poisoned," adds the other grimly. "Would that hurt the cat that ate it?"

"It would. Pesticides bio-accumulate in the cells of the body."

"Bio-accumulate…? As in… they accumulate *naturally* in the cells?" Jacob nods and notices the hard blinking as the boy's eyes scan the field and margins while his brain processes the interconnections of life. "That means the cat would not have to get the **l**ethal **d**ose **l**evel in one mouse meal, but when it ate *enough* slow moving mice to reach its LDL, it would… *die?*"

"Yes, that is exactly what bio-accumulate means. Good reasoning. Humans aren't much different from cats; we're just bigger and have a higher LDL." Noting the admiration on the face of his second son, Jacob whispers "okay, where are our birds?" The boys exchange a glance and smile and set about solving the puzzle while walking gently over the land.

"Ten o'clock," whispers one "its quail, a covey of… maybe seven."

"Could we get all seven if they scatter?" hisses the other.

"How do you know its quail?"

"See how the heads of the grass moves together, like a flock of something short brushes it low on the stalk. It's a covey of six or seven quail."

Jacob grins, "Remember when you asked why I had you to bring grain here and sow it around?" His head tips back in silent laughter. "Grain fed quail…, what a rich man's feast we will share tonight. First son, what bird have you found?"

"A pheasant cock. Alone, I think."

"Where? Why a pheasant, and why a cock?"

"Four o'clock…. Pheasant because the grain heads whip like a long-legged bird turkey-walks past" the boy bobs his head back and forth to demonstrate, and they see his mime reflected in the heads of the tithed grain. A cock because it moves alone to test for danger while the hen or hens stay alive.

"The birds don't know we're here yet."

"Well then, since there are three of us and eight birds, what do we eat tonight, and how do we get enough for all of us?"

The first and eager son grins and whispers "give me five minutes to circle around the quail and then you drive them toward me, we'll have them in our cross fire and we'll drop them all."

Jacob's laughter trills like the call of the morning hawk singing dawn-delight "how do we know where you are, and you where we are, when we take off the safety and start shooting quail…, that scatter in every direction, as quail will do?"

The eldest tucks his head to cover a grin "oh…, bullet in body…, hurt. I *like* the safety catch now, and not getting a bullet in my body. We'll stay together, Dad."

"Good plan. How'd that bullet in your leg change the way you feel about hunting for food?"

"We kinda *grow* it Dad, we feed it, we even talk to it…" he glances away blinking quickly.

"Ever talk back?"

"Dad…, does it *bother* you that you are the adult here?"

Jacob grins, "Not at all. The animals *do* talk. They talk to you too, but you don't hear…, or *do* you?"

They walk seven paces in silent unity. "Do the trees…, do the trees talk too?"

"Yes, but trees are very old energies and the things we find important they don't understand, so trees will always just say that you are perfect and do no wrong."

The boys grin warmly as they walk to the quail willing to serve. "I *like* the way trees talk."

"So, son, how did being shot change the way you hunt?"

"I hoped you'd forget I didn't answer."

Jacob chortles like a whippoorwill "not a chance," he whispers.

The sun dips slowly, casting alien-long shadows ahead that glow in a nimbus of light. "I want to kill clean," the boy replies, "with one shot to the head. No pain. No *time* for pain." Looking long to his father he adds, "I need to know I can do that every time, Dad. The Spirit - as you name it - that feeds me deserves no less. How do I shoot that true?"

"How did the Indians do it with only bow and arrow?"

They pass a long silent pace and then the answer sighs "they called an animal to volunteer to feed the tribe and be their clothes and shelter."

Jacob's eyes crinkle. "Yes, we need only to remember the circle of life and man's role in it.

That was a worthy bullet you took then, son, and you a worthy man to learn its lesson so quick and clear." Reaching into a pocket Jacob pulls out a spent bullet holding it to the light. "I saved it for you, for the day you knew gun safety has less to do with the safety catch than with the heart of the hunter. Without heart, the hunt is carnage. Keep the bullet as a reminder that you are a circle of life hunter."

"Do I have to shoot myself to be a circle of life hunter too?" the younger son pipes.

Jacob hoots like a barn owl "No, son, only heart. You *can* shoot yourself though…; oh, and if I bring home another son with a bullet in him, your mother is likely to put one in me and then make me drive us all to the doctor."

The Barren Wife

"The Daughters should have a say in what's done about Father. It's our children too who are spoiled by his randy love. The Daughter mothers *should* also have a say in protecting our children."

"And the Sisters…?

Hester flashes a lopsided grim grin, "The Sisters got their message to Father soon after the pregnant nun 'retired' to the nunnery. Our sons and daughters came at risk then.

Jacob nods amiably, "the Daughters have as much at risk as the Knights." He looks away, irritated, then snaps, "And, Father would not have owned the problem in the presence of women, nor would he have willingly been part of the solution, and we didn't leave much but agreement for Father to contribute."

Hester steps away to refresh their coffee keeping her eyes averted. Firmly replacing the pot on the burner she says "he never…," She frowns tight, "Father didn't do anything to *our* sons did he?"

Jacob chortles, and when Hester looks up he beckons her back to her chair. "Remember when I invited Father to come bless our herd, and I just *happened* to be castrating a yearling when he arrived?" Hester nods; Jacob continues, "Well, they say a picture is worth a thousand words, so I gave Father a picture so crystal clear that he didn't need one spoken word to take my message." Jacob's eyes dance with glee, "The boys were helping with the gelding, and when Father saw me with my pliers and both boys helping with the castration, he went a *very* unlovely bilious yellow and excused himself until we finished. As Father left the barn he assured us our new steer would get a very *special* blessing when we were done. Our sons' eyes blessed *me* when Father left us to our work; and we shared an openly conspiratorial clucking, crowing, bawling laugh." He nods agreement, "Unrepentant…, to the man."

Hester studies her husband and murmurs "You *planned* that. You gelded that animal for the sole purpose of showing Father what he puts at risk if he doesn't keep his pants zipped when performing his priestly duties."

"With intention, planning, and premeditated aforethought; yes, I did that." He adds a defensive, "I feel bad about the bull though! He'd have sired *many* fine calves to the herd." He winces and moans "and *so* much money lost in stud fees...."

"Husband, you are disconcertingly like your father when you have decided on a thing. You are one eyed and uncompromising to the end." she grins despite herself, "and you do it with sinister innocence." She is silent a moment then asks? "What if Father had *not* gotten the message? "Wait, Jacob. On second thought, I do *not* want to know." Smiling faintly she adds "I am continually thankful that you are on my side. Tell me what happened in the Knights' meeting with Father."

Jacob frowns then slides a hand over hers. "Father admitted that he is a randy son who winked at the vow of celibacy and took the penitent's path of silent and frequent confession and 'purifying' self-castigation. Knowing that complicity inspires secrecy Father made it an *honor* to be chosen to 'help' him on the altar and always stressed the need to keep their secret forever, and to never tell anyone."

"Jacob, *stop*! Hester gasps; "you *must* not tell me this. I too know how to use your *special pliers* and I am *sorely* tempted to use them for an altogether other objective other than growing large meaty beef for the table. This man is our parish priest...." Fighting a grin and failing, she revels in glee "It would not *do* for a Daughter to castrate her Father; and throw his balls to the sea, I suppose. Our parish is far too small to house that mighty myth, Jacob.

"Tell me about the Knights' solution instead."

"Hedda Geis is a Daughter isn't she?" Hester nods with an arch-browed frown; Jacob sips coffee. "Well, as it turns out, Hedda loves Father – her words, according to Rinhold; and she will happily serve as housekeeper and cook for Father, and take care of his physical needs while she's there." Studying the steam curling off his coffee Jacob whispers surly sour stoic "so that Father can keep taking care of *the spiritual needs of his parishioners*." Despite himself, his last six words come out as a tearing growl.

Hester inhales sharply, and whispers "Hedda's barren." Jacob nods. "What did Reinhold say about this?"

"I quote. 'She's barren. She loves sex. She'll take care of me before, and after, she takes care of Father. I'm retired. The extra income will help.'"

"He said it that *dispassionately?*" Jacob nods. "That is *painfully* cynical."

"Or practical." Jacob defends to the jury of his cup, then adds "Words don't change reality, Hes. Perfect solutions are of God's realm. They are as rare as hen's teeth where man lives. Human plans cannot anticipate all the ways an issue shows up in life, Hes." Sliding a hand over hers, he adds "life is imperfect, wife-mate, sometimes only an imperfect solution meets the life need."

Hester sighs "I know. Still, I want to protect Hedda from what she knows is wrong and wants anyway!" Lowering her eyes she admits softly "I have a passion to punish Father for the harm he's done the people he came to shepherd and to protect. Why *not* ask the Church to assign him to another parish, or to another role in the Church?"

Jacob numbers the reasons on his fingers "That moves him to other people who don't know his problem. That's avoidance, not a solution. There is nowhere *else* to move him. He's too young to retire. We are a small parish, insignificant to a global church *with* a past Pope that took the name Innocent to declare his blamelessness for being born *the son of a Pope*." He clicks his tongue and spits, "I'm not over that yet…, and it's only *been centuries* ago.

"We either resolve the problem with Father, or we keep living with the outcomes and adapting to them because ignoring the truth *does not work*. There is no perfect solution, Hes, but this one works. Hedda and Reinhold will make it work," his fierce eyes meet hers, "with or without Father's help. Reinhold agreed to the plan first to protect the children, then for Hedda," he shakes his head in awe and perplexity, "for her *good love* for Father; and then for the parish, and for the community."

The couple silently studies the order of the willing Knight's advocacy aims, and Jacob speaks. "Sheriff Ben was there. The Knight in him goes militant when talk turns to the pregnant nun, and it did. He wants to go strike the head off a serpent, or dethrone an arch-demon, or some other-worldly worthy deed."

"I think Father remembered my special pliers because he glanced my way, and *quickly* assured Ben that when he became a priest he believed he could be celibate, that he *could* manage his urges by censure, denial, and penance. Now he knows better, and willingly accepted the Knights' solution."

"Did Father tell the truth, do you think?"

"Truth is more a journey than a destination, Hes. When she prepares the favorite meal of a guest, Hedda will eat with Father and his guest. Father will *never again* call children from school to help him." Jacob scratches his palm vigorously, "My hand *aches* to use my good tool on our good priest."

He sobers sipping coffee, "Maybe Father heard the truth this time and let it set him free to be the priest he always hoped to be. He's not the first to feel shame for his physical needs and act in guilty, shameful ways. Did you know Father was zealous about mortification to discipline the body into obedience? I'd hate to be his dog." He grins and shrugs, "Maybe not; for I surely *would* bite the hand that feeds me.

"Father owns some punishing beliefs, Hes, and has scars to tell the power of those beliefs."

"Scars?"

"Before Father arrived; and after the Knights were sworn to confidence, Reinhold told what Hedda said him about seeing Father's scars when she was 'cleaning his private office'.

"Private office?" Hester's eyes dance dangerous delight, "Tell…."

"I *thought* you would go there…, the Knights certainly did. It seems that Hedda sometimes prepared special meals for Father and quickly noticed that each special meal she prepared was the favorite food of Father's guest. One day, after talking with Reinhold, Hedda asked Father if she could prepare for him *her* favorite meal and be his guest to eat it. Before Father could catch his breath to speak, Hedda quietly and pointedly confessed to Father that she was barren and could bear no child.

"As it turns out, Hedda's favorite meal *is* Father's favorite meal, and soon the Knights are calling it a shake and no bake meal; and that rampage continued until our watch Knight came to say Father was on the way so we could settle down and be knightly before Father arrived."

"You *planned* this? You set a watchman?"

Jacob nods solemn as a judge, "Indeed we did. We Knights did *not intend* to need Father's forgiveness *before* our meeting with him began. The unexpected blessing of spending our anger in high camp is that no one got down the ceremonial sword and rebuked Father into a gelding before the meeting began." Hester tips back her head in opening, easing, healing laughter. "It was an uncommonly dramatic evening, Hes," Jacob manages his glee to add "one of the strangest Knights gatherings I have *ever* participated in."

On Being a Keeper

The problem with being a Keeper is that I have no choice, which means I have to protect the innocent from the predations of the fallen angels. I am bound to protect those who are innocent of blame, harm, or sin.

Without 'proof', whatever that means. As a Keeper, I may not judge by my own lights. Instead, as a Keeper, I must assume that all are innocents until I have proof positive that they are not. What Nephilim spawn would be simple enough to assume that a thinking man would not see the unceasing evil of their ways, and know them for who they are by what they do? And their belligerent bullying ways are time tested and repeatedly proven since the time of Lucifer's challenge to the Maker God that he'd made Earth too rich, and too lush, and too ceaselessly abundant for man to ever be tempted to turn away from the Source of all and every good and blessed thing..., and have a go at it on his own with his own personal band of militantly sociopath sycophants.

Ergo, as Keeper, I have no functional free will. The Divine Maker gave away that priceless gift He'd given exclusively to man and woman in Eden's Garden, so that He could enjoy his Seventh day rest, and not have to contend with dangerously deviant fallen angel demons itching for an excuse to wage another bitter battle royal against God to take from Source more power than Source has? Es totalmente tonto!

So I have to ask myself, why would the all-knowing Divine Creator of all and everything, sit on his divine derriere and do nothing to keep Beelzebub and his fallen cohorts from taking their war of attrition to Earth and preying on the life force energy of man that God created as caretakers of the new blue planet, and all the winged, footed, fined, and hooved creations he just made? Es totalmente tonto!

I personally believe that the first maker is not loco, and is not slap-dash out of his divine mind. But why did He make Keepers? And Keepers of what? And of who?

And what does a Keeper do? Why does he do it, and most of all how does he do it?

Those are my thoughts since Mati made me..., then forcefully expelled and propelled me to my exile half way around the world from where we were..., and they still are..., living among the walking dead.

Mati made me a Keeper though, not a feeder bleeder. There's the good news, and my praise report, but I don't know what to do with it and why. It is curious though that I know who the Nephilim are. I see them now, or more truly, I feel the weight of the energy of them. I didn't before Mati made me.

And..., I don't suppose I could *protect the innocents among us from the predations of the fallen angels who stalk the earth in human form if I can't see them with my physical eyes – and I can't. And I can't see them with my inner eye either. Fighting blind that would be..., and Mati didn't put me in this Keeper role to fight blind or outnumbered. I hope.*

Still, I do wish I could take out some of the Nephilim among us who greedy feed off innocents through fraud, lies, and exorbitant interest rates. We have 'a fair and equal' justice system to take care of that for us the Nephilim overlords assure us, while patting us down, picking our pockets, and the gold from our teeth! G-r-r-r-r-r-r-r!

God, I really do *wish you'd let me kill 'em and transform 'em because I know them true and sure for who they are. And, I want to do this because* Mati made me *to be a Keeper of the innocents against them.*

And, dad gum it, yes, you did say 'justice is mine,' and you said that you are a jealous god. Still, I was never a patient person, let alone obedient. Don't Tisk your tongue at me! You made me this way..., just so the record is straight between us.

I hear you laughing. It's not funny, nor loving..., when you laugh at me and I'm baring my heart and soul and telling you my very truth! Loving God indeed! That brings me full circle to why you let Beelzebub have control over Earth. If you were on this side *of life, you would be called criminally insane!*

Or divinely inspired. Words are tricky things. I don't use words that much because there are so many synonyms for human words in any linguae franka man uses. That whole Tower of Babel thing is an edifying myth of man. And it's not my tale. Its man's tale, and it shows man's tail of arrogance that says that man can somehow outnumber and outsmart the divine numberless and infinite intelligence. I AM a circle whose center is everywhere and whose circumference is nowhere. Man cannot comprehend the divine I AM. And you aren't supposed to.

I gave man free will – alone among the creatures great and small I made to purify, enrich, recycle, and, ultimately – to destroy the blue planet called Earth. How will I do that? Through the mind, brain, hands, legs, and body of man exercising the gift of free will and dominion – in my usage, being Keepers of the planet – through all its evolutionary phases.

Did you know that every sun was once a blue planet with a life giving sun? Just like Earth, and its life giving, spirit inspiring sun. 'Sun rise, sunset, swiftly go the days, one season following another, laden with happiness and tears'.

Suns burn out over time, and without the sun, blue planets fall out of orbit and become the fodder for new suns that support new blue planets. You could think of it as a cosmic recycling process. It's all good.

Except maybe from the very personal perspective of a human one, like you. One who, in his humanness, has utterly forgotten and forsaken his godliness, and so he miscreates..., as a Nephilim does.

Nephilim have no power to hurt or harm you. I did not grant them that, though they demanded it. They cannot hurt humans physically anyway. But they sure can fuck with your minds. They can make you think you can and should take the law into your own hands, and make right what you know is wrong.

There's a difference between knowing a thing in your mind, and knowing the same thing in your heart. The greater mind lies in the heart, not in the skull, as most men think. Even you, made a Keeper, imagine your way is to justify a fiercely forced solution because you think it is in the best interest of all. Really?

So, tell me this, how is it in the best interest of your neighbors, and your community, for you to take out the bankers, who are the money lenders of today with a newer name? Bank collapse..., mean anything to you? Stock market crash? You can bring that trauma/drama right home here to your small community.

Tell me, what happens to the mortgage you and most of your neighbors have on homes and property and the mortgage is held by the local bank run by Nephilim you want to take out because you see their greed and judge it evil?

Remember the run on the banks when the over inflated stock market crashed and the value of currency plummeted? Who was hurt most in the end? The fat cats who jumped from tall buildings? Nah! They chose their way out of the consequences of the crash they precipitated. Their wives and families now, they paid the price due for the men's venial vacuous rape of the masses at the bottom of the pyramid.

Interesting symbol for the back of the US dollar, don't you think? But that's a discussion for another day.

What does your heart say is the right way to keep the greater good for the greatest number of people, right now, today – this one day that the Lord has made?

My heart says that I pray for them without ceasing. It also says that I don't kill them..., even though I know how to make them dead, and how to transform them into inert mineral matter. Not yet. That comes another day.

The day Mati comes home..., here, for the first..., and the last time. Wing home sweet spirit, I await that day with a grateful, and an achy breaky heart. Lord, this is hard for me and it isn't even real right now.

This is what a Keeper knight does though. And I never promised that my work would be easy for man to do, only that submitting to my unfathomable will is always in man's best interest.

The conflicted pain that twists and knots your gut though — that's optional.

Thank you for helping me know this truth about being a Keeper. It does give wings to my heart knowing that I will not act on the power of my personal human will that is unenlightened and untempered by the Power of Understanding.

Get the first understanding, the Master said, and so I do, and I am fortified and borne up by the wings of angels. Make me your instrument....

How many angels can I call to guard, guide and protect me from the pervasive assaults of my E.G.O. will?

The infinite unknowable is not bounded by the numbers man has devised to count and order and make 'rational' the work of his own hands. The number you ask for is for the comfort of your rational mind — it serves no purpose nor objective of Divine mind. Put another way, I cannot tell you the number of angels you will need or want to call, because I don't know. That makes no logical nor heart-centered sense to me. Pretty much I get everything but man when he's still bound like Prometheus to chains he forged and set deep into rock so a demon lord could be captured and bound there.

What are your personal and self-forged Promethean chains? Yeah, dammit, pick a number in your rational mind, one you're comfortable. Tell me that number.

Oh, thanks for the helpful personal example. I get it now, any number my rational mind would choose is both too limiting, and too expansive to be functional in picking a 'rational' number of angels to call. So, I must willingly yield and surrender my conscious mind need to know the numinous number of angels.

Hah, good job! God. That lifted me, on angel wings, above and beyond the conscious mind's need to know all the physical world facts, figures, and data points, and still stay rational right here on physical plane where truly shitty Nephilim energies walk the earth in human form.

They have no aura, God, the Nephilim. Why is that?

You tell me.

I don't know. That is why I asked you.

You do know. But not in the conscious mind of you that looks not beyond physical world 'explainable' reasons using empirical evidence to 'prove' the primitive body wisdom of the fight or flight response I designed into man.

It's an ancient wisdoms that was encompassed and wisely taught and applied by pre-priestly ancient masters of every people. The ancient wisdom is denied and denigrated by the priested ones who bend knee only to the fictional law of not enough. Like the All and Everything has any capacity to be not enough? Que tonto!

Yet, Nephilim in habits pulpit preach penance and payment as ways of mitigating and even obviating the wages of sin for those bold enough to follow their own inner light-way to their indwelling still small voice always calling from the heart center. When was the last time you went into your inner closet and spoke in silence to the one who hears and speaks in silence? Come soon.... We have missed you.

'By their work ye shall know them', my chosen Keeper. Only by the work of the greedy feeder bleeders do you know them. Because you are a Keeper and need to know that you do clear see into the muddy aura that is the hallmark of Nephilim. That is always how you will know them.

By enticing the unenlightened, the Nephilim open in him an unchallenged and unfettered direct access into the mind of man.

*Why do you imagine I would have even tolerated that, let alone permitted it? And beyond that, you have decided that I was unconscionably negligent because I wanted to take Sunday afternoon off? Really? Que tonto, hejo! That is an assumption I find irritatingly irrational on the face of it — as in: make an **ass** out of yo**u** and **me**.*

But I AM a God who is slow to anger.... Now, back to the question you are avoiding, how will your fellow man know you other than by the work that you do? They will be looking at outcomes here, not motives.

And 'need' has nothing to do with it in any event does it? It's all a God job and there is no need or lack in the Divine One. Covering a 'need' cannot be part of my work as a Keeper. My work is only to stand guard and to protect the innocent from the dark delusions of the Fallen Ones.

And where have they fallen from?

From grace.

And where have they fallen to?

To Earth..., where man walks.

Why would I let that happen? If the fallen ones are my creations, as all of life is, why would I allow fallen angels to walk like men among my defenseless creations of man? Es increable tonto, no?

It is.... Ergo, you did not make man defenseless..., nor needy. You made man to be Keepers of Earth and every living thing in, on, under, and around it. Oh my! That's a paradigm shift. It changes everything.

Do I throw out my Bible then?

Do you throw the baby out with the bath water?

So then..., the Bible is in its infancy? Barely a toddler? Is that what you are suggesting? You're laughing *at me for asking that..., so then, I must already know the answer.*

So well that you don't even know that you know it.

Ours is a blue planet, still in its infancy. When it reaches its cosmic 'best by' date, like man, Earth must naturally begin to devolve and dissipate into source energy, and it does that by releasing the density of the matter of it that enables it to appear as substance on the physical plane. And it goes out like a big bang, doesn't it?

That's a question only a human could ask, and then, only from his E.G.O. consciousness.

Ouch! That hit close to home.

Was that hard hit by chance a product of a big bang of Nephilim energy imploding inside you?

Hum-m-m, interesting thought. I can work with that. Disenchantment is never pleasant, but being released from the captivation of misconception is a decidedly saving grace. So..., being a Keeper doesn't automatically make me a hero?

In whose eyes do you want to be seen as 'hero'? Who cares other than you? Will you also covet a tomb of an unknown to vaunt your E.G.O. to a relevance it does not enjoy in life? Where is Scotty when you need an E.G.O. man beamed back down to reality of life on mother Earth?

Now you're laughing at me.

Laugh with me then. Or bitch and moan. Make of your navel gazing self a babe that does *get thrown out with the bath water. Your call.*

I AM the creator of all and everything manifest and unformed. That is my work. Period. Punto. The end. Why do you suppose I created man?

To be the Keeper....

Of?

Earth, and its inhabitants..., everything you created.

And the Nephilim?

Yeah, Nephilim too. You are the Source of all and everything and that has to include fallen angels. This makes my head hurt.

That's because you are trying to explain a Divine call that you imagine man would not do. That is only possible if you believe you are separate from me because you have a body mind brain Earth suit and I don't. Which of us is incomplete do you think?

Hum-m-m, you are the creator, and you made man the Earth Keeper, and you made Nephilim who embody looking for all the world just like man.

How do you know them then?

By their works..., I shall know them. I feel you grinning at me now, what's so damned funny?

Just thinking about your assumption of the work of destroying – or undoing – what I made, because you judge it evil. Where do you suppose evil came from if not from the creator of all and everything?

You simply will not tolerate me thinking rationally will you?

How's that working for you?

Why do you suppose I endowed the greater mind of the heart into man if man believes that the only arrow in his quiver is the mind brain of man? Stop trying to reason it out because logic is incompetent of higher level thinking. You're thinking like a Nephilim by the way.... Just wanted you to know that. So, to rephrase my question, 'where did the destructive impulses of man come from if not from the Creator?

Gees, you are one twisted mind. So let me think this through – because I have to get it in my conscious mind so it is functional for me... as a Keeper. You created evil as well as good....

I created day and night too. And, I set the greater light of the sun to give meaning to 'day', and the lesser light of the moon to enlighten the night.

Metaphysically the moon represents personal intelligence, the intellect. The moon's light is supplied by the sun, which is the metaphysical symbol of spiritual light. Methinks you are moon blind right now, meaning that you are blinded by how brilliantly endowed you think you are, my hesitant Keeper.

So, to remedy that, please allow your intellect to be enlightened by your own personal spiritual light that resides in your heart center, and ask your heart self why I'd create Nephilim energy, and give them equal stride with man who has 'not fallen'? That's an oxymoron actually since the spirit that inspires man is always a unique expression of the divine. 'Not fallen' may be the very definition of oxymoron.

Then, the good, the bad, and the ugly..., are all fallen from the grace of God, and all are in the process of regeneration that begins the unification of Spirit, soul, and body in spiritual oneness.

It's a divine do-loop, you dizzying deity you. And all of it is part of your cosmic scheme to perpetually evolve and expand the universe through a perpetual process of contraction and creation.

So..., I don't have to kill anyone do I?

No, you won't.

The caldera vamp feeder bleeders and their made ones will be delivered to you already rendered mostly dead, sun-dried, and pre-packaged in a locked gilded cage.

It is the vampires that will Mati call to follow her to your home… made a safe place for people like them in a whole other country, where bats are only night flier voracious insect eaters. They do make really foul slippery reeking guano though. It is not a redeeming quality of the night fliers.

And you will have help those bat matt black full moon nights. She'll teach you how to shoot too. Don't get huffy with me! She is that good. And, she's a gifted healer. At the end of each full moon night she will softly blur your memory, and that of your son, so you sleep restful and well in the dark hours remaining; and awaken rise rested and refreshed when the sun rises again and a day's work calls you.

Time to be Calling All Angels

Can we call angels?

Why not?

Um – because we are fallen ones, spawn of the Arch Demon. Mati equivocates.

You're not. You haven't been made yet. That comes later today, when Mater wakes up from her long day's nap, and comes downstairs to do her dastardly deed on you. Where do you imagine that you are at fault..., for what has not yet happened?

You're so fucking logical it makes me crazy sometimes.

You're welcome. And if Mater heard you say the f-word, she'd wash your mouth out with her handmade lye soap."

Augh! That's a disgustingly disturbed thought! Would this be before or after she makes me her vamp man slayer whore?

Does it matter?

No.

So back to the question you try to evade – why can't we call angels? Start with you, please, and then you can explain why the Divine Loving One would punish Naomi and me because we were made feeder bleeders for the blood drinkers against our will and without our prior knowledge of what was going on in the castle, or that the castle masters were blood drinkers. And then explain why we are blamed for the mostly dead part, because I am personally grievously offended that my free will *wasn't even considered by the forever thirsty ones, including Mater. The brat boy master made her. She had the hots for him anyway mostly because all the really good stuff was in his room — oh fuck, his suite of rooms. He may be the Dictionary definition the word 'bastard'.*

And we cannot control that! But we damned sure can change it — and we will, *Mati.*

Will is one of the Twelve Powers of Man. By trial and error, man has demonstrated proof positive of the outcomes that flow naturally when the Power of Will is exercised without the prior application of the Power of Understanding. We live in a time when the war-makers of the world and the financiers who profit from the cost and carnage give proof positive of outcomes when man's will is unenlightened by understanding. It is the signal mark of the Nephilim — the unredeemed fallen angels. Never before has man devised so many vile new ways to eliminate the opposition that it created.

Witness the wholescale carnage of Hitler's war of attrition.

Witness the number of stunningly vile petty tyrants who seized control of European governments, and the military, and ordered nationalized local militia to fire on the protesters, people they grew up with and went to school with, until the protests dissolved for want of protestors. *That's just wrong! It is pure Nephilim evil! Nice segue back to Mater if I must say so myself.*

Mater was made by the vamp master who made her in his stunningly elegantly appointed suite. That was the year we moved here at the invitation of our newfound noble cousins.

A year later, Mater led me like a lamb to slaughter to the first vile vamp sister – probably named Lucretia – of the brat master because it was now her *turn to be the maker, and the first drinker.*

A year after that, Mater came and led Naomi to the second sister because it was her *turn to be the maker and first drinker.*

This year it's Mater's turn to be the maker and the first drinker. The brat boy vamp demands first rights again. *He's way tired of being second drinker, bad enough to yield maker's right to his sisters, but to yield first rights to a* made *one? Preposterous!*

No way will Mater yield! She knows what he demands like a spoiled first child. Mater is not a happy camper. And you will remember, please, that Mater doesn't take revenge. She takes her rights..., and lets the chips fall where they may.

And this is the cool part, Mati, Naomi interjects enthusiastically, *Mater will preemptively defend her making of you because, she will say, that she made you to be her spy at the best little whorehouse in town, and to report potential threats to her so she in turn can report them to the masters so they can preemptively defend – or eliminate – those threats.*

She's good, don't you think? It's not every woman who'd have *the balls to defy her vampire maker let alone teach him to like it brilliantly much. We are her daughters. We got Mater's brass balls!*

Our only question is, do we lug 'em around like lead weights, or do we apply them to incline an outcome all of us want, to leave the world a better place than it was when we came? I know what Da would do. I know what Mater is doing, and why; and I know what we will do and why we will do it. Shall we intentionally *make it a class act?* There are amens and clinking wine glasses all around. Gotta love Lambrusco.

We'll best begin our mission by calling in a squadron or so of angels. She shrugs a defense: *The Master did say that we have not because we ask not. Let's not compromise the success of our mission for want of asking God for what he said he'd send, if only we ask.* Their linked hands form a pyramid with a sister as grounding point of the trilateral star.

Does this mean we call three angles?

Or thirty. Cora poses.

Or three thousand, suggests Phoebe rationally and eagerly.

Amen that! They agree in one mind vibration that induces musical tones into their body mind brains. They feel a sudden down rush of air as falling angels land to ring rosy cozy around them. *We are so loved. We are so blessed.*

I see the angels beside you..., Archangels, actually. Mati muses with a smile for both sisters. *Which suggests that we need to call the architype angels, the ones known as Archangels. Who's your Archangel Clara? Oh, don't think the answer! Let the Archangel tell you, they are God's messengers after all. Let the Archangel tell you his name. Or her name. Angels don't have gender. They are genderless, and genderful.*

Who's your Archangel? Clara asks stalling for time.

Jeremiel, the truth teller who goes into shadows comfortably. Hence, I can be the double agent courtesan Mother has 'destined' me to be, the dark side; and still be the principled truth teller who cannot *profess to believe what she knows is not true in the 'Truth' sense of the word. In Truth, made or unmade, I am* not *a vampire. But I can play that role to the hilt, and Mater will believe I am her obedient courtesan, and totally not see that I am also a double agent spy. That's Jeremiel.*

Your turn, Clara.

Clara smiles and counters: *Since you went first, Mati, Naomi is second, and I, the first, am the last, as the Master foretold.*

Excellent line, Clara! You are good, Naomi enthuses. *And I see through you.* She smirks and adds: *And I will go second..., as it should be...,* she bridles a chortle, *so that the first can be the last.*

My Archangel is Zadkiel, the sociable but studious multitasker. Fortunately for our mission, I am a studious multitasker, and, I am also sufficiently sociable to make Mater feel dominant even though she is decidedly *not dominant in this castle inhabited by thirsty, entitled, blood lusty walking dead vamps.*

In case you wondered, Mater is in another space and time just now and she can't hear us even if we were to talk aloud, which we won't. Naomi zips a thumb and forefinger over her lips. *Your turn, Clara.*

Metatron, is my first Archangel, the hardworking, industrious, inventive, curious, serious perfectionist. Which I am, and a good thing for us too. The sisters nod agreement. *His colors are violet and green. My colors. His signal stone is watermelon tourmaline.*

And, my lady Archangel is Jophiel, the lover of beauty and orderliness. Her color is dark pink, her stone is rubellite.

You are unquestionably a perfectionist, sister dear, and you do love the beauty of orderliness. Naomi is impressed, *you could readily tame a savage beast without a fight, Clara. I am in awe, once again.*

So maybe you will support Mater when she goes to tell the sucky vamp man that she made Mati, in her turn; and why that is a very *good thing for the vamp family. I so want to hide and watch, so keep your mental link with us open when you cover Mater when she baits the beast in his own man cave.*

Yes, please, Mati agrees. *So..., why did you get to call two angels?*

What, do you think God as a maximum on the number of angels any one person can call? Clara poses.

If you will remember, on the seventh day when Jehovah God rested, Beelzebub and his most prickly militant seconds came to the resting Creator, and Beelzebub fawned and gawped and gaped and could not say enough nice things about the beautiful blue planet He'd created, Then the devious demon lord pointed out the obvious — du'oh!, that everything man could ever possibly need, was provided for in excess. The whole planet was an exquisite Garden of Eden, and as such, God's human kind would be his untested and untempered minor minions. Absent temptation, they would never have any reason, cause or motivation to assume their inherent duty to maintain *the pretty blue planet.*

Well, it was his day of rest, and God didn't really want to explain to the more brawn than brain fallen angel leader and his prickly sycophant minions, everything you ever wanted to know about the universe and everything in it, including that the divine ultimate recycling effort is *for every blue planet to — consume itself, I suppose — at the hands of its upright primary caregiver occupants, thereby evolving itself into a sun that supports the next blue planet thrown off in the creative cosmic recycling effort. It was the Sabbath day, okay, and anyone who thinks that has any relationship whatsoever to doing mental or physical combat with fallen angels is simply dangerously dumb, disturbed and disoriented. A foolishly misguided one who denies that the role of man in life is to devolve pretty blue planets into suns. Oh, where are the Pleiadians when you need them?*

Clara, I can't decide if you are utterly brilliant, or dangerously disturbed, Mati snarks with a frown.

What's the difference? Functionally? Clara demands with utmost indifference, then adds: *What's the functional difference between me calling two Archangels and you two calling only one?*

And, if that is a problem for you why don't you simply stop being the eager victim, and stop demanding to be a victor instead, and just call another angel? Both victim and victor roles are inherently serpentine, which means both choices are to be powerless and powerlessly cast down like falling leaves in autumn winds.

Clara backs a hand to her brow, contorts her face into a crying clown mask and whines: *Oh woe! Poor powerless Mati will be made a vampire by mean manipulative Mater, and there is not a bloody thing she can do about it. Except wallow in her currently fave rave victim trauma/drama.*

Victims need victors to push them down and keep them helpless and abused. She pauses for a clear eyed look at Mati. *You really are terribly torn about your victor of choice being Mater or the vamp masters. You cannot even conceive of yourself in the victor role can you?*

No. Mati thinks with downcast eyes. *I don't like the femme fatal dominatrix role, even on stage.*

Too much like Mater?

Well – yeah – except for the femme fatal part. Mater's got the dominatrix part down to a T, except for the clingy femme fatal getup, which she will not wear since Da died.

Can you criticize Mater for that after what happened to her after Da was killed? The hot topic of debate among the neighbors was whether Da inseminated you into Mater before he died, or if you were the bastard child of another man she took to her bed before Da died! They hissed like serpents that you weren't Da's daughter at his funeral. That is mean spirited vile slander worthy of Nephilim! For all that, Mater never stinted in her love for you, Mati, through the years of her shaming even after you were born and were clearly a full genetic sister of me and Naomi. Clara smiles and confesses: *We did protect and defend you from the hatefulness of your schoolmates who were as mean-spirited as their own maters in victimizing innocents simply because they are smaller. Mater knew..., when we came home from school with raw knuckles and paddle marks from the hot rod discipline of the teaching sisters.*

You see, the know-nothing nuns would not believe that the well-dressed polite little daughters of tithing parishioners would know a thing about how babies are made..., innocents every one. Despite the fact that most of them grew up on farms and know that 'the woman lies like fresh tilled soil while the man guides his plow and plants his seed'.

Mater protected you from cruelty by innuendo neglect when you were a child. She protects you even now. Whether or not you know and accept that, Mater still protects and keeps your innocence. You're an excellent actress, Mati, but this is real life. This is not a stage. The curtains will not fall dramatically when our last act in the play of life is ended. The curtains will not be opened for you to receive applause and tossed roses of your adoring fans.

In real life right now, Mati, you are more likely to be tossed a hand grenade than roses. Pull up your big girl panties and behave like a wise, well informed, and at will adult. Or – I can slap you into next week – and catch up with you later.

You're cold! Mati shivers.

No. I am a clear eyed realist. By making you and sending you to spy for her, for the vamp masters, Mater still protects you from the hard realities of life; and instead of appreciating that, you have confirmed Mater as your personal persecutor – you need no other – including the vampires who will *make you if Mater does not. Mater is your protector. Still. Hers is a brilliant strategy – if you will allow that – because she protects you from the greedy needy feeder energy of the Masters. Yes, I know the vamp master is sexy beyond belief, and that there's a dangerous exciting sensual edginess to him you have not found in any other man, so you skip carefree through la-la land more enchanted by his conniving illusions than Mater ever was. And, you should know that Mater was 'honored', her word, that he personally*

*wanted to be her maker and no other. Let me be the first one to fuck you…,
and Mater's all weak kneed and pussy wet.*

*Whew! Cold, Clara. Why don't you just say it saw-tooth edgy like you
see it.* Naomi intervenes pacifically. *It's almost like you want Mati to
despise Mater.*

*No, I want her to get over her small self-consciousness and make room
in her awareness to comprehend a higher self, and a higher calling than the
victim's revenge, and a higher self than the victor brutality she's claimed as
her next exclusive role in life.*

What's left? Mati asks, her native inquisitiveness liberating her tight-
laced habitual small self-awareness.

Verity consciousness, Naomi replies, releasing Clara to be a listener
and observer for a while.

Truth *consciousness?* Mati poses.

*Yes. What do you suppose verity consciousness is? What do you imagine
it feels like? How do you see yourself differently when you see yourself in
truth consciousness?*

*Verity consciousness is when I get, and I accept, that I AM a beloved
child and a unique expression of the infinite Divine Maker. Wow! That's a
quantum shift in consciousness.*

*What does it feel like? Faith, that God did not waste or misplace one
Divine atom in the ideation and manifestation of who I AM in truth. The*

waste has been mine all the years I spent jealously protecting my starring roles of the abused victim and the dominant dominating victor. I'd have gone to the vamp master's room as innocently and unprotected as Mater did.

OMG – that's a hugely transformative *reality bite. Thank you, Naomi. But for your clear eyed slap upside my head, I'd still be hating and fighting Mater and she's not the problem. Sorry, I went all Nephilim punishing edgy there. Not fun from here either.*

I do see myself differently now, Naomi, because by my free will and choice, God's script now charts my life and my life purpose. That is the only one that matters now because that is the only role that is true and challenging and big enough for me. I will be the most notable and noble courtesan at the best little whorehouse in town, and I will be the consummate expression of the Divine full focused on changing the world in positive and uplifting ways.

Mati moans softly and confesses, *I do see a John beating me brutally..., making almost dead physically. And when I recover enough to turn tricks again, he will return. And I will take pointed pleasure in making the bastard beast a dead man walking. Then, when I tire of that torment, I will make him totally and permanently dead. This lifetime anyway. The Divine One can reorganize the subatomic particles that made up his body mind brain and return him to life if He chooses.* She shrugs and adds: *I'll be happy to make the bastard undead all over again, then triple substantially transform him again, if that's what the Divine One needs to redeem his soul from the clutches of the Nephilim overlords of Earth.*

Remind me to never get you pissed at me, Naomi declares round-eyed.

So, we have a high-level plan then that we will evolve as we execute it, and we are all agreed that our objective is to take out the caldera vamps and make them permanently dead. My question is how do we execute the triple substantial transformation of all the world's vampires when we too are vampires?

Brother! Mati says with open-face wonder. She turns her palms up and scrunches her face in dismay. *Angels, in the interim, she punts. Anybody else up for asking God how many angels he can spare to guide us through the hidden twisting way we have chosen simply because we believe it's His work we do?* The three nod agreement. *Let's call angels for Brother too, he will need all the wind at his back he can get.*

Let's do it! The three sisters pray in one silent voice and hear and feel the silent soft flutter of angel wings as they bask willing yielded in the warm light scented downdraft from a host of heavenly wings.

And so it is, amen.

Help Me

It still hurts, that Mati threw me away like she did. It still hurts that she made me to create a safe place for people like us…, blood drinkers, walking dead, a dead man walking. Why? It makes no sense to me!

Well, actually some of it makes sense — in the way a follow the numbered dots picture makes sense — at first it makes no sense whatsoever, then when you connect most of the dots you do begin to see the picture, it begins to make sense.

And twenty years later I still can't see the whole puzzling picture.

I don't cry. And I want to cry. Until my eyes turn red and salt gritty for all the tears I've shed — over how that blindness has shredded my mind to confetti.

And I've no cause to party and throw it up in happy celebration. It still hurts, dammit!

I didn't lose Mati.

She threw me away like yesterday's newspaper. She pitched me a dozen klicks beyond the caldera where we'd been living and working four years, with no more than a heart stopping threat…, that wasn't a threat. Mati meant it…. She was dead serious and unflinchingly determined.

Mati made me. My sister made me a vampire. Like her.

Like Naomi.

Like Clara.

Like Mater.

Like the family of caldera masters.

Mati told me this with silent words and petrifying pictures flickering in her eyes fierce lock set on mine, she said that I'd be the next to be made a bleeder feeder to the caldera vampire royalty unless I left that night, and she wasn't standing by and watching that happen. She didn't bite into my carotid artery though. I though that's where vampires always drank from their victims. Still can't watch a Frankenstein movie. I get the heebie-jeebies so strong I hide my eyes, and then, I must *to peek between my fingers to see the 'EEK' box after the bite, because there is only silence otherwise and I might never know….*

On the sane side of me, I believe that royalty is a lifeless and socially ham-fisted concept, so the overreaching of royalty was the one thing I could align with among Mati's reasons the reasons for me getting out of Vamp town before sunset.

Otherwise, I was not at all happy with her doing what she was dead set on doing. Mati didn't call it that, but she was throwing me away. It's the 'doing for me' part of her telling that didn't make any sense to me. That remains an illogical, irrational, and incongruous brainteaser riddled with conflicting opposites.

Why throw me away to America? Why by way of Amsterdam? Why stow on a freighter bound for New York City? Why stow? I was the groundskeeper at the caldera keep, for God's sake! I saved enough money to have paid for a cabin and suffered no lack or discomfort because everything I needed would have been delivered for the ticket price. Coulda been a vacation. Never had one of those.

I'd not have co-habited with rodents of significant size through a very, very long and tedious stow-away passage to America. Instead, I would have eaten in a dining room. I would have had baths, and I could have had my clothes cleaned, pressed and returned to my room ready to wear again. But no, I had to stow. I had to do as I was ordered to do, and I could not do what made sense to me.

Beloved bully big sister Mati gave me those orders. Mati didn't give orders come to think on it. She didn't have. All she had to do was ask, and it was done willing and willfully well and thoughtfully compliant – for the pure pleasure of pleasing Mati and seeing her meltingly heartfelt smile. Genuine, genuinely Mati.

Mercifully, part of the pre-processing for entry into New York City, meant bathing and ways to clean clothes. I could have stayed in that heavenly bath forever, but that luxury is not part of entering a port.

On the up-side of Mati's throw-away from the caldera, for whatever the reason, I ran like I've never run before. I was silent and swift under the heady influence of a lung pumping, self-sustaining oxygen high that pushed ample power to flood my heart mind brain, and lull me into the deep rhythmic breath that most without doubt propelled the sure-footed fleet feet of the messenger god Mercury on a vital mission.

Maybe then I did have a Mercury message to deliver then. Maybe I still do have a message to deliver.

That may be my problem in a nutshell. I have not functionally received the message. I don't know what I'm supposed to do, and what I do know is conflicting opposites. I don't have enough data-points to connect the dots and get any sense of the confounding conflicted mission Mati sent me on. I don't know who's to deliver the meaning to me, now that Mati is gone from my mind. More to the point, I don't know what I am supposed to do on this mission and I don't know how to do it when I do what it is.

That's my whole confounding crazy-making conundrum. Why did Mati make me? What did she make me to do? What's my mission, why am I here eleven miles outside of a town of 2,500 people in it? Remote..., like Mati is. I can't even hear her think any more. It's almost as though she's not alive now. I reach out to her in my mind like we always did; and she's not there. She's a gone girl. I'm alone and lonely.

I ponder this conundrum and always come back to the same place. I'm abandoned and alone. I pretty much have no option but to surrender to trusting faith and good fortune that when it is time for me to do a thing, I will know clearly and well what I am to do, and how I am to do it.

And that feels like I'm sitting my big britches in my rocker passively letting my life questions squeak themselves out of me like farts from a tight ass while listening to the meditative mantra of my rocker's sad sorrowing song. Especially so since I'm currently hunched in it rocking out my aching isolation that makes not one lick of sense to me! It still hurts.

Macy Gray – Still Hurts

Maybe Mati's been tapped dry of life vitality, like she told me Mater was, and Clara, and Naomi after they were made bleeder feeders to the caldera royals.

Maybe she's mostly dead now and no longer gives a shit about anything but feeding on the life force energy of others. Such a defeating deflating thought.

Maybe she's simply loving living in a whore house and playing double agent spy.

Maybe she doesn't want to risk exposing me and my location to the vampires by communicating with me even telepathically.

Why would she do that? She sent me on this mission. She ordered me to do it. I wish there were a kinder word to explain her demand that I create a safe place for people like us — feeder-bleeders, to live free —and to free feed on the life blood of innocents.

Innocents like we were before, when we still lived on our farm that Da built and maintained for us..., before he was murdered in cold blood.

I miss the innocents we were before receiving that damnable invitation to come live at the caldera with our 'royal' distant cousins, and leave our home behind. On a fool's errand!

Of course Mater insisted wasn't foolish at all and would be wonderful life for us!

Wonderful indeed, living like slaves to our new found and imperiously haughty and hostile distant cousins. Que tonto! Que totalmente estupido! Mater fueren una puta forever dressed in widow's weeds of mourning.

She never laughed again after Da was killed. Rarely even smiled. A defamed woman does not smile. There is no joy left for her when her neighbors and former friends gossip viciously and slandered her behind her back without thought or remorse or even a personal or polite apology.

Maybe it was inevitable that Mater would fiercely grab any possibility of living with self-respect and beyond reach of the vicious vile insults of our neighbors, Mater's traitorous, slandering, betraying best friends forever.

I can't say that I blame her. Those BFF bitches were brutal. Better to let them think they were seen as important and even necessary for her living of a connected and centered life.

The bitches' husbands were worse though. They'd sneak into Mater's room in the dark of night wanting to fuck her..., but not like their wives fucked her over, they wanted to play hide the peepee. Mater had a pistol, and Mater knew how to use it. I can't tell you how many nights for how many months I'd awaken to the sound of her gun going off, how many nights I'd hear the angry curses of married men wanting an easy lay free only because Mater had been so thoroughly slandered they fervently held she'd betrayed her marriage vows on the night Da was killed.

There should be a law against a man being that venially and vilely insensitive and insulting to a newly widow woman. But men write the laws..., for others to obey. They exempt themselves for they have a dangly dick and that gives them an entitlement to be bastards. No wonder their wives despise them and their children want nothing more than to go away to college and not come home for holidays even.

I miss Clara, my beautiful big sister and 'other mother' who cared for me and loved me because Mater could not.

Self-defense by the defenseless is inevitably twisted and perverted by the small-minded into implied complicity and even willingness. Slander..., such a foul deadly sin. And slanderers still live. Still live on the life force energy of others even if they don't drink human blood. Slanderers sour and curdle the milk of human kindness. They make it unpalatable, sour, and unhealthy with their deadly sin of covetousness.

I miss my big sister Clara who mothered, loved, and protected me..., because Mater could not, nor even pretend that she did. Wow, what a powerless victim consciousness that evokes in me. Tisk, Tisk. How human I am. Clara would have a thing or two to say about me playing small as a helpless victim, and even more discouraging words to say about the vile veniality of me playing victor.

I miss Naomi. If she were here she would make me laugh at myself for my self-induced navel gazing pity party. She'd put her arm around my shoulder and say: 'sticks and stones may break my bones but words will never harm me'. Then she'd tell me that how I feel about the words is my own choice, and she'd remind me that I don't have to give my free will to anyone, not even to a demon dancing in human drag.

Then Naomi would show me the scrapes on her knuckles and fists and she'd whisper secret soft and low how she and Clara defended me on the playground when kids slandered me. She told me even the nuns couldn't make them stop protecting me because it was the right thing for older siblings to do.

Besides, she'd say, if there was a fault it was not mine; and I didn't have to accept it as my truth. Instead, I could use my free will and choose to hold my head high against the cruelty of children trying their best to be compliant with the expectations of the addlebrained adults in their lives. Poppycock! Mind control!

Naomi's word, not mine. But I do admire 'poppycock', even if I've used only once in my life. Twice if I count thinking it as use. And I don't. I learned how to doctor their bruises while they healed my heart. Gotta love big sisters. Even when you don't like them because they don't communicate at all now.

And then there's my dream girl Mati, two years older than me and light years wiser and more loving and compassionately powerful. How I miss Mati now that she is silent in my mind and I can't ask her why. I can ask, but it's pointless. She doesn't answer. It's like she doesn't exist anymore, like the Spirit of her is long gone and she's no longer anything more than an empty husk.

How can something so alive become suddenly dead, unresponsive, and utterly lifeless? She must be dead. Or mostly dead. As inanimate as one small lump of coal in a bad boy's Christmas stocking that isn't big enough to even produce heat when burned in a fire box.

I'm alone. On a solitary mission impossible that makes absolutely no sense whatsoever. Where is God when you need Him? And why has He gone distant silent and incommunicative too?

Wonder who left first, if it was me, or if it was God? I think even my guardian angels have gone AWOL. Damn, I feel alone, and unloved, and abandoned!

'Get thee a wife', the absent goofy God directs me, as though a wife is the ultimate answer to everything you ever wanted to know about life and living it. Poppycock! Bogus! Bullshit!

Damn you God if you do exist! You make devout atheists of lovingly good and loyal men, and then you feed them the insipid Pablum of 'get thee a wife'!

Well, God, get a life, for man's sake! Try something novel for you, try to give a shit what goes on here on Earth where you gave the fallen angels' free reign over man on Earth for three bloody millennia!

I'd ask you what you were thinking, but apparently aforethought is not one of your overhyped gifts, only milk toast warmed over. Yet you do lavishly pour out your 'gift' of cruelty by neglect on your mere mortal creations of man. You're are more spiteful than Mater in her most malignant of moods.

Besides, you never answer any question I ever ask you. You just do that whole infinite silence thing that appears to be the only generously given 'gift' you have to offer man. If you exist, you are not worthy of my respect, love, nor honor, let alone my worship.

On your knees first, asshole, for you will beg me to come back to you before I'll do it of my own free will!

Or, you can make me dead and send me straight to hell to be poked, prodded and basted by Beelzebub who is at least open and honest about who he is. At least he doesn't lie about being a kick butt bad-ass Nephilim spawn of a demon bastard. Honesty is a synonym for the Divine, and you have none. Liar, liar, pants on fire....

You lie about being a loving father God who gave his only son to a horrific death 'to save the world? Really? That is pure, unadulterated Nephilim bull-shit! No loving human father would even dream of doing that! You are Beelzebub's own demon spawn.

That's the only thing that makes a lick of sense to this human..., you loutish Lord of Lies and laziness, dementedly demanding your Sunday afternoon of rest and to get it, totally willing to free forfeit your own free will, and in the bargain inherently forfeiting the gift of free will you gave to man.

'It's my Sunday of rest. Ya 'all go play nice with the devilish demons and don't bother me again.

'And do not *damage my beautiful new blue planet in the process! That's an order. I will hold man answerable in the end, so we may as well start it right man's first day of life on Earth.*

'Call me tomorrow, maybe I've got an open twenty minutes then, I'll check my calendar. Nap time now.'

You must be the first, full and complete definition of A.W.O.L. You made humans to care for the planet and set up a double-blind making it impossible for us to meet your requirements, A.W.O.L.

And, you biting bitch bastard, you will be vigilant venial and profuse in meeting out your punitive punishing penance through blessed *hands of your permitted pious prurient pestilent priests and Popes! Nephilim in robes, with tonsured hair, dirty habits – double entendre intended – and a taste for virgins, of any gender, preferably before they get the full concept of free will so they will be easily intimidated into shamed silence pretending nothing at all happened and silently bearing the mind and heart hurt of their loss of innocence and the security of their own bodies.*

And, you bogus bastard, your habited child rapists will give your Nephilim pals penance when they confess. You are a despicable excuse for god. You make Beelzebub look like a nice guy bully bastard by contrast.

Still Hurts

She was a charmer with a full face smile that lit her eyes and melted my heart. I thought I would never marry – before her – and very soon I knew I would never marry anyone else. She fit me like water. Where I was empty, dry and barren, she was my generous slow soft showers that utterly filled and loosened all the empty dry places in my heart.

I wouldn't let her in my mind though, not where all my self-consciousness rode me like Nephilim bandits bent on keeping me small, separate, self-conscious, selfish, but not self-aware. E.G.O., edging God out, for I denied him all and any power over me or my life.

Still I prayed. Out of perverse habit maybe. Maybe because I thought denial was not only a river in Hell, but that it was also my ace in the hole that would proudly prove me clever enough to take the trick like a one arm bandit, leaving God with no option but to push his whole pot over to my side of the table.

Yep, I planned to use my trump ace to win the game of life with or without God's impotent help. Angry arrogance, pure and simple. That's who I was…, before I met my wife.

By age, she was young enough to be my daughter. By wisdom and understanding, she was ancient old enough to be my great, great, great, great, great grandmother.

But I had no use for Mother Wisdom then. My E.G.O. self would not allow time, mind, nor space for the wisdom of the ancient mothers who squatted to pee and weren't upright in doing their business. And yes, that was a judgment; and the arrogance of it was stunning.

On the upside, stunning a bellowing bull always was the quickest way to demonstrate to the semen stupefied beast the wisdom of compliance. Get a grip on reality, bull-head. Keep obedience out of the mental picture where it's irrelevant, if you'll allow obedience to be irrelevant because it is, it always was.

Regrettably, there was no one brave or bold enough to stun me into accepting the prudent practicality of compliance. Yet, there was my remarkable woman wife to be, who stunned me silly, simple, and willing with a smile and without raising a hand or voice to me. Would that I had done the same for her. God forgive me. How can God forgive me when I cannot forgive myself? Que tonto! Que increable estupido!

I weep when no one can see or hear, when I'm locked in alone in my man cave cellar with my whisky still making me high on the fumes of grain alcohol and rye while refining it into a mind-altering god nectar that makes everything okay, even when you know isn't, and you made it so.

With my bare hands, I killed the one good thing I had going for me. I stubbornly, bull-headedly, willfully, and negligently allowed her die in tortured agony and alone in our marriage bed. The Nephilim have nothing on me. If I were God, I would not forgive that. I could not forgive that. Ergo, and logically, I cannot forgive myself.

The devil will take his due. It still hurts!

| Macy Gray – Still Hurts |

It hurts worse than an abscessed tooth treated with chasers of rye whiskey to dull the riding abiding buckling pain of my own stubborn, willful, and knowingly brutal manipulation of a good woman who was a good and generously loving wife, despite my spiteful angry punishment, for I what believed in my own rye addled sexually deviant delusions of what a good wife is 'supposed to' be.

I willfully destroyed everything that was good and worthy about me, full self-deluded that it was she — not me — that was the cause of my grievance. And all the while it was me. Me, who would not know love if it was a snake and it bit me, its maker! It was a snake. But not the pretty liquid serpentine things that slither shiny, beautiful, and silent along the ground and take us by surprise because we were in la-la land and not present in the body mind brain Earth suit that Spirit inhabits and animates into life with a purpose that has nothing to do with human judgments. The only judgment I would own and allow.

In denying a One Source God, I denied my own true reality. In truth, my body mind brain is only a magnificently designed and amazingly adaptably capable Earth suit that is inspired, inhabited, and grace filled only by the I AM presence, the sole and only One Source of all and everything.

All the while I thought it was all and only about me. Delusional. I so need forgiveness. And forgiveness now must begin with me, and be given by me, for me. And I am incapable of forgiving me. It still hurts.

*My wife, my wife..., how inconsolably my heart weeps, my knees bend, I fall flat with dead dry gritty hard eyes in the face of my faithless, cruel stubborn punishing abuse — that **I** cannot forgive.*

*That I **will** not forgive. I vowed to love, honor and protect her. And I did not. Yet I know that I would choose again to not to protect her from me, the one she opened her heart mind and body to, the one man she invited to her bed, the one man whose children she bore and raised in love, honor and respect. And high expectations.*

Help me..., it still hurts..., it's the angry, empty, persistent pestilent twisting pain of self-betrayal.

Macy Gray – Help me

Who can help a man with forgiveness of others when that man cannot forgive himself? A question worthy of the indifference of the Divine Mind..., and light years beyond the mind of this man.

Who can straighten the way of a man who denied his wife the comfort of the marriage bed because she kept on being the charming disarming beautiful laughing girl I married, because she was different from any other woman I had ever met.

I tried not to love her.

She was barely a girl woman, and I, a man old enough to be her father. But there was nothing in me mature enough to not get a hard on just seeing her across the dance floor making grown-up nice to the married ladies with children her own age.

I remember once when she was charming the mothers telling them all the reasons she adored their daughters and sons, and reporting all the ways and times they'd been thoughtfully witty and wise. She had an intuitive heart melting ways of making everyone around her feel brilliantly special, all the while leading them to see true and clear with new eyes the unique gifts of their own daughters and sons.

Because of her I learned to love our girls with my whole heart, my whole mind, and to the nether edges of my own soul. I was full able, willing, and delighted to let them see, feel, and gracefully receive, every iota of my open-hearted, right-minded admiration of the unique gift of each one of them.

They bloomed like star flowers. Each of them uncoiling themselves upright daily like they were weaving a beauty basket formed from the very sinew and essence of their true selves, formed on the fly from their mind body brain, and blessed straight, upright, and disarming in the confidence of divine spirit.

Each day, I watched my girls grow deeper and ever truer and more upright into beautiful, outgoing, lovingly generous and perfectly amazing human beings they were made to be. I loved them to and beyond the nether regions of own self-love. Loving my daughters made a better man of me.

It's the way I'd loved my sisters, come to think of it. Same outcome, only the names were changed..., to protect the innocents, and I was not an innocent.

Except when it came to my witty wise wife, that is. I loved her possessively. Ravenously. Covetously. Selfishly. Greedily. Jealously. Harshly. Brutally. Pitilessly! I could go on, but what's the point? Judgment is mine sayeth the lord....

But we don't talk much anymore. I never did listen anyhow.

Instead, I allowed my separation from source anxiety, my perpetual fall from grace, to be my downfall. I fell flaming like Lucifer in his swan dive from the heavenly ramparts of saving grace.

That actually seems practicably predictable in hindsight, for I became a man who first reflected, and then became, the mirror image of the god I judged too absently abusive to deserve my respect. My self-made Beelzebub had come home to roost in my chicken poop coop through the long dark night of my soul.

God help me! Hear me! I call for mercy from a god I do not believe exists. My god is dead! Que tonto…, que increable estupido! Only a man desperately in need of help could think such tight torqued tortured thoughts. Help me….

Macy Gray: Help Me

There is another reason I killed my wife. And, that distills down to an insanity defense against murder. Even when I just think it silent in my stuttering stupid mind. That is not a reasonable! Even at the time it wasn't. There was nothing reasonable about what I did, nor even why I did it.

*I thought she slept with another man because I would not lay with her in the nine months before my third son was born. I would not lay with her in the way a man lays with his wife, the way he makes love **with** her. I couldn't do that then. Not then. I denied, stuffed down, and forgot how to give and receive love with her as my partner in life and as living it. I lost that knack…, if I never had it to begin with.*

But I did! I did love Clara, and Naomi, and Mati, without recourse and with no remorse. I never gave less than I had to give, I never stinted, I never held back.

But then, every sunrise was a first day. Every sunset signaled a new first night of rest in heavenly peace. There was no 'wicked' in my world, not even Mater who could not love me for a fault that was not my own. For, in my innocence, I found nothing wicked. It was all good.

Wicked came later, when I brought home the hard black walnut of doubt and planted it deep in the garden of my heart, and tended it with fierce fury. I force-fed the fire in the belly of my inner beast. I gave it its demon name: Jealousy. Wicked was my beastly jealousy roused and made ravenous by my E.G.O., making it subject to my hand, and to my will.

You see, my wife was not obedient! Not to my wily wicked whims and ways, nor to my brutally selfish isolation of her, nor in my devilish depriving her of the inspiring life force energy of her, not to her precious gift of an unstinting loving generosity of spirt.

My beloved never met a stranger, and for this I loved her beyond reason. For this exceedingly greedy love, I killed her. It still hurts..., as it should do. Shame alone should seal that devil's bargain to a far be gone.

Macy Gray: Still Hurts

The Still

I had a still. And I had a skill, native, pure, and true; a divine gift of turning barley, rye and distilled spirits into an utterly amazing and tasty rye whiskey.

Please keep in mind that I was not only the distiller of my rye whiskey, but the taster, and the final judge of the quality, and the inspiring spirit of my distilled of rye whiskey. Dang but I was good!

That is not bragging. That is a true story.

I used grain alcohol – that I distilled – in a still that I created and formed with my own hands that were guided by the blueprint embedded in my mind. Who put it there? The jury's still out on that point. Personally, I believe it was divine inspiration. But that comes from my own E.G.O. conscious mind of me and admittedly not from my higher consciousness that is one with the Divine.

That's always been my major problem with holding a firm fast faith in an un-seeable, unknowable, non-physical divine deity. So, prove it to me! Don't just give me a mucked up world filled with mostly fucked up people and expect me to make divine sense of it! Who's in charge of it in the end? You, the Divine, or man, who is nothing more than the muddling Muppet puppets of you, an alien, other-worldly, and reputedly divine string puller? Do you care whether the play of life makes any sense at all to man? You seeded man here to care for and preserve the Garden of Eden you made of the blue planet Earth.

You won't answer. Never do. You are always MIA, Missing In in-Action, you bogus djinn behind the muttering mask of mendacity!

Dang I like words.

Even if you never hear them.

So, there's my still, and my exceptional rye whiskey that hasn't sold since my wife died..., since my wife was killed. By my own hands. Because I was jealous, I thought she had betrayed me. I believed she laid with another man in her fertile time, when I would not lay with her, as a husband is vow-bound to do. I would not comfort her. I would do nothing to assure my vivacious vixen wife that she was my chosen one. That she was the one dearest beloved of my life and of my world.

So, why would I not lay with her? You might wonder. Fair enough.

I would not lay with her because I was punishing her – for not being obedient to me – for not quitting being the person she was when I fell in love with her and asked her to be my chosen bride wife life mate.

I didn't know she was a shifter. Not then.

But I did know my wife was fertile and 'in heat' if we were talking about a dog. I knew she wanted another child. A son, she told me it would be, and he'd told her his name. I believe that now. I believe without doubt, that the spirit that inspired the body mind brain of her third son gave her the name that was right for him in this lifetime with her as his mother, and me as father of him.

I sincerely wish at times, that man really could un-ring a bell. Given that power I'd not un-ring our marriage bells. But I would swiftly silence the sounding gongs of my pounding punishing possessiveness. I'd not pin a beautiful iridescent butterfly to a board and frame it airtight in glass to preserve it forever..., mostly dead, fully unreachable, still beautiful, and still unreservedly mine. I open my twisted tight fist and it's still empty. There's still no hand to hold, still no eyes to sparkle, still no warm kissing lips, still no soft caressing hands.

It still hurts.... And it's still my fault, for I can love no other better and more kindly than I can love myself. Oh how I despise and hate me! I cannot live with me, and I cannot kill me. My opiate and my chosen form of death wish are one..., slow death by alcohol poisoning. Snake eyes..., again. I still breathe.

Macy Gray: Still Hurts

The alchemical art of being helped lies in the magic of a willingness to surrender to being helped. That takes reaching out and taking firm hold of the helping hand that's poked out in front of you, and then graciously receiving the help being offered.

Personally, I've always found it more effective to demand, and then to take what I want, and let the chips fall where they may. Bully boy abandoned strikes out on his own and makes a success of it and himself. A Horatio Alger classic of pulling yourself up by your bootstraps. That, in itself, is a puzzling paradox.

So, there I was, in my cement cellar man cave stewed to the gills on my very excellent rye whisky that I couldn't sell nor give away since my wife died. Five days after I hit her for the last time.

Oh, God, I cannot forgive myself!

How can I rationally hope that a kind, loving creator God could continue to love a man who beat his wife to death out of insane furious jealousy, and then let her stew for five days in the sour yellow bitter bile from her ruptured appendix?

I deserve hell! And hell is not deep and forbidding enough. I deserve the seventh level despairing depths of hell, and even that is not deep enough to house the infinite immensity of my self-loathing. Help me!

Macy Gray: Help Me

Sheriff Ben came by mid-morning. Said he was in my neck of the woods and thought he'd stop by and say hello to me. Sure, that makes sense. My farm is only eleven miles from town; and more than half those miles are on poorly maintained dirt roads.

That said, even a gloomy, died-in-the-wool navel-gazing skunk drunk fellow will eagerly accept most any distraction, even a patently bogus one. I did that.

More unexpected still, I invited Ben to join me in my man cave cellar and have a toddy or two of my most excellent year for rye whiskey – if I do say so myself.

And then, truth be told, since my wife's funeral, I haven't sold one bottle of my very fine rye whiskey. Not one. Serves me right though. If I were God, or were I Beelzebub, I'd sit back and watch me stewing in fruits of my life labor for good or for evil as I silent rode the twin bobbing platters of liberty's silver scale. Not at all sure I'd ever be free though, even when the scales of justice do finally balance.

So there I was in my man cave cellar with Sheriff Ben sipping my fine rye whiskey and thinking it was a danged dark place I'd made as my man cave. Ben's a good man, he's a peacekeeper more than he's an enforcement officer.

He did his signature 'heh, heh, heh, and asked me why my man cave was so dark and dismal because it simply had to encourage my dim view of people and of life and the living of it. Said maybe if I'd made it so some natural light and fresh air could came in of its own accord, then I'd not have fallen so deep into the dark hole of my punishing misery over my senseless jealousy that made me mad enough to kill my beautiful charming beloved wife. That whole thing was indeed fueled by my acute separation from source anxiety, my perpetual fall from grace.

It's a good man who can say hard edgy things in easy and comforting ways that leaves no room for taking offense yet soft pushes a mean, navel-gazing man like me get up enough self-preservation sense to actually give a shit about the nature of the changes he's making in the world and the people in it.

Like my kids. All of them took the first stage out of Dodge – my dodge of responsibility – for the likely outcomes of my own choices. My girls left to marry and move to their husband's homes, as a good woman will do in anyway. Wasn't my girls.

It was my daughter-in-law, Anna who put her foot down hard and fierce faced me down without putting me down. She did speak the truth about how I made Hitler look like a sane man for he only destroyed the lives and bodies of his victims. He didn't make them live with him. He didn't make them take orders from him. He didn't force them through the mental thumb-screwing I did of my sons. And my daughters. And my wife..., my wife.

It was my daughter-in-law Anna who put her dowry money down to buy a farm of their own for them and the family they'd have. They were taking their things from the house, the shed, and from the animal pens, and they were moving, lock, stock and barrel, away from me, and out of my clutches.

It took months to get over that, and I never really did. My E.G.O. was sore bruised that a mere woman dared back me, King of the board, into a forfeit on a chess board and then take my King, and the game.

In a different way, and with an altogether other objective, that is pretty much what my wife did. She shrewdly played her game to win, and a boy child was born to her. Nine months after I laid with a neighbor's red haired temptress cousin visiting from Chicago, who liked a man with big britches.

Big britches. Small mind, hard heart. Quick to judge and judge harshly. What an E.G.O.! I knowingly and with malice and aforethought took the Queen of my wife off the chess board of life. I smashed her to smithereens. I punched her in her soft spots where bruising is hard to see and easy to cover, over, and over, and over again, until my blind rage was spent and my body utterly exhausted.

When I recovered, I realized that had shattered my very own chosen Queen of my heart. I battered her body viciously and in blind fury because I believed the son she delivered, my third son, was not my child.

You see, I would not lay with her then. She was not obedient to me. She did not stop being the charming, witty woman she was when I made her my wife. She was not being obedient. Not in exactly the way I demanded. For that, I made her mostly dead so that she would never again shame me and lay with another man. Not any man. Not even me.

She was all but dead save for the torture of dying alone, in our marriage bed, from an untreated ruptured appendix.

I didn't know then that she was a shape shifter. I didn't know that even though saw her shift every morning of my life with her. This is the honest truth: she'd wake up as ugly as a skunk on a bad hair day, and by the time she'd toileted and bathed, she was the heart-stoppingly beautiful reborn queen of my heart.

Funny how a man won't see daily miracles that go on around him like free falls of fairy dust blessing a common world with uncommon grace.

I..., I could not, I would not take her to the doctor. The self-shame of my vicious abuse of her dry froze my heart until it imploded like a dried prune. If I took her to the doctor, I'd have to own up to being an oath-breaking, adulterous, slanderous, and abusive husband.

There aren't any marital vows I didn't break perversely, decadently.

The agony of my self-loathing puts me on my knees until they are bloody raw from my sorrowing shame. I bull-headedly and mulishly chose to reject my vow to love, honor, and respect my beloved wife..., the light of my life. Oh, God, it hurts, it still hurts!

Macy Gray: Still Hurts

So, there we were, Sheriff Ben and me not talking much but hearing a lot, and both of us pretending there was nothing to hear but silence. I finally got around to asking him why he'd come, and I said I was pretty sure it wasn't the rye whiskey, no matter how good this, nor any other batch was.

That man never answers a question straight up. Not in his life that I know of. Maybe a law enforcement habit, or training, or something along those lines. Ben could talk up a storm though. And all the while be charming the socks off you and opening you up like a cutter to a tin can top. Ben wasn't doing that this afternoon. He was enjoying my rye whiskey though. He was sipping it like a gentleman does, like a gentle man, who has nothing to hide and no dark secrets obscure by abusing strong drink. Not like I had to hide.

And none of that ever mattered a whit to Ben! He is a straight-up straight talking young man, if ever I knew one.

A man like I used to be before Mati made me and threw me away bound to complete the peculiarly puzzling mission of making a safe place for folks like us to live safe and free. A dark safe place where we couldn't be burned out by vampire hunters.

It's a curious thing though, with that history that I never wanted blood, let alone human blood. The look and the smell of warm blood pudding, made me gag and puke my guts out until I thought I'd never need to shit again and knew I'd never eat again. Didn't happen. I'm a plump puff ball of a man for all of that.

Long about then in our silent meditation, Ben asked me how my whiskey sales were. He didn't say 'since you killed your wife' though. There's no point whipping a dead horse. So I told him the truth. There had been no purchases since my wife's funeral, nor even intimations of any since then day. My wife was my bond help mate, bound always by her own choice. I'd see her make it all over again when I'd done something stupid and bossy that couldn't be undone without losing face and she knew I'd not do that.

Pride! It goeth before the fall, that's sure and true..., as the words of Good Books always are.

I couldn't shed tears the day of her funeral. I had no tears. I have none to this day. I got dry gritty eyes that look irritated red all the time. They say eyes are the windows of the soul, and I say 'amen' to that.

I must a plumb blew out and debilitated my tear ducts. This is not a good thing for a farmer living on the high plains of western Kansas where dusters still sometimes blow. Man devastated this once rich and productive land; and my red raw, waterless tear ducts, but I am the man who fashioned that.

If I could forgive myself, then maybe I could heal. Doc sure as hell can't. If it's to be done, it's mine to do. And..., I don't love myself enough to go to that effort. Compared to the price my precious wife paid with her life, dry eyes are small compensation for the evil I've done. I need help.

Macy Gray: Help Me

Which leads me straight back to silent somber Sheriff Ben and his unannounced visit, and his as yet unexplained reason for being here in my man cave cellar. Ben's a pretty gregarious good guy when he's carrying the badge and not wearing it, like he is today.

He's not drinking much — but he's wearing the badge, and he never drinks liquor when he's wearing — so this is not a social call.

So I'm asking myself 'what does *bring Ben here to spend 'silent meditation time' with a cantankerous old coot he doesn't' really like at all'? I can put two and two together and get four, and I think that's Ben's point. I think he wants me to connect the dots, to get the picture, and to make the first move.*

The liquor! That is *the missing dot. Now I get the picture, but I still don't know what it* means. *What's Ben-with-the badge-showing angle? What's the outcome he wants? He's making it pretty dang clear he wants compliance, and maybe not obedience. That could be good. And, it could be rotten bitter too.*

Take the bull by the horns you phony old coot! Man up and get sober, or as sober as you can do under the circumstances. What's my *desired outcome?*

Oh, of course, I want a compliant, peaceful, and helpful, resolution for whatever reason Ben is here. That means he's left room for negotiating.

I need, and want, his help. That means I have to make it easy for him to ask for my help. I know how to lead into getting that done, and it means I have to lead with my trump card so Ben knows he now takes the lead. 'Oh what tangled webs we weave, when first we practice to deceive.' Always liked that line. Never before applied it to me though.

Ach! He knows why he's here…, and so do I. And I have to ask, I have to play the first card.

So what brings you out this way, Ben? He's silent, as though he's just now thinking about his reason, and he can out wait me.

It's a far piece to drive on dirt roads with no names or markers; and I know you didn't come to drink whiskey this afternoon and make small talk. I do hope *we pay you enough to not make the trip just to socialize awhile and drink my rye whiskey. Why are you here?*

I need your help. And you need mine.

Macy Gray: Help Me

Always happy to help, Sheriff. That said, tell me about the help you need from me, and say why I am the one to do it.

Wouldn't hurt for you to say what's in it for me too, but that's lagniappe in light of the fact that you're in uniform and wearing your badge. Official business then, if I read you right?

Yes, I am here on official business.

And, I'm also here on personal business. Personally, I'm here because you are my neighbor, and I'm here because you need my help to walk away free and clear from what will happen next if our business today is not concluded to my complete satisfaction.

Wow! No options then. That is a whole other kettle of fish, sheriff. In which case, I reckon the only thing I can say now is: how can I help you, Sheriff Ben?

'Heh, heh, heh, you waited me out on that one; and you baited me out too. Well done.

I want your still.

You want my still?

And what's in it for me?

You live as a free man. And not as a man running a still against the law of the land.

I know you do that to make ends meet when the brutally abused plains are cruel and vengeful and won't give back a day's work that is productive of income, nor even animal feed. It's a hard choice for a farming man to make.

And you have no other.

You really have to get that. Or..., I can call you 'Caleb', because you behave angry and pushy, just like him when he was drowning his failings in whiskey and using it as an anesthesia too. Just like you do.

The only difference between you and him is that he chose a cheaper brew than yours. And, for that 'discount' price, he got and drank rot-gut whiskey. He hasn't done a day of work since. He's nothing more than an addle-pated alcoholic with a bleeding gut and nowhere to go but to the grave.

You, on the other hand, have got your own high-quality grain alcohol going for you. Caleb didn't. He used the cheapest alcohol he could buy or brew. The end of that con was that he's rotted his brain completely out. He's mad as a loon, and that's an insult to loons, whose only fault is an enchantingly haunting call.

If I'm hearing you right, Ben, I really have no viable option other than to 'turn state's evidence' and surrender my still, and my stash of really fine rye whiskey.

You are hearing me right then.

Why would I do that?

Because there are government revenuers in town. They sniff the air, that's part of their jobs. They smell the fumes from an illegal still hereabouts but they haven't found it. They're with ATF, alcohol, tobacco and firearms.

They know there's an illegal still around here. They can smell it. They know it's illegal because they know the operator doesn't have a liquor license, and that he's not collecting liquor taxes, and he's not paying liquor taxes on the sales. 'Moonshiners' is what folks like you are called. The ATF job is to find and shut down moonshiners like Caleb. Caleb took himself out of the bootleg business ahead of the ATF. And that, is the only difference between you and Caleb.

I'm a farm boy myself. Don't know if you knew that. I've lived a lifetime of knowing that a farmer's got to have a whole market basket of income sources just to survive, let alone thrive or get a bit ahead every now and again.

As a law enforcement officer, I also observe that sometimes a good man will do things he knows are just not right in order to make ends meet. I know that without the 'extra' income from barter sales that throw off extra 'butter and egg money' for the family, most years a farmer can't make ends meet..., and there are a lot of hard candy Christmas's.

I understand the need for barter exchanges between and among farmers and farm families. I also know it's against the law, and I do no favors to those my badge protects by turning a blind eye to the make-ends-meet things they do that are illegal under the law of the land.

Just like you, I am a Keeper. My job is to keep the peace and order among the people living in my jurisdiction. You're in my jurisdiction. And so is the ATF, and their badge trumps mine.

If I can't give ATF what they need, they are oath bound to take it.... When it comes to jurisdiction, ATF has the trump card in every pursuit that involves federal, state, and local law enforcement. I want to help you, and I cannot help you unless you freely and willingly help me peaceably do what I cannot do without your help. Without your willingness and your surrender by choice it won't look like you repented and turned yourself in, that you chose to turn a new leaf and freely surrendered your illegal still, ATF will take jurisdiction from me.

I assure you that will be to your detriment. Help me. Help me help you

Macy Gray: Help Me

In that case, Sheriff, we've drunk about all of this fine rye whiskey we will need in one lifetime, and since I have no choice in the matter, let's dismantle the still, cart it out of here, load it in your truck, and then come back for the whiskey. Reckon I could keep one bottle?

Heh, heh, heh, not on your life..., not on your life.

Then let's get her done so you can get back home by supper time.

Vamp Act Rebellion Redux

The past three months had been a whirlwind for Interpol selecting their Interpol team of dedicated ardent coven breakers – or hive hunters – as they came to be called among themselves alone.

Each man and the few women on the Vamp Action Interpol team had willingly sworn to hold their mission top secret for the duration of their lives. Each agent knew that included their families, backward and forward across time. Interpol briefings identified the unexpected ways association with the mission would expose their loved ones to lusty resolute predations of night fliers globally. They understood and agreed that they would be 'missing in action' to the world to their families as well. No letters. No calls. No visits. No *nothing*, and *know* nothing! They would forsake their families during the mission and trust and rely on Interpol to shelter and safely sustain their loved ones.

After a long private talk with their personal Divine, each mission candidate soberly and solemnly vows to forget their name and never speak it nor respond to it for the duration of the mission. Each knelt to be knighted to a new role and a new self with no name and dedicated solely to their role in the Interpol mission. They would be free agents without names. They would be one team. On one mission. With one life to live, as one team.

They *would* take out the vampire hive, and live to remember it but never tell it, and they would take those memories to the grave. The newly knighted swear their oath and turn to meet and greet their seniors, who are now on their feet moving to applaud, meet, greet, and welcome their new member knights of their team.

"When do the de-briefings begin?" as a bold eager one who speaks for all.

"Well," the chief smiles and glad hands the next plebes in line "they begin now." His commencement date is cheered by the plebs as riotously as if each had a cap and tassel to toss aloft.

The chief chuckles and takes his place at the teacher's podium. "Ladies and gentlemen, "Welcome to the Interpol version of the vamp act rebellion."

He expects puzzled expressions from the plebes and knowing smiles from the leaders among them. "A key part of your training program..., in fact, the first part will taught by a lady vampire." He also expected exclamations of dismay, denial, and fear. The chief waits for the plebes to subside on their own inertia as curiosity overtakes the cat in each of them, and they sit quietly to watch, to wait, and to hear. The chief chuckles. "I hope future mission candidates choose curiosity over fear even as you have done." He sweeps their eyes in recognition and in honor.

The chief focuses now on the women plebes, then adds: "Not *especially* because you are female, but *because* you are female..., and you do not have the same knee-jerk response that men do because a female vamp will teach them core awareness and knowledge we will all need to survive this mission. It is my intention that all of us return – together, as we leave – together. One unit, each member looking out for his own safe return, and the safety of others.

"Gentlemen, there are ladies in the group because women have inherent skillsets men do not have. Deal with it. Ladies, the men in this group do not have the skillsets that you do have, but they are bigger, stronger, and more forceful. They will be your protectors on this physical plane as you will be their protectors on the metaphysical plane..., or this mission has no chance of success."

The student body silently ponders the interconnected interdependence of each gender member of the one team of them. Bias dissolves as though it never existed, leaving only one web of life with countless hubs of interconnection. Each and every one see and understand that no team member is more than five degrees of relationship from everyone else on the planet. Backward and forward, across time. The chief gives them time to assimilate that stunning revelation.

"Gentlemen, do not decide who your partner will be with your eyes, or your mind. That's not enough." He grins mischievously, "Ladies do not pick your partner because he's a hunk-a-bunny." The room erupts with ice-breaking laughter, and the chief knows he's achieved his first mission objective. "Find your partner, people; and remember, this is *not* a marriage contract you enter into." He watches in wonder as new trainees and old meld and merge in amazing energetic ways forming the core teams that will be needed if the mission is to succeed. When the plebe mating and pairing is complete, the senior team members gravitate to their teams. He watches amazed – but not surprised – as the master climbers gravitate to experienced climbers, ski masters connect with plebes who ski and want to do it better, hunters gravitate to hunting masters, shooters instinctively find the shooting master; and those who do Kung Fu, like 'cricket', gravitate to master of that art.

One master, a silver smith stands alone awhile patiently waiting for those with the innate or developed ability to master the arts of metal to find their heart way to him. But he is a she; and she is an ice hard fierce fire hardened avid artisan and master teacher. The wandering ones find her eyes and know her for their master and one by one spiral into her magnetic field and find themselves home again.

When the groups have self-ordered and aligned with their units, the chief spins the wheel of life to see where the pointer lands. *Time for Mati,* and thinks, as she appears in a dramatic flourish of sound and motion stunning the room into silence. She has appeared as a bat..., unaggressive, stalking the podium and sumptuously strutting her vamp bat stuff.

"Ladies and gentlemen, meet your teacher." The chief says in a commanding voice. "Be seated, all of you, in your groups please.

"This tutorial is a prerequisite for each and every member of each and every mission team. Do I make myself clear?" He sees the wide-eyed nods of agreement and spots the blind-faith holdouts. He lets the doubt weigh and compound in the uncommitted an edgy uncomfortable time. His words when he speaks them are silver edged and razor sharp. "If you cannot allow your intelligence to overwhelm your blind faith in a feckless god you've known forever, you are *incapable* of being a contributing member of this team." He eyes each and every hold-out, his eyes glinting silver pure and fierce fiery gold. He waits a telling moment..., "Get up and go now." They thought Mati was intimidating..., before.... "Or change your mind and stay. Your choice." He pauses a hairs breath, then severs the option. "Make it now." No one gets up to leave but the holdouts eye Mati still looking like a pissed off eagle. Some of them grin. Some chortle softly. None rises to leave abandoning his or her sanity vanity in what we must not see.

If you cannot see a vampire you cannot slay it. They know the voice in their mind is the voice of the vivacious vixen at the podium who has projected onto their mind. And..., they are okay with that.

"I'm in." A lady holdout stands to announce. She remains standing, right arm held upheld calling to mind a statue in a harbor, awaiting only man's signal salute to claim, own, allow, and announce freedom's boundless indwelling shores.

In a moment of truth another holdout stands, raising his right hand in a salute to the very concept of liberty and freedom. His inspiration, like the second domino fall, galvanizes the other doubters who one by one stand with upright arm raising freedom's fiery light.

In the end, their choices had nothing at all to do with statues and shores, either mental or physical, and everything to do with spirit, free will, and choiceful dedication to a singular desired outcome. Mati releases a breath she didn't know she'd held, and smiles easily into her wise master teacher role. "I could tell you… what I know." She smiles knowingly, "Or, I can show you. Show and tell is altogether easier and more profoundly effective. Fasten your seatbelts, ladies and gentlemen, we are about to depart on a once in a lifetime show and tell time adventure." Mati seats herself near a window opened by the light lieutenant who then places a silver gilt birdcage on a table at her side. Mati thoughtfully rests her hand atop the cage, disengages from who she thinks she is in this time and place, and lets go. She just lets go. Mati closes her eyes and calls the eagle in her mind. Unawares, she emits the shrill sharp scree of an eagle shattering the rapt attention of the students who, as one, are taken aback when an eagle descends to alight at her side and step complacently into the cage drawing the consciousness of Mati into every sinew and soft tissue of its being.

The students experience this. It is disturbing. Even to the seniors among them who still feel the shifting stability of transforming form and consciousness. Mati's form appears to sit comfortably in a chair near an open window, her right hand, resting on a silver birdcage, is lifeless. Now only spirit has the com of Mati. Only spirit charts the course of the eagle's flight the plebes and pros see from the eye of the eagle.

Ladies and gentlemen, Mati's voice blooms in their minds, *I will be your flight coordinator and tour guide, sit back, relax and enjoy your flight. Here is what your city looks like from a bird's eye view,* Mati says, and then comforts: *Take slow deep breaths to bring air deep into your stomach because that will help mitigate the nausea you experience in your physical bodies. You are safe and secure where you are. If you look around at your the senior members, you will see that they serve as your physical grounding while you swoop and soar with the eagle. And people, the keepers give hugs…, if that's what you need. And they aren't touchy feely types either, so honor the role they play for you today keeping you centered in your bodies while your mind flies free with the wind.*

You should all now be able to feel the wind in your face as the eagle flies. She feels the plebes smile and relax into their maiden eagle flight. She also feels the keepers go at ease in their alert grounding watchfulness even as the spirit of them beams up for their second eagle flight. She senses the light lieutenant monitoring and updating his maps with coordinates and notes even as his mind and spirit relish his second overview from the eye of the eagle. *We will follow the south gate road, for this is the route you will follow when you come to the caldera.*

It is the nature of eagle to watch over whole areas, and not man's byways alone. Your first task is to take note of manmade structures, their location, their condition, any signs of human or animal inhabitation..., and any and all risk factors associated with those structures.

Eagle is also keen to know where footed predators prowl. Eagle finds and follows a wolf pack. *All pack animals are led by an alpha male, and the ruling alpha is always subjected to relentless competition from younger alphas, until he is taken down and a new alpha leads the pack. The ousted alpha without a pack is a lobo, a singleton. He lives in a treacherous world ruled by pack mentality and no loyalty. Competition is the name of the wolf pack game.*

To survive, the exiled alpha lobo subsists on small slow game and domestic animals such as inquisitive sheep and penned hens, for they are easier prey for a lobo.

Most humans cannot outrun a wolf, even a bony slow lobo. She lets the implications steep into their awareness like tea in hot water. *Archers among you, you will bring bows and arrows, for you will be front line defenders for your team as you travel. While I think of it, those with knife skills will silver edge the knives that will be used inside the castle to make the vamps mostly dead again. Keep an unsilvered set for more ordinary uses while you travel.*

Hatchets?

Mati hears the question and agrees, *yes, hatchets are excellent for clearing trails and cutting wood for the campfire.*

She waits a heartbeat: *As for axing a vampire, if you did actually succeed in putting an axe into an undead, that would simply* seriously *piss it off and it would fast snatch the axe from you and use it to make you dead. In your case, totally dead. And, you would have alerted the whole hive that is now pissed off and fully dedicated to taking vengeance for you awakening them against your mates.*

Okay..., that's *a good idea we won't use.* Mati hears the laughter of the remote watchers as though she is in the room with them. And there she is..., sitting atop the desk at the head of the room with a hand resting comfortably on a silver gilt cage, laughing with her fellows.

Meanwhile back at the eagle, Mati resumes her show and tell narrative. *Silver edged knives will be the hot setup for making the vamps— including me — mostly dead on the day of the raid. Then you will put all of us mostly dead ones into this pretty silver cage, lock it with its silver key, and cover it with the sun bright cover so we undead won't notice that the sun's gone down and it's party time for night fliers. Vampires are eternally hungry and that won't wake them, only darkness stirs them to their mostly alive undead condition. Knives are silent and punch deep into the eye and brain of an undead. It will shift to bat form — I don't know why. Cage the bat immediately and lock the cage with its silver key. I'll come back to that.*

Attention passengers, please note that we are approaching the turn where the south road turns east. Vamps are master illusionists. The castle masters can, and do, charm this place and others, to deflect eyes from the path leading up to the caldera. Hang on to your seats ladies and gentlemen, we are going down. At Mati's warning words the eagle tucks its wings and falls from the sky like a lead weight. It's not a freefall at all, but it does a *masterful* job of impersonating that into the bodies of the watchers.

Deep breaths, folks, pull oxygen to your stomach and pump some back into your brains. Alert will keep you alive. Terror and fear are strong attractors to bleeder feeders of all kinds. Look around now and see who's alerting on eagle and me since they sensed your alarm. The predators are associating your fear with an eagle they cannot reach, but it came from you, not from eagle.

This as a master level lesson on the power and feeder force of fear. Inducing fear is a highly favored draining tactic of predators of all stripes, think alligators who will pass you peacefully by…, unless they scent on your fear.

The caldera vamps use illusion not only to deflect eyes from what you should not see, but also to expose their hunters to irrational fears and to predation by their wolf familiars.

Fear is fatal, ladies and gentlemen.

Life is breath. Breathe into your fears and learn to master them so that you stay alive long enough to have awesomely amazing *memories — to take to your grave — many full years from now.*

Perhaps one day, Mati muses absently, *in another life and form, I will write all our unbelievable adventures into books of amazing amusing fiction. It could happen.*

Now, back to the lesson plan. Eagle and I are at level again and flying at a 100 foot altitude toward the bend where the south road turns west. Spot the illusion, ladies and gentlemen. Mati and the eagle hover in place facing away from the road turning west, and toward the foothills of the mountain atop of which is the caldera keep. *Who sees the illusion? Common, folks, eagles cannot fly in place forever.*

Mati lets the silence extend into its discomfort level before someone speaks in awe filled tone, and eagle takes his ease. *There's a trail, a path, and it winds up the mountain. Can you ask the eagle to go higher please?* Mati and eagle eager wing to a higher altitude with a scree of exploding joy and laughter. They hear Mati's laughter too, and the oddly easy way it echoes through the distinctly other throat and voice box of eagle. *Yes, there it is, I see it now. Mati, you are a genius and an innovative and powerful teacher. Thank you.* Mati hears the multi-voice chorus of 'amen' that sweeps the room of watchers. Having been on this trip before, the keepers, knowing their wards are well warded, alert and eager, they settle back into a very personal enjoyment of the eagle's wild ride.

Go back please, and let us see that approach again. Eagle, you can skip the rock drop if you will.

Not a chance. It is not Mati's voice that speaks these words and all know it.

You like *the rock drop?*

You betcha!

Putting your life on the line for what you believe is important and right is worth every risk, even the inevitably eventuality of death. The body mind brain earth suit was not designed to last forever. And that is why the undead live such a hellishly long and licentious life. Eternity is not for the faint of heart. Nor for the cold of heart, for them it's hellishly long. We do them a favor here, humans. It is good to remember that and to hold that in your hearts as a compassionate mission objective.

Mati — we've found an altogether more profound teacher than you.

Why do you *think I asked eagle for a ride..., and not some* other *bird?* Mati coos dove-like cool. She is cheered with high fives and jubilant laughter. The Mati sitting on the desk caressing a silver cage does not move nor even smile.

Okay, the approach redux. We'll take it easy slow so each of you has the time to clearly see the illusion you already know is there but do not see.

Try forgetting everything you think you already know about life and revert to the mind of a child, where it's all *new, every singular sensational moment of grace that free fall flows by day and by night. There is no judgment in innocence, there is only eager receptivity in the heart and the eye of a child. Receptivity, my fellows, not grace, will decide the outcome of this mission, and of your lives. Live long and prosper.*

Eagle is hovering in place like a helicopter can do. Why do you suppose he is doing that?

I see the illusion! Me too, me too! The watching room below erupts in cheers, words of wonder, and hoots of celebration. The gone girl Mati sitting on the desk hugging a gilded cage raises silent praise for ever flowing guidance and grace. *Receptivity is the hidden key that unlocks the golden door. There is only one golden door. All else is illusion.*

They get it! Every one of them. They *don't* have to change what is, they have only to own and allow it – and then, they can receive the singular grace of knowing the truth of at-One-ment where a higher order of awareness and conscious choice to change themselves, their life, and their world in loving and godly positive ways.

If you hate the fallen ones, the Nephilim, they have power over you. They can, and will, control your minds because you *have personally surrendered your power to them through your unrecognized and unresolved personal petty habits of fear, inadequacy, anger, and hatred. Your personal manifestations of your unique separation from source anxiety. The emotions excited by* all *of those lazy mental habits of thinking yourself powerless, defenseless, rage, and inadequacy, are strong attractors for the Nephilim fallen ones.*

The caldera vamps – and all the others – will manipulate those dark energies you hide and deny, the truths of your fear motivated determination to keep you small and invisible – to the slings and arrows of cruel fate. Only the truth will save you. The big scary truth. There really are Nephilim walking among us. Mati by the cage smiles – as does eagle in flight, which is a chilling sight for the wingless ones feeling it all from a classroom below.

You are a unique expression of universal spirit, a singular child of the Divine. Across time, though the spirit that inspires your body mind brain is the recombinant DNA of the Divine. Mati flies and spies and shows sensitively silent. *The Spirit that inspires and guides you through all of this walk of life is the truth of you, the person that you chose to be before you had body, mind and brain to enable the physical you to choose. This illusion operates at a uniquely visceral and intensely personal level.*

Experience that! Own and allow it. Breathe into it. Experience the aching emptiness that is your innate Nephilim energies. Own and allow all your anxious evidence that indeed you are inadequate. Own and allow all the ways you judge others better than you as proof to yourself that you're not good enough. Own and allow that you fucking don't believe there is a higher power that you can turn to and find solace, comfort, and support. Keep on nursing and nourishing your small self-consciousness and you are bat bait. You will keep on dithering and being incapable of free will and choice.

Or, you can just check in with your Divine and ask to see, own and acknowledge that your human self is incapable of doing great and noble works, but with the inspiration and reception of Spirit, you can do all things. Through God which comforts me. Surrendered to that comforting loving guidance, your small self-consciousness will accept the truth that you truly are more than your body mind brain – awesome as that is – it is still small. Oh look, eagle has spotted a snake shedding its skin, what a good guide you are, eagle.

Imagine that you are a snake in a tight skin. The skin of who you think you are..., well, you have simply outgrown that, have you not? Feel how corset tight the skin of who you think you are wraps you so close bound to the past that you are mentally and functionally out *of the present solely due to the cruel compression of the tight laced courtesan corset of who you think you are.*

It's illusion, ladies and gentlemen. Be supple and surrendered as a snake shedding its skin. I assure you that in the process exposing your new and expanding skin to the air and elements of your environment you will be sensitized – and not desensitized *to what's going on in the world around. We may not change the world..., but we won't leave it the same.* Mati hears the cheers from where she sits desktop in the training room. She feels them from where she flies with eagle.

So, who do *you think you are, vampire bait? Or a chosen one, a keeper?*

Keeper, affirms one multi-toned voice from the room of observantly interactive keepers in training, and the mostly inertly inactive uninhabited Mati body perched on a desk.

How does that not hurt? A trainee asks the still life Mati who starts alert to the space and time inhabited by her body mind brain. Her hand jerks involuntarily from the gilded cage raising a stinging singed flesh smell.

Mati eyes the trainee levelly and snarls sinister soft: *Obviously, it does hurt. Don't ask me that again.* It is not a request. He takes her point, and slips zip lipped back to his chair.

Okay, people, time to focus on the eagle flight, even an eagle tires of hanging in the air immobile. Let's roll! The eagle does that in the air, then settling again into a smooth upright flight circling the area where the south road turns west. *How many of you can now see through the illusion and into the truth? If you're still having trouble doing that, tell your conscious mind to sit down and shut up!*

They do that, one by one, and then as one cohesive mind with one singular choice. *I see it! I see* through *the illusion. Oh,* thank you, *God! Show us through the trail at the bottom please.* Eagle complies flying low and slow through the disarmed illusion and slow up the trail swinging left and right through and beneath the scattered full leafed trees in the foothills. With lazy grace eagle rises in his singular swinging grace up the path that increasingly rises in the upper foothills. *This is a cart path we follow, it's the path you will follow when you come on your mission. Remember that predators of all stripe are the servants of the vampires. They will do all in their estimable power to stop you from reaching the caldera alive.*

Climbers and skiers, I trust as we fly you are spying places where you can best use your gifts and skills to help assure the success of our combined mission for Interpol? She feels and hears their open-eyed and willing affirmations of attentive awareness. *You are also seeing the risks then? And mitigating them, please.*

More of that will present itself when eagle and I fly high to view the mountain from higher perspectives. Mati sighs and adds: *This flight of the eagle is the only practice run we'll get people. Archers, keep a keen eye out for where you will position yourselves during the climb. Some of you will roam ahead of the group, others will follow behind as the 'cleanup crew' if back cover is needed..., because that's how archer teams have always operated when providing protection for travelers. Get your team on now, folks, this is our only practice preparation time before we undertake the assault on the caldera castle.*

Always the case. That's why it's called a higher perspective. So, groupies, what interesting and useful things are you seeing from below the trees?

Campsites.... There's a titter of golden glee from the grounded group.

That's as important as eating and sleeping for travelers.

Water, where it flows, and where it pools.

Notice where water flows. Those are good places to refill canteens and water barrels. Water where it pools matters because those are just excellent places for swimming in the process of making bodies clean and cool again. Note where water pools in rocky shallows, those are ideal places for washing clothes, tools, plates and utensils.

What will we use for soap? As an attentive and forward-thinking participant.

Soapstone. It's natural, and a hundred percent biodegradable. It won't harm the environment nor hurt anything that drinks from the shallows or swims in the basin. On the actual expedition, pick up some soapstone rocks and tuck them in your travel pack. Not all pools are blessed with soapstone, and you don't want to travel with soap that man made. It is unnatural and the scent of it will attract the keen nose of predators of all types and stripes.

Good girl. Mati affirms. *Take note, Teamies, no one of you has all the good ideas. Let that come as a relief to you. Better still, be aware that you are experiencing a mind meld with every person in the room. This is how unique individuals grow and lean into the grace that evolves into a group mind that still respects and honors the multitude of ways each of us is unique and in reality, have little in common with one another. It's a two-step, peeps, let the weight of you be fluid and comfortable in the instability of motion. That's how you consciously grow the grace of Spirit into your body mind brain earth suit.*

Dichotomy, the spicy dice of life, dear-hearts. If you know that, then the dice game of life changes from random to aware, and every number you role must be *the right number.*

In your right mind, if you need to roll dice and to win, and sincerely ask Source for that grace, then you can and will always roll a winning number. I want to eavesdrop on your chat with the Divine if you ask to be granted the uncommon grace of always winning at a worldly game of chance.

Yet, if it doesn't matter a whit to you if you win or lose, and you ask for good reason that blesses many – greed won't cut it – God is truly likely to comply. His master servant did say 'you have not because you ask not.' A wise guy asks, and asks for a God like cause. Like, helping Nephilim exit from existence in all worlds where man walks covered only with thin skin for predator protection.

Okay, folks, eagle grows bored with the slow low close-up view, we're circling above the trees and back down the mountain to the foothills. Then we'll be flying at a higher altitude with sights you can't see from down in the weeds. Climbers and skiers, this is what you have been training and waiting for. The rest of you, you aren't watching to enjoy the scenery, that's a trip bonus courtesy of eagle. How does the view of what you see from this altitude help you? *How does the higher altitude view help you help your team? Your team mission? Your whole world?*

If even one of you is less than one hundred percent committed to this mission and the success of it, that person is a weak link, a place where the chain of the team is week. Mati smiles eagle beak wicked and cutting. *In what ways are you choosing fear, equivocation, and withholding over conviction, dedication, understanding and the understanding exercise of free will? When you are not so tightly bonded to earth and its trauma dramas, is the time to claim and exercise your higher will over your E.G.O. will.*

Edging God Out, a trainee thinks, initiating the shift sequence that claims, owns, and allows Oneness consciousness to over-write, upgrade, and remove from the software of the mind small-self fears and trauma dramas. In lightness of being, the group of One takes to Spirit wing and soars with the eagle.

As one, they feel the clarity of mind and the focused will that converts a leap of faith into a visceral awareness that this whole batty vampire mission is a God job, and they are the self-chosen and willing participants fully committed to fulfilling the mission they now know is divinely inspired.

I hear and feel it folks. God's in. Nephilim's on its way out. We are taking them out. Amen and so it is.

Mati, if the vamps are already dead, and we take them out with silvered knives into their hearts...,

Knife to the eye is the better way to go. It will pierce through the eyelid, the eye, and straight to the brain before the mind even has time to register the assault and prepare to defend.

She feels the asker's grin. *I like the way you think, Mati. So, from your personal perspective, what's the end game to making the already dead caldera vamps, dead all over again?*

That is an excellent question. Pay attention to the eye of the eagle and what you see far and near, and I will explain a part of the mission that begins when your part of the mission ends in success.

The afternoon of the raid, I will fly to the vamp mansion to give trick money to Mater, that's the reason for my visit. I'll stay the night. We're already dead, what is *the objective of making us dead again?*

Transportation of European vampires to America. That's the short story. Mati hears and feels their unease and their militant determination to know *why* Interpol is knowingly and willingly engaged in transporting vampire bats to the heart of America.

Ladies and gentlemen, we are now above the switch back where foot and cart traffic enters the bowl of the caldera. We follow the switchback leading into the caldera. Notice the crows. Watch where they roost and where they fly. Crows are day guards for vampires. Their raucous caws will awaken the vamps even in the noonday sun. You do not want the attention of ravens or crows, both raven black birds serve as day watch over the caldera keep.

Some of you will walk in with servants or traveling craftsmen. You must think of yourselves and behave like, and walk, talk, and act like everyone else coming to serve the castle masters. The ones you walk in with will not be looking at crows. You must seem to not even see the silky shiny, sun-sparking ebony winged ones that raucously demanding your eye. That is what warning claxons are intended to do.

Do not look into the eyes of a caldera crow. You are a simple servant. You've come for day work, nothing more. And just like the rest, you will keep your eyes and head low even when you are not in the presence of 'your betters.' Work and a day's pay is your only cause for being in the caldera and the castle keep. Be humble. Be what humility looks like. Keep your eyes down and your brain on full alert.

Dudes! I just felt all of you do that. And, all of you shifted into a fully present, alert awareness in one holy instant. Awesome teamwork people! Amazing individuals, by free will, becoming a team of one. Mental telepathy among a team of committed individuals is to be expected. It is not unnatural. Mortals aren't designed to be separate from one another, nor to keep only unto themselves and only for themselves. That is a classic example of Nephilim energy. By their works shall you know them, sayeth the master.

Now eagle and I will roll back outside the caldera so you can see the outer rim of the mountain cupping the caldera bowl. That looks pretty danged inaccessible to me, but I'm not a climber. Eagle loves flight though, and among all the options, he best loves riding air currents funneling up mountain walls. These were formed and faceted by shifting fault lines some ages before man appeared on earth. Eagle wheels and screes aloft on an updraft, taking a comfortable cruising speed with time to explore breathtaking views and vistas to tailor and map their work to best enhance and advance the mission objectives.

Why are we killing you, Mati? A trainee asks.

Because I will come for you if you do not. Only the soft sound of eagle's feathers whispering to the wind disturbs the silent flight.

Oh. I mean, you're already dead, but only mostly dead. If we make you dead again you will still be only mostly dead for all of that, and your mates too will be only mostly dead. Maybe I should as how instead.

And your plan is to make all those mostly dead, dead all over again, put them in a silver cage under a sun gold cloth, and take you all the way to America. For what purpose? What's your end game objective?

Triple substantial transformation of the bat bodies so they are transmuted into inert mineral matter. My brother in the United States knows how to do this rite, and he knows it must be done in order to protect innocents from the persistent predations of Nephilim blood lust.

Can't that be done here?

Not feasible. I am the only one in Europe who knows how to perform that rite; and I will be one of the undead in this silver cage. I will be otherwise 'occupied', and incapable of performing that rite.

And in America, is my brother. Who I made. To be a Keeper, not a feeder bleeder Nephilim. Brother will stand unwavering firm and focused on his objective. He will be eagle eye clear. He will be bear heart courageous in holding an energy tone that attracts and repels the feeder bleeder energy. The Nephilim will come for Brother, every full moon night. They will be one communal mind focused on achieving their objective of shattering the invisible boundary between what is and 'what is not.'

For 'what is not' can be nothing but illusion, and only innocent people can see the illusion for what it is.

You still have that innocence. It is not gifted by the Divine so you can waste by falling like Alice into a wonderland where everything is illusion and everything is good and beautiful. La, la, la, la, la, la, la. If it looks too good to be true and all is good, beautiful, buttercups and rainbows, it is probably illusion.

Keep your innocence, people. But refine and sophisticate your inner child so through your inner innocent, you can feel *Nephilim energy far* before *your physical senses are capable of registering it.*

Mission Rule: Do not pick a fight with a nearby Nephilim. They're all nasty. A key mission objective is: Avoid eye contact with Nephilim. Do not look into the eyes of a vampire is a core mission value. When the strike team goes in to take out the caldera vamps that rule is a critical *mission* objective.

When the mission is accomplished and the file is closed, go see a good movie with someone you love. It is an excellent way to help your inner innocent child to again feel safe, secure, and unconditionally loved.

I taught and trained Brother by thought transfer, how to turn mostly dead silver shot bats into inert mineral matter. He's got a rough road ahead of him, for every full moon nights for months on end, Brother will be shooting blind into a matt black sky full shrouded by the sheer number of vamp bats sweeping and swirling overhead. They'll completely black out moon and star light.

It will be hard for Brother because Brother loves without condition, without intent. Even in the face of his keen knowledge, aforethought, and purpose, cause, and personal objective. And I cannot protect him. Magi sighs low, soft, howling mad mournful, *because unconditional love given willing and free, is the bright light heart marker of my brother, who is sworn and pledged to his role as a Keeper.*

Brother will eat, sleep, and bear the sins of every feeder bleeder he silver drops from the matt black sky. There will be enough night fall bat bodies to fill full the meter of barrel space above the hot spot of the flames leaping off the gasoline soaked windfall wood tucked tented inside the drum. He will know all the Nephilim by their energy. He will silver shoot them without mercy, even those who are his beloved ones. What terrible torment I have laid on you Brother, because I have no viable option. There is no other Keeper. I failed you by the very act of making you a Keeper.

Mati shakes herself free not unlike a puppy fresh leapt from water and splashing away the light sun bright liquid weight of it. She inhales fully and moves on. *On the good news front, there will be so many mostly dead bats on full moon nights, that every silver bullet will hit a mark, or more.*

His son..., just a lad now..., will help. Her silent wail of raging sorrow is barely a whisper of wind heavy weighted by her divided soul fallen in fear and remorse for what is not yet done..., what is still to come.

I can help with that. Offers an Interpol agent with sparkling eyes and a strong, confident air.

Tell, and show. Mati challenges with a fragile but resolute smile.

I heard your hinted logistics concerns around getting you, the caldera master attractor bats, and all the other globally interconnected bat hives dislocated to the new world. I heard about your brother in America, and his young son, and it occurs to me that have some solution ideas that I believe will mostly mitigate the risks you have conceived but have not revealed in words. Want to hear? Mati and the student body nod as one and settle in eager to hear her full fit solution.

Like you I'm a woman who does not fit the popular profile of a docile decent woman.

Like you, I can be compliant.

And like you, I am a total rebellious disaster when it comes to being obedient. She gives a lop-sided grin and continues: *What that produced in me is a determined will to be not just as good as those who look down their noses at me,* and are mind staggeringly better than the holier than thou consciousness of the world. I don't fight it. It just is, and I let it be.

And then, I go within where I find and reconnect with my higher self, the self of me that God had in mind when he created the singular expression of life that I AM! And ya know what? I AM good enough for me. My faith lies in the 'I AM'. The one I AM does not arise from nor is it subject to the rules of the physical world and so the weights, measures and judgments of that world cannot, as in is incompetent to, define the boundaries of who I am in the mind of the divine. I am not obedient. Personally, I don't give a flying rat's butt about the opinions and attitudes of light headed, heavy handed know nothings. I'm not obedient, and I already said that.

And that's the background you need to know. Here are the specifics:

1. I am a marksman par excellence. I've been banned from many notable hunting clubs because I regularly out-target and out-shoot everyone else. Even the gunslinger members aren't fast enough to empty their six-shooter quicker than me. And all my bullets hit inside the black eyeball of the target. It's rather like Maeve hunting with kings and taking more and better game with cleaner kills and one arrow loosed per deer. Or, like the Indians of all lands who mentally call the spirit of the animal and ask one who is willing to serve to feed, clothe, and house our hairless bodies through the winter to come to step forward. They come, with light heart and quick hoof.

2. There is always at least one other one who is willing to serve. I can *help* your brother, but only if he willingly overcomes his ingrained gender bias that because I sit to pee, I can be of no real help to him in holding the line of the Keeper against the bleeder feeders. Only with my unobstructed and un-resisted assistance, can your brother hope to hold his invisible the line against the swarming hordes of vampire bats that will befall him every full moon night for painfully long months. Your brother must own and allow that I am a Keeper. I am equal with him in that role. Your brother will yield, and will hold, a space for me at his side and in his heart, for I own the Mother's skill of healing. Her grin is macabre. *Masters of my art know how to cause pain as well and easily as how to invite and instill healing. Those counter-weighing skills are inseparable in Mother's eyes. Together they can be applied like a healing balm, mostly without touch, to ease and release the nightly horrors of the boy; and of your brother.*

The memories will remain..., tucked deep into the darkly receptive and retentive subconscious areas of the brain, and into the keeper places of the heart. This process is something akin to an energetic application of shock therapy but without the physical component of electrical shock therapy. She shudders. *My mission name, by the way, is She Keeper.*

3. *I am a master of numerous oriental arts. All of them are martial arts. Some of those arts do not look at all martial, they look instead like an amazing freeform graceful dance..., and they are just as lethal. The art of life is to clear see the ugly dark shadows and see that they are locked in an eternal dance with the bright liquid light of the sun..., and of the Son, who saw evil and dared call it by its name.*

4. *I am aces with knives: and I walk as soft and silent as a breeze. All of that intimidates the shit out of every vamp I have ever known or heard tell of. From my mouth to God's lips. My name is Gabriela by the way. It's the lady version of Gabriel, the Archangel Healer messenger pal of Michael, the Warrior. I try to travel in good company....* Gabriela grins. *Is your brother good company?* Mati's unsubtle snort is her only response. *I'm a healer too. If your brother isn't so crusted cracked like dry clods of dirt, I reckon I can show him how to have a good time even doing dirty work that, when it's done, will dissolve into history sorta like the dusters did.*

5. *And if you still have any doubts, Mati dearest, project the second floor hallway just here, to scale, with every obstacle and squeaky joist just as it is in the vamp house. Don't worry about the second floor hallway not fitting in this room, it will.*

Mati is puzzled but more curious to see the proofs Gabriela wishes to demonstrate, so she does. And the long hallway fits perfectly. *Is this magic?*

The trouble with magic is that no one has ever been able to define it. Nor has anyone ever been able to tell the difference between magic and hocus pocus. The art of life is to live in the world we live in with all the good, the bad, and the ugly, and not only survive, but to thrive. Okay, people, I'm ready to dance. Attention please.

No one sees Gabriela take her first step nor do most of them not trained as dancers follow her steps as she free form fleet feet flies down the long polished mahogany floor twisting and spinning silent swift as wind over silent squeaky joists and safe past precious porcelain hazards perched atop their obstacle course positioned tower stands.

At the end of the hallway, the healer stops and turns to the gape jawed watchers. Gabriela smiles winsome winning. *Shall we all agree then that I will be the one to go to the top floor and take out the vamps napping there?* She sees the nods and smiles. *It will be good though that those of you who can scale walls and towers to be quietly on the roof near windows in case something unexpected happens – or something expected doesn't happen.*

The first rule of preparation is always have a back-up plan. And, Gabriela vamp coos, *a woman always adores having smitten admirers and avid imitators in her company.*

The mission doesn't care *who backs me up. The mission cares about success. Punta, period. So,* she smiles, *any of you up for defense dance classes as part of your training program?*

Yes, we are. Affirms the wide eyed astonished chief. And of course, everyone else avidly agrees.

Gabriela smiles to the chief and declares. *Put it on our schedule then, Chief. I will be your trainer…, for the same pay, of course.*

Of course. The chief smiles at her playful negotiation and nods a bow to her attentive planning skills. *A hundred percent committed.* He thinks: *And she's got something else up her sleeve too.*

Gabriela turns to Mati and declares: *I will carry with me your gilded cage, its silver key, and its sun gold close fitting cover on the mission. When I make the caldera vamp bats mostly dead again, I will put each one in the cage and will lock the cage door against improbable escape. I will go from room to room, first taking out the male maker vamp and locking it in the cage. Then I'll go to the room where his sisters sleep, make them mostly dead bats again, lock them up, and then I'll go to the room where your Mater sleeps* Gabriela closes her eyes against the words she must now say, *and make her mostly dead all over again, then I will lock her bat body in the cage with the vamp master and his wicked stepsisters. There's nothing about vamps that's natural.*

And then I will creep silent as death into the room where your sisters sleep, and you, on a mattress on the floor. I will take your sisters first, you must know that.

Yes. I must see…, and know that. Mati tips her head: *If it's easier for you, Gabriela, I will walk willing into your silver edged blade while you only stand still and hold the blade still, straight, and firm.*

Gabriela is silent a moment, considering. *Maybe that would be easier for me. It seems that I've become quite attached to you – Your Vampness.* Gabriela drops a courtly bow to hide her grim grin and liquid blinking eyes.

And, Mati, you have my word that when I put your vamp bat body in the cage with the others, I will lock it, cover it, and I will personally carry it with me all the way to America, and then all the way your brother's farm on the high plains prairie of western Kansas.

I will ask you to release me, so I can help Brother. Mati counters.

No. Gabriela says bluntly. *I will do – for you, Mati, in your stead – all that needs to be done to support and assist your brother before, during and after the full moon night bat night flights.*

I am a master of the healing arts. I give you my personal assurance, Mati, that before they sleep each full moon night, I will soften and smudge the hard memories of your brother and his boy so that they will retain some sweet semblance of sanity, and some traits of child-like innocence, which is the true nature of man held safe in the arms of God.

That is what Keepers do you know, Keepers like you made your brother to be. It is the work of Keepers to hold high the fierce flame of faith and the spirit of freedom against the persistent pernicious assaults of Nephilim.

Your faint faith, Matilda, is a signal symptom of persistent pernicious Nephilim assault on your self-confidence and self-awareness. Who do you think you are...? That's the question. You are not *who you thought you were a decade ago. Who are you now?*

Those vamp act assaults have continued and increased for almost a decade now. It is highly unlikely that you have any effective capacity to even choose to kill one of your own kind, let alone triple transform your vamp master makers, for God's sake! Get real, girl! Your former humanity has been small sip sapped out of you, Mati. It is not there anymore.

Gabriela smiles and gently promises: *On the last full moon bat night flight, I will uncover and unlock your silver cage. I will remove all your mostly dead bat bodies, and I place you and all the vamp royals atop the pile of bats shot from the sky that last bat flight night. And, when the gas fired windfall and all the mostly dead bats are sundered to ash, your brother and I together will perform the rite of triple substantial transformation turning the carbon of you to ash, and the ash of you to water, and the water of you to earth, turning your Nephilim self into inert mineral matter.*

You have my word, Mati, I will stand side-by-side with your brother as his fellow Keeper. Together we will protect innocents, including your nephew, against the ravening raging persistent nightly assaults against them.

I know what making you a bleeder feeder did to the true nature of you. I know what it meant to you to be made a bleeder feeder by your birth mother. I know what it did to your innocent faith in goodness and love, to be power whored by your wicked witch Mater to satiate her own ravenous faith in lack, not enough, and needy feeding greed.

It would be natural, in your circumstances, to think of yourself as the victim. For you have been victimized by your mother. Gabriela's soft side self disappears illusionist quick.

It would also be natural for someone in your situation to seek to avenge yourself against your abuser by taking revenge. In doing that, you step into the mental and emotional tones of the victor..., and then you are no better than Hitler, Mussolini, and the other greedy-guts provoking, promoting, and boldly profiting from the World War instigated by their ravening Nephilim greed.

The caldera vamps supported the war, did you know that? She waits for Mati's sorrowing nod. *The caldera vamps traded the currency and gold they'd collected over centuries in exchange for a plentiful supply of daily fresh spilt blood of wounded warriors, the newly dead, and the nearly dead, on battlefields all across Europe. They made, and claimed as their own, many of the MIAs of that war. In most cases, their bodies were never found for being made newly undead. The caldera vamps were and are the influence makers of vampdom. Vamps globally will follow their call to converge on the new world isolated and an ocean removed from the feeder bleeder legends of the old world.*

You are a caldera vamp, Mati, call it guilt by association or anything else you please, but know well and clear that nothing you can say or do will persuade me to allow you, in mostly dead bat form, out of your gilded cage before the night of the last bat flight. On that night when I place all your silver struck bat bodies atop the fire and watch you burn to ash, then your brother and I will collect your ashes and triple substantially transform you and the vamp bat bodies into inert mineral matter.

Your art of illusion is exceptional, Mati, even for a vamp. It is not good enough to cloud my eyes.

Amen that, confirms the chief. *For what it's worth, Mati, you will be traveling in style, and that goes far beyond your gilded cage. Gabriela will travel by ocean liner to America keeping the gilded cage in her personal possession at all times. When Gabriela is cleared through customs at Ellis Island and then through to New York City, she'll travel by a train to the west most station in Kansas. Then she will travel by car to your brother's farm bringing your sun gold covered silver cage with her.*

Gabriela's Interpol mission will not be complete until all the vampires summoned by the caldera bat man master to fly to America have been transformed and made totally dead forever amen. Do I make myself clear?

Mati nods. What's a girl to do? Except to graciously receive what she really wanted all along, and all along thought she'd have to do alone. Instead, she will have nothing at *all* to do once she is captured in the gilded cage before the mission crew leaves the caldera castle. *It's a relief actually, not having to do it alone as I thought I would. But not getting to watch is an unexpected and disconcerting disappointment. A bit of a bitch actually.* She gnarls a growls in her mind only. *Oh well!*

I do hate being a prisoner though. And, that probably comes from Mother's predatory confinement in the pretty upper whore room. I guess you and I will be close companions for a while, Gabriela.

Hum, Gabriela murmurs. *That's not how the Stockholm syndrome works actually; but if it gives you comfort, go for it.*

Okay then, I guess I'll just be depressed then for the rest of my nearly natural life.

That'll make it easier to let it go, Mati, when your time in the flames comes on the last bat flight night. For whatever comfort it affords you, I will be the one who takes your bat bodies from the cage and puts them atop the last bat flight pile. To save your brother and the boy from that trauma, I myself will perform the rite of triple substantial transformation once your bodies are burned to ash. Carbon to ash is the first step, ash to water, the second, water to earth, the third and final transformation. There's an abandoned well on your brother's farm and that's where the final water to earth step in transformation will take place. And, your brother and his son will forget that well, for I will put an occlusion spell on it so they won't even see it when they pass it by.

And, if you hadn't been born to that bitch of your mother, we would not *be having this totally preposterous conversation, Mati. Cest la vie, cest la guerre.* She shrugs. *If it's any comfort to you I will make damned well sure your mother's bat body is dead center in the hot spot of the fire.* She makes the sizzling sounds of greedy well fed flame, at first emitting a sizzling singing sound, then the z-z-z-z-z sound of brazing, then hell-fire raging roar of broiling flesh.

And I will take care of the Keepers, Mati. I will make certain and sure that we three Keepers stay upwind of the smoke rising up off the fire hot flames. Gabriela gives witnesses to Mati's powerful full body shudder response to the images she willfully evoked into Mati's mind. Her eyes are sad, sorrowing. Yet the rest of her face and demeanor is determinedly, unrepentantly and devotedly forcefully focused on the mission objective.

Look on the bright side she suggests. *You'd be like a fifth wheel again – like you were to your mother even before the caldera vamp illusionist let her see only pearls, gold, silver and precious stones in multi-carat sizes, where before there was nothing but shadowy death by deep small bites. Death to Source that is. And Source is the sole source provider of life eternal. For you it's a win-win.*

Your mother is a bitch, can we just say it like it is? She stops abruptly, then recalibrates. *Um – and I'm repeating myself aren't I? Well, at least I used different words this time.*

Mati giggles gleeful glad again to be alive and to still be an integral, if a somewhat narrow, part of the Interpol mission. *Even if I am nothing more than a guide and then a piece of luggage that Gabriela will faithfully tote half way around the world. Still, I will be made one and whole again with Source.* Mati sighs smiling in sundered wonder, *by the work of my Keeper brother, and the soothing salve of my angel Keeper Gabriela. Oh, God is good! I am so ready to return to my personal at-one-ment with Source. Whatever 'personal' means in this curious convoluted context of me not being who I was, nor even being who I am.*

You know we can hear everything you think in the silence of your mind, don't you?

Mati starts upright on her desk perch by the gilded cage, then recovers her place and time in the classroom. *Of course. Mater told me double daily that my habit of thinking aloud imagining no one could hear would be my downfall one day. Guess she was right. Seems to me though that today is my up-fall day, and it is a strange and uniquely disturbing day for all of that.*

Are you feeling detached and removed from who you think you are? Mati nods, keeping her eyes low. *That's a first big step, dear heart. There will be more, but probably none more disturbing. I will teach you Kung Fu, an oriental martial art that looks more like art than dance. That will distract you.*

Like what you did when you danced down the vampire hall hazard map? Gabriela nods and smiles. *Oh, I am so up for that. When do we start?*

O seventeen hundred hours. 5:00 PM for civvies like you.
Where?

Basement exercise room. No mats. Lots of sweat and salt water in the eyes though. You will discover muscle groups you never knew you had, and they will aggrieve you even when you turn in your sleep. But, in a couple of weeks the bulked up tears will heal and the muscle tissue will lengthen, strengthen and build mass as you master small and long muscle strength that will grow from the tears and stretches. You will be one bad-ass bat woman.

She scans the student body naming by eye contact each trainee as a participant. She prefers willing participation…, and she'll work with the unwilling until they get it too. *How many of you think you can kick stretch so your toe touches the I-bar supports up there?* She points to the ceiling. *None of you then? Well, I'm telling you it can be done – and you can do it – because I did.* Allowing no time for debate or argument, Gabriela toe steps a spinning leap, followed by a split leg back over flip that lifts her sure footed as a gazelle into an elliptical upward upside down three step tap walk along the bottom of a handy I-bar. Surrendering to gravity's law Gabriela does a back over flip to plant land upright on her feet, palms on her knees, thighs bobbing her hips, shoulders, and torso up and down in syncopated rollicking rhythm with the upwelling gleeful bubbling laughter welling up from her lungs, throat, and mouth.

Okay, dang! I'm totally good with odor of liniment for a handful or so of days of really not wanting to be alive in this achy breaky body right now. I'm in. Same reason. Comes the alleluia chorus in one voice. Then a lone voice asking: *Is there a spa nearby?*

Gabriela eyes the boy with bemusement. *You are one spoiled, overly indulged young fellow aren't you?* She laughs gleefully, drawing him into her joy. *Maybe next time Mommy sends the chauffer to pick you up for holiday she can arrange a spa stop for you.* Half way through the sentence Gabriela is hooting with glee teasing the Plebe's reaction into a tickled acceptance of his gaffe so that he can laugh it out of his mind, or at least those parts of it where he secrets and hides his deepest darkest dreads and pretends they're not really there at all. *That's classic Nephilim illusion/delusion, dear heart. I am a healer. My master gift is helping you release the demon dreads you have buried all of your life in the deep dirty darks of your subconscious mind, and turn them to your side – as I have done – so that your fears are not your enemy, but your stern, pushy, in-your-face instructor. . Make it easy – or challenging, your choice. I am your instructor though and you should keep that in mind.*

Let's dance first, and then get practice mats in here so we can start learning some kick butt Kung Fu moves and do aerial battle with our personal deep dark secret scary things.

But Kung Fu isn't about battle is it?

Gabriela shakes her head. *It's about mastering your scary dark dragons. It's about learning to master yourself, and also about mastering your fierce dragon fears so that you can ride the strong updraft of that fierce fire as a master dragon rider.*

Oh, I am so in for that.

Matt, we do need mats! Matt and a bevy of plebes swarm from the room and back with mats that quickly blanket the floor of the training room while others move chairs clear of the training place.

That was an impressively quick start, Gabriela. And it was a powerful healing you skillfully embedded directly into their training practice – arousing enthusiasm in them in the boot. I'm impressed.

Thank you! Gabriela grins. *Did you know, Mati, that the word 'enthusiasm' is derived from the Latin words 'en Theos,' meaning 'in God'? The healer in me says those words are especially meaningful for you right now.* She waits awhile comfortable with Mati's silence.

Ca-, ca-, can a vampire..., ever be..., en Theos?

No. But in a handful of months that won't be a problem for you because the Nephilim energy that possesses you by illusion will have been transmuted from your body mind brain earth suit, and your Soul returned home and reunited whole and pure to Source again. Gabriela grins, *and then, when the Spirit of you embodies again, there will be no residual sludge of slugs or other nocturnal feeders left to weigh down the spirit of you when it re-combines and enters the newly inspired self you and God design and arrange for you in your next game of life on Earth. You may as well be prepared, because of the wounds inflicted by Nephilim in this lifetime, there is sure to be a primary mission in your next embodiment that involves healing yourself of both the victim and the victor consciousness.*

What's left?

Verity consciousness. Truth consciousness. Gabriela eases into the depths of the peace permeating those four words in timeless space and lets them free speak in the silence only her inner ear hears.

There is no body...! Mati is stunned senseless for an infinite eternal instant. *It's all illusion.*

Until Spirit needs a body mind brain Earth suit that is uniquely designed by the Divine to do a thing that Spirit has never done before. It is a transformative concept for the vamp amped mortal mind of Mati, and she knows in an instant that she can dance on air with Gabriela even if the woman *is* an archangel in human form. *And she is. And she doesn't give a damn whether or not I know it.*

I can work with that..., verity consciousness..., in which I know the truth of the illusion of body mind brain as a physical form. Verity consciousness is utilitarian. It confounds the illusion delusion of the body mind brain. And I am past tired and bored with this body mind brain deluded into submission by the mind numbing illusion of the fabulously long life of the living dead.

I can hear all of that you know, comes Gabriela's silent sullen snap.

I know.... I was counting on it actually. I am just now learning — all over again — that wise words wielded in wicked ways desensitizes the mind body brain, and emboldens and embeds 'the victim' consciousness, the first grand illusion that invokeslevokes the tepid torpor of Nephilim dead men walking. It's criminally creepy.

And the victor consciousness, well that's the at home in control personal persona of vampires. She grins, *that thumbs down controlling, and intimidating vamp act dire domination is the iron fist inside the velvet glove that takes blood in punishment for minor imagined offenses so the victim is made to blame. That is the dark side of the victor consciousness. It's pathologically creepy.*

That, my dear archangel Gabriela, leaves me only the third option as rationally viable, and that is iffy. Verity consciousness — despite the iffyness — or maybe because of it. Mati smiles into Gabriela's eyes, *Truth consciousness inherently means that I have to choose to be an alert, aware, and fully informed co-creator with Source mind energy. My personal will doesn't amount to a hill of beans.*

A hill of beans?

Yeah, Da used to say that about a thing that wasn't worth the time and effort to gather, bundle and cart to market. Mati sees all the blank puzzled faces around her and explains. *Think of tall growing pretty wee weeds you once left in your garden or field. How'd that work for you? More work, that's how. Plus, in the process of uprooting all those tall shade giving weeds from your garden so your plants can grow, you uprooted the vegetables and herbs you planted there on purpose, am I right?*

She sees their answer and counsels. *You cannot change the past, people. You can only change the future, and you can only do that by changing your mind about what it is you value. I used to value long life, power, and luxury; and then I had it, I lived it, for cold countless decades. I had made a mobile mountain out of a hill of beans!*

What are the beans piled up in *your hill of pointless passions? What are you treasuring that in reality has no value to you? Is it money? Is it power? Is it social status? Is it being a **bold face type**, a name everyone knows from the society pages even if they never met you?*

Those are your vanities! *They are not your values. Don't go vapid vamp over vanities, make a fierce fire of them. Get a grip on reality, peeps.*

Let's engage a wee mental practice of starting a roaring fire here in the middle of all of us. She smiles and observes casually: *The fire of spirit can indeed burn in us. But it will not burn the flesh skin or clothes of us…, because spirit is a God job.*

It is also true that if you step close to a fire asking it to let you feel the heat of its flames, you will feel them. Mati puffs a sigh of pique, *No, dear hearts, you cannot toast marshmallows on the fire of spirit you silly saps!* And she chortles along with the rest of them. *Well, that broke the ice.*

Sunflowers and seeding weeds that have medicinal, herbal or healing uses, and can be let grow along fences, beside well managed flowering vines that offer uses other than beauty, which is a virtue in and of itself, yet beauty alone does not balance a scale to an ounce of weight.

I hear you…, all of you, having an 'aha' moment about what it means to be human and to have been given custody over all the rooted, hooved, clawed, winged, and footed things in the Garden of Eden. You can eat 'em. And that dominating, controlling, thumbs down energy comes from the victor consciousness. It is voraciously creepy.

What is your verity consciousness? What does that look and feel like to you? Mati watches the transformation as each one uproots the overgrown weeds of victim and victor consciousness and lays bare the fertile soil of their souls now rising wingless to return to the One, the verity, the truth of the Spirit of the Divine implanted in the egg of them before it was fertilized into life by the inspiration of Spirit. *Nice work, people! Your auras are rainbow bright and shining light with Spirit Divine. Do you feel it? Do you see it? Is it now more real to you than your 'reality' ever was? Good. That pleases and gratifies me more deeply than I can express in words and concepts. That being the case, I'm coming over to your side as a trainee. I'm leaving the training to the Master among us.*

A stagnant puzzling pause settles into the echoing silence in the room that is broken by a hesitant question posed by a tactician among them. *Gabriela, how does that work tactically, that Mati is sitting on the desk by a gilded cage and wants to work on the mats here with the group of us?*

Ah, Gabriela replies, *you are face to face with the self-imposed didactic dichotomy of balancing reality bites of the temporal world as you see and know it, in one tray of a triple-beam scale, and timeless Truth and fiction in the other scale tray. Spirit has weight on the physical plane, it's just buoyant, like weighing a balloon filled with helium. The triple-beam is out of its league.*

The only way that 'truth' can be weighed against 'fiction' is metaphysically. The only scale capable of weighing truth is in your heart. The counterweight of heart is choice. Your question is another take on Shakespeare's 'to be or not to be' soliloquy. The answer is what do you want to be?

O-o-o-o-h, wicked.... The class takes a laughter breather and puts things right again. *Mati is sitting on the desk, and sparring with you verbally and physically on the training mat.*

The man boy rises with a rueful shrug and says: *I never liked being a bench warmer. I'm on the mat with you warrior women masters of mental, metaphysical and physical warfare.* Despite his obvious insanity, he growls: *I'm coming for you, Ladies.* He steps on the mat in a wide eyed aware and alert fluid Kung Fu horse position. Divine Director shouts: 'action', and all hell breaks loose.

There is no one on the bench. No one in the bleachers. No one shaking crepe paper pom poms by the field of play. No one planting poppies in a faraway field. Only spiritual warriors training for spiritual warfare are present on the field that day.

Metaphysical training class – day one, hour one.

One hour later: *Oh,* one weary warrior grouses, *I do believe that every muscle, tissue, and tendon in my whole body is stretched sore and trembling.*

Back on the mats, everyone, Gabriela counters their body orders. *It is now time for us to do the slow dance of martial arts that lengthens and strengthens all your Kung Fu abused muscles.*

Tai chi is the name given to this fluid soft dance of grace. Even as she speaks Gabriela is teaching by example, her body mind brain slow dancing itself into physical motion as fluid and flexible as the piping tune of the uninhibited dancing Pan, the faun and forever muse of music in motion.

Metaphysical training class – day one, hour three.

Slow swimming lessons, A.K.A.: Cool down float, slow strokes, dead man pose; no laps.

Gabriela leads the hot smelly masters in the making along a forest trail that is resoundingly silent and alive with song and slithers and snaps and sighs of wings stirring the air and leaves above them splashing rainbow dots of color flashing through sun lit shiny winking tree leaves recent washed by welcome rain. *Remember to use thigh and stomach muscles to hold you upright and alert as you climb. Nothing makes you more dull and careless clumsy better than climbing or walking like an old man stooped and bent low in arthritic agony.* She pauses atop a rock standing upright and at ease in the sun kissed air and woods surrounding them and offers wisdom of the ages. *Awareness precedes choice. Choice precedes change.* She announces from her lofty ledge of their climb.

Awareness is a gift. A gift that is often not effectively and genuinely received by we mere mortals. She grins, raises a hand of admission, and watches as other climbers, then all, raise their hands in acceptance, recognition, acknowledgment, of stumbling humble gratitude for homely gift of grace.

Choice preceded change. People, understand this: It is our work *as co-creators with God on this Earthly plane to change the world in which we live. We can do that in our head like we've always done, or we can do it from our hearts where the inspiration of Spirit first inspires life in us. Did you know that the heart is fully formed and functioning and assigning developing cells to specific roles, places, structures, and functions in the body?*

For six weeks, people, before the vertebra of the spine are formed and hung in place by tendons strung in fluid place with sinew and muscle before *that thin blue line flows up the spine and initiates the brain — that is fully formed and loaded with all the atavistic memories written in the Book of Life before electrical currents of the brain are even activated? The heart is the sacred inner dwelling place of the Most High God.*

We can shut God out..., but He's still there, inspiring and animating us. We're just ignoring and not hearing the soft sweet voice of spirit. The only thing that changed for us is that we willfully expelled, barred, and locked our conscious mind, our co-creator portal, against the infinite, eternal, inspiring and lovingly indifferent Source Mind of God. God gave us free will, he will not revoke that gift because we use it with ignorant indifference and heartfelt meanness of spirit.

In our free fall from grace we turned our hearts and minds against the indwelling sole Source provider of everything that is, and all that is not as well. We rebelliously willfully stripped ourselves bereft of the truth of who are. We forfeited the help of angels, we turned a blind eye to the inspiring spirit that guides us to who we came to life to be and what it is we came to do. We stumble like blind beggars in the dark night of the soul, cursing and damning the Divine for giving us free will and allowing us to use it freely.

Gabriela pauses a thoughtful moment, then offers: *It's Nephilim energy. The question is: did we come to life with the disability, did we choose it, or did we just capitulate to the victim consciousness out of social and familial habit? Does that reason change anything? Not on the physical plane, no.*

Today we work on the mental plane, our meditation focus is: Who do you think you are?

This is a walking meditation, folks. Up, up, on your feet. Let's go, we've got soapstone and a swimming hole ahead of us; and miles to go before we sleep.

By the end of the excursion, all the participants are exhausted, enlivened and refreshed, and ready for the next unexpected aspect of their evolving and unfolding Interpol mission to make the world a safer place for humans to live absolved of the Nephilim obstruction to their Oneness with Source.

Add some soapstone to your travel kit, and plan your life to be a Keeper of the rights and freedoms assigned by God to each and every one of the infinite beings created as humans…, who believe they are little more than consumers collecting the pointless pleasures and treasures of the physical world. Abject spiritual poverty by choice, is what that is. I expect better of you. And I expect my expectations to be met, or exceeded, by each and every one of you. Fish, or cut bait. Do it now.

Conditionally committed is not commitment. Conditionality is the half-way house for the spiritually impoverished. If you think you are one of those, this is the time to step down from any role in this Interpol mission. If you do you can count yourself a failure, or a wise and prudent decider. It makes no never mind to me. It makes a world of difference to you. Who do you think you are?

Here's our swimming hole, announces Gabriela gazing down with a satisfied smile at the invitingly shaded, breeze cooled swimming hole she found when she was but a free-spirit child of a farm family that flowed organically whole from their devotion to the integral oneness of all of life in all its manifest forms.

As it turns out, Gabriela is the last of the travelers to reach the pond now gone turbulent and riotous with the righteous gleeful energy of the new-born Keepers. *It is good,* she smiles with unspeakable gratitude to the One, and the wondrous ways his grace appears on the physical plane of life.

And Mati herself is an amazing grace. Thank you for that. In exchange for the praise, the Divine drops hints and intimations of immortality while unimagined and amazingly perfect outcomes appear in Gabriela's open and absorptive mind. And she is transformed yet again. And again she meets and exceeds expectations, and is giggling gleeful grateful for that grace. Amazing grace indeed!

We'll do this every day? Comes a question from a swimmer.

Every day while the mission continues, Gabriela assures while slicing into the water without raising a wake or wave. She spies Mati swimming deep and easy beside her and smiles.

We need a plan for what happens to the caldera, and to the people who keep and maintain it once the vamps are removed…, and the caldera is bereft of human inhabitants and the work they do to maintain and enhance the space, the castle, and the keep.

Forward thinking…. Gabriela knows this as an exploratory mission on Mati's part. She's curious. She waits, knowing Mati has the lead. Gabriela soft silent probes the feelings of Mati's energy, finding her every intimated idea harmonious and copasetic. She's curious. She knows better than to ask.

The caldera is an amazing and beautiful space and it has been kept so by the people who come here to work and maintain the caldera lands – and the castle and the keep. Without maintenance the caldera goes wild and…, ugly, at the level of the energy in the basin. Without love, best administered by man, the whole space reverts to the wild; and it will be inhabited by the wild things that were obedient and beholden to the coven of living undead that owned the place…, although I doubt they had a deed or anything like that.

So, what happens to the people who kept the caldera? What happens to the castle once it's been abandoned and falls into disrepair? What happens to the people who make an honest living keeping the caldera, the keep, the castle, and its kitchens and serving and sleeping spaces? What can be done for the workers on the day of the raid so they are not taken out by marksmen as enemy combatants? What happens to them without the income earned from doing the jobs they did to keep the caldera orderly, and comfortably safe, and naturally beautiful?

I see the pictures in your mind of what that looks like. Not pretty. Gabriela says deflated. *I feel what happens to the workers who kept the space while the mostly dead vampires still live. I know how hard it will be for them to live without wages earned from working inside the caldera…, in a post-world war economy made brutally bankrupt by the cost of turning living, loving, thriving humans into permanently dead ones.* Mati blinks her eyes rapidly, like an eagle does when seeing too much too clearly, and none of it is lovely or good. She ups her altitude and makes an attitude adjustment.

But there is a way…, she whispers prayerfully.

Tell me.

Mati smiles, gives a soft giggle of excited opportunity, and presents her case. *The caldera is perfect for a ski resort and hunting lodge, a high-end resort, with castle rooms priced at a premium.*

Rooms in buildings within the keep are priced at a moderate – high end ski resort – per night rates.

The rooms outside the keep can be converted into a hunting lodge for hunter gatherer guests who really want *the stinking bug-bit luxury of sleeping, bathing and eating in a hunting lodge setting. Ugh! They can have that – at high end hunting lodge per night rates. Checkout at noon, of course.* Gabriela giggles boggled knee weak glee knowing it will work.

And there are the people who work here. They know the place, they know the space, they know what's great and what's not so good, and they know how to keep the place and the space clean and productive enough to satisfy prickly prissy picky vampires who've had centuries to perfect their down the nose distain for lesser beings. There are some amazing cooks at the castle, they'd be called chefs and paid a chef's rate at any ski chalet on the planet. I lived there, I ate the food they prepared. I also lived as a courtesan eating on the tab of my customers at top dollar restaurants, and I assure you that the cooks working at the caldera are culinary virtuosi by comparison.

The grounds keepers are without par, the hunting guides are the best in their field, the carpenters, craftsmen, and artisans are amazingly gifted and creative. These people create collector items because their masters were collectors, but mostly because they know how to invite, receive and create inspiration..., meaning 'in spirit, or inspiring spirit'. These people know how to judge art from craft while still seeing the art in *the craft. They value both and each.*

They know the art of weights and measures, and pulleys and planes and forces and harmonies. They take natural things and turn them into things of unnatural beauty. Those perilously placed vases that look like Ming vases..., they're not. They were created by craftsmen working at the caldera. The crystal bowls, vases, and ornaments, were made by caldera craftsmen and women. The real Ming vases are kept in the vamp lords and ladies sleeping spaces. You'll find none in Mater's room, nor any in the room my sisters share – with me when I come for an overnight stay – which is rare because a working woman is expected to work afternoons, evenings, and nights, and bring home the pay to Mater whore master. Mati hisses the last three words with serpentine venom.

Gabriela leans away looking askance at Mati who just now looks very snaky, and not in a good and loving way either. *Time for a diversionary operation,* she thinks. *So what are you suggesting? The big picture I think I have pretty clear, it's the practical details I'm not getting, like what happens to these people on the day of the raid? If they are allowed inside we've got an unacceptable risk to them, our mission, and our operatives.*

Someone with administrative skills and authority meets them at the entrance to the caldera, and offers them a week's vacation with pay.

And how will we pay for that?

Mati smiles smug and replies: *People who live long and prosper collect currency... in addition to pretty priceless breakable things. And, being discriminating collectors, they do not collect German marks, nor Italian lira, nor Russian rubles, nor any other currency of any country that systematically shakes down their citizens by dispossession, theft, extortion and iron fists in leather gloves. Those currencies had thoroughly been rendered trash cash by the Nephilim leaders of those countries.*

The caldera vamps adore greenback dollars, the currency of the U.S. That money they did not sell nor even lend at lend at exorbitant interest rates to any failing dictatorial governments. If you live for thousands of years, you are bound to learn things a person who lives four-score and twenty years simply does not have the time to absorb, let alone master.

You're suggesting that Interpol uses the U.S. dollars to pay the caldera workers to not *work the day of the raid, and pay them a week of 'vacation pay'?*

Mati shrugs her shoulders and one bow arched eyebrow as she meets Gabriela's eyes for a count of five..., then says: *I'm not with Interpol, so I don't know this about Interpol, but history and life itself teaches me that confiscation is traditional, long-standing, and functional rule of war. That truly must be true for even the wee small unofficial operations that Interpol runs. It is an international police operation.*

Now you're teaching me my business?

You asked. Mati's eyes are searing sober and cautionary. *And we never had this conversation.* She snaps and turns away, letting Gabriela plainly see the pugnacious pugilistic jut of her jaw a jarring silent while. *If you are unwilling, or unable, to be a collaborator with principles and reasoned logic, you are wasting my time. Why, are you are throwing up illogical and counterproductive roadblocks against doing what is right, just because in the process of doing what is right, you will also be doing the right thing?*

Given a name like Gabriela, how *are you able to oppose an idea that incorporates taking the right action* and *doing the right thing? When did the*

Nephilim drop into and possess your mind effectively negating your Interpol training? Those two mission objectives must be taken, and planning must be comprehensive enough to anticipate risks and eliminate them when that is possible. Interpol will use greenbacks, and an Interpol agent will pay a week's wages to the caldera workers to get them safe away from the caldera the day of the operation. The next day the caldera craftsmen, cooks, maids, and forester/hunters will come back and do their usual work in the caldera, the keep, and the castle.

They will already have been given vacation pay for a week's worth of work..., challenge them to use that paid time to apply their art to bring into physical form a vision, an idea, a concept that makes their heart sing, into manifest form.

The small pretty fragile things can be sold at the caldera castle gift shop. The work of artisans can be sold at their stalls. Any craft that needs heat to create, needs an open-air fire pit. Any art or craft needing lead based paints needs to be done outside. We need containment and disposal for those wastes. Mati looks deep into Gabriela's eyes and pleads, *there is so much to be done to turn the caldera into a high-end ski resort and hunter's lodge, that we* really *must not be wrapping ourselves tight around the axle of your moody prudery.*

Prudery? Gabriela is aghast.

I call it like I see it. Mati juts her chin and goads: *Prove me wrong.*

Gabriela hides her grin but her giggle makes its escape through the tight bars of her fingers. She nods. *Okay, I take your point.*

I know the Interpol agent administrator who can do this 'community outreach program' of yours perfectly and precisely well every step of the way. Perhaps the greatest boon is that during his post mission debriefing, he will account for every greenback to the penny, from his memory. All of this is classified.

Given that information, Mati, please imagine the strings I had to pull and the promises I had to make to get Interpol's permission to use you as an operative in planning, executing, mopping-up this raid. Your debriefing will be brief. The window is between the time when I kill your sisters and the time I kill you. Gabriela grins, *I won't be in any particular hurry, but do know that you will be dead and caged an hour before the sun sets.*

I am very much looking forward to seeing the caldera ski resort and hunting lodge painted luminous bright by the fire of the setting sun. And, you will not be part of that, Mati. Only your remarkable vision of the resort and hunting lodge will outlive you. I want you to be complete with that, Mati, for I have come to love and admire you in unexpected and brilliant ways. Your inspiration and insight will be, and remain, a guiding light for the chalet ski resort and hunting lodge that you have envisioned, and that Interpol will make manifest for the benefit of all the hunters and skiers who will come here to live for a few weeks and live their fantasy vacation so very distinct from their mundane lives as hunter gatherers.

Will I hate them? I'm pretty certain and sure that I will, and I'm not happily satisfied with that.

On the good news front, Mati, I know the perfect administrator for the caldera resort and hunting lodge. He's not an Interpol employee, and that is as it should be, because the Interpol mission will be complete and ended on the day the caldera vamps are killed, caged, and prepared for my personal transport to your brother's farm for the final conflagration that destroys and transforms the last of that vile energy into inert mineral matter.

You will be dead in physical form, Mati..., and you will live forever in my heart and mind as a Divine director of the transformation that banishes Nephilim energy and converts it into Divine grace and love..., the hallmark of the Oneness consciousness of the Divine One. The One, who will celebrate and honor you even I do, my dear, unique, and infinitely irreplaceable Mati. I will miss you..., even as God welcomes and celebrates the infinitely unique and beloved essence of the spirit of you, who came to life and living the cold cruelty of man in his time of transition and transformation in the third millennium of man's life on Earth.

The Creator God did grant Beelzebub and his minions' control of man and Earth the first three millennia of human life on Earth. And, the Divine One did wisely reserved the right of man to call on God's angels to protect and preserve him against the persistent, pushy, and devious attacks of the fallen angels. Gabriela grins: *It is unlikely that the Divine One did not grant to humans made vampires, the same ineffable, infinite grace. You called, Mati. You asked for total control of the issue and its outcome. God said no.* Gabriela shrugs. *But he knew that wasn't in your best interest, nor in the best interest of anyone, most especially those made Nephilim without their own exercise of free will. You got that grace, Mati. The grace available to you now, is to accept it with gratitude and joy. Or, you can keep on warping your fingers and hands into Nephilim claws – for want of grace – that is free for the asking. Time to get down off your high horse and get down on your knees – emotionally, not necessarily physically – but you can do both,* she grins wickedly, *and it's easier that way anyway. Your choice....*

Moon Bird

The rhythmic clip-clop of the mule's hooves following a familiar path home lulls Bam White into an unexpected euphoria in which his physical senses are profoundly hyper-alert to all the expressions of life settling into the retirement of the day as its fiery light casts slant shadows into shade of deepening night. He experiences and shares the passion of all the forms life inhabits and manifests on the physical plane; and gives thanks with special delight for the life and love he shares with his wife, and for his earnest amiable children.

Bam eyes the western sky where the sun burns down like hot coals, still flaring liquid gold rays across the bowl of the sky and tinting lingering vapor clouds with the hues of fire and flame. He smiles feeling the extending shadows on Earth tint heavenly hues just for man's pleasure and joy at this one singular sunset on this one holy night. He praises Great Spirit for the forever growing giving gift of life wisdom that ever guides him sure and safe along the twisting twining ways of his red road of life.

He surrenders, and mourns, that sometimes his personal wisdom is purely inadequate to the tasks laid before him. In that acknowledgment, Bam recalls, then forgives and releases all of his shortfalls, and those like his that appear in others. In the release Bam is overwhelmed by a flow of confidence and certainty he never before allowed his conscious mind to entertain. His personal sense of self, who he thinks he is, and who he thinks he came to life to be. He finds with sound shock that he is pathetically too small for the constant confounding callings and challenges of his life. He humbly admits that he is woefully and forever inadequate to competently cope with life's surprising twists and turns. He owns that.

He exhales that deficit in one powerful puff. *Release and let go*, he advises himself. Empty now Bam gasps great gulps of air and is filled to overflowing by the sometimes privately personal and always astonishing ways the Abiding Wisdom of Love subtly, slyly, subtly, reveals itself into his life. In functional ways too. *That's important!* Bam affirms in praise for that persistent presence.

A humble man before the throne of grace, Bam lifts his praise pack and slide steps from his cart, doffs his cap, drops to his knees in exaltation before the setting sun. Reverently placing the praise pack before him, bows to touch forehead to earth. He feels the fiery glow of the sun press the crown of his head, then penetrate livid light streams embracing his mind and brain. He melts liquid into his obeisance.

As amber light shot with rainbow flame filters through his skull and to his mind and brain he pulls deep slow breaths inhaling this singular grace. Holding his breath in the breadth of Spirit to a count of ten, he exhales, knowingly allowing a slow release of the small sticky stuff of life to be transformed into only love that seeps like warm honey through him. Bam observes his brain/mind rigorously recording mental release notes from the universe and methodically plants them to thrive and reside inside, his on-demand guide to a life practice of compassionate listening to all he meets on his red road walk.

He smiles knowing that his vision of a healed earth is already manifest although his mortal eyes cannot see it, nor his mind know how it comes or flows. He cannot even guess how Life will reveal itself in the flowing grace of time. He chooses to be a mind, and a heart, freely and willingly made whole, to be and to become the lover, and the beloved, of the myriad manifestations of the Divine into life in this benighted land now a wandering dust desert. Wandering dirt, Bam thinks, in a land once called the Great American Plains, the breadbasket of the world…, when the war still raged and ravaged Europe.

Surrendering the pains of the day, and of a lifetime, Bam gives sundered and surrendered praise and gratitude to the Source of all that is, all that is not, and everything in between. He is especially grateful for the unknown and the yet unseen blessings that will come for the people and the places of his beset beloved prairie. He is awed by and gives gratitude for the indigenous people of the land, and a great awe for those who crossed an ocean with little more than the firm will and the intention to make and call this land their home. Even when their living space is but a windswept dugout. Bam is wholly humbled by the grace and strength of the persistent prairie people in their diligent determination to restore fertility – albeit necessarily of a new kind – to their benighted chosen land.

Bam is grateful for the generosity of his neighbors in receiving his help and for their equally generous sharing of what is presently at hand when cash is not. He warmly praises the openhanded fair exchanges he regularly receives for the help he gives neighbors and town folks. He sends up a special smile of great gratitude for the inexplicable and ever timely generosity of Mistress RO.

It seems to him that she always clears her pantry and can cellar when food is more limited, or more costly, than can be had for the money he earns doing odd jobs around houses and yards. *I am grateful that you receive my special thanks for Mistress RO. You done a right fine job making that woman. And I'm plum delighted that you guided her and her great helpful heart to live and love in our town. And so it is, amen.*

Bam rises now, his surrender and praise complete and his heart healed and whole again. He picks up his praise pack and turns to his mildly munching mule, steps into the cart, pats the weighty bag beside him, takes up the reins, clicks his tongue, and his faithful mule resumes their habitual homeward way in the fading light of a day chock full with surprising burdens and blessings.

Home Again, Home Again

At ease in the abiding pacific peace of his sunset surrender of burdens and blunders, Bam whistles and tweets bird calls, and smiles anew at each reply of welcome home again to their nesting places along ridge rows and ditches, and to the brave branches of trees toeing roots deep enough to draw the water of life to branch and leaf. *Our land will live again. Welcome home my dear singers and tweeters,* he grins big and wide, *welcome home again…, welcome home!* He pats his praise pouch thinking of the 'extra chicken feed' Hester gave him and smiles so warmly at the winging singing birds his eyes cloud with happy tears. He tips back his head so the tears cannot fall and warbles joy to the soil, the sun still burning down in the West, and to the stars blinking Morse code odes to night; and to the ever cyclic order of life amidst, and despite, the random witless predations of man.

Though he will never tell of it, Bam sees and hears angels winging and singing odes of joy for the redemption and healing of earth that man will perform one day…, when man remembers again with the creation of man in the mind of the Divine as enlightened and knowing stewards of Earth and its atmosphere and its soil and its water. Caught up in the mystical magic of Oneness with Source Bam's voice box chest and lungs expand like a gently filling balloon setting free his throat and tongue to warble and wail and trill and titter and croak and caw, and speak and sing in the tongues of all winged warbling, footed and hooved things living on Earth. It is, in Bam's peculiar voice, an Ode to Joy.

So embraced in Oneness bliss is he that Bam can see nothing amiss until his mule stalls and stutters on the path home, bobbing her head until harness traces jingle and jangle in the deepening dark. Tensing the reins and talking gently to calm the animal, Bam blinks to refocus his mortal eyes to see what bothers his basically blasé beast. In the way a man does not see what is not there, so Bam does not see, then blinks to clear his eyes. He leans forward resting chest on his thighs and knees and lowering his head to mule head high. Still Bam does not see what is not there to see. Until he does.

He sits upright blinking his eyes, opening the aperture of his pupils, and sending his curiosity ahead of eyesight to lead it on; and then he sees what is not there.

Light. Where there should be light. Where my family is. He clicks his tongue and speaks with soft urgency and strong faith. "Let's go, Becky, let's us go see what's going on at home and put some light on the problem. If there is one. And it is sure looking like there is…. Let's go find what's not working, make it right, and get you some good healthy food."

Bam pet pats his praise pack, and breathes deep and slow. He sends faith and love ahead of his pleasantly plodding mule winging swift and true to the house – where now a feeble flame flickers fretful flaring light against the raised glass cover of the hurricane lamp. Their only light at night, save when the moon comes in. *It's not Lizzie…, her hand is sure and quick. These hands are new, small and slow, she doesn't know how to light the lamp. She's never done it before. Where is Melt? Where is Lizzie?*

That alone would have me worried if worry ever did any good, and it don't. Ever. Where is Lizzie? He worries anyway.

"Step it up, mule, get us home fast as you can, we got some fixing to do, let's go." Contrary to her reputation as a mule, Becky quickens her pace to a steady clip-clop, tosses her head to ring the harness traces and trumpets a charge. It is unproven, but amiably claimed, that a mule is physically incapable of anything reasonably called *a charge*.

As they stop, Bam grabs up his praise pouch, scrambles from the wagon and into the house where he sees Lizzie curled into a ball on the floor, Melt crouched near in fear, and his tiny eldest daughter on her toes trying to light the kerosene lamp with a stick match burning black too fast to light the wick and not singe her fingertips. He drops his pouch beside his fallen wife and steps quickly to the lamp lighter touching her shoulder softly and taking the match from her fingers to fan out the fire.

"I didn't know how, Daddy, I tried, but I couldn't make the light." She is near tears but holds them back bravely, stubbornly, until Bam wraps her close to absorb her fears and free her tears.

"That's okay, Aggie" he soothe strokes her thin back and shoulders, "You tried. That's what counts. You tried even though you were afraid." He pulls her back to look big-eyed into hers, "You *were* afraid weren't you?" She nods admission. "Because, you didn't know how to light the lamp, did you?" Sucking singed fingertips she shakes her head. "That is *brave*. That is *bold*. That's my *daring,* darling daughter." Aggie giggles up at him safe and sure and home again, though she never left the house to come again. *Home isn't a house*, she thinks with conviction, *until the house has lots of love in it and people who care whether you're happy or sad, and love you anyway, no matter what.*

"So, let's learn how to open and light a hurricane lamp. Come over here you kids, Melt, Abbie, you two may as well learn how to make light safe and sure along with your sister. No shoving now," he fusses, "there's enough learning to share, and some to spare. Melt, clap a hand on each girl's shoulder, and help them *not* squirm and push." He wins Melt's grin and one from each darling daughter.

Lizzie peeps now from between her fists to watch the warm, still fireless scene. *The wick can't reach the kerosene,* she thinks numbly. *There's no kerosene to put the lamp. There is no light,* her inner lost child wails woe; *and no way to make or find it.* As though privy to her thoughts, Bam smiles with calm confidence and steps across her to pull from his praise pouch a thin can with the word 'Kerosene' across the label. He holds it for her to see, smiles, then return to his lamp lighting safety training program.

Wonder what else he's got in that praise pouch of his, Lizzie thinks but does not stir to peek, nor seek or find any words to ask.

When the lamp is filled, the wick trimmed, children trained; and the lamp casts a warm dancing red gold glow about the room, Bam tells Melt he needs help unloading the wagon. He sees Melt stand tall and straight hinting at the man he will be. Smiling, Bam adds, "There are some things a man simply *cannot* do without the help of another man. You're my man, son. Let's go get 'er done shall we?" Man and son leave and return soon with armloads of wood cut to lay in the fireplace over a nest of kindling to flash the flame that fires the wood and prepares it for cooking, and later for warmth when banked for their sleep. When the fire is rosy warm, they leave and come again with wood to fill the wood box for later fires. Using hand signals Bam signs to Melt the number, pieces, and sizes of hardwood they'll want to fill the fire box by the stove to lay for later meals. Melt's stomach growls hungrily imagining what might be cooked and eaten, wholly ignoring the fact that he checked every cabinet, cupboard and closet, and found no food in house or garden. *I'd be glad for a hard candy Christmas,* he thinks but does not say.

Hungry is easier when you're warm, Lizzie weeps weak woe as her stomach rumbles restless refute that *hunger is never warm.* She waits silent spiraled in a natal coil, incapable of volition, voice, choice, nor even hope. *It's so cold…, so craving craven cruel cutting cold. Bitter, bold, sharp biting cold like a foot long icicle fallen free to pierce through the soft spot and into the brain pressing it down-down-deep into suspended animation while the body breathes still…, breaths chill…, air that holds no warmth and exhales wheezing whimper blasts of cold, like black snow air, just like black snow air.* Rushing, dark, dirty, despairing thoughts beset and burden her bright and brilliant faith in good and new and possible. *Where did all the possibilities go? Blown away maybe, with the wind and the crops and the grass land even the locusts…, leaving me alone half buried in a pit full foul with sifting sliding dusty grit and dirt and nothing to hold on to, to hold on, to hold, just to hold…. Dear* Lord, *give me just one hope, just one possibility, one sign, one small sign.., just for a moment.*

Though Lizzie's eyes are bloodshot red no tears form to flow to wash away the darkness from her eyes, lids or dust laden lashes. *Maybe I'm dead and don't know it yet, like a lamp left burning warm in a dark dead house. Wonder when Bam will see and say….* She tries to raise her eyes to find him, but her eyes, suddenly disobedient, will not respond, will not even to blink. *Maybe I'm dead and don't know yet.* Lizzie sobs silent into elbows and knees and pleads. She has no hope. Nothing like faith or its substance stirs in her heart nor in her sullen, angry, withdrawn and beaten down mind with no safe space left for hope or grace. Feeling forsaken and denied, Lizzie rejects and turns away from her bright inner core to trudge like a convict through a life without hope or power or even enough food. Still she bows her head into her hands and whispers her last hidden prayer. *Give me grace…, grace to hold for* just this one minute, *this one moment of this one howling hungry empty day on this hard barren land without mercy.* Her body shudders silent sundered dry sobs, *Give me* this *grace, this one gift, this one time, this one day.*

Lizzie hit her overload limit, and knowing it, she let go. She just let go. What's a girl to do? She didn't plan or practice it, she told no one, she just let go. She is adrift weightless and giddy lost from the unyielding command of gravity on her body. Part of her bobs along the low ceiling like a balloon untethered and beyond reach of the sticky hands and minds of the physical world. With no thought she is through and long beyond the roof and into the quiet place of the infinite silent Present Presence.

Peace reaches rushes through Lizzie with her gentle slow exhale release of things no longer working for her, clearing room within her to welcome, embrace, choose and cleave to a wise, gentle and devoted diligence. The love she longs to encompass and consume her and to enlighten and brighten her life and her living of it. *My children…, how frightened they must be…, when*

I fell, and couldn't get up. When I wouldn't *get up for want of will. For want of* hope. Sundered by the total absence of love in her and standing separate and apart from the firm rock of faith that might stabilize the shifting dust that shavings her life, her home, her body, her mouth, her nose, her ears, her eyes.... She is bereft of even the salty wetness of tears falling to trace her face clear and muddy along their gravity track to the dusted floor under her head. *Everything looks so* big *from here..., and I so small.*

When the lamp is lit and burning merrily, Bam claps Melt on the shoulder saying "I need more help from you, son, get on your coat, hat and gloves, we got man work to do." He grins invitingly affable for he thinks he hears Lizzie's soft slow laugh and her warm inhale at the end of it. "We'll make it son, never you fear, when God's on our side, who can be again' us? None. Not one. Not ever. No matter how dark and alone we feel, we only got to remember that God is on our side. All *we* need do is stay on God's side and walk our red road of life in *his* stead, in *his* step, in *his* place, and doing *his* work. Its fine grand work we do too, and we gotta keep the faith that the Good Lord made us whole and hale enough to do the work he places before us to do each day."

He scratches his head below his hat and grimaces. "We humans made it kind of hard for the Good Lord, tearing up his prairie like mad gophers the way we did, then walking away and leaving it cut open raw to blow away in God's harsh rebuking wind."

"Pa," Melt looks at his father, his face adult serious and sober, "I don't think God is punishing us. In any way. For any reason. He gave us free will, and mostly we just pretend we are free...." The boy pauses pondering; "but when we fail to *will* a thing done, it doesn't get done; and nothing changes. Nothing *can* change because man *didn't* will to do a thing that God wanted done...; and *it didn't get done*! The outcome can be *clearly* seen, even by a blind adder. That probably *has* no faith..., and *certainly* has no power of choice." Melt tosses a lop-sided grin to his father and says: "The question is whether – or not – *we* have the sight of a blind adder, and the *will* to do what is before us to do."

Bam scratches the whiskers beneath his nose, snort sneezes a tickle, and hides his grin behind a hand. "Your eyes are laughing...," Melt observes wise to him, "let's get our chores done, and put Becky away with some hay. I *did* see some hay on the wagon didn't I?"

"You did. Let's get done all that's there for us to do this day, son." He glances back at Lizzie with a gentle smile, "Then we'll rustle up some food for us to eat."

"We got no food." Lizzie whisper whines from the icy cold floor.

"Pluck up your faith, woman! In God – if you have none in me." He grins to soften his words. "We didn't have oil for the light, nor wood for the fire before I got home neither. Don't you worry your pretty head about food, dear Lizzie, we Men will take care of that when we get back. Hustle up, Melt, your ma is hungry and so is Becky, who's still standing patient like in her traces *longing* for hay and grain laid in her stall in a warm barn."

"The barn's not *warm*," Melt hisses Soto voice.

"Becky wears a fur coat, and is chock full with the fire of her orneriness." Bam retorts calmly.

"She's a good mule, Pa, you got no call saying' she's ornery!" He grins pulling the door behind as he adds "She *is a hot* little beastie though, that's sure and true."

Lizzie grins behind the mask of her hands, slowly allowing herself to be comfortable being taken care of sometimes. Especially when the world is too big and too hard hearted and she too small and far too unworldly to be called wise by any common measure. She puffs a soft sigh, nestles her face into her cupped hands, and closes her eyes in peace and rests. *It is good to just let be what is. Especially when you can't fix or change it anyway. Not alone now. Bam's home. He has food. He'll cook for me…, for us.* Drifting dozy Lizzie comes only faintly aware when cozy soft cotton warmth drops over her. She feels two warm bodies with *very* cold arms plop into the curve of her body to rest against her and share their warmth of love with her, and receive warmth from her body, her arms, and heart. Too soon, it seems to warm dozy Lizzie, Bam and Melt return, practically insisting, to no strong resistance, that the ladies stay warm and cozy while the *gentlemen* manage the kitchen duties.

When the scent of savory stew and baking cornbread make the ladies salivate in a most unladylike fashion, Lizzie can no longer contain her curiosity. She asks Bam to name each and every thing in the praise pouch. "Wha…, it's almost empty, practically nothing to see!" he protests petulant pretense. She grins. So do the girls. And Melt. He saw what came from the praise pouch to be cleaned, browned, and cut into a stew that simmer savor flavors to burst like star fire in the mouth. Melt knows that what remains still hidden in the praise pouch will be tinned or crocked and stowed in cupboards, but not yet. First there is a great healing that must come. He wants the healing more than anything – except school that is, which is closed, the teacher unpaid and gone home to start again somewhere, sometime, later, when hope returns – to travel with his father, to watch and listen and to learn his trade skills, and his gifts for the trade itself, which are very different talents indeed. Mostly, Melt wants to master the practical magic his father knows so well he doesn't even know he knows it, or how to practice it.

Pops can't make water though. He thinks as he grins a hidden soft smile. *He's a natural water witch though. Gets good, paying work witching land to help farmers find the best place to drill* their *well..., into the Ogallala, to make their homestead green and lush like it was once – or never was – except in land shark fliers. The liars.* Melt never speaks these dry dirt hard discouraging words though. Still, a restless ruthless anger torments and tosses him when dusters come. Still come. To his beloved raped and ruined plowed planted prairie where once oceans of buffalo roamed and Cheyenne were the sage steward warrior Lords of the Plains.

The past is done. He reminds himself sharply. *Only the future can to be decided, chosen and lived. Only that.* Melt melts into a smile imagining watching the moon rise later tonight. He promises himself that he will and knows it is already done. "So, Pops, the stew's stewing, the biscuits browning, Becky's fed and warm, and we got time for you to show us what all else is in your praise pack. Bring it here by Mom and the girls and lets all get cozy nosy together."

Caught by surprise Bam yodels a chortle and joyfully joins his cozy clan on the bare board floor. He feels about in his praise pack and murmurs "Oh! Of *course* you want to come first..., and so you shall!" he exclaims, pulling out a fluffy sweater knit of eye bright brilliant hues, shades and tones, to drape close over Lizzie's shoulders and arms, and pull the end of a sleeve to gently stroke her cheek. She sighs a smile and stirs from the floor displacing her giggling grinning girls eyeing the bright warm prize.

"Put it on, Mama," the girls cry in harmony helping her pull the sweater over her head, across her shoulders and down her body embracing her in a warmth deeper and more complete than any yarn alone can give no matter how masterfully knit and sewn.

For the first time she can remember, Lizzie feels embraced by love as warm and light as the kiss of a butterfly wing in the morning sun. She hugs herself and feels Bam's wiry strong arms embrace her from behind. She curves her back against him, snaking her knit warm arms around his neck holding him curved close and tender the way a mother comfort cuddles a worried child. "Welcome home, Bam," she whispers near his ear. "Welcome home.... I have missed you..., the strong faith of you, I have missed you for that." She sighs sorrowing second thoughts and daunting doubts and yes, barren bare cabinets, cupboards, bins and bowls. Most soul shattering of all, the hope empty eyes and bare bone bodies of her children warded warm only by lean muscle and thin clothes. *Bam is home now, come with fire and light and love, and him. Him, brought himself home, his homely hopeful helpful beloved self is home now and I can go on. I can breathe full and deep. I can hope. I can even plan! Without hope no plan can stand against the fury of nature raped and scorned and savage mad. Lord, forgive us for what we have done to this land you love so well and true.*

"Amen that," Bam whispers fervent near her ear as though he overheard her thoughts.

"Da-a-a-d, what else you got in that praise bag a yours?" Abby inquires innocent interest.

"Well, let's see then," Bam agrees reaching in his praise pouch and pulling out a square tin can painted pretty and capped with a matching lid, which he holds with one finger as he tips and turns the can evoking a hissing cascade from inside his spontaneous percussion instrument. Melt steps close curious as his sisters who rise from the warmth of their mother to eye the handsome hissing humming box, even Lizzie turns from her funk to see what Bam holds and spills in such enchanting song. When all eye are fixed on him and the singing box Bam, prompts a guessing game, "Who can guess what's in the box?" A long silence follows while the conscious minds of them attempts a reply that makes perfect sense in all ways. He smiles like a magician about to pull a rabbit from a hat and Lizzie almost sees a black silk top hat upon his head. Until she blinks. Then it's gone like momentary magic. "Well," Bam poses, "how else might one get data points about what's in the box?"

"What's data points?" asks Abbie, still too young to fear asking what she does not know. Bam grins.

Then straightens to see her better eye to eye and to let her see into him, "data points are information you can get from the physical world." Bam pauses a time for thought outside the scope of the brain where the conscious mind lives and rules. "And when figuring out a puzzle – of any kind – you need all the data points you can get. But then you need something else."

"What?" Abbie asks innocent and open to possibilities, even the ones she can't yet imagine nor guess. "I know…," says Abbie thoughtfully. "You have to let your mind go inside the box, so it can see and smell what we can only *hear* from outside."

"Can you do that?" Bam asks in heartfelt surprise.

"Yes." Her confidence is clear and cool like an unruffled pool, and Bam wonders what it is she sees with inner eyes and hears with inner ears that are beyond the range of the senses. It is always disconcerting, and humbling, to Bam when one of his children becomes his Sensi Master teacher. He waits for her…. She grins at him holding the pretty quiet tin, "I need to touch the box," she says stepping forward hand outstretched. He does not touch her where fingers and palm touch the box. He silently waits. Only that.

"It's popcorn!" Abbie whispers awed, as she jumps tiny hops, "I can smell it, I can see it; I can taste it." She frowns out of her hop, and adds curiously, "It's got *butter* on it." Puzzled, "and there's no butter in the can!" she clarifies her confident confusion.

Bam grins, "Sometimes facts just won't add up to anything useful. Gotta collect 'em anyhow. Never knowing when or how they'll matter, or, when it'll matter that *you* know about them."

Abbie eyes him a solemn silent moment, sets an arm akimbo, and demands: "Where's the butter? I *know* there's butter, I smell it." Mollified, Bam paws the pouch until he finds and formally presents the butter to his queerly queenly baby girl child. *Awed again,* Bam reflects. *Nobody warned me that'd happen to a man when he's with his wee wise ones. Still it is good to know they are wise in the ways of Spirit and can see problems coming long before they start to show up on the physical plane.*

"Okay!" Bam concedes cagy crafty careful as he hands her a hinge lidded clay pot with butter inside.

Abbie's smile glows with new confidence. "I *knew* there was butter," she whispers. "I knew it. And, now it's true." She turns her hands palm up and gives a 'what's a girl to do?' shrug of giddy gladness.

Aggie, the lamp lighter girl, is profoundly thoughtfully silent, then asks wistfully *"How* did you know?" Abbie looks at her with a kind small smile and says: "Sometimes, sister, you just know a thing *so well* you don't even know that you know it. Pretend!" She commands queenly small. *"Pretend* you already *know* something that's in Papa's praise pouch. Pretend *so hard* that you can see it, you can smell it, and you can feel the weight of it like it was already in your hand. Then you will, that's the magic."

Aggie nods, closes her eyes, focuses her mind, and opens her heart. She is silent a long while gazing into the infinite and eternal space between what is and what is not. In this awareness she records no image or input from the outer world, and does not see the pouch nor anything within the small lamp lit fire warm room. She now sees only from the mysterious inner eye with no lid and finds herself *inside* the praise pouch on the floor. She gasps, eyes large and wide, "we got eggs! We got eggs!" she sings dancing about like a stiff legged fawn caught in dawn light delight. "We Got Eggs!" she laughs, then suddenly stops still, blinks three times, grins tentatively, as though taste testing the word for what she thinks she knows is inside the pouch. She giggles a whooping trill and shrills "We got *bacon!*" Suddenly unsure and insistent she demand begs, "Show me, Daddy…, please, let me see…."

"Proof is a good thing when you can get it." Bam smiles, "As you wish, my darling daughter." He pulls out a packet of butcher paper smelling of pork and smoke and seasoning and time. He hands it to Aggie with a papa proud grin. "Reckon you're big enough to help make breakfast in the morning?"

Aggie blinks three times and says, "Not *alone!*" She steps beside her mother, drops to a knee, and asks "will you help, Mom? Please. If you help me I *know* it can do it…, but I *think* I can't do it alone. Yet."

Lizzie chuckles and nuzzles Aggie's belly making her laugh in tickled delight. "Okay, I will help you. And I think we will need Abbie's help too, don't you agree?"

Aggie nods full serious, "Yes, we do. I will need Abbie's help, because I'm the big sister. I have to teach her what I already know. What do you want me to do tomorrow?" Abbie asks willing and eager.

Abbie frowns patently puzzled, takes a full breath, decides, and says, "I gotta know, Aggie, do you smell biscuits or bread in the praise pouch?" Aggie disappears inward awhile to see with inner eyes and heart as she breaths slow and easy, still frowning softly. "Yes," Aggie says surely certain at last.

"*Which?*" Aggie probes with pointed brows and hungry eyes.

Abbie retires within again a bit, cocks her head as though balancing weights on a scale. "Both. I think. Definitely biscuit makings though. It's biscuits for breakfast for us for sure!" She grins, "And there's bacon! Plus, cornbread for dinner with the beans and ham still in Papa's pouch. We'll need chopped onion too, so pull them out at the same time." Arms akimbo Abbie faces her father waiting confidently –if not patiently – for him to pull from the pouch all the things she has named. And so he does. What's a father to do? He hands them out to her in the order she named them, and her smile grows and glows each time a thing she named is pulled from darkness and appears into light.

Aggie nudges her mother as she curls against her again, "when I grow up," she whispers solemnly, I want to be like Abbie."

"Me too, Aggie," Lizzie agrees with a serene smile, "*me* too." Nobody notes that Lizzie is already grown and has children of her own, and in that eager empty silence, Lizzie affectionately embraces that possibility as the very and only true truth of her and all her tomorrow days. In that calm, confident flagrant flouting of reality, she sings "I want to be like you too, when I grow up" softly and gently, puffing truth words into Aggie's hair that now smells sweet of green grass and clover. *How I have missed that smell..., and I can't think* why.

"Tell me about my name, Mama."

Lizzie stirs alert to the new and eager focus of her child. She smiles alert and quietly eager to tell Aggie her naming tale in a mythic manner, for only myth will suit to sound the spirit, the weight, the nature, and the subtle substance and sound of a naming name. *"Agatha,"* she whisper thinks the name that came when she called the spirit of the babe to say its name and to speak its nature. *Agatha,* came the breath of the word. In that whispered word were the persuasive portents of the pure power and the pulsating potency of her crime investigators, Hercule Poirot, and Miss Marple. The book I enjoyed most is called: Murder – on the Orient Express," she speaks each word with sibilant dramatic flair, eyes and sparking smile alive with enthusiasm and zest.

"Best of all, I rode with Inspector Poirot from London, through the Channel train tunnel to Calais, and then to Paris where we rested a day – except Poirot never rests, but keeps looking and seeing even what isn't there to be seen. It is a gift to write like this, and make the reader experience the excitement of boarding the Orient Express bound for Lausanne, Milan, Venice, Belgrade, Sofia, and then at last, to Istanbul. Oh the sights I saw in those faraway places she took me to and let me smell and taste and touch and hear and see in my mind's eye plants and vistas and people and places and every wonder word I read while traveling with Poirot. I even smelled stale tobacco, gin, the sooty oily smell of smoke puffing from the stack at every stroke of a cylinder of the diesel engine pulling that snaky train of cars.

"Oh, Aggie! I saw the night sky cold and dark and sharp pointed with dazzling stars, and smelled the gin and the waxy odor of tacky lipstick residue at the rim. I went with Poirot to the kitchen to look for what wasn't there, where it should be..., maybe a missing knife of just the size and shape to have dealt the deepest cut, perhaps the purloined pistol that fired the fatal shell. I went with Poirot to the engine of the train and talked with the Engineer about "the 'hog', as he calls it."

The minds and thought processes of Poirot and of Miss Marple, Agatha's uncommon female crime investigator whose lively minds and springing spirits every reader came to understand and know intimately well. And, understand they did, they do. I was there *with Poirot,* beside inside him, behind his eyes. Writing like that is spellbinding, captivating, complex, and singingly beautiful and full throated. You, my quiet, observant Aggie, have that same full five sense aware attentive way with words. For this I named you Agatha and call you *Aggie* to keep the sound of you near and dear to my heart." Aggie gentle stretch breathes into her new knowing of her old name and asks with thanks, that an Agatha Christie book she feels weighty in her hand, reaches out and inclines itself to her.

Abbie, leaning and listening close and smiling, uprights herself, circles her mother to drops and curl beside Aggie facing Lizzie. "Hello, you," Lizzie coos cuddling Abbie's cheeks, "I'm glad you came back."

"Me too, Mom," she says simply as she snuggle butts into Aggie's warm embrace and leans into the curl of her mother's body. "Tell about *my* name now. Who's Abbie?" What's her big girl name?"

"Her 'big girl name'…," Lizzie chuckles, "how well and carefully chosen are your words, my Abbie. So very like Abigale, a wise mother of the Bible who was called the woman of great understanding." She gentles a soft strand of stray hair from Abbie's eyes, "A woman like you." She tickles her belly, "A woman who can see into and all the way through the void and beyond that, all the way into the abiding abundance of life. You understand abundance, and know its appearance is a product of faith. And you have a psychic sense of smell in the bargain!

"What remarkable gifts came alive into our life with your life, my wonderful little woman of great understanding; my darling Abigale Abbie." Lizzie dotes with focused eyes and pointed purpose. "How confidently you use and apply your gifts to heal, even the invisible hurts that break and bend us. The one of us…, sometimes. And the each and all of us, most of the time. Like the Bible Abigale you think with your head and love lead with your heart. You show the way to meet, learn, know, forgive and love ourselves again as whole, when we've been beaten down, broken and forlorn. You shine your light on us and reveal us free and strong, more capable and creative than we ever imagined before."

"Will you read us about Abigale, from your Bible? I think Aggie would like it too," she grins, "until our magic daddy finds and brings Aggie an Agatha Christie book to read."

"Yes. I will do that." Lizzie sees it already true in the eye of her mind projected through her heart and so she creates. "We'll nestle close together so everyone can see the words as I read them and learn to read while listening." Bam smiles and snuggles close to Lizzie, setting an example – as a father should; and his clan cuddle huddles all close and snuggly.

"Melt," Lizzie finds and cuddles him close with a smile, "come here close and comfy, and I will tell you how you got your name; and the true meaning of your name. You too, Bam, you're a part of this story," she pats the floor until he sits warm at her side, an arm loose over Melt's shoulders.

"Your name," Lizzie says, earnest eyeing her son, "was given you by your father," she pats his leg, "when he first saw and held you newborn gentle in his arms, his eyes full with wonder and love and filling your eyes with it too. It was a golden rain of love that passed between the two of you, son and father.

"'*Melt*,' your Pa whispers soft and low looking at you with love eyes, and you looking in his eyes, and both of you falling into love in the eyes of the other." She is silent cherishing memory a moment, then she adds strong and firm, Bam declares: '*His name is Melt…!*' He is silent then as he just holds you and looks at you in wonder a lazy long time and then he says the rest: "*Because my boy…, my son…, melts my heart and makes my eyes leak love…, so he shall be named and known as Melt. I am father now. I am washed clean and purified of the man I was before. I am new reborn – with my son – on the day of his birth. From this day forward I am no longer the man I was before my son.*'"

Lizzie's eyes smile soft love light gazing at Melt in silent wonder, watching and waiting for him to melt, and then to speak and own the truth of his name and his naming.

Melt toes the praise bag and finds it still heavy laden. Crossing his ankles Melt drops Indian style to the floor beside the pouch. "What else ya' got in the bag, Pops?" he asks looking at his father from the floor.

"Well," Bam replies, "there's a story behind that."

Melt giggles, "there's *always* a story, Pops. Behind everything you do, there's a story." Letting admiration sound, he adds: "You're nothing if not a terrific tale teller. Tell us your tale, Pops, and tell it tall," he grins, "the way we like it."

Bam lowers himself slowly to the floor keeping his head down to hide pain winces pinches behind the bill of his cap. Melt alone sees and feels the reborn aches and breaks taken from XIT horses unwilling to be broken to saddle or rider. Not even by the man gaining standing as a first rate bronc buster, and a canny cattle driver.

He never admitted it to anyone, but Melt knows. He's been told, cautious and careful, by Mexicans and Indians and cowboys who love telling tall true tales. From these ones close to the earth, Melt learned that Bam always had a mysterious way with horses, and then…, that something changed. Sea change level. Bam got better. No one could say how, no one knew why, yet everyone knew, and all could see and more intensely, feel, the change in the little man easy to not see. Bam was gracefully masterful now, and calm confident in it.

First to feel and then to think, Melt recognized the change first. Long before others either sensed or saw, Melt felt it, he felt the energy of his father in change, first subtle, gentle, slow, then expanding exponentially into a pure potent power and presence. Bam had a presence. That was oddly unsettling and comforting to the boy who long judged his father too weak, too pliable. *Too darn much attention to others; and too little reserving even the harshest stingiest shreds of compassion for himself.*

This was a new man Bam. A man wholly comfortable in his skin and in his mind – at least when governed and guided by his heart more than by mind. The new man Bam courted, cooed and cossetted his trainee horses. Bam contracted to train the horse under contract terms and conditions, specifically including that Bam the Trainer, had a minimum of six weeks alone with the horse before the owner was invited to come for owner training. Melt grinned thinking of the owner's blustery bullying that it was *his* horse and he'd damned well see it, and ride it, any time he wanted. The compromise was a training contract between trainer and owner specifically specifying that the owner would be in breach of contract and would immediately pay the full training fee to the trainer.

Bam hired and contracted for two months of exclusive use of the stables, training track and running field of a horseman rancher neighbor. The new man Bam was proudly quietly confident. He moved with a fluid grace belying the effects of bone breaks badly healed and muscles torn beyond reasonable repair.

Looking back later Melt admits he never knew clear and sure if the exclusive lease was for this horse alone or if was Bam's habit and practice to contract for exclusive use of a stable when gentling and training a promising pony. The new man Slow and easy, Bam eases his trainee horse to the weight of his hands admiring stroking the proud head and neck while softly whispering love sounds and praise words into the ear of the animal. He sweetly curries his honeyed generous words deep into the horse hair coat until love light shines from and through each strand even when no outer light touches it. *Horse magic,* Melt thinks, and wonders if it's true.

Odd Jobs

Melt eagerly accompanied Bam on a job to break a horse to bit, saddle and rider weight for an owner who couldn't pay the time to do it himself; but could afford the fee for a top trainer who'd give him back a fast, agile show horse readily responsive to the horseman's weight and firm rein. Being a watcher by nature and choice, Melt felt first. Then watched to see all the ways Bam gentled the horse with praise prose and patted poetry. He feels the curried comfort of Bam's copious praise reports and his easy heartening way he raises the bridle and bit to the horse to let it sniff and snort the rig even as he slowly rubs raises the harness twined between splayed scratching fingers, to the crown of its head. Moving fluid and slow, Bam draws the bit up along the soft nose and curious lips and pauses there letting the horse explore the unknown and find peace with it. Only the heart in peace can see the gift full.

Creeping near his father Melt watches the horse explore the bit, harness and fittings with its soft sensitive nose and lips, even as Bam eases the halter up and around the long ears of the beast. It snorts. Bam snorts. The horse eyes him, as a silent picture show passes between the two sets of eyes in which horse, and willing rider, race the wind for the pure physical joy of the run.

Bam lowers the halter now, takes the bit ends between thumb and finger, and lifts the length to the horse's lips. It huffs. Bam's free hand finds the white star on its crown and settles there softly stroking, soothing, comforting, as he speaks slow low chanted charming words communicating easy wellbeing in the fleeting flickering mind picture images that now race and run in the mind behind the star. The eyes of man, and of beast. Neither equal to the other. Neither as good alone. Both know it.

Stalemate.

Still, to either, both, or neither, it matters not a whit to either. They both know that too. Yet both are afraid to *not* be separate for neither knows how…, how to even *begin*… to be so much bigger than their skin, or to run wild free on the wind. True to his name Melt slips slow, low, loose and silent to crabwalk the ground flowing near to see and hear yet not be seen.

"Horse," Bam is saying, "You are good alone. I gotta admit that. You are *good*.

"I am good. And I'm good alone.

"Together – by choice, yours and mine – we can become something altogether amazing." He pauses dramatically, "You interested in talking?

"I'm better than good *without* your help," the horse sniffs, a noble in a snit.

Bam does not laugh. Aloud, at least. "Why with your great and noble strength and spirit, combined with my estimable skill at letting a horse see its own nobility, strength and power, we *can* win." The horse bobs its head enthusiastically.

"But we gotta run. Together. You and me. Me astride your back, like this blanket," Bam croons his cozy chant while stroking the pad smooth over the curve of its spine and down its sides, calming the beast's natural nervous jitters under the weight of the unknown.

"Now I'll just lay my arms across your back…, like I've done before, and I'll stroke you all the while. Then, I'll put a bit of more weight on the pad so you get used to that…." the horse jerks aside, Bam follows, "And all the while I'll stroke you and tell you what a fine horse you are, I'll whisper that you are one of the *handsomest* horses I ever laid eyes on." Horses, like all heart full beasts, respond well to lavish praise and to gentle coaxing stroking reassurance and affirmation. *Just like the human animal.* Bam thinks.

"And you run like the wind," he whisper whistle adds as an afterthought. The horse raises its head, arches its neck nobly, and then bob whinny snorts its active accord with the accurate acclaim into Bam's near ear provoking a lilting laugh. Then come the sober words, "question is whether you will willingly take the bite of the bit and the weight of the saddle. For if not, you will never learn and know why God made horses love man, and made man love horses. You will never be the magnificent and singular horse you can be…, you see, a horse needs a rider. Just like a rider needs a horse." Without another word or thought Bam flows with the inspiration lifting him. He gathers the loose reins firmly at the neck of the horse and without word or effort, grabs a hunk of mane, and jumps smoothly astride the wide-eyed dancing animal, twining legs and feet around its girth as far as they will go and tucking them with firm resolve into the crevasse between the forelegs and the barrel belly. The horse jumps straight up in a stiff leg leap, eyes round wide wild, nostrils flaring in its furious indignant snit at being jumped and mounted without so much as an 'if you please.'

"But running like the wind don't mean one thing – to a horse, or a man – without a rider astride." Patting the arched neck appreciatively Bam adds, "I'm astride now, whether you like it or don't. Show me how you run on the wind." He clicks his tongue, tugs the fistful of hair and bumps heels into the horse. Uncertain what to do in the novel situation, the horse does what is natural. It runs. Away.

Until it isn't running away. Not now. Not from the weight nor the smell of the man, nor from his guiding grip on its mane, nor does it flee from the firm fluid leg, knee, heel and toe muscles that wrap and relax muscles in the chest so they readily rhythmically transform shallow breaths into full long powerful pulls of pounding air that carry him and the him above, on their enchanting jubilant run of pulsing pounding joy. The horse trumpets a whinny and yields to the joy held tight inside, locked away until it allowed, welcomed, and invited rider weight, strength and wisdom on his back. The proud beauteous beast willingly aligns itself with the command of the firm easy guiding grip on its mane and about its girth.

When he does, his whole center of gravity shifts subtle soft sure and singular; and the man becomes the beast, and the best in the beast becomes the man. *Perhaps a bridle would be better...,* the subtly stirred mute mount muses. *Perhaps it would help — us — both of us, if I learn to* enjoy *the warm weight and sinew strength of a two legged one on my back. Perhaps I could come to understand, and to even like, all the odd jingling ringing things he brings..., to amuse me, I believe.*

To teach me perhaps. Maybe only to distract.... Ah-h-h, but there is the wind, and the sun, and the run....

The horse finds length and strength, breath and heart, and forgets there is an*other* aboard. Forgets there is an*other* at all and knows only one on this together run.

Melt watches the run in the golden sun. He sees his father tuck his feet on the horses back and under his butt; then eases his knees atop the pumping shoulders, balancing there like an acrobat. He raises hips above his feet, balances there, and rides like a jockey standing in high stirrups. *Good Lord!* Melt thinks, *I want to have muscles strong enough to move like that..., when I grow up.*

A shrill piercing as a parade whistle stills every motion and thought to a startled stop, every sound to a sudden shattered sibilant silence. Bam spins to the source of the shrill trill. He freezes, then flares blast furnace hot.

Melt is stunned hyper alert by the swift power of his father's energy shift. He is jolted the insight that every other father anger he has ever witnessed was less than a whisper, merely an intimation, of the scope, force, and the dangerous power of the fury that possesses his father. *Heart stopping anger...,* Melt thinks, awestruck, *and Pa ain't said a word yet.*

He turns eyes to the shadowy intruder, parade whistle still bit in teeth. The man is perilously oblivious to the energy shift that overtook the man hired as Trainer for this most promising horse yet. Across the horse pen and front yard Melt hears the man's thoughts as if carried by the wind and whispered in his ear. *A man has a* god *given right to see his horse when he wants, and no seedy cowpoke trainer-come-lately will change that. Not even with a written and signed contract will he take that God given right from me.* His lips curl. *I got a gun* he pats his holster pointedly, *to back me up and protect my rights.*

"You are in breach of our contract by coming here, Chester. Under our contract I have a minimum of six weeks alone with this horse. Alone. Me and the horse. Without you. It's in our contract. You agreed to it and signing it. You also agreed that you will come here only when you receive my invitation to come. When you signed that contract you agreed that if you ever violate this provision of the contract, you are immediately obligated to pay me my fee in full. Bam touches the brim of his hat, gives a bob, hard-eyes never leaving the man's face. You were not invited. The contract is breached. I'll be over this evening to get my fee in full."

"Like hell you will," the ornery owner snaps surly sour staring down his nose at the small man who now isn't small at all.

"Yes...," a calm voice intrudes, "yes he will." The quiet courtly older man eyes down the intruder. "I will ride with Bam and the boy to town this evening, and I'll alert Sheriff Ben to your trespass against me and my property in violation of my restraining order against you." He eyes the intruder calmly, "I will tell Ben and Counselor what I heard of your bullying intimidation of Mr. White while you breached the terms of your contract with him. Tisk, tisk, what an ill-mannered human you are! Did no one ever point out to you that a man will catch more flies with honey..., than with vinegar?

"Maybe I should have guessed from your guns and bluster, that you'd take that homily at face value, and never consider for an instant, the intrinsic and functional truth of the adage." The mind of the intruder is busy parsing how his confident assertion of his rights somehow soured the sweet milk of an all-around good business deal for everyone involved. Including the cowboy he currently hated for his calm assertion of contract rights in the face of breach to collect his fee now. Not later. The intruder will not meet the eyes of his neighbor, with a restraining order against him, and a calm will to *not* allow either his contract with Bam or the penalty for breach, to be disregarded and foregone under the weight of threats and an impressive array of physical world weapons.

"Let's talk vinegar, *Chester*. Your puffed chest bullying of this man," he points to Bam who's not small at all; and looks away quickly, "is vinegar. Nobody wants it around. Including mosquitos. Little good can come of it, and you know it." His exasperation shows. "From *experience* you know that.

"Yet you are so bull block-headed dull that you imagine that *this* time, something good will come of your belligerent baiting bullying violation of contract rights under the agreement you signed, and magically, you won't have to pay, or to obey. Delusional is the word for it. So deluded that you bring me a preemptive violation of your contract with Mr. White." He grins small tart pleasure. "In addition, there is your *present* breach of Mr. White's training contract giving him a minimum of six weeks alone with the horse. Without you. Under any circumstances. Except..., his express written invitation.

"And then there's the training you're paying for. From what I saw of the commotion, you implanted a *fierce* fearful distrust of man into that fine animal of yours. No trainer worth his salt would abide what I witnessed from you today." Comfy on the shaded porch, the man puffs his pipe awake and continues.

"Vinegar, Chester. You hoped I'd not get back to vinegar didn't you? You are in breach of your contract with Mr. White to train your horse for you. Under that contract, Mr. White has the right to collect his training fee, *in full* upon your breach of contract terms by coming here before his six weeks of solitary training of your horse is complete. And by coming before you receive his written invitation to come. Contrary to your bluster, Chester, it is Mr. White's *right* to declare you breach for being here today, and it is your contract *duty* to pay his the training fees in full, on demand.

"Is there any part of that you did not understand, Chester?" Chester does not reply.

"Vinegar, *Chester*! You are on *my* property. Without invitation. You are in violation of my restraining order against you." His eyes are dispassionately firm and fiery. "Your deliberate trespass on my property this afternoon, with shouted threats and drawn guns, is *unacceptable*. To me.

"Now you would pardon your abhorrent behavior to Mr. White by trespassing on *my* property in violation of *my* restraining order against you." He stares unflinching hard at the sullen horseman. "Nothing to say then? You should know I will be riding to town this evening with Mr. White and Melt to talk with Sheriff Ben. And with Counselor to discuss these legal issues and how best and most quickly to resolve them. Tomorrow Sheriff Ben will ride out to your shack to tell you where and when you'll pay Mr. White his training fee."

With mindful molten motion, the land owner pumps a chamber into his rifle, raises the butt to his shoulder, and sights along the barrel until he sees into Chester's eye. "You gotta know, Chester, that after I talk with those gentlemen, I can no longer kill you '*in self-defense*.' He grins amiable unamused at the humbled horse owner. "It is best and wisest for you to be off my range and beyond range of my Winchester as quick as your horse can get you *off* my spread, Chester." The chastened man scrambles to his mount to spur and whip it away into distancing dust.

Forgiving Trespass

The land owner calmly un-chambers the shell from his rifle, pockets the shell, and notches the weapon into an elbow. He pulls a pipe and puffs it awake, inhales, and meditates awhile on the uncommon occurrences of this unusual day. He watches the lowering sun with a soft surrendering smile. *Guide me firm and strong to what is mine to do this day. Lead me along each step of the way, my Good God, for without you I will surely go astray of your will, and your grace.* He adds with a grin, *"Honestly God, I do wish you could let me kill that man!* Exhaling now, long and slow, he adds: *Forgive me for that. Amen.*

Forgiving trespass, the land owner knows, is closer to a Godly act than a manly one. He puffs an exhale as though spitting sour acid thought and tang. He snorts, clears his nose, then growling long and low, hacks phlegm into the garden by the porch, hawking the foul flavor of un-forgiveness from his mouth. He inhales now slow and long and becomes present again, full aware of the scents and flavors of the season and of the afternoon still full with hours to complete and fulfill. *And I with hours to go before I sleep.* Smiling from his wee walk in the woods with Robert Frost, the land owner turns his thoughts to what remains for the hours of this waning day. He smiles now, knowing and claiming, that it is all good.

He turns back now to his stable and yards. Bam looks frightfully like a fourth of July firecracker that didn't get to pop. He smiles him a warm eyed healing and moves on to Melt who willingly waits for his eye and smile. The land owner gives it to Melt's heart melting smile and a quick step to the stable door, where he clicks and coos the suddenly shy horse out from the dark and into the light.

"Bam!" The land owner cries, then waits in silence for the raised head and met eyes. He waits awhile. Smiling inward at how keen are be to give tit for tat and slight for slap; and how great the gap between us and that, and me and them, and we and one. *Words…, the Good Lord was right. Of course. He shouldn't have given us words. Perhaps to amend for that too precious gift given too soon, God gave us twin gifts of thought and feeling. There's a price to be paid for that outwardly bigger boon though. We invest the very days of our lives in and through our words. Most of us don't even know that. Or, most of us are blind afraid we will misuse the great power invested in us by God as co-creators with him. It takes a bold and courageous heart to inhale that much unstinting love, and it needs a mind fully entrained with the soul to make the enlightened and open-hearted choices of a wise co-creator working with the One.*

More coldly stern now, the land owner barks: "Bam! Snap out of it, now! The man has left! How *long* will you stand there shooting eye bullets at the sand of a man whose long gone out of sight? That is *far* too much separation anxiety anger for a man like you to contain, Bam White.

"Puff it out of you now." Bam is statue still. "Or, I will come over there and gut punch it from you." He eyes stiff scarecrow Bam, and shouts an order "Inhale, Bam White!" As he steps focused from the porch toward Bam, he sees the blur of Melt flying to his father from the stable where the perplexed pony stands still a bit wild wide eyed. Melt rounds on his statue still father and punches him, quick and sharp, in the diaphragm. Bam's body behaves as a body normally does when its gut punched. He exhales explosively. The body need for air demands a swift inhale. Bam obeys.

His brain gets a swift shot of blood oxygen with that gulping gasp of air. He winces out of his mental stupid stupor to blink shock and astonishment into the fierce fire eyes of his son. "I didn't know you could hit that hard, son," he whisper wheezes, straightens, and silky strokes his stunned abs.

"I didn't hurt you did I?" Melt melts, touching his father's shoulder and arm with cautious concern. "Did I hurt you?" he whispers face to face, eye to eye. Bam shakes his head a fast no.

"I'm okay." He breaths deeply, rubbing his gut, and eyeing his son somberly, "Don't ever hit me again."

"Don't ever go stupid crazy *pissed* like that again!" Melt snaps and does not soften nor melt at the edge.

"Who taught you to say foul words like that?" Bam demands.

"You!" Melt retorts, eyes sharp and chill. "You keep on baby brat behaving like the owner of that horse, and we ain't even *begun* talking ugly words, Pa."

Bam frowns "You don't say 'ain't'! I never heard you say the word 'ain't' before in your life."

Melt's eyes hold hard and harry, "never before today did I see you behaving like a spoiled manipulating brat. No better than that brash beast horse owner." Bam is mute. "Even *more* stupid! *Silent* stupid."

"Stop!" Bam wheezes raising a hand. "I – I got it - son. I lost myself in anger and I became the man I most dislike." He bows his head sorrowful "I'm sorry, son…, that you had to see your pa behaving…," he can't stop the grin, "like a brat."

Melt giggles gleeful glad and says "It is *good*, for an observant son, to see his Pa behaving like a man he does not respect." He eyes his father canny, "So tell me, Pa, how are you planning to work with the bigheaded beast during *his* two week training period?"

Bam grins and cap slaps Melt's belt. "By then, son, *you'll* be ready to train the owner. Trust me on this."

Waiting for the Moon

Melt returns from his recent reverie to the warm huddle of this family nested around his mother and Bam's praise pack. He smiles his fresh appreciation of his father, and of his family. *Home is anywhere you feel fully loved.* He thinks, *Home is where the heart is,* the correction pleases him. *I have a whole Divine portfolio of homes! I aim to have more. Though I need only one physical place to keep my stuff, still I live in a universe of heavenly homes.*

"*Ah God is good! God is great! Praise God forever!*"

Lizzie turns to look at Bam, curling an arm cozy around his neck and shoulders, and smile invites. "Tell us about that praise pack of yours and how you came to have all the things that are inside." She narrows her eyes at him, "when nobody has *anything* green or fresh or fleshy, when was the last time we had meat? Meat that wasn't ground, meat you could *chew* on it, meat with bones to gnaw marrow from when the meat is gone? *Who* has greens and growing things in this dust blasted land? Who has *water* to make greens grow and carrots and potatoes fresh and firm enough to snap when they're cut into?" She grins away her caution, casts a twinkle at Abbie, and adds airily: "I can smell them, Bam White. I can feel them, and taste them…, and my mouth waters!" She says touching fingertips to wonder round lips.

"Well," Bam squirms into his tale "I was about to tell you that." Raising a cautioning hand he adds, "And you won't believe it. Any more than I did. At first." He smiles, grabs into his pack to pull out an assortment of fresh plump vegetables. "Smell," he directs his small clan. "Each and every one." Come on," he waives a hand to all, "there's enough for everyone to have a smell of each. To taste and to remember the smell of each one when it's fresh, and cooked to its whole healthy goodness."

"Um-m-m this smells good," Aggie coos over soft leaf stems with dainty flowers at the top. "I want some of this under my pillow tonight."

"It's Basil," Lizzie answers, sift stroking a stem then smelling her fingers. Her family follows suit.

"What is this?" Abbie asks holding a deep soft green spike bristled stem to her nose and inhaling fully.

"Rosemary," Lizzie answers, curling a palm around the brush of the herb and scrubbing it gently into her palms smiling as the fragrance scents the room. Abbie, and then Aggie follow suit, and the guys soon follow. "I want some Rosemary under my pillow too!" Aggie adds. She smells her fingers and reconsiders, "Or, maybe I'll just rub Rosemary all over my hands and sleep with them by my face."

"Always the pragmatist," Lizzie grins nuzzling noses with Aggie.

"I like that idea," the clan, as one, agrees. Lizzie shrugs only a tad contrite, "We *should* use the herbs while they're fresh anyway." She hears her own words, and smiles wise willful; and Bam falls in love all over again. "So, back to the source of this mysterious manna from the desert of our land," Lizzie prompts lazy easy. Bam smiles shrewd recollecting all the whys she is his chosen one.

"The mysterious manna…," Bam begins thoughtfully. "Mysterious is an apt word for it, yet there is no mystery at all. All except one, and that one I can't believe my own self. Even though I know it is true."

"You know…, but you don't *believe*? How does that work?" Melt puzzles aloud and all nod agreement.

"You are my doubting Thomas, son." Rubbing the back of his neck he admits, "And I don't know if I can get used to that. A son isn't *supposed* to be smarter than his Pa."

Melt pops a brow arch up, peers at is father long and deep, arches the other and observes, "Seems to me you should be giving a thousand thanks to God for breaking your rule…, that never was God's, rule…, who forever makes all things new, even musty old rules that don't work." He round eyes his father and says, "Maybe it's time old Bam White made room for some *new* possibilities, and fewer *old* man-made rules." He flat-lines his brows and mouth and round eyes his dad. "Else you teeter dangerous near *being* the ass of a horse owner who tied your scarecrow tongue this afternoon."

"Melt!" Lizzie snaps upright slapping his hand. She inhales upright hard eyeing her defiant determined young man of a son. "You have no right – to speak to your father so disrespectfully. I raised you better than that!

"And such a loud smart mouth you got on you, son! Where'd *that* come from?" Her frown is fierce fiery, and Melt melts into a bow of contrition. Now Lizzie chuckles and her eyes laugh into Melt's rising ones until he knows with a melting slump that the only viable choice she left to him is to laugh with her. And so he does. First with the durable duty of a small smile with lightless eyes above, and a tight-lipped he, he, he wheezing out below.

Abbie giggles tickling a finger under his chin. He jerks his head away, beyond her short reach. She giggles gleefully hopping up to straddle his curled up legs and tickling his ribs with one hand, under his chin with the other. "Stop it!" He growl shouts sourly.

"…Where never is heard, a discouraging word, and the skies are not cloudy all day," sings Aggie, knee walking to torment tease Melt tickling his armpits and ribs to melt him into a better mood. In his head. Or, he could go to his room and be alone until he's fit to be with others. She'd be okay with that too.

Lizzie sits upright and spins to full face her son. She takes his chin in her hands, raising his eyes to hers. They stay lid down, closed. She smiles and blows air kisses into his lashes, knowingly tangling them, and making him blink open his eyes – at least half the time. She could work with that. *Melt is still young, still without enough life clues to know, or even guess, how to deal with impotent rage. Wonder where* that *came from.* She taps his chest where his heart shelters and asks, "What happened today?"

Melt melts away far beyond apart from what he will not say. She clamps his jaw between fingers and thumb until his eyes and jaw pop open in astonishment and agony. "A-O-w! Stop!"

Lizzie smiles, "that's better. Nothing can change until you talk about it. What happened? Tell me."

"In front of everyone?" he asks casting wide eyed dart glances to his father and back to his mother.

She smiles. *Damn her!* She sees/hears that, her laughing eyes join her lips in easy acceptance. She pats his knee and comforts, "you will never be a mother, Melt. You will never truly know nor fully understand the depths, and the heights, to which a mother will go to save her child," she cast him a bold grin, "even when it's to save him from his own folly."

"*Folly?*" Melt hoar ices, "*Nobody* uses that word anymore!"

Lizzie's brows arch dance over soft light laughing eyes, "I do." Her brow arch intimately invites amused opposition. "Ergo, meaning: therefore, your rule of *nobody* is proven false and faulty on its face. I love homonyms, don't you?" She coos casually.

"On it's *face?*" One eye challenges, ignoring her word *homonyms* and the veiled mystery of its meanings.

"Yes! The words 'everybody' and 'nobody', means there are no outliers. There can*not* be even one person who is outside the scope of those two words, 'everybody' and 'nobody'. Make sense?"

Melt chews on it a bit, nods, and says, "Yeah, in a snake eating its tail sort of way it does make sense. And, it means I can't be mad at the horse owner for being such an ass, and I can't be miffed at dad for letting that bag of hot air turn him into a beached fish panting for air from water and not from sky."

"So-o-o," Lizzie poses, "in what ways was the horse owner a commendable man?"

"Whoa! You start with the hard nut first, that's hardly fair."

"What's fair got to do with it? Any of it?" She watches while he takes this in and adds, "For any of *us*?"

Melt grins and eyes his dad, "Pa, you gotta help me on this one, you have more of Abbie's great understanding than I do."

Bam giggles, "well that won't help us much either. But, together we can do it, don't you think?"

Melt shrugs, "like we got a choice?"

"Good point. Okay, here's mine: the man has a good keen eye for fine horse flesh. Your turn."

"I don't know him as well as you do." Melt gripes guarded.

"Danged near! And 99.9 percent of what I do know I don't like. Maybe we do need Amos to help us."

"Think like Amos then. He's an amazing man, Pa, I'd like to be like him some day."

Bam breathes a chuckle, "We share that aspiration, son. So, what might Amos admire about the man? Maybe his passion? Do you think?"

"Passion?" Melt waivers wondering.

"Yeah, the man has got a wide swatch of fierce hot energy pouring through him, that's for sure. What's good about that?"

"He makes things happen. Fast and even furious sometimes…, or so I hear. It's amazing what a lad can hear when pretending not to listen or even care."

"Eavesdropper, eh?" Bam grins.

Melt matches him, "you can name it that, or call it listening, mostly because adults never want to hear what a kid says."

"Mom does," Abbie contends. "She hears everything we say, even when we think she's not listening."

"True that," Melt agrees with a wry grin, and turns back to his dad. "So, do we admire him because he makes things happen? Even if he doesn't think it through first?"

"Even then," Bam agrees. "Well, that's two. What else you got?"

"He's passionate."

"Yeah, and dumb as a post."

"And as stuff shirted as a scarecrow." Lizzie snorts solemnly.

"That's a *good* thing?"

"Well, you can see him coming from a block away."

"And smell him a mile before that."

"That's not helpful," Bam snorts.

Melt giggles. Lizzie and the girls grin. "It's an early alert system if you keep your nose to the wind, and if you do, you don't have to meet him. *Especially* across the barrel of a loaded rifle, the man hasn't got the sense God gave a snake."

"Then we could be grateful that he shows us how to admire snakes too."

"I like their skins, they are pretty and very soft and silky."

Lizzie turns on Aggie, "you've petted a snake haven't you?" she whispers breathless and doesn't want to hear what she already knows. "Never mind. I'd rather you did not answer that question. And I agree" she adds with a grin, "They do have striking soft silky skin."

"You touched a snake?" Bam asks owl eyed.

"Yes. I'd just killed it in the woodshed. I picked it up, took it outside and slung it as far as I could thinking a coyote might find a meal morsel in it."

"You feed coyotes?" It's not a question, but it begs a reply. Bam doesn't expect the stern eyed look.

"What would you have had me do with it instead?" Lizzie's eyes are steady level on his.

Bam breathes full and slow gaining time for a thought, perhaps a wise one. "Exactly that, Lizzie, exactly that. Okay. I got another reason I'm grateful for Caleb, because except for him, I might not know what a self-sufficient, fearless, and disturbingly creative woman my wife is." Lizzie starts the laugh that rings the room luring and lulling each and all of them into radiant rosy peaceful delight.

When the energy of her people and place is joyful, peaceful and calm, Lizzie says, "Tell me, husband…, your tall tale of the fresh vegetables you will pull from that praise pouch of yours, like a magician taking rabbits from a top hat.

"Tell me where you found them, who grew them, who gave them to you, and…, tell me everything you know about the rain that watered them, Bam…, because all the wells are dust dry; and I do so want to believe in miracles again, at least for a little while." Their eyes lock wide angle open, and both forget time and its passing and simply are. There. Present. In this moment. Not expecting a thing, and open to whatever comes. It's a peaceful easy feeling, and the kids nestle close to enter their rose glow space.

Sounding sleepy, Abbie simplifies, "Tell us especially the magic parts, Daddy. There *must* be magic parts to make a dry dusty day fetch fresh food for five of us for a week of days."

Bam smiles, "You are so wise, my Abigale. I didn't see the magic before your eyes let me see. Until then, I thought it was just a surprise blessing come out of the goodness of God and his good people who live here. Well, that in itself is a miracle, but it is every day magic. The story I will tell you is *real* magic. The only magic there is. The magic of miracles, when what *can*not *possibly* happen, happens anyway."

Abbie's eyes brighten and her sleepiness disappears. Melt, the only one to see and hear the improbable tale his Pa will tell, settles close to hear and watch and guide the weave any story strands his father drops or omits. He grins seated at the right hand of his father, knowing the master tell teller will not negligently drop a warp strand or woof, but only leave aside when its color, heft and weight are not right yet for the pattern the tale itself takes as it spins from his teller mouth and master muse of mind.

"Well," Bam begins as he tucks a calf and thigh under Lizzie for her head to rest comfortable on and see him well, for Bam knows Lizzie's love of tales well told. For her, he will tell his best told tale; and enchant his children in the boot. "Well..., where to begin...."

"The veggies," Lizzie prompts with a playful grin which Bam returns full round and deep into her eyes.

"Yes, my love, as you wish." Bam chortles, chest open, spine arched back, then settles quiet upright. "Yes, that's the major minor miracle tale that I still can't believe in my logic mind; but that I see with my eyes, smell with my nose, taste, yes, I have, with my teeth and tongue, hear crunch and snap, and feel fat water full in my hand." He pulls a handful of various vegetables from the praise pouch and hands them around. "Because this tale is so very hard to believe, I want each of you to hold, see, smell, while I tell my improbable story."

He hears a soft nibbling like a squirrel worrying the shell off a nut and his eyes follow the sound to Aggie who is nibbling wee small chips from a carrot. Aggie looks up into the silence and sees all eyes watching her. She ducks her head lips kissing the carrot tip but not nibbling. "He didn't say we *couldn't* taste or hear. He just left *out* those two senses. And I *like them*!"

The circle is silent a moment, and then Melt snicker snorts silly, snaps a sweet pea with his teeth and crunches with a satisfied smile. Bam backhands his knee, "I like peas," Melt defends with an unashamed shrug. "Hand me a tater, I plum *like* gnawing on raw potato." Melt hands him one grudging, "Okay, but don't go spitting tater tads at us when you get over excited" he grins, "telling your improbable tale."

Bam chin bobs quick up and down, eyes round. "I am most likely to spit chips then." He says softly. "You was there, son. You heard and saw, you gotta help keep me grounded..., under the angle wings."

Melt melts and presses a palm to Bam's spine between the shoulder blades and behind the heart. "I got your back, Dad. I'll keep you near and under the angel wings so the tale won't be too big for telling." To the weight of his father's hesitation, Melt adds, "And, if you come to a place where you just *cannot* tell even *one more* impossible thing, I'll tell the telling, and you can listen and say 'no way!' with Mom and the girls."

Now Bam laughs chuckle hearty, considers being a listener and not a teller, and remembers that every listening he ever did made him a better teller. His heart softens full and sure as he imagines listening to a fine first told tale narrated by his first and only son. He knows he glows. He feels it and even sees it, when he's not really trying and only allowing. He nods, "I'd like that, son. I'd like that a lot. Why don't you start? Are you ready?" Melt's heart melting smile is his reply. Father and son butt walk, Bam back, Melt forward. He feels Bam's hand on his spine and hears the unspoken words *'I got your back'*.

"This will *sound* like a tall tale, just like it did to Pa and me." He pauses for a smile and met eyes around the circle. His brows bob, "'It cannot have happened, you will think. "'It is impossible', you will say, and say sure and reasonable.

"We did too, Pa and me, even as these fresh sweet vegetables filled our palms and fingers to overfull. Was it magic? A miracle?"

"Was it magic?" Aggie asks eager.

"A *miracle*! It was a miracle, wasn't it, Melt?" Abbie demands impatient to know.

"What if it was *both*?" Melt consciously and conspicuously complicates the debate and, in the process, magnifies the tacit tension between trust and proof. *What is a miracle anyway? Each breath, every heartbeat, every morning sun, all star strung nights, even waiting for the moon to rise, is its own wonder and awe – for the open heart to see, feel and experience. Every* heartbeat *is worthy of awe and praise. How do I tell that tale?*

"Water," Lizzie speeds past Melt's question. "I want to know about the water that fed and held the roots into soil dark and rich enough to pop the smell of them right through the pores and put a healthy shine on the skin. Even on the skin of Bam's plump brown spud." All eyes are on Lizzie now. "Tell us that first, Melt, about the water." She prompts with deep thirsty eyes.

"Water is the hard part to believe." Melt grins. He bites a sugar snap pea for grounding and inspiration. "There is no proof for what I'm about to say...; except what's in your hand." Bam bobs a solemn *amen*.

Aggie nibbles crunchy carrot chips drinking the sweet water of them pressed between her teeth. For a reason she does not know, but is sure she will if she needs to, she savors the flavor of raisins and doesn't wonder why. Easy entranced by mystery and its curious clues, she is full peaceful for Melt's water tale to unwind in its time, slow or quick, by its own rhythm, at its own pace. *I'll listen for clues,* she thinks, *just like Agatha would do. Soon enough, I'll collect so many clues I'll begin to know what to do with them. I'll watch how they relate, and how they weave themselves together clear as a puzzle full laid.*

"Where'd the water come from, Melt?" Lizzie demands suddenly impatient with the pace of the tale.

He looks her clear and steady in the eyes for three eye blinks, then replies, "angel tears."

"*Angel tears.*" Now Lizzie sits up squaw legged facing her son, eyes and mouth round.

"Don't you taste them? In the food?" He clasps Lizzie's hand and bites her sugar snap. "They're sweeter than they'd be with even daily water from a well." His eyes hold hers hard and fast, "And you know there is no other water because all the wells are running low or dry and not recharging like before we plowed under the fruited plains and *really* pissed off Mother Nature."

Bam backhands Melt's shoulder, "*Don't* say those words around your mother, let alone your sisters! I taught you better than that."

"Yeah. And you taught me how to tell tales. Sometimes spicy words add the right tang to a tale."

"Melt," Aggie takes his hand, patting it softly and looking into his eyes, "you just go back to telling your tale about the angel tears, that's all that's important right now. Ignore everything else."

Melt's brows arch over round eyes, "You're talking about *my* mother here, little sister. You should know that I am not planning on ignoring her, so put that right out of your mind." Aggie's face falls. Melt leans close with a grin and peeps up into her eyes, and all is forgotten forgiven.

Abbie pats Aggie's hand with a pudgy palm and says "Don't worry sister, Melt's going to tell about the angel tears next. We just have to zip it," she pulls thumb and forefinger over her lips, "until he does." She adds, "For now, all we gotta do is listen. We do that all the time, and we're already really good at it."

"Our first source is Hester." Melt begins, "There's something about that woman that makes me *believe* what she says even when I know that it can*not* be true in 'real' life. And then, I saw it with my own eyes and I know what she says *is* true. Here's the Hester Hester told Pa and me about these juicy fruits of her garden, which continues, by the way, to be as green and lush as Eden."

Lizzie smiles soft into the swift silence that follows Melt's unexpected announcement and says, "Attribution accepted, Melt. Back to the angel tears, dear." The sisters snuggle into Lizzie's sides and in the circle of her arms where she hold them close and free in the warm embrace of mother love. The kerosene lantern flickers fleeting dreams of impossible things that may nonetheless be tastefully true.

Melt grins appreciating Lizzie's tale telling guidance and the ease it introduced into the task of telling his tale faithful and entertainingly well. "And then I will tell of the angel's tears as the girl claimed, saw and knew it to happen."

"The girl?" the girls harmonize in one more keenly interested voice.

Melt bows with an inward melting smile of conscious gratitude for acting on his intention to integrate tale telling guidance from hearers. Their active engaged exchanges somehow enhance the tale and its telling rendering the whole of it more integral, full faceted and true than any teller alone can do. Raising his head dead slow Melt sets his eyes on hers and asks, "'the girl?' you ask? *Before* 'angel tears'? What don't I understand about this?"

"She's a *girl!*" Abbie replies, "*That's* why!"

Melt's brows and head elevate cautious slow, his head bobs mechanical maniacal fast. "I get that now." He assures mock scared, "I get that now." He grins fast and off-sides, peers deep into her eyes with barefaced bewitched enchanted love. Abbie melts. He sees that. Feels it too. He leans down to rub noses with her. He grins eye to eye, perhaps I will tell her a prairie princess whose tribe is hungry and weak without food to eat and…."

"*Yes!*" Abbie interrupts, echoed almost instantly by Aggie now on her knees keen to hear the girl's story told as a prairie princess tale.

Aggie puts an elbow on a knee, raises her forearm, rests her chin on her palm, smiles, and says, "I vote with your sisters, Melt. You cannot reveal Elder Wisdom through your telling of the *girl's* tale…," the emphasis is soft supple strong. *You* must tell her tale as she told you, with her mouth, her eyes and her little girl heart.

"As for the girl, she is simply too tender young to be burdened with the weight of the way and the rhyme less reason of Elder Wisdom. She has neither the weight nor the right to speak it." She masks a smile with and hand and her eyes give her away. "Let her *be* a little girl, Melt, who still has neither the wit nor the way to explain what is happening that is far beyond her control, but for which she was – and is – no more than the necessary catalyst."

"Catalyst?" Melt repeats curious.

"Yes, a catalyst is a reagent, something that activates, facilitates and spurs a reaction." She smiles into his eyes, "Does that make sense?"

"Yes, it does, and it's exactly the right and perfect word to use when telling the girl's tale." He smiles, "She was indeed the necessary catalyst and only that. She is a bit of a chemical compound too!"

"What do you mean by that?"

"Ever hear her explode?"

"Can't say that I have…," Lizzie replies uneasy uncertain while Bam is startled silent seeing dots connect to dots that he hadn't even seen before. She peeps over his shoulder and into his mind at the gap toothed line drawing he plotted there. *Interesting,* she thinks.

"She doesn't do it often. Even her mom says that. "But when she does, nothing false, not one thing, still stands when the rattling shattering sundering stops."

"Oh my! And she doesn't…, *do* anything?"

"Define 'do'." He arches his spine and relaxes against Bam's chest soft dropping his head on his shoulder. He can feel his father's mental distraction absorbing his weight and warmth while puzzling how *no* action can possibly produce *right* action. *It's a do-loop for sure. <u>Do</u>ing has nothing to do with it. Simply being peaceful with what is changes things; that and being grateful for all of it, even the prickly parts. That's the power of the girl come to think of it. She has no power at all…, and that's the greatest power of all.* Melt waits comfortably until all eyes are on him. Then, Melt speaks aloud the words he heard in the silence of his mind and heart. He watches as transformations move through them like a flight of silvery shooting stars lancing them through in places where smallness and separation hide and abide, healing, clearing and lighting their repressed of smallness lies made for security's sake.

Knowing what comes next, and feeling the fixed focus now, Bam strums from his guitar notes, tones, and sounds fit to engage the hearts and ears of humans, and angels too, when Melt tells of angels come near to Earth to see, to hear, and to weep. Melt soften to the sentient presence of ethereal energies of angelic faith and power in the company of his small clan.

When the time has come, he says: "First, the *highly improbable* things that Hester told me and Pa, and *then* the girl's telling of the tale. She told only me," he grins, "and, she said I could repeat her telling only *if* I told the tale well." Everyone laughs imagining the feisty fair child putting *that* condition on her consent to the telling. As one being they focus eager eyes and excited ears on Melt. *Can it get any better for a tale teller?* He wonders idly and begins.

"When Pa and I finished helping Lady RO clean out her cupboards and her canning cellar, again, she said we should stop in to see Hester, for there was a thing she needed help with. So now you know where the canned goods came from, including the pickled beets Pa just pulled from his bag of tricks known as a praise pouch." Bam gets a round of applause for his apparent magic trick of turning time and effort into food, and sometimes into sweaters and shoes.

"So, Pa and I stopped to see Hester, and to our surprise, the work she wanted was help *thinning* her garden! Well, we didn't leave the kitchen for a *long* time after that. Hester's is a hard tale to tell because everyone knows before she even speaks that it *cannot* be true." He lets the puzzle rest with his audience for a bit as they bite and flavor the fruit of that Eden green garden that currently bloomed and fruited in their minds.

"Angel tears." Abbie assures shrewdly, getting ahead of the tale. And, to a story teller like Melt, elevating the tension of the tale by early anticipation of its resolution. A resolution that is impossible, however. He smiles, *lovin'* it.

"Hester told Pa and me that she was in the kitchen doing 'kitchen stuff' as she put it, when she heard something sub audible shrill and piercing that it even bit into the marrow of her bones. It was agony, her word, so intensely overpowering she feared she might die, but knew she would not. It was not her time to die, she said. But something else equally compelling as death when it walks in, inhabits her body mind brain, and possessed it more wholly than she herself ever had. Her body trembles and she knows not why. She can't help the quaking, she can't control it, and she can't stop it. It possesses her. She is terrified that she's having a seizure and no one but the girl at home to help."

"Was it evil?" Aggie asks warily suspicious.

Melt squares his shoulders, lowers his brows, looks into her eyes, and asks, "Can you *imagine* an evil…, even the *Great Evil, ever* winning possession of Hester's mind, and *if* it did, finding *any* comfort staying there?" The girls giggle at a tormenting demon in a personal hell hiding from Light in a circular cell.

"It was not evil. It was a sound she heard piercing pure and rich in her inner ear, but not at all in her outer ears. Hester covered *both* ears," Melt demonstrates, "and nothing changed in the volume or the agony of the shrill singing sound.

The girl felt a grating tearing sundering thunder like 'heaven ripping a tear through the fabric of time and space to open a new door. A door *very* near to this place where she and her family live. She knew without doubt that something new and powerful would pass through the time space portal that now being rent open. She felt the portal tear open inside of her, and knew beyond doubt that the portal opened outside too. Both were true at the same time. What she felt, she said, was the composite force of repeated subtle soft shreds of infinite agony fiercely invoked and imposed on Earth Mother as a direct consequence of man's separation from Source anxiety. *She* talks this way…, I'm just telling.

"Yet that buckling pain that rode Hester down carried welcome Hope safe and gentle in its uplifting arms, in *her* arms. That surprised Hester. It meant, she said, that the portal she now faced across space and time, was about *her*, in a very intimate way. And she wanted to know how, and why.

"Hester follows the subtle sound of falling tears. *Many falling tears*, she thinks as she closes on sound she cannot hear with outer ears. Now comes the tinging tingling tune of tears dripping from high and higher onto something hard and close and cracked and earthy dry like clay left too long in the sun. The smell is earthy, close, careful, and intimate in an infinitely personal yet cosmically indifferent way. Her words, not mine," declaims Melt palms out and high. He grins loving his art and performance of it.

"Hester comes quiet and soft into her room where the strange weeping wailing energy is soft and safe and beyond her window, where the girl sits in wide eyed weeping wonder watching something she cannot see. She moves soft and close, bending to look over her shoulder.

"She sees angels alighting in a ring around the garden. She watches as the angels morph into etheric gentle giants falling together in linked arms to dome the garden high. They cry fresh water tears into the parched garden and before her eyes her tattered plants transform from scarcely surviving to blatantly thriving. Hester has blinked perhaps thrice, she says, since entering the room and watching pitiful plants miracle grow to thriving due to something rich whole and vital within the tears of the angels.

"That's where Hester's story ends and the girl's begins.

"But what *happened*?" demand the sisters in one voice at a tale ended too soon and sudden to satisfy.

"Well, next, I went to Hester's bedroom where the girl was still apparently in shock and awe; and there I sat and listened and heard what she said and saw what she happen. I wanted to learn why it *did* happen. And that's where the girl's tale of angel's tears begins.

"So, there they were, all spring and summer long, she and her mom and sibs all working hard and smart in planting and caring for their garden. Daily they drew water in pails from a weak well and toted the water to the plants they grew. Their work was paying off, the week well still gave water."

Unexpectedly, Melt melts at hearing his retelling and the weight of what tells next. He is silent a dramatic moment slowly inhaling and exhaling. Just that. Then he opens and clears his throat, and continues. "That afternoon another duster came pelting the plants with sand and rock hard soil shredding the leaves, pelleting the fruits, and teasing tearing the well-tended plants up from their roots, and their roots from the soil.

"The girl got mad! She got *so* mad at that dirty duster that she yelled a blue Norther' straight at God' ear for allowing yet *another* danged deranged duster rage cruel as a mad arch demon over the *very* land the Lord Himself made, and shred to sunder the fruits of their labor! And *they*, the people who love and serve Him, would starve staring at empty cupboards, bins, pots and bowls!

"You are a *good* God of abundance and love!" She rages soundless above the storm. "The demon duster that attacks us IS NOT YOURS! COMMAND IT TO STOP, NOW!

"WE, are yours! Save *us*! Save our garden!" She does not ask the High God for this boon. She demands it. None of this did girl say out loud to the Lord. She raged silent, she yelled sub audible, she hissed words shaped and formed only in her mind…, where only He can hear.

"In her mind she imagines the simple smiling joy of sharing the fruits of the garden with others, and receiving from them from their own abundance, their own 'too much' that gave and got such simple pleasure from recognizing and paying *their* 'too much' forward. Or back. Said she could never really grasp *how* an Infinite God whose center is everywhere and whose borders are nowhere, would grasp concepts like forward and back.

"Time and direction must be just so *squishy* for God…," she told me, "and I have no idea if, or even how, we could *possibly* pay forward or back. Or why we'd even want to know," she shrugs, "I mean what *good* is there in that? With God what we call 'reality' is really just a big infinite, multi-dimensional circle whose center is everywhere and whose circumference is nowhere, forever forming and flowing."

"She talks like that?" Asks Aggie in open awe at the way and play of words that is the gift of the girl. "I want to *think* like that," she smiles, "so I can talk like her and speak music and poetry like she does."

Lizzie rubs Aggie's back and says with a soft smile, "You just did! I heard you. We all did. *Wish granted!*" She turns back to Melt, "Back to the duster, the tear in heaven, the angel's tears, and these veggies. By the way, I agree with the girl on that pay back/pay forward thing is a terrible waste of time and mind."

"Well, I reckon the good *Lord* God got an ear full because that's when the wailing angels descended to peel the sky apart, muscle through the breach, and make that *dreadful* inner ear shredding shattering sound Hester mentioned that made Earth rumble tumble and left her stumble clumsy on her feet." Melt meets appreciative giggles grins and huzzas from his attentive fans, bobs a wee bow, and continues.

"What happened is no mystery," Melt assures certainly. "Nor is it magic. It may be a miracle, but surely it is divine intervention. Whatever name we use, it was called by a girl too young to know the meaning of 'impertinence' who stood boldly before the throne of grace to *demand* God send angels NOW!

"I would laugh, but I can't inhale that deep. Awe takes less breath.., and has no truck with laughter." Melt melts, allowing the power of awe thundering through him to pervade his tale and to exude the incense sweet serene silence of wonder into the room. The soft wet kissing sound of chewing water laden vegetables makes him smile. He feels the growing yearning for more of the girl's do-it-now requisition of angels of God from God, and why her impertinence didn't render her a crispy critter among the brown blown vegetables left by the duster.

He feels his own sweet passion for the angel tale grow and bloom in his mind and heart, and in his mouth and knows it is time again to tell tale. He breathes deeply recalling on the inhale all the words and feelings he heard and learned as the girl spun herself out, exhaling expelling the whole intimidating horde of impossibilities that spew like fiery flow flare flames of lava oozing and spewing from a livid lurid volcano.

He should speak, but he cannot. He is gut punched breathless mute and still stunned stammering stupid by the weight and measure of the girl's tale that is his alone to tell. He imagines his heart stops but he breathes again so apparently not.

"Um, Melt," Bam bumps his elbow for attention, "you might want to breathe now, son. Getting light headed for want of oxygen to the brain makes as much sense for a tale teller as getting dumb drunk does. Breathe!

"Do it again! Deep and slow now. Hold it in, give the brain time to absorb the oxygen and for the heart to still and calm to a steady easy rhythm. That's it. Do it again three times." Bam waits with his son in silence as he faces his dark demons of doubt without proof. Short on faith to believe what he cannot prove, Melt may not tell what he does not believe. Storyteller stalemate. No tiebreaker.

When Melt is calm and alert again, Bam smiles encouragement, sobers and says: "You are the only one, son, who heard the girl tell her telling. You're the only one can tell it true and whole." In the face of silence he adds: "I can't cover for you here, I didn't hear. *Can you* tell the girl's tale, Melt?"

His eyes are open, deep, calm, and the fear in them has melted into molten liquid passion again.

"I don't *believe* it, Pa!"

Bam grins, "A crisis of faith. I thought that'd be it. Did you ever tell a tall tale?" Melt nods. "Ever lie?" Melt eyes him flat and looks away silent. "I'll take that as a 'yes'. Did you tell a *good* lie then?" Melt is sullen sudden slit eyed silent.

Bam grabs him roughly by the shoulders shaking him solidly sternly shouting, "You-will-not-fade-into-fear! If you do that, the devil in you has won without a fight. Whites are not quitters; and you, my son, *ain't* going to be the family first."

Melt's angry beset eyes meet Bam's stern ones without remorse or apology, but with a profound sense of doubtful distress. Bam grins toothily, wraps Melt in a bear hug and consciously and forcefully expels air from his lungs leaving him open mouthed gasping and fish eyed, a child again in his father's arms. *Pa's face ain't smiling though,* Melt frowns foggily, head bobbing.

"When you need oxygen again, nod your head" Bam coaches comfortingly.

I gotta ask *for air?* Melt thinks foggy fractious, still surly sour, separate, and securely denying even the possibility of miracles.

Not in this *god-forsaken dust dashed devastated desert we made by plowing too much, planting too much too soon too long, and forgetting everything we knew about making dry land farming rich and productive and ecologically sane. We became thick hick suckers leeching life from the very land we were born to or came to live with and on. We no longer enrich the land as we work and reap and live intent on making every day a* Guten Das.

Melt's head tips softly slowly to Bam's cheek, eyes surrender closed. Bam smiles and gentles the circle of his arms as the rhythm of Melt's breath deepens and slows while his brain, still in a do-loop, repudiates and reprimands what was. *No, God left this land when we raped and despoiled it and would not give it succor, support or respect.* He breathes a deep, slow rhythm and his oxygen fed muscles relax and ease. His neck opens and arches until his head rests soft against Bam's shoulder. *A rock. Like Peter. That's my Pa, a warm strong rock.*

God though is like President Roosevelt and the rain makers. They come, they see, and then they go, never to be seen again.

Bam hears this with growing unease, not all of it arising from hearing his son's deep asleep views. His face creases deep, brows bunched bothered above eyes fixed firm on Lizzie's, "He thinks God left this land when we raped and despoiled it and would not give it succor, support, or respect."

Lizzie is taken a bit aback by the force of the words Melt chose. "You heard this in your mind?"

Bam shrugs tipping his cheek to Melt's crown, "He's so near to me," he explains rationally.

Lizzie cocks a brow, gives a grudging grin, then a see-through sweet smile, and notes, "It's not the first time I've known this about you, Bam. It is the first time you mentioned hearing thoughts though."

She gives a playful grin, "I think being close had nothing to do with hearing his mind speak. You have the gift of knowing a man's heart, and then being there with them. In minutes of meeting a person they come away feeling like they know you like an old friend, a bosom buddy, even a *womb mate!*

"That can be keenly disturbing to a mere mortal, my dear husband. Even a son. Perhaps it is good that you didn't hear his thoughts before the head touch…," Lizzie stops mid thought. "You did." She touches her head absently, "You hear mine…," she stops, smiles, then laughs soundlessly, open eyed amazed.

"That's *it*! You *do* hear my thoughts, even when we're far apart. That's how you *always* and without fail bring home with you the very thing I need and am without. Today you brought staples and fresh vegetables, and you feed us from a tale that we, all of us, have powerful and abiding need to hear.

"Most of us, like Melt, are terrified *silly* at even the thought of believing in God, let alone having faith in Divine intervention and things that look *exactly* like a miracle but *cannot* be!"

She grins now, "And you, my dear heart, are very probably the one who told him most about how we plowed up the Great American Plains and in under a decade, turned it into a wind-blown desert of dirt." Bam bobs his admission.

"Give him some slack, Bam, he' still a boy, who is so avid and eager to become a man just like you." She chuckles knowingly, "even your passion for the land and living with it, not just on it." Bam smiles up at her, eyes clear and bright now. "Maybe when Melt wakes up, you can ask him to let you tell the tale of the angel tears."

Bam hoots a hollow holler and says "Oh, like a true tale teller like Melt would let another teller tell his tale? Not likely! Besides, he's at the part about what the girl told him, and I didn't hear that." His brows form firm flat over his eyes, "I can't tell it! The boy's got to be the teller. I get to be a listener."

"U-h-h-h-o," Melt moans as he raises his head, "like I'd *let you* tell my tale telling? Not going to happen, Pa," he says pushing off from Bam's chest and straitening upright, "I just needed a few wee winks to get restored."

He pats his pa's chest, "Thanks for the shoulder to lean on. I'm restored now. I'm good to tell the girl's tale. The way she told it to me." His family circle straightens and relaxes at attention on Melt.

"After she told us her telling, Hester took my glass, nodded to her bedroom where the girl waited for me alone, that the girl would to talk only to me; and when I was done, I'd find them in the kitchen or maybe the garden. I hoped the garden, if you want the truth; and I got my wish.

He pauses shifting scenes and senses. "The girl sat on her knees on the cedar chest facing the window, her palms up and open as though blessing something beyond, outside. I came close to see over her shoulder and into the garden that was more deeply green and lushly in need of thinning than it was the day before.

'Impossible', I thought. I leaned near the open window and inhaled the heavenly rich smell of fresh green, red, amber and gold and saw the glow of life shine through them. I was stunned silent stupid, I was. She felt it and turned to me with hope filled eyes and a silent prayer for humility.

"*'Humility'*, I thought, curious at the choice of word. I sat beside her on her mother's hope chest and put a palm on her back behind her heart. I felt her sag almost, at some release and comfort she found in the touch. In silence she slow pulls her lungs full, holds easy and long, then exhales easy through her open throat and mouth.

"She does this three times, and each time she becomes stronger and more confident. I feel her heart beat slow and strengthen, her energy expand and glow through and beyond her skin like a whole body halo. I felt my hand inside her halo glow grow warm and begin to vibrate at the jubilant rate of joy. I must have laughed aloud because she turned to me surprised and looked in my eyes and was surprised again to see and hear her Ode to Joy sung silent through me too.

"We bonded." Melt assures surely. This is what she *confessed* to me with a hand on my arm, praying forgiveness and expiation.

"I was angry, Melt. Hellfire spitting furious with God for not making the duster *stop,* stop destroying everything we worked steady and smart to have and to eat and to share. We had nothing, Melt. Nothing but hope and that garden, and without it, a long lean winter ahead. I was so mad I cried…, and that's not worth the salt that's spilt in doing it.

"So then I felt sappy silly and that *always* makes me mad! At *me…, that's* a snake eating its tail!

"And so I *yelled at* God. In my mind and heart only…, where he alone can hear." She smiles below lowered lashes and makes her first confession. "My self in my mind wailed raging wild in a fierce voice fit to shake the walls of Jericho and sunder them down." She adds in a slow small voice, "And God heard. And the sky tore a shrieking shred open to let the weeping angels press through."

With wonder in her voice she adds: "The angels fell to earth like a hawk dives down in a wide centering spiral, each landing to form a circle around the garden, hands linked, wings scooping to slow them as they soft touch down to the powder dirt of earth in a garden *decidedly* outside of Eden's bounds."

"She talks like that?" Aggie interrupts.

Melt smiles a nod, "she does."

"Good, 'cause I'm going to write like that when I grow up."

"Start now," Melt advises soberly sure.

"I can't write yet, nor even read!" she defends.

"But you *can* talk and speak." Melt counters, "and that mean you can *tell* tales." He leans confidentially close to add, "It's called the 'oral tradition' in tale telling circles. And then, when you do learn to read and to write, you can *write* your best told tales quick and easy because you know them so well. I'd start there," he advises, "writing the ones you best love telling first."

Aggie gives Melt a heart full smile, and he melts. Practically predictable. "Where was I when you interrupted me?" he demands with a stern sour face.

She giggles, "The angels just tore a hole in heaven and falling to earth to circle the not-Eden garden. That's where you were."

"Ah, yes, that's it. Well then, the girl tells me that the angels stretched and grew to the size of giants and then, as one, they fell together into the arms of others forming a dome of angel and wing over the enclosed space. That's when the angels wept, she said, while their wings and hair whipped into dreads in the bitter hot winds and they wove and wound the dreads into air baffles as they expanded and stretched to tower over the leafless trees in the nearby grove.

"The girl heard a sub audible tone song of longing and loss that mourned, moaned wept and wailed and then threaded through with sweet surging sweeping lyrical harmonies that so *ardently* loved and moved the wind, that it settled itself into a quiet and peaceful attentive breath 'of fresh breeze that cools as it whispers through the screen to kiss away the sweat of my brow'. The girl's words," Melt clarifies with an outturned upraised palm.

"Methinks he protests too much," Lizzie quips to Bam provoking a smirk and a smile shared among the clan. Especially by Melt, who *likes* being seen through by an engaged group of attentive listeners. For what is measure of the *worth* of a teller if not the ears that hear and the hearts and minds that hold?

"I'm a *teller*!" Melt hisses through smiling lips. "I must tell my tale tall and true." Then he adds with an eye wide dramatic flair. "It is yours *alone...* to deny or believe, as you will and why. So then, the girl says, those mile high angels fell together catching shoulders as they went, collapsing their bodies heads arms and wings into a baffled dome over the garden. And then the angels wept...."

Melt has puddle melted and can't tell on just now, overcome *again* by the tale telling girl and the decidedly dubious deeds she described and the wayward timely timelessness of them. Taking a slow full breath, he holds aloft a floridly fruitful red bell pepper like an Impromptu torch of Truth and gives a contented salute to proof. Melt is poised again, in the center of him, where the best stories always begin.

In the core of him, where there still stalks the fierce and Faithless One with greedy livid eyes trapped snapping in a rage of denial doubt. *This beast will not be bested!* Melt knows. So he meets his inner stalker, and eye to eye, face to face with the Beast he demands: *Grandfather Teller, is this fierce conflict within me* truly necessary *to me telling this tale?*

A cat tail whips within, gold emerald eyes spark flare flame, strong lithe body whip tail torques through a taut and tightening Mobius strip loop, his eyes flare fierce with a fang flaunting heart searing mind jolting fury. Melt is impaled and imposed by those eyes. He slow breathes three exhales and inhales, eyes never leaving the angry ones of the enchanting beast. Suddenly Melt *knows,* in a silly senseless sort of way, and with a certainty that both embraces and exceeds the reach of faith and doubt thereby transcending both.

While opposition by opposites is a necessary and natural part of the flow of life, that does not mean man must be stymied or stopped when the dark side shows up in life. Melt could give you a long list of ways and whys he has let the dark side stop and stay him long and wrong along his pilgrims path of life. He is not proud of that past. Nor can he change or delete it from his history or memory.

"He almost hears Grandfather Teller's amused breathy easy laugh and the wind whisper of his thought words carrying easy breezy release receive rhythm to entice, tease and ease the duals within into being and becoming a compatible fluid floating One energy, two equal, opposing and embracing flows.

"So," Melt's one word captures their eyes. He smiles. "Here's the hardest part of the telling for me. I could not find faith to *believe* what the girl told me next.

"What'd she say?" Aggie demands to know – to be her own judge. Even of Melt's own doubt and his blame and shame of it.

He meets and holds her eyes, silent solemn still, as she takes her own measure and weight of him. Melt pulls a full breath and replies from behind shame lowered lids. "The girl said that they had planted – from seed – last month." He holds a dramatic pause, "Then she said the plants were only two or four inches high when the duster hit…, yesterday."

He holds the bell pepper torch aloft waiting, feeling ripples of shock break on the shores of their minds hissing sibilant singing across the sand then sucking soft away leaving sea and shore wholly changed, yet in a subtle and unremarkable way, leaving sea and shore comfortingly the same. He lowers head and lashes, and breathes within the truth and scope of what he has not yet said. What he must say.

His family feels his retreat and without understanding it. They honor it anyway with gentle caring free flowing energy sharing. He smiles and raises his head, "Thanks, Abbie," he whispers. "I needed that."

"We know you did, Melt," she melts him with her exasperated smile and warm sparkly eyes. "Now, what the heck was *that about*?" she demands, fiery eyes flaring wide. "What can you *possibly* have done that shames you so deep that you cannot tell *us*, your family? We who have to love you *any*way."

Into Melt's surprise shocked face she grins a singing melting, "*That's* what unconditional love *means*! "So, whatever it is that's so hard for you that you can't tell it's telling…, to us, who must love you anyway! Get *over it*! *And tell her* tale, not yours!"

Her eyes brook no nonsense, she spins on a heel to step to and plop where she was, draw herself up regally tall, and with tender firmness mandate: "So, brother, first tell us *what beastly* thing you have done, and, when you have said that telling, say how your dastardly deed, whatever it is, fits inside the *girl's* tale, and tell how your despicable deed keeps you from telling *the girl's tale*…, full, true and fair?"

She frowns doubt, "And when you spin out the *whole* tail of your telling… *of the girl's tale*," she grins lopsided sloppy indifferent, "*we* will decide if we will forgive you for planning to skip key parts of the tale *simply* because *you* don't believe them!"

Now, she is not at all indifferent or unconditional. "Personally, that sounds like a self-sounded death knell for a tale teller."

"Whew," Melt sits sharp erect, head back, eyes round. He thinks he has never before been dressed down so properly, so thoroughly, and in so few words. He lowers his eyes hearing her words echo in the privacy of his own mind. "I think I have not been dressed down so thoroughly and in so few words ever before this day. Thank you Abbie. I needed that."

"I know you did," she agrees amiably while licking her tingling palm.

"You, Abbie," Melt presses on carefully, "from your great understanding, have thoroughly and completely destroyed my ego and its decree about the kinds of telling I will do and those I won't. Without your potent protest," he touches his cheek tenderly, "I probably would have edited the girl's tale *solely* because *I would not* believe the things she told me. Out of my own lack of faith.

"You were right, I already tell tall tales I know aren't true. I even know what 'metaphor' means well enough to know better than to edit the girl's tale or change the telling of it. Thank you, sister dear," he says sincerely, "for *demanding* I shape up so that I can grow into being a true and truthful tale teller.

"Okay, the next part of the girl's tale is what scared me senseless. Because it makes no sense, I believe it cannot have happened. And yet, her telling is the only way that all the data point dots connect and actually *do* make sense." He takes a deep breath and continues:

"What the girl showed me today is that the garden is growing bigger. There are new plants volunteering in the space *outside* the border of their garden. She took me outside and showed me where plants are filling the circle where the angels stood…, and wept angel tears."

He groans as though pressed down flat by a great weight, "And she showed me plants that were *new*. Plants they didn't plant! Not from seed, nor from starter pots. It's illogical!"

"Miracles *are* illogical to the human mind, Melt. That is why they are *called* miracles, dear. They *do* defy man's powers of reason and logic." Lizzie chews a pea absently and asks "When did you go athei…, *agnostic*?"

She growls pugnacious as a mother bear defending her cubs, eyes slit a fiery stiletto goads as she hisses, "An atheist has the integrity, at least, to take a position and make a stand for it, even if it's unpopular. Sometimes even when just plain bald face *wrong* from the get go!

"Not so, an agnostic.

"An agnostic is someone who willfully puts on blinders, twists in ear plugs and sourly sings 'La la la la la la…, I can't *hear* you. Then, the antic agnostic ties on night black blinders and yells screech owl hollow loud, 'Ne ne ne ne ne ne, I can't *see* you'. The agnostic then declares from that most hoisted high place that what *he* can hear, and he *will* see…, is the sole and only reality.

"And the no-eyed man who cannot see, and the man without ears to hear, yell tell us that *they* are the one and only *right* source of truth.

"Bogus, Melt!" Aggie snaps. "We taught you to *do* critical thinking. We taught you ways and methods to *not* let doubt and fear to turn you into the wooden headed puppet plaything of the brute pusher scared bully thug that lives inside you!

"Can *you* turn *you* into a mindless reprehensible drone, Melt? I am *very* disappointed to see and say that I believe you can. I'm looking at proof of it." She snap raps her word gavel of judgment on his wide eye baffled un-bowed head.

"Mama," Aggie shakes Lizzies arm firmly. When she turns, she asks, "When did we plant our garden?"

"Last month. Like every farm family did. Because the Farmer's Almanac said it was the best time to plant. So," Lizzie grins from behind a hand, her eyes spilling spewing sparkling laughter, as she says: "I personally believe we have a verifiable miracle here. And, *not one reason* any of us should name or claim it." She mime zips her lips, and everyone follows suit. Everyone except Melt, that is.

"So," Lizzie challenges the ice hard un-melting Melt, "What's your holdout, Melt, what's going on with you?"

His eyes and one side of his mouth grin as he says: "I *promised* the girl I'd tell her tale…," he bobs his head, "so she'd never have to. Not *ever* have tell that terrible telling to anyone after me." He frowns, "I think she used 'never' and 'ever' more times than I did."

Bam giggles and claps Melt's shoulder, "It is the art and craft of the teller to tell tales tall and true. Hearers never know where the line between the two winds, loops and forks through the tale. Every time you walk with a tale it takes you down another path, one you never found before. Hearers know this. They'll only mention it though when you surprise 'em or tell 'em something they hadn't heard before.

"And, son, nobody but you even *knows* what the girl said. If she called it a miracle and you are telling her tale, then you have *got* to use her word." A small sentient silence follows.

Melt smiles and says, "You're right, Pa. If I am to tell the girl's tale, I have to use the words she used.

"I'm good now, Mom. I will keep my promises to the girl." He grins, "She *also* made me promise to come tomorrow and tell her how the telling went while Pa and her ma go 'pick a peck of peppers and stuff'. Her words. Tonight is my trial telling of the girl's tale. I will tell it true…, and tainted with titillating temptations to believe or to deny. Just the way she told me."

Lizzie soft strokes Melt's cheek, "there's my good boy," she says tumbling Melt back in time to each and every occasion she found to say proud words into his eyes and heart. He catches her hand in his and lets her see through to the true truth teller he intends to be and become. First as good as, and then better than, his dad. Bam sees this. He smiles humble honored and filled. *You make me proud, my son, and so very glad to see the man you will be and become when you get your whole grown up body.*

"When we got to Hester's this morning, the girl was in the kitchen helping her ma. Hester poured a cup of coffee for her and Pa, and the girl took my hand and let me outside. The hot red eye of the sun beat down with the force of an ungoverned blast forge that forcefully transferred its heat into us through our shirts and our shoes, into the core of us. First my lungs and then my heart caught fire within me. I engaged with the thought that I would melt to a puddle where I stood just like the tar baby did.

He grins, "But unlike the tar baby I had an option. It was presented just then by the girl's easy ring around my already rosy wrist. She led me slow…," He huffs a sigh, "okay she *dragged me* slug footed to the garden gate. That wasn't there yesterday.

"Every step of the way, my inept beset EGO *jibbered* insanely petulant, pushy, that I DENY! Just deny it ever happened and make it not real." He is silent through three slow centering breaths. "Even while my EGO mind was *terribly* uncomfortable with an outright denial of the data points my eyes collected and automatically fed to my brain. Both my EGO mind, and I, are stunned simply speechless by the myriad *majorly impossible* things I am seeing with my mortal eyes. That very same EGO even now hounds me to accept, allow and admit that what I can and do see, cannot be, and in EGO's tale, well, there is nothing to tell." He straightens and adjusts his body upright and free of The Great Denial, and picks up the tale.

"Without reprieve or release, EGO likewise cautiously counsels and comforts that, though it's nice to believe, it is *not* true that what I think, imagine and claim confidently, will be attracted to me. EGO is like a fellow I know who's a self-lauded and self-appointed expert on everything I am, can and ever possibly become, and truth seer is not one of them. And I may not be a truth teller either, because all those jobs are already taken, thank you very much. *That* too is impossible, to me, personally.

"I may *not* think big," they snarl, slap attack and throw down." Teller waits for the image and experience to clear before he softly tells the EGO lie.

"I may *not* show or use my power. I must hold my hand close and curled lest what is there be taken and lost to me.

"I must stay small.

"I must not make ripples on the placidly submissive lake of life.

"I may only expect things small common in life.

"I may expect that none of it will come generously.

"I may not say that a thing that *cannot be* there… is, in fact, actually there!

"I may not speak of what cannot be and yet I see… with my own eyes.

"I must *deny*."

Melt waits while he and they, both and one feel and find the ways they, and all, play dull and small and will not see, say, or be, anything that cannot be. His inner teller knows that until the hearers own and allow what they will not accept, they are powerless to end or change it, or their innate responses to it.

"That part of me that edges God out…, my EGO, needed to simply let go! That shift in consciousness enabled my conscious mind where the co-creator lives, to capture and process *all* that it saw, while allowing it time adjust to my inner eyes to see clear and well, that it was fierce forgotten familiar fear in me that made me deny out of hand – and mind – what I *knew* with all my senses was totally true.

"My inner battle was not about faith in God, nor in all the *not secret* things that God can and does do. Those things I know with firm faith, even the new and twisty. No, that battle was all over my paltry puny pugnacious petulance over *parsley*!" He slump sighs another countless remorse, this one not coarse or callow, but open broken hearted railing remorse. "So…, I just let go. I just simply… let go.

"And on that instant I could see as though blinders were lifted, and in the lifting revealing me as a blinking lash-batting peckish pre-teen selfish naval-gazing ninny!

Bam bats his leg and in a harsh whisper says: "I taught you to talk better than that about yourself!"

Melt grins semi cocky proud and stage whispers: "I caught you up in the teller tale, didn't I? That blinded you to the arch of the art of tale telling that tells dark and light. Go on, Pa," he urges, "you can admit it."

Bam quick changes into a listener scarcely aware of the teller or his telling. He hears only to the next soft sweet sigh of a page turning in a teller tale now teeming alive in his ears and flitting firefly free in his mind. *Unfettered.* The word slithers in Bam's mind hissing sibilant echoes through its twisting corridors and caverns. Blood hound like, he sniffs out scents of the word mingled and mixed in the slow eddies of Melt's quicksilver mind and melodic mouth. Bam smiles contentment. *It is good to be just a hearer with ears to hear and eyes to see…, oh my…! <u>Unfettered</u>. I do like that word.*

Unfettered now, Melt returns inward to walk by the girl to the garden, and into his veggie tale talk. "I stopped…, as we came near the garden. I could *not* go one step closer to the shimmering *illusion* where the garden was. The girl stopped too, watching me with infinite attentive and present compassion. I looked… her in the eye knowing she'd unload on me for a faithless fickle fool I was, and she did. But not once was she mean to me.

"Instead she channeled into me all the free flowing radical love and forgiveness God could spare to her to flow through to me." My head bow of its own weight against the weighty weightless weight of love. The Good Lord diverted all of His abundant surplus of unfathomable love through the girl, and into me. I fell to my knees for I could *not* bear up under the ferocious force free form fall flow of His *unjustly* lavish grace. It felt like that, like love gushing in lavish liquid forming flow form.

"Justice has nothing to do with grace" she says soft gentle, as though she heard my private thoughts that brought me to my knees and pinned me to the dirt dry dust.

"Justice is powerless… to initiate or to alter the flow of God as a river of abiding love." She says, and I know it and knew it too, before. I simply do not *believe.* That is a very other proposition altogether.

"We can…" She frowns puzzlement, "*refuse* to get in the river though. We *can* choose instead to stay on the banks to watch the river of life pass by. We can do that because we have the power to deny a thing and make it gone." She looks away far and distant as though peering through the membrane of a cosmic web and into another dimension.

"As we have the power to affirm a thing, to name and claim it, to give praise and gratitude that it is already done, and then to sure and certain make it so." A long troubling troubled silence follows, then she adds frowning. "We also have the power to un-make a thing. And, destroying what is already made is easier and sometimes more blameless than creating something completely new and *other* from new cloth…, woven seamless from threads formed in the spinning mending mind of God.

"The un-making power of your determined denial of what is," she turns her eyes away so I can't see in, and continues, "is the reason you will not enter the garden with me."

I am bereft. I am rejected, rebuffed, repudiated, and barred forever from entering Eden's gate. She waits there with me..., until I melt in the pelting stinging sun.

"We do have to jump in that river though...." She says in almost a whisper. We must do that to learn to trust and follow the flow of the river of life. And do that over and over until we feel faith in our *bones*. We inspire that inspiration flow until faith is all we know, all we comprehend, and all we are.... In the way that all and everything a fish knows is frank faith in fluid flowing water.

She eyes me now, testing, poking, probing, and is silent all the while. "Faith acts on the conscious mind the way baking powder acts on biscuit ingredients. Faith activates the perceiving power of the mind and that initiates a chain reaction that is *needed* to turn biscuit ingredients into something *else*, something *substantively* unlike what it was before." She nods to the garden, eyes not leaving mine, "Faith alone..., had the alchemy to turn Saul into Paul. I think that like Paul, you are on your road to Damascus in a fanatic fury to throw down, destroy, punish and plague the disciples. So great is your anger in your own self-doubt that you feel impeccably and utterly demanded to destroy the faith of others, and all evidence of it, and to *throw down* the altars and holy places of all the gods *you* name false!

"Well, my young and ardent denier, in the Holy Book – all of them – there *is* no god before God. No god *but* God. From where *come* all these gods you name false if there be but One?" I cannot face her wide crystal clear diamond hard eyes..., and I can't avoid them, it's like she's looking at me through the full spectrum eyes of Infinity.

She paces me slow and appraising"

Her eyes narrow and focus on mine; "And I *know your* God!" She says staring down sharp and hard on me from the same height. "That dark disturbing detached dirge of a trying taxing taskmaster Reason, whose warped words you hold keen in your mouth and webbed through your denying mind. Thus he plaits you tight and tauter into the beguiling fiction that *his* words are pure gold and living water, and the Word of God you cannot trust. Nor, dare you even *contemplate* the *possibility* of miracle happening here because your default factoid god of facts will not allow something so utterly unprovable as a living breathing growing thriving self-generating miracle! *Faith... boy*!" Her eyes are white sun hot as pierce searing as her words. I lower my eyes but the fierce sun of her piercing passion sees and seeps through my lids…, deep… into my brain, where it lays dust to my dallying dreams of bright brilliance and potent power over 'false gods' Golem god. Formed and fed in the womb of my brain and mind, patched together from all the hurt, anger and doubt I fiercely repressed, that haunts and hunts me still." He sighs bowed low. I could now faintly see foggily into God's newest Garden of Eden meagerly sheltered in a shallow bowl in a parched prairie ocean in motion. The girl felt it…, that I doubted what my own eyes saw. She felt the weight and warp and wallop of my lack of faith. She said I could not enter into the garden for my disbelief would shatter and sunder the miracle space created by the angels and spoil it sour and stingy and that would utterly destroy the dynamic creative harmony the angels had made…, and then all of us would lose the gift of grace space the angels had formed and the fruits of it. The girl was fiercely cold in her rebuke…, and it cut like a blade set deep and twisted viciously."

"You want us to feel *sorry* for you?" Abbie asks innocent and aghast.

I grin, I have to, she is so owl eyed wise and solemn and serious and stern. "No, no more than I'd give kindness to a golem gone mechanical on a rampage incited by a merciless mortal. In its defense, the golem, lacks the power reason, knows not right from wrong, and acts only reflexively obedient to the mind that gives it breath and a mission. No…, your sympathy won't heal what was broken in me. *I needed* to admit out loud, in my own voice, that *I am* the one and only one, to induce my inner golem to rage and destroy the miracle Light *I saw and would not accept*! *My* callous faithlessness barred me from our Eden glen! And the girl Joan of Arc defended the faith, and the plant people, and the people in and near our lives who will thrive and survive on the plants grown on angel's tears." Melt releases his spirit of his self-inflicted wounds, and melts into the fertile rich softness of the soil in Divine Mind. He sends tap and support roots to sink deep and spread far and brace his faith…, not in man nor in man's fearful designs, but in the incomprehensible inescapable everywhere present Presence, the shoreless restless washing healing stirring ocean of God's wondrous love. *A tree in an ocean…, an ocean in a tree….*

Aggie, who's been a silent watcher awhile sits suddenly sharply upright, head tipped to a side listening to hear something beyond sound. She nods, frowns softly, pulls a nostril wide slow easy inhale, and then turns to Melt to demand, "Do you smell apples?"

"Apples?" Surprise puzzle pieces Melt's face and eyes.

"Yes! You *said* the girl told you there were new plants in the garden, didn't you? Ones they didn't plant, right?"

"Yes…," Melt agrees cautiously wondering where his solver sister will next go. She demonstrates to all by long leg crawling to the praise pouch, poking in a hand and feeling around its bottom and sides. She frowns and wide nostril sniffs above the bag. She sits back, pale brows meshed in a puzzled arch. Melt almost feels her brain carefully analyzing collected data points, sniffing like a blood hound on a trail for scents and clues she hasn't yet found. She comes up empty. They feel it. Together they watch as she re-processes data points, hear her sniff small wide again, see the second frown, and, when she gets her second wind of will. She smiles then, only a small smile, raises a hand, frowns, and drops it, and raises the left, intuitive side hand. As though drawn by an invisible strand Aggie's hand moves slow low and near, then plunges into the pouch and pauses. She breathes a full slow smile and in one trance dance like motion, surely lifts her hand from the pouch, turns it palm up to present an apple sparkling a red bright enticing invitation to bite, chew, savor, and to enjoy. Aggie rotates her wrist letting the fetching fragrant fruit catch the light and show itself plump proud and luscious lusty in her palm.

There is silence. Awed silence. Silence so deep and pervasively present that when Bam moves, the soft whisper of his shirt shifting startles them to attend to him and watch as he takes the apple from Aggie, pulls out his pocket knife, and unfolds the blade. "I'll cut it for us," he explains wiping the knife blade on his pant leg until the juicy fruit is steady in his hand.

"Dang that smells good," Melt says, "give me a wedge."

Lillie brushes his hand away protectively dominant. "Wait!" It is an order delivered soft polite and pointed. "It *was Agatha* who found the clues you dropped while telling the girl's tale. *Agatha* who put those clues together, and Agatha who made sense of them. More significantly, it *was Agatha* who stayed strong, firm, and unquestioning in her unshakable faith in Source and the love He revealed when He sent his angels who came and who wept angel tears for our mindless methodical rape of our once fertile and fecund land. *Angels* do not chasten us. That is God's work, the chastising and chasing and challenging until *you*, of your own free choice and will, turn 360 around and come *willing* and choice-fully into the healing arms of God. Then you could enter the garden as the girl does and you cannot.

"Aggie knew, without doubt…," Bam picks up without a pause, "that if Source already creates new things to thrive in the angel tears in his mini Eden *west* of the Mississippi, then that same God could *certainly* make apple trees grow, leaf, bloom, flower, *and* fruit, in the hours between dark and dawn! And," his palm stops protest before any sound, *"Agatha* will have the first cut of the apple." Bam leans close holding a wedge of apple against the knife for

Aggie to take. He says lover soft and sweet, "I made this cut bigger than the rest, to honor your gift of sweet heart full connection with life and all that lives.

"But mostly, I made it bigger because you were *so beautifully brave*, certain and sure that there *was* an apple in that praise pouch that even though it was empty before, you were able to take yourself *beyond* doubt, *through* faith and *into* understanding power. It took my breath away watching you apply that powerful strong focused mind to keep faith *and know*, even in the presence of doubt. There *was* no apple there before. I looked too. No apple." Abbie ducks her head to peep well and purely pleased between lashes as her tongue absorbs the luscious liquid apple meat exposed by the knife.

"That *alone*," Bam continues, "would have crushed the firm faith of most; and dashed the high hope of strong men. But not you. Somehow, my woman of great understanding, you *knew* that the God who made a rainbow of skin colors for man on the day Adam and Eve were banished from Eden's glen, could *indeed* make fruit trees set, root, sprout, flourish and fruit in what looks to man to be one single day.

"You seem to know all along that God does not *get* time the way we do. You accept and abide that, Abbie. That is faith firm as a rock and not daunted delaying nor diminished by doubt. Powerful!" In Bam's approving words Lizzie hears his near dear hopes for, and firm faith in, each of their children. She marvels at how easily he has melted Melt's doubt and anger by loving him through and beyond it, refusing adamantly to leave him alone in his dark night of doubt and fear.

Feeling Lizzie's attention Bam purrs a soft sensual satisfied sigh and coos "Did I ever tell you Lizzie dear, that you are my moon bird?"

"Moon bird?" Lizzie's brows dance a high arch. "No, you never told me that, Bam White." Her eyes tease tempting incitement; "I know this for certain because never before have I heard *anyone* say the words 'moon' and 'bird' together. Nor have I seen 'moon' and 'bird' side by side looking like they belong together. So, my dear husband, it is time now for you to spell our boy teller awhile" she pulls Melt across the circle to sit beside her facing Bam, "and tell us your moon bird tale. Spin for us your best bewitching snare of moon bird telling and net us deep and wide, Bam White, for I need both tonight."

Lids low, Bam straightens and lengthens his spine above hips and his Indian style crossed legs. He inhales slow, deep and rhythmic, setting and centering himself liquid relaxed and alert in his favorite tale telling pose. He invites and welcomes the Spirit of all birds who stay secret silent in the dark waiting to trill and tweet jubilant joy to the moon as it rises to light the star decked dark night sky. He smiles feeling the strong force of moon bird bliss surge through him, and he cannot *not* tell the tale true and tall and deep seeded with love. "Moon bird…," he muses distractedly as though trying to recall a memory held deeply rooted not long ago, yet gone missing without a trace at this particular pointless point in time. *What is the* point *of a pointless point? No* matter *the time! It is good* Bam muses, *to sometimes forget the whole lot of it, every tit and tittle of a tale you ever knew. Yet this tale is new and there's little I know of it to have forgotten.* That momentary mindful mindlessness mental meandering clears and opens a cluttered space within Bam. He enters that inner space to find it newly empty. Vacant. Void, and available for something *else…,* something *new.*

He has not a clue. But he has a trust. "Moon bird…," he begins, savoring the plump round humming of the words in his mouth, mellow between his teeth, sweet under his tongue. *Sweet,* he thinks. *That's it! The tale is told sweet…, open…, and sincere.* He savors the moon bird telling before it even begins.

"A moon bird, my dearest Lillie," Bam begins, "is a bird that is silent – as a *breath* – waiting for the moon to rise. And, when the moon rises and its light hits its eye, the moon bird sings.

"Wise ancient elders, and new ones too, say that the moon represents personal human intelligence, individual consciousness, the intellect and reasoning power of man. The moon receives light from the sun and reflects sun's light to Earth when Earth, and man, are in our daily darkness called night.

"Well, those same wise elders believe and teach that the sun represents the realm of human conscious that has been illuminated by Spirit." He smiles knowingly, "The sun, the greater light that rules the day. Thus our good God gives us daily reminders of the bright light and the deep dark of His impartial, impenetrable, imperturbable abiding love for us. Each and every one of us.

"Lizzie," Bam takes her hand in his and strokes it smooth softly and meets her eyes with smile that warms and melts her core to skin and beyond. "You are my moon bird, dear wife. When days are hard and nasty mean with empty apology and hungry eye, my spirit just buckles under the weight of icy doubt, serial separation, and abiding oppressive *other*-ness. I feel so alone, like an abandoned child on a cold dark night passing under windows of light seeping sweet smells from platters and plates piled with food, and I feel so *damned* sorry for myself that even Becky doesn't like my company and brays and spits in my eyes." He pulls and puffs a fish eyed sigh at the trivial indignities navel gazing gathers into its deepening dark downward spiral. He vows never to do it again. As he has done before.

Bam slumps sounding so painful pitiful that everyone turns away to hide wide laughing eyes and hold within the giggle that wants *so much* to come bubbling joyfully gleefully free. And then it does.

First from Abbie who understands that laughter heals when it is shared, and that it *must* be shared simply because humans are hysterical…, but not funny, and they can't see that when feeling sorry for themselves alone. *They are simply not funny then, or fun to be around either!* She thinks snappishly.

Quietly, quickly, Aggie gigs Abbie giggling gay again. "Stop! Stop…," she cries, "Enough!" The girls share eye contact and unspoken words, grin as one, nod together, then index fingers at the ready, pounce on their Pa, tickling his ribs and armpits until he laughs himself breathless and can no longer endure his private powerless pity party. Their dramatic work complete, the girls return to their places by Lizzie, sit, and look at Bam attentively…, expectantly.

Under the gun, he thinks appreciatively. *Nothing like it to focus one's attention and sharpen his wits.* "I take it that I have said *enough* about my navel gazing pity parties. And, *apparently*" he barely suppresses a snorting snigger, "you don't *want* to hear nary *one* discouraging word about the mule…, so all I got left to talk about is Lizzie," he takes her hand in his, my chosen mate, my beloved, my moon bird." Her chicks click and peep as they tuck themselves into the feather warm nest of Lizzie's love to hear her moon bird mate tone tell his towering tale of love in the moonlight.

"A moon bird, my Lizzie, is a bird that sits silent as a breath," he breaths, a palm cupping an ear, "one eye on the sky," he touches an eye and up, "waiting for the moon to rise. The moon you see, represents personal human intelligence, the intellect, that has gathered, collected, and now reflects the light of Spirit…, that realm of consciousness that has been illumined by Spirit. That abiding present awareness of Spirit in man is represented by the sun, the greater light that rules the day.

Bam bows to the weights and woes of the world and whispers, "when I come home some days the weight of this world is too wicked and heavy for me to bear. I give all that to the sun…, yet at times some dark weight of it tarries inside me and comes home with me. You are my moon bird, you help me to sing it away and to praise raise the light of spirit again when the dark is deep and echo empty." Bam's words are both admission and confession. He lifts his head overcoming high, neck turkey long, plucky playful supple and as swift as his smile. "I stopped at Smithy's to have a look at the Farmer's Almanac and I'm here to tell you moon rise is at 10:15, which gives us time to pop some of this popcorn," he shakes the can like a castanet, "in butter, and take it outside and wait like hungry moon birds for the moon to rise."

His idea, from beginning to end, is delighting and enchanting welcomed and a repeat request flavor savored lifelong memory of sometimes tear slightly salty love.

My Master's Mark

Jacob drives slow through town to catch and exchange smiles, waves and nods of townsfolk, and to spot the rare stranger. He assures himself that it isn't nosiness that inspires his attention but rather his native awareness of self as body, mind, brain, and his abiding affection for his home town and people.

Strangers…, now that's where the vinegar hits the galushkies and gives the juicy tang that brings a man back for seconds, Jacob muses. *Nothing uncommon today…,* except *for that magnificent Rolls Royce,* he smiles admiringly, *of a vintage when a Rolls came with a chauffeur, butler, mechanic, and jack-of-all-trades in one man. Interesting there be a Rolls where there is no want of one…, and a scowling black woman on the porch of the Feed and Grain. Interesting….*

Jacob parks beyond the Rolls to set up his slow stroll to the Feed and Grain to explore his curiosity. Letting the truck come to a steady idle he checks the rear and side mirrors before switching off the engine. Stepping leisurely from the cab to the bed of the truck he pats about for something or nothing as his eyes, ears, skin, nose and tongue, measure and weigh elements of the scene as he casually ponders the virtue and vulnerability of each.

Stepping to the Rolls Jacob enjoys the art of car as a cover for observing the woman, reading the mute language of her taut body, and sensing the nature of the anger that radiates from her. *Something burns in her, something that twists her gut with fear and fury. Interesting…. She watches now, edgy as a deer in the gold glow of panther's eyes…, now she wraps a shawl around her neck like a muffler – to hide the mark that's there I'm thinking.*

She blames herself…, Jacob is enlightened, *"Victims often do.* Refocusing on the Rolls, Jacob puffs his pipe alight and notices. He notices no footprints by the rear door where a Rolls owner would sit, peeks inside to see the unoccupied rear seat. Spotting footprints by the driver's door, Jacob squats for a closer look. *A man's shoe, long and thin, like the man surely is. Muscular, but thin…, maybe even skinny.*

He grins despite himself at his next discovery, *Shoes with holes in the soles, plugged with a coin and taped in place. Interesting.* Bending closer, Jacob scowls, frowns, then takes another look. *Copper coins, a telling choice. Both Lincoln head pennies…, both face down to the dirt. Interesting!*

Mississippi license plates, Jacob notes as he ambles to the passenger side of the car. *No prints by the rear door on this side either. Unusual that the owner didn't come on this long trip in his Rolls Royce.*

Jacob steps to the front passenger door and notices prints of bare feet with plump toes and foot pads and high arches. *Goes barefoot a lot.* Without rising from his reading, Jacob follows the prints through the dust to the porch. Tipping the bill of his cap to shield his eyes, he follows the dust prints across the porch to where a wary woman waits.

"What you looking at?" the woman asks, sounding more inquisitive than challenging.

"Tracks" Jacob replies with an infectious grin that doesn't catch.

"Tracks" the girl echoes with a neutral tone and a raised brow. Jacob nods. "*Why* you looking at tracks?"

Tipping his head he invites, "It would be easier to show you than to tell you, come, and see for yourself. Watch your step so you don't blur the telling of the tracks before I can teach you to read them. See the prints there by the front passenger door?" Jacob points, "Those are the tracks you made when you stepped from the car; they show you were barefoot when you walked to the porch and across it to where you now stand."

"Oh." She smiles softly, "I can see that track tale now."

"There's more telling here, and on the other side too, if you're interested in reading tracks." He rises and she steps to follow. "Notice there are no footprints by the rear door where a Rolls owner would sit. That means one of two things, that the owner was not in the car, or, that he got out on the driver's side.

"Come read the telling of the tracks on the other side." The woman freezes, knowing what the prints will teach about the driver and hint about the true master, then, prompted by curiosity about telling tracks and by no other motive, she trails the sign reader around the car.

"There are no footprints by the rear door on this side of the car either," Jacob points out, "that means the owner probably did not come on this trip." He waves her to follow.

"What if the owner was driving his own car?" The girl-woman asks.

Jacob studies her as he puffs his pipe awake. "That's unlikely. Most Rolls owners never learn to drive. Did you know that?" She shakes her head, surprise telling her veracity. "The Rolls Royce Company provides a driver with each car it sells. If the driver doesn't work out for any reason or none at all, the owner contacts the Company, it recalls the driver and dispatches a new one to the Rolls."

Noticing her puzzled frown, Jacob steps away motioning her to follow. "Look at the tracks by the driver's door. Notice how both footprints are the same depth from the plant of the feet, to the stand, to the rise up on the balls of the feet. It's an unusual man with leg and thigh muscles strong enough to stand up and out of a car in one move."

The woman's face puzzle puckers, Jacob grins and expands, "For any set of muscles to be unusually strong they have to be tested and toned every day. Jockeys and horse trainers have leg and thigh muscles able to stand a man out of a car and up on the balls of his feet in one move."

The woman squats to study the prints with a new eye. "That man" she points at the prints, "was the Master's jockey and horse trainer," her voice holds a trace of wonder. She leans closer and adds "He got holes in *both* shoes, and he put something in both holes, but I can't make out what it is."

"Good eye," Jacob approves. "That lift to the balls of his feet blurred the print of what's in the sole holes. Come, read the print sets where the driver walks away and tell me what you see there."

The girl stoops to better see the sole holes, reads the tracks and then flinches away hissing. "Lincoln head pennies *face down* in the dirt."

"*Copper* pennies." Jacob offers absently watching her closely.

"*Copper?*" He hears the tension in her voice and adds the clue, not weighing measuring or judging it.

"A penny is an interesting coin choice for plugging sole holes," Jacob muses. "Most men who can't buy new shoes or pay to have old ones resoled, use a bigger coin for holes that large, nickels, or quarters if he has them." He is silent a moment then observes, "Nickels, quarters, and dimes are cast from silver." He puffs his pipe and ponders, "Makes a man ponder the choice of copper pennies too small for the job and needing to be taped to hold them in place."

"*Taped?*" The girl starts, and then tips her face again to the treacherous tale teller tracks but mostly away from the man who reads them clear and well. Her untended shall falls from the mark on her neck.

"Tell me about the mark," Jacob invites neutrally, consciously drawing his energy close to leave space for silence, or for her to spell her telling. As he waits he curls his toes, curves his arches, tightens and relaxes core muscle groups in his calves and thighs into the squat. As he slow inhales into the silence sunbeams sprinkle odes of joy into and through his mind body brain. Exhaling in easy rhythm Jacob serenely surrenders to what is yet to be. In the boundless space of no breath, he enters the infinite and eternal peace between the formless and the formed where there are no choices, only potentialities.

"It's my master's mark," the woman whispers, not lifting her head nor moving save to breathe.

"Your master, is he the man with the copper pennies in his shoes?" The woman nods sullen small.

"When did you leave Mississippi?" She eyes him warily. Jacob opens his hands palm up and flashes her an arch-browed grin, nods to the rear of the Rolls, and says "it's on the license plate."

She blinks, smiles small, relaxes and replies. "Must be two, three months now."

"Where you headed?"

"Don't know," she shrugs, "he don't tell me nothing." The words are flat, cross and pinned with sins.

Jacob ponders what she would *not* say and allows the few new clues seek and find their own level of worth and meaning. "When did your master give you the mark?"

Unaware that she moves the girl covers her neck, her face wilts but she does not weep nor sound other than weary as she replies, "'Bout two months ago – when we was too far from home for me to find my way back – nor even a way to get away. Away to *what…*?" She exhales, choosing no answer over birthing hope too soon lost buried and forsaken. *Dry pits,* she thinks but does not say.

Jacob's eyes soften watching her; he asks gently "Your first master, was he the plantation owner?" The woman nods. "And your new master is the old master's chauffer?" She nods again.

"How a chauffeur comes to have his master's Rolls Royce on a long journey without the master and becomes a slave owner in the bargain is a tale worthy of the Old Testament…, yet yours is a new story. Will you tell it to me?"

"'T'was a devil's bargain, if you want the truth," she breathes abandoned apathy.

"Who's the devil, do you think?" She retreats to silence and Jacob joins her there, flexing and relaxing muscle groups in turn from his toes to the crown of his head.

"I was given him by the old master," the woman hisses anger into her sullen silence and feels Jacob's energy presence there quietly collecting clues and letting them find their own level and worth.

"Both and neither…, is a devil. Both are possessed by demons more powerful, demanding, and insatiable, than they ever can be." She shrugs,

"It is the nature of the Beast to be its most beastly when it is world-weary or uncertain…, or afraid…, and ashamed to admit it." Her mood shifts quicksilver fast. "Nothing I can do about it. The man owns me. He can kill me quick or slow and nobody will never mind."

Jacob counters peacefully, "yet it is the nature of the Spirit that animates man, to name, see, and claim a *greater* truth than existing facts alone allow, and then to choose and to express a higher potential into form." The statement is not a question yet it expectantly and patiently awaits a reply.

"Something beastly that way came…," she whispers, "I felt the beast, I heard it, I smelt it. Once I even met it, but never did I know its name. Both men bowed low to that Beastie thing that gave them their dry daily bread and charmed them into believing they feasted on a rich banquet heaped on platters of silver and gold all chased with gemstones, and forever laid, hot and ready." Crickets, earth worms and wind in leaves create white noise for the silence that follows.

"The chimera of the beast blinded both men to anything more real or true, even to hope, let alone faith in something bigger and more powerful than the EGO they serve. My minister back home says E-G-O stands for Edging God Out. The more I live and learn the more I know *that's* the plain truth."

"Man's perpetual fall from grace…." Jacob muses. "Are *you* willing to name and claim a higher truth and begin to express a higher potential into form in your life?" He waits awhile in the stillness. "I'll take your silence for a no." As he rises from the dirt he asks "how will I know your new master?"

She casts him an impertinent impish grin "he ain't dressed like you."

Jacob's grin matches hers "then he ain't dressed like anybody else in there either. I will know him by his clothes." Touching the bill of his cap he adds "I appreciate your candor, *and* your humor, young lady."

The Mark of the Master

John Adorney: The Meeting Place │ Jacob pauses at the threshold to the common room hearing familiar ethereal music. He inhales fully, holds the breath for ten counts, and as he exhales lets his inner and outer eyes adjust to the deeper shadow inside and gently expands his mindfulness into the energies in the store. He locates the familiar known ones and the position of each, then gently probes the energy of the outlier, the one the woman called "master." He hears and feels the cadence, beat and energy of the unfamiliar voice, noting the accomplishment in the oratorical style that forms the base line to support the lyricism of the words. He hears a profound insecurity rare among orators. *Interesting.* Removing his cap Jacob slicks back his hair, inhales slowly, and while exhaling casually expands his energy into the room feeling his early recognition by the regulars though he is not yet seen. He steps inside to "hellos" and welcomes and gives a nod and extended hand to the stranger saying "I'm Jacob, you must be the driver of the Rolls Royce outside."

"I am the *owner* of that fine automobile," the man affirms firmly. "*Before*, I was only the driver," he pats his breast pocket self-importantly, "*now*; I hold the title to that fine vehicle."

"And the woman?" Jacob tips his head toward the window where the cocoa woman silently sulks.

"I own her too." The man replies with casual indifference, curiously oblivious to the edgy energy his assertion arouses in the locals.

Interesting…, Jacob thinks, letting his eyes touch each man in the circle and with a soft smile, then light on the visitor as he voices their puzzlement "How *does* one man own another one?" Into the alert and probing silence, Jacob grins, "Honestly, I cannot say *which* tale I want more to hear you tell, the tale about how you come to own the Rolls, or the one about how you *can* own another human being."

Counselor rumbles amiable interference, "Jacob, you came at just the right time, the man was commencing to tell us those very things, pull up a chair and join us." He turns back to the visitor with an open smile, "why don't you step to the center of our circle where you can see all of us and all of us can see and hear you too."

The visitor steps eagerly to the center, rises on the balls of his feet and spins a grand slow round meeting the eyes of each man in turn. He tips a nod to Sheriff Ben – *the uniform*, Ben thinks – pauses a moment before Jacob – *the skepticism*, Jacob fancies – then turns to Counselor executing a practiced bow generally reserved for gentility.

"It is my pleasure to enlighten you folks on how these astonishing happenings occurred. Since the tales are intertwined, I shall tell the story as it happened, injecting humor as I can." He clears his throat dramatically while supple snaking his tongue up his throat until it settles softly into his mouth ready to carry his words to all who have ears to hear.

"I am the owner of the Rolls Royce. That's mostly because the old master never learned to drive – due, I believe to his *great* admiration for having a chauffeur deliver him to his appointments and festivities. At the end of our time together, the master gave me the auto because he could neither drive nor maintain it." Striking a most gallant pose has little effect on the locals, but it looks good, so he continues. The master still needed me when we parted company, but he had to let me and the auto go because the pitiless carpetbaggers stole him blind leaving him with no choice but to release me from my service and send me on my way to a new life in the great American west."

Counselor murmurs, "Never before have I heard such an *extraordinarily* generous act. Surely the master knew the Rolls Royce Company would assign and send a new chauffer at his request?"

The raconteur sighs dramatically, "Yes, he did know that, and he and gave me the car anyway. The master is a saint, or will be when he dies, may that day be many years from today."

"How does your master get to his appointments and parties now?" Sheriff Ben asks, lids slit narrow.

"The folks back home love that man and will do anything for him. They'll get him where he needs to go."

Ben notices a double edge sharpness in the last five words and frowns "*Why* would even a good and godly a plantation owner rely on the kindness of neighbors to get his business done when he could use his *own* auto and his own chauffeur? Why would he allow a departing chauffeur to even *use* his auto for a long trip to…, where'd you say you're headed?"

"I didn't. I don't rightly have a destination. You see, I never before had I a chance to see this great land of ours. I'm starting a new life, my plan is to drive into the sunset until I find a place with friendly folks where I'll settle awhile, and then head off to see what's around the next bend in the road."

"Sounds like a drifter to me, Ben growls to the circle, "except for the car."

"What's a drifter?" The visitor asks anxious.

"Someone just passing through with no contribution to make along the way." Ben smiles friendly, agreeable, insincere "Here on the plains, drifters are about as popular as carpetbaggers down South."

The visitor eyes Ben evenly as he says "The old master assured me he could take proper care of his business *without* the auto before he gave the title to me."

"A remarkably generous act," Counselor reiterates redundantly imposing calm courtesy.

"Tell us how you claim that you own the woman outside," Jacob prompts.

"The master gave her to me so I'd have someone to take care of my needs." The orator is oddly oblivious to the edgy energy aroused by his last words.

"Does taking care of your needs explain the mark the woman bears?" Jacob growls tap-tapping his neck with two fingertips, "The one she calls *my master's mark*?"

"Dang, Jacob," Ben growls, "here I was thinking the woman was his *sex slave*." Turning back to the guest he asks pleasantly. "Tell us how you come to own the woman, and about the master's mark."

"I got her ownership paper too" the man defends, slapping his breast pocket, "the master gave the slave to me legal and true. She's mine; just like that Rolls Royce is mine. I can do with either whatever I please, and it is *no never mind* to anyone else."

Jacob growls, "*Why* would a plantation owner give a healthy young slave to a driver leaving his service and taking his only vehicle?"

"The master is a good man, I told you already that."

"Indeed you did, and we have heard what you said," Counselor cautions casually. "Jacob is asking the reasons *why* even a good man would give a healthy slave to a chauffeur leaving his service." Silence extends into prickly points prodded by the steady tick tock of a wall clock.

Turning to Jacob Counselor says "while our guest is auditing his *accounting* for us, why don't you bring the woman in so we can hear what she has to say and have a look at that mark." Jacob leaves and quickly returns with a woman the color of sweet cocoa and eyes round with doubt, dread and dismay.

Counselor is the comforter "Thank you for joining us, young lady. I know this cannot be easy for you." Her eyes dart to the orator and back to Counselor now robed in black with a curled white wig. She blinks. Jacob lays a hand on her shoulder giving her courage for the challenging mile ahead.

"Come, sit by me, child." Counselor invites moving his chair to one side as Doc moves his to the other. Counselor calls "somebody, bring a chair for the lady." The orator snorts at the word, but holds his tongue for Jacob edges barrel-chested close on his deliberate deviant path to his chair by the door.

"The man on your left is a medical doctor," Counselor informs the woman as she sits between them.

"Jacob tells us you wear the mark of your master." Doc declares. The girl nods but does not meet his eyes. "Will you let us have a look at that mark?" Unaccustomed to consideration in matters of her body, the woman dashes a glance to Jacob who nods calm assurance. Holding his eyes, the woman releases the shawl letting it fall to reveal the mark. One soft inhale stirs the room to silence, yet none save Counselor hear the words exchanged between Doc and the woman. He watches as the girl nods, eyes wide with doubt and dread as though she has just agreed to jump without a rope from a towering bluff and into the infinite heart of creation. And so she has.

"This man," Counselor motions to the dandy, "is he your master?" The woman nods but speaks no word of ownership by another.

"Did he put this mark on you?" Doc inquires with professional detachment, her head bobs. "When did he put the mark on you?"

"Five, six weeks ago…, it started…, I think." She sighs, "I forget things now, like the time, or the date, or when I ate last, or when I last had a good night's sleep."

Doc nods and murmurs "Does he – *urr* – penetrate you in – *urr* –other places?" The woman locks eyes on his, cocks a brow as one might to a village idiot, then turns away without reply. "I'll take that for a yes," Doc says behind a hand hiding a grin at his silent comeuppance. Leaving the question of pregnancy aside entirely, he assures the woman, "we can help heal that mark."

The woman studies him through eyes slit thin with abiding wariness born of neglect, misuse, abuse, and of primeval terrors come savagely alive. *Too pale,* she thinks, looking away, *his hope of redemption, like tea when the ice is melted in the glass.* Yet thirst blooms in her mouth and she dares not speak to ask, to know, to trust; so she simply receives the hope like a cool breeze over a blistering field.

"We'll need the Daughters for the healing work, Jacob would you…?"

A chair clatters into a fall calling eyes to Sheriff Ben snatching a chair from its fast fall. Casting a quick grin at Jacob he says "I'll go – Jacob." Stepping quickly to Jacob's side he claps a hand to his shoulder, locks eyes, and bares a toothy grin "You know, Jacob, *he, he, he,* the ladies always come when I call."

Jacob tips his head back in a chortle and Ben laughs with him, intent eyes never leaving Jacob's. "You stay *by the door* while I'm gone." He whispers the command casting a quick eye to the visitor and back.

Jacob smiles a nod. "Good speed, Ben, the healing art of the Mother/ Daughters is soon needed."

"What is your name young lady?" Counselor asks the woman at his side.

The woman is silent a moment, "I – I never had a name given me." The orator's head snaps up but he does not turn to look at the woman.

"Indeed?" Counselor eyes her solicitously. "Tell me how it is that you were never given a name."

"My mama was a slave," the woman reports remorsefully, "she was taken by a plantation guest she despised and never would name, and I don't know the name of my father." She sighs a sorrowing hum, "My mama was shamed and blamed by *her own people,* for not speaking his name, for never saying what happened or how, never telling me nor anyone else what happened the night I was conceived.

"Mama could never accept me. Maybe for her, maybe for me, but *always* because of the shaming that was done her. Other slaves say my mama was bright, happy and affectionate before me, but I don't know because she was never that for me. Oh she saw to it I was clean, fed and clothed, but she had no love, nor joy left." Words fail where memory holds no key nor cause nor reason but only nameless loss.

Counselor silently studies the evidence and turns to the orator. "What is your name then, young man?"

Caught off guard, the orator stammers "I – I…. The master called me James," he says tucking his head. "James, I have an appointment, bring the auto; James, get the door, James, my guests have arrived; serve the drinks on the veranda, James.'" The orator stammers to a stop.

"And your given name…?"

"I…, was never given a name… that I know of."

"Two strangers in our town in one day, and neither with a given name. What do you make of that, Doc?"

Doc brackets his chin with thumb and fingers, broods awhile and says, "Beats anything I ever heard."

"Well, young man," Counselor cautions, "the transfer of property, chattel or slave, requires the transferee's name to be binding; and since you have no name, I don't see how it is legally possible that you legally own the auto or the woman. Let me have a look at those papers for you." He extends a palm until the papers are there; studies them silently, then raises his eyes to the orator and rubs his chins. "The line for the transferee on both of these documents is blank."

"Can I see?" The man gazes intently at the papers, colors softly and shoves them back to Counselor meeting his eyes, "would – would – you show me what you're telling me, please, Sir?"

"This is the auto title," he says proffering the parchment document, "See this word here? That word is "Owner," the name of the master is entered here. This word," he says pointing, is "Transferee," it means the name of the person the item is transferred to. The line beside it is blank, and that means the title to the Rolls was not put in your name, the master still owns the automobile." He shuffles the documents, points to the second and says, "The Transferee line on the slave document is blank too, the Owner is your master. Legally speaking, you do not own this woman who now bears your slave mark."

"He *don't own* me?" Shrieks the woman punching the air at all the invisible indignities that rise now like ghosts to dance with her stiff body in intimations of the intimate injustices the man suffered on her. She paces the ring, a cat in a cage in a rage, gulping great gouts of air in her battle to control herself against the revelations of this day and of the day the carpetbaggers came to take away the life she used to live. As though in the safe hole again, the woman hears the master's firmly cool reception of the intruders and their snapped impertinent words, catches the shoving and scuffling, the grunts, cries and protests, feels the impotent futility fury of the master's effort to protect and defend his home, family, and people. She hears the echo as the invaders slam through every door driving the family, servants and slaves with whips of word and fist into the great hall. She feels the herding and the weighty intensifying anxiety that trickles like coarse meal through the floor and into the safe black hole below. Silently she moans, wails, screams, and denies again, again she covers her ears to *not hear* the futility of the family's defense of self, home, help and friends against the bullying braggart raiders. *How do these men not know the wrong they do to this family of* good *people? How can they* not *stop, not go away peacefully after finally admitting that it was all just a jolly jest, purely a punkish prank played for foul fickle fleeting fun.* Again the man in the safe hole by her claps a hand over her mouth, pressing a blade to her throat the moment the mistress cries out, hears her scuffle, and her fast hard fall to the floor. As the blade bites her neck, she pictures the fallen woman as powerless as she trapped in her silent safety.

An agony of hours later the family is taken away and the house falls silent as night. She is safe now. As safe as one can ever be, subject to the whims of an eager sinner in the hands of an angry god. The dancing memory ghosts dissolve to dust before her inner eye and she begins to allow the new dots of today connect with the old ones of the raid. She balls her fists, inhales sharply and howls "can I *kill* him?"

Michael's Mark

The orator shrinks away from the black fury of the woman and turns to the faces in the circle, seeking shelter, support, sympathy, security. Finding none, he shifts.

Jacob sees energy at the edges of the man's body flicker telegraphing a shift and without thought surrenders himself and his own will to the indwelling infinite Source power of life.

Michael Gott –Thy Will Be Done as you sing it, insert as hyperlink, with credits and contact information.

In first breath no-thought surrender Jacob experiences the familiar dissolution of self and the subtle inhabitation by another greater awareness that instinctively meets and matches the transformation. From his watcher awareness Jacob sees the clothes of the visitor drift vacant to the floor, sees the small dark shadow take to the air and wing for the door where he now stands absorbed by the energy of Michael the archangel, clad in his shining armor and bearing arms. *"Welcome,"* Jacob thinks and feels his awareness fade, dissolve and collapse as empty as the orator's clothes.

It is good to be in form when the foul sin of separation, the original fall from grace, takes a favored form of Satan himself. Jacob feels his teeth bare into a grin worthy of the grim reaper on a mad bad night. *The master of lies, deceits and deceptions returns to stalk earth where man walks. Thanks for keeping your body in shape by the way, Jacob, I like working in you, I like working with you.* Jacob feels the angel smile rise on his face as a son of man willingly blends his joy in knightly service with Michael's fierce fiery grace. As one, Archangel and man step choice-fully surrendered into the endless ever-evolving multi-dimensional sinuous supple wondrous springing will of the Infinite Eternal One. *The game's afoot!*

At the speed of light that is the Truth of Being Michael's eyes follow the flight of the bat across infinity through the slit in his silver visor. A spiraling gold wheel set with diamonds and pearls and centered with a heart shaped Hiddenite stone adorns his helmet over his third eye catching light and spinning an ever evolving reel of reality on to the flat physical plane reality. In the blink of an eye, the wheel reverses to rewind reality across time until no trace of it remains at all. *Interesting, that.*

A rush of dislocation overcomes Jacob as a separate awareness, thought, ego, multiplies into a fully present and lucid mindfulness of the sometimes startlingly fluid frontiers between what is and what is not in the eye of an Archangel. All the will, judgment, order and strength ever applied by man in using the power to change the physical plane hold no weight where Jacob now resides aside inside an angel peering into an infinity where a bat flies and a slave bleeds. Michael breathes deep and touches the jewel at the bottom of the seven set in his gold embossed breastplate from sternum to clavicle.

Ruby, the stone of nobility, the star fire of purity, imparts vigor and passion for life, it is protective and leads to vibrant visualization, clears the path (to the true self) of negative energy, and promotes dynamic leadership, vigor and passion for life. Ruby is an abundance stone stimulating wealth and passion for all of life, imparts a positive, courageous state of mind, and heightens focus and awareness. It amplifies enthusiasm, stimulates power and vigor and protects in controversy and conflict by focusing mind and heart on desired outcomes. Sometimes known as the resurrection stone, ruby allows the user to rise above martyrdom and all forms of suffering, anguish, and turmoil, as it holds the power of beginnings and endings of all that is, was or will be made manifest. Ruby facilitates wise and loving change, promoting creativity and expansiveness in manifesting along the golden spiral stairway to enlightenment. Ruby pulls the creative urge from the base chakra into the throat chakra under control of the mind, to direct life from a safe but distant position. It gathers input from all the senses and imparts heightened intuition allowing one to direct life from a safe place and minimizing the risk of speaking harshly and without wisdom and compassion.

As Michael touches the Ruby, he is inspired with courage, passion, power and abundant life force energy to neutralize all negative energy in his mind and body. He smiles as the words of Luke bloom in his mind: *Take heed therefore that the light which is in thee be not darkness. Luke 12:35* and considers that it is the darkness within *him* that sees and recognizes the darkness in the bat/man. As within, so without, as without so within; and Michael frees his darkness, releasing it into the light where duality melds into polarity and spirals into infinite possibilities and prospects. *Thy will be done*, Michael breathes surrender to the Higher will; and so it is, was and forever will be – according to the will of the Divine.

From his mastery of metaphysics, Michael recalls that the ruby is the stone on the breastplate of the high priest that is associated with the apostle **Judas** who was a man scrupulously devoted to **life** – as it appears on the physical plane – and especially zealous about its principal weighty form of *money*. Judas held the purse of contributions made by the followers of Jesus, and the man was purse proud! That said, more than any other apostle, Judas believed *without reservation* that Jesus would escape the attempt to capture him as he had so often done, that Jesus *would, could* face no risk of death. Judas believed so unflinchingly that he was blind to the willing will of the man he called Master. Judas bet on the run, and on the cache of thirty pieces of silver the plotters added to the pouch of contributions he alone carried "to feed" the followers and those who came to hear Jesus tell-tale Truth in parable form.

Judas also believed without doubt at his inner core the truth Jesus spoke, that death was not an ending (for those at one with Source), but a new beginning, and that Jesus would/could actually resurrect, and he really, *had* to die in the flesh in order to *demonstrate* the truth of what he taught. Through the power of **regeneration** abiding within the ruby, Judas awakens to the call of the risen Jesus and is regenerated into Jude – with the surname of Thaddeus.

Michael strokes the ruby absorbing the power of the stone that flares with life sufficient to awaken the healing regeneration of the stone to animate the newly resurrected Judas now manifest within Michael.

Those in the circle of friends observe that the ruby among the twelve stones of power chasing from tip to top of Michael's sword scabbard flares with the vibrant vitality of life always regenerating, reforming, reshaping and reappearing into life in manifest form.

Michael strokes the **Jasper** and experiences the grounding of the "self" of consciousness into the truth of the Self of Source balancing dualities in mind and body and imparting tranquility and wholeness. Contact with the protector stone grounds Michael and inspires a shamanic journey through which he dances balancing dualities in mind, body and brain with the etheric realm, and recalls inspired visions of resolution gained by assertive honesty and assurance of support should conflict be required. As he absorbs the protecting, neutralizing energy of the jasper Michael chooses to find a way to inspire, nurture, renew and to realize tranquil balance into the manifest form of the man in bat drag trying to wing away from consequences of past choices made. Michael's decision absorbs, neutralizes and releases stress, re-energizing him in confident wholeness that opens a path to completion and renewal of his blossoming idea into manifest form, and he is refreshed in mind body and spirit.

The apostle **Simon** the Zealot is associated with the jasper stone that inspires right use of the power of **zeal** and **enthusiasm**. The stone stimulates honesty, imagination, quick thinking, organizational ability, zeal and the courage of enthusiasm to boldly get to grips with problems and transform ideas into action.

Smiling, Michael strokes the jasper igniting the power of zeal and its helpmate, enthusiasm to scope, resolve and heal issues, to blend polarized energies into complimentary opposites and to quickly transform ideas into action. The jasper flares with passionate, dynamic creative power. Thinking quickly Michael considers possibilities for the man bat winging across infinity for a date with destiny and opens himself to see and embrace the highest outcome held in Source wisdom for the man and woman. As he touches the jasper on his breastplate the jasper on the scabbard of his sword flares with tranquil light.

Next Michael strokes the **Topaz** on his breastplate and as the stone flares a pure yellow gold light and enters the abiding place of substance setting

him on the path ahead and inspiring in him wisdom and its companion
judgment, the twin powers of the shaman and wise elder. Holding contact
with the stone, Michael experiences an empathetic flow of energy that soothes,
heals, stimulates, recharges, motivates, promotes forgiveness, lights the path
to highest goals, and taps inner sources to center him into *be*ing rather than
simply habitually *do*ing.

Michael experiences a clarity and certainty that inspires joy, generosity,
abundance love and good fortune, releasing hidden pools of tension evoking
an ever-evolving flow of spiritual energy within him. He can't help but smile
at the inner riches revealed, nor resist a silly-boy grin at the exuberant passion
to teach and to enlighten that sets him on the problem solver healing path
that is the way of the warrior.

This problem-solver healer path is a bit of an awakening for Michael so he
probes it, tapping inner resources until he finds his inner problem solver who
guides him to the right use of knowledge gained in visualization to gather
and focus his passion in support of the Universe in manifesting Good God
on the physical plane. As Michael's self-imposed precision eases, passion flows
and he experiences an infilling of love from all sources. He exhales like a Zen
master opening to love and good fortune and knows the Truth that all is One
and that is good (root: *goot*, a Germanic word meaning 'good' and 'God').

The apostle **James**, the son of Zebedee, and brother of John, who expresses
the twin powers of **wisdom** and **judgment** that sweeps him into the abiding
pace of substance and remembers again with the truth that Judgment day
is every day where the effects of the body/brain causes and choices made by
man and angels is revealed in daily life. Michael smiles recalling that Spirit
choices reveal ideas and inspiration, and ponders whether the dualism of life
prompts evil, or only paradox. James discerns that the right use of the twin
powers in the creative universe that enables him to *be* rather to *do* his desired
results. In good judgment inspired by wisdom, James confidently places his
joyous trust in manifesting only divine right outcomes.

As the topaz on his breastplate flares Michael senses an ever renewing
awakening of wisdom and judgment and knows his contact with the stone
inspired a spark of fire in the one on his sword scabbard.

Now Michael strokes the **Emerald**, the stone of enlightenment,
inspiration, infinite patience, and life affirming relationships, love, bliss and
loyalty, and is inspired by and is in filled with those graces. He finds he has
lost, or simply misplaced his separate sense of self and has been flooded with
flowing unity that enhances love and heals and balances all relationships.
He feels and senses a clear distinction between negative and positive energies

and experiences a balancing of those polarities across his meridians and up and down his spine, legs and head. As his consciousness rises, only positive outcomes leading to positive decisions and actions remain possible for him.

In that insight, Michael inhales fully and owns and allows that he *has* the strength of character to overcome the trial and test winging toward him, and he *has* the power to recover from, to regenerate, and to bring healing wholeness to himself and all the wounded ones. This mental clarity enhances his memory, expands and focuses visioning, inspires wisdom, discernment, truth and eloquent expression. Under this influence, Michael recovers unconsciously known truths that aid him in understanding himself and all others who wittingly or otherwise, play roles in the presently unfolding bat man drama.

The apostle **James II**, or James "the less," the son of Alpheus, is associated with the emerald, and with the power of man known as **order** and **processes**. The power of order and process demonstrate that man can never exercise true dominion until he knows who and what he is. Emerald gives strength of character to overcome the misfortunes of life by applying the process aspect of this power to heal and regenerate negative emotions. James demonstrates this process by expressing the power of order into external life by a three step process, which is mind, idea, and manifestation.

Michael surrenders himself and his will to divine order and process trusting in divine right outcomes, and as he touches the emerald on his breastplate it flares, exciting a flash of greening of the emerald on the scabbard of his sword. Words bloom in Michael's mind: *To whom little is forgiven — the same loveth little. Luke 8:47.* Perception opens Michael's heart to know the orator forgives little and loves too small to have capacity to recognize the need, or to believe in the power and saving grace of God love. *He has lost himself and been cast away — by his own judgment born in his own unforgiving mind and heart.*

Touching the **Lapis Lazuli** on his breastplate, Michael is enlightened by a release of stress and a deep inner peace that eases and opens his third eye, balances is throat chakra, and feels his personal and spiritual power expand as he opens to contact with spiritual guardians. He recognizes the psychic attacks the man in bat suffered in his lifetime, and those he induced and then inspired in others. *Not inspiring*, the Jacob within Michael's armor thinks as he blocks and returns the energy to its source under the influence and inspiration of the Lapis stone. *Interesting…, the man in bat is* not *the source of the shifter energy.* He flashes a toothy grin. *Michael…, shall we send the curse of the shifter power back to its source, follow where it goes, and there apply a liberal* *dosage of energy medicine? I'm in. And my sense is that the man in the bat did not speak out in the past, because if he did he was disciplined harshly. He learned to be sly, evasive and always quick with an excuse. He wasn't limited by factual truth to begin with, but he liberally created fictions as truth. Knew I didn't like the man before I even laid eyes on him,* Jacob observes placidly. Michael smiles with Jacob's lips cheeks and eyes and assures, *Lapis harmonizes physical, emotional, mental and spiritual levels of awareness and brings harmony and deep inner self awareness. Shall we send the wee winged beast a stream of Lapis energy? Let's do. And let's add the Lapis skill of active listening as a way of harmonizing conflict, and ability to dissolve martyrdom, cruelty, suffering and emotional bondage.* These ideas calm and inspire the pair in one body to consciously co-create a higher order of being in the man bat that is forceful, energetic, objective-oriented, enlightened, and that instinctively taps into available inner resources before taking action.

The Lapis Lazuli is associated with the apostle **Bartholomew** who represents the power of **imagination**. The man *Nathaniel* fell asleep beneath a fig tree and imagined/dreamed through his third eye to see a new vision of who he is newly awakened as a man named *Bartholomew,* which signifies a field plowed and ready for seed. The awakened Bartholomew is impassioned to see, hear, experience, and follow the Spirit call to attend a master he has not met and confidently rises to follow the call to find and follow Truth in the form of Jesus.

Eternally fired by imagination and the enchanting light of the blue topaz, Michael touches the stone knowing its twin on the scabbard of his sword sparks and flares its blue flame dance. Michael steps into the blue flame dance and recognizes that the war dance choreographed for his battle with the devil and fallen angels has been transmuted and now vibrates with power, clarity, confidence, focus, peace, and the easy grace of a shaolin master facing a skillful rival with jubilant keenness for the challenge.

Michael touches the **Sapphire** and experiences a streaming upload of joy and peace of mind that opens him to facets of beauty, intuition, dreams and Divine passion to knowingly and wisely evolve conscious mind desires into the physical and metaphysical worlds. Sapphire brings a confident energy of cooperation and collaboration to the cellular level of body and mind, joyfully re-membering the user again with the truth that when you change your mind, you change your life. Willingly surrendering his militant mind-set, he feels his energy and intention focus and experiences acceleration of joyous manifestation of idea/thought into physical form. He now perceives a facilitation of his approach to metaphysical realms that grants easy access to esoteric principles of manifestation and opens him to his intuitive, psychic and astral natures. Michael smiles to be feeling what he already knew of the power of the stone. Spring-boarding off his smile, the Sapphire infuses him with peace and the serenity of knowing that when he is in service, his spiritual attainment is accelerated.

Claiming the power of faith, Michael peers into the infinite and eternal space where a bat wings with fierce determination toward the exit from a physical place temporarily appearing in time and space. *Interesting,* Michael thinks in Jacob's voice.

With the mystic music of the Sapphire pulsing through him, Michael touches the stone near the top of his breastplate and is electrified by the words of a wise caution: *the spiritual path is not a destination; it is a journey,* and he quick-steps away from his old walk of life to enter into the dance of the peaceful warrior.

Sapphire is the symbol stone for the power of **faith** physically expressed positively by the apostle **Peter** when walking on water in utter conviction that if Jesus said he could do the same impossible thing…, then he *could do* the same impossible thing, and more. And Peter did!

Peter, originally known as Simon, was given a new name that better anticipates his spiritual progress to truth. Simon means "hearing," or receptivity, listening to Truth in a receptive state of mind that opens the way for receiving the next degree in the divine order, faith. Peter means rock that represents faith that is strong, unwavering and enduring and a necessary foundation for building spiritual consciousness that unites receptive hearing of Truth with a dynamic expression of faith. Without the firm foundation of rock there is only changeableness, the capacity to deny what is known as Truth. When the storms of fear, doubt and faint faith plague Peter and he denies Jesus and enters a consciousness plunged deep into and subsumed by a foreboding faith in the power of hostile physical forces, trust in the physical form, and thrice denies knowing his chosen master. In this way, Peter reveals his greater faith in things of the physical world – like many of us do.

Taking responsibility for his thoughts and feelings, Michael surrenders himself to faith and hears: *"Faith never knows where it is being led, but it loves and knows the one who is leading."* - Oswald Chambers. As Michael touches the sapphire on his breastplate, its mate on his sword scabbard flares into a midnight dance of stars on water that alters Michael's war dance to the sure light footedness of a gazelle running solely for the joy of body in fluid motion.

Now Michael touches the **Amethyst** stone and feels a powerful protective energy with a high spiritual vibration guarding against psychic attack by transmuting the energy into love. Amethyst blocks negative environment energies and enhances higher states of consciousness; and Michael experiences the dissipation of negative energies and expansion of higher energies that enhance spiritual awareness. He is transported to another reality. He focuses and controls his faculties and feels the subtle strong energy of Jacob's confident control of his faculties and flows with him into an assimilation of new ideas that connect cause with effect, and enhance decision making by blending common sense with spiritual insights. This practice calms, synthesizes and supports transmission of neural signals through the brain of the archangel and the human he channels through. He experiences an enhancement of memory and motivation. In one mind with Jacob, Michael absorbs the Amethyst power and feels anger, fear, anxiety, sadness and grief dissipate. Led by Jacob's slow full inhale, the archangel sets realistic goals, comes to terms with loss, and, as one with his host, Michael experiences true selflessness, spiritual wisdom, and enhanced psychic gifts. *We can do this,* the two minds think as one.

The Apostle **Philip**, whose power is **power** and **dominion**, is associated with the Amethyst stone. The power center of Power is the throat that produces sound and emits all the vibratory energies of the body. Alexandrite is the open door between the formless and the formed worlds of vibrations that express only as sound.

Michael touches the Amethyst stone and is propelled into spiritual awareness, clarity, healing and confidence that he has the power to bring Divine ideas into reality.

The Ancient Adversary…, Archangel Michael smiles toothily within the silver helmet sheathing Jacob's head, *still imagining he can be separate from the Creator, still enthralled by the mad delusion of isolation from Cause; and more besotted still, willfully embracing Beelzebub's lie that a bat – man or angel - will one day, gain more power than Source and be thus be empowered to overthrow the One. Fool! Still besotted by the mad delusion of separation and the arrogant conceit of imagining it is even possible to wrest from Source more power than Source contains, and thus overthrow the One. Delusional!*

Battle fury overwhelms Michael again and he tiptoes on a needle point of control, past drunk on the thrill and fill of battle, blood, fury and an impatient passion to at last extinguish the original sin of separation. Gulping great gasps of air, Michael feels the giddy grace of an oxygen high that engulfs his mind and flows hot, rich and consuming through his body until he *is* the heat of battle, he *is* the eager lust for death and devastation, Michael *is* the Four Horsemen of the Apocalypse….

Cool it down, Michael, comes Jacob's firm, fatherly, unyielding command. *What this situation does* not *need is two uncontrolled and uncontrollable men…, while I am stepped back making room for you in my own body and my own mind. Or, if you prefer, I can tell everyone later that a man in bat form terrified an Archangel into senseless stupidity.*

I'm not afraid! Michael snarls.

That was not *a request, Michael, in case you need clarity. I allow you in; I can let – or boot– you out, your choice; but make it now. Even the Eternal cannot make time on the physical plane stop forever.* Jacob grins toothily and adds, *Fear isn't the only thing that makes fools of angels and men…, sometimes one small bat can do that – to an archangel too caught up in the past to clearly see what lies before him now and what can be done now to create a better world. Kill one bat, you've killed one bat.*

I don't like you sometimes, Jacob.

Mutual. Check the course of bat man.

Sighting with inner eye through the seven enlightened stones on his breastplate and scabbard, Michael checks the progress of the man bat winging through space and time. *Judas unredeemed,* he snarls; *capable of comprehending only personal, worldly power in all its forms, enchantments and illusions. Able only to grasp fleeting faith that the playhouse of the physical world the* only *show in life. The Ancient Adversary…,* Archangel Michael smiles toothily within the silver helmet, *still imagining it is even possible to be separate from the Creator, the first Cause of all that is and all that is not; and more besotted still, willfully embracing Beelzebub's lie that he may somehow gain more power than Source.*

Ancient enmity boils through Michael and Jacob feels his own passion rushing slow like molten lava to curb and cool the archangel's ecstasy in his first purpose and mission that blinds him to the wisdom of the seven stones. Jacob rides the polarized passion like a living surfboard over the sweeps and swells of the battle fury that possessed Michael at the original fall from grace when he countered and contained the willful winged wonders who thought to claim more power than Source power. *Fool! Still drunk on the illusion of separation from Source, and the entitlement to seize from Source all of Source power and more. An arrogant affinity for separation,* Michael sneers.

You got a wide streak of separation anxiety yourself, Michael. Curb your temper. Zeal, not rage, is one of the twelve powers of man; and rightly used, zeal can heal…, you, and the bat man. Light the other stones of power; we'll need those powers soon. Do your sensei master fight dance this time, I like that, good rhythm and beat, great fluidity, dazzling footwork…, who knows, maybe the bat will stop to watch.

Next time I come I'll bring you a sense of humor. Michael snaps.

Bring two – you'll need one yourself, Jacob replies evenly. *The physical world* needs *comic relief more than it needs a militantly dogmatic archangel who's* still *fighting fallen angels from eons ago. It is time for a wise consciousness of cooperation and collaboration…, and the sapphire is the last stone you touched. Short memory for a semi-divine being.*

Michael stiffens eyes wide and hard with exasperation. Pushing against Michael's resistance, Jacob forces his lungs full with air intentionally pressing the archangel hard against ribcage and spine, then holds the breath for a slow count of ten forcing the angry rigidity out of the winded archangel. The angel champion does not go down easily so Jacob begins his slow ten count again. *All right already! I take your point. Inhale now so that I have room to breathe again.*

Still overtly crabby for a semi-divine being. Still punitive and irritable. No wonder *the Good Lord doesn't give you important world changing assignments these days. On that note, what* are *you doing here?*

Michael is silent a long moment breathing slowly and rhythmically until his heat cools from volcanic intensity to mere driven purpose and memory of his mission returns to his conscious mind. *Thank you – for your strength – and for your wisdom and good judgment in calling me to task for reverting to a time when my sword could be unsheathed in anger and vengeance.* He sighs a long release, adding; *and for making me move beyond the past and into focus on the present and my mission here and now.*

What is our, your mission this time?

I am to save two souls who are lost in their own human minds, but never lost in the mind of God. I would have failed without you, Jacob. I know that now…, I remember…, how you persistently pressed the angry vengeance out of me and held me fast, Michael chuckles, *until I blessed you. In truth, it was you that blessed me – and I'm glad it didn't take an all-night fight this time.*

Couldn't, Jacob replies; *we don't have that much time to complete this mission.*

We have all the time we need, Jacob, all the time we need. Turning his attention now to the five unenlightened stones among the twelve jewels set from tip to top of his scabbard, Michael clasps the sword grip levering it down and tilting the scabbard so it crosses his body like a guitar. His dancing feet lead as he strokes a thumb over the un-lit jewel above the ruby.

The **Garnet** jewel flares, filling the archangel with cleansing, revitalizing, purifying, balancing, energy and inspiring love, devotion, courage, fortitude, hope, expanded awareness and mutual assistance. The power the stone dissolves habit patterns that even archangels have, and bypasses the habit of self-sabotage by obsolete dysfunctional beliefs.

Michael chooses to reform error thoughts that still serve so they produce happier outcomes and to eliminate the dark hidden ones that beguile him to believe in what shows up in the physical world that is *not* true in Spirit. With knowledge and intention, Michael releases, removes, denounces and denies all delusion that anything made by and from Source could ever be or become separate from Source. *Illogical.* Michael hears the words *"To whom little is forgiven, the same loveth little.* (Luke 8:47), and ponders the possibility that the man in bat has forgiveness issues for always giving small. *Except for horses…, they gave with no holding back. Interesting. He never found that with people.*

A russet red flame quickens as Michael strokes the garnet gem illuminating chakras and expanding mindfulness so he feels and experiences the frequencies and harmonies of the springing, swelling, inspiring, and passionate energy that animates life. He can't *not* dance. *Pointless.*

Michael surrenders lead-footed ingrained behavior patterns that no longer serve him, to tap with and around resistance, inertia, and self-sabotage. He stomps out old and dysfunctional ideas, antique inhibitions, a closet full of shoulda, woulda, couldas; belief in primordial enemies, and all the ancient taboos he'd picked up cheap at a rummage sale. *Nonsensical.* Michael is inspired with hope, clarity and courage and his dancing feet step lively with joy.

The Apostle **Thaddeus**, with the given name of Jude, modeled the power of **Elimination** and **Regeneration** by open-heartedly releasing error thought and ideas that no longer serve and inspiring hope for a better self and a more loving life. Thaddeus is known for abiding compassion and the restoring power of *being* rather than *doing*, and his generous use of the healing virtue of the soul that instantly transforms discord into unity. Eliminating thoughts that no longer serve to make space for ideas from Universal Mind, he gives jubilant thanksgiving for the healing that already comes.

Eyes now prismatic projections of the nine powers already invoked, Michael takes a second look at the spiritual truth of the man bat and the woman who bleeds and is amazed to see a shared destiny leading them to this place and time. *Interesting,* Jacob/Michael muses, *whatever happens to the bat happens to the both of them. It will be grand discerning the path the Divine has prepared for these foes. And for us!* Affirms Jacob with strong confident passion, but without aggression. *Maybe I* won't *kill him then…,* Michael muses. *There's an idea whose time has come!* Jacob encourages as he moves to strum the next stone.

Before Jacob can act, Michael touches the **Carnelian** stone and is filled with life force and vitality, motivation and creativity that stimulates his acceptance of what is while inciting a passion for finding the resolution that enriches everyone involved. *That is* creativity in action he thinks, that's Carnelian. At his touch, the stone activates in him vitality and acceptance that leads spontaneously to release, resolution and re-visioning of what is yet to be created into form and relationship. Michael smiles his true smile as love and compassion infill his angelic mind, body and brain.

Carnelian is the stone associated with the apostle **John the Baptist** is the apostle of **love** and **compassion** that is generously applied to all of life and every situation in it. He signifies a high intellectual perception of Truth, but one not yet quickened of Spirit, and an attitude of mind that is zealous for the rule of Spirit. This attitude is not spiritual but a perception of spiritual possibilities and a passion for creating conditions in which Spirit rules. This perception leads to striving with evil as a reality rather than a transitory condition. John knows that culture does not make people honest nor evoke their natural virtues. The power of love washes away the sin of separation from Source and gives birth to the inner Christ child reborn in one aspect of the One. Love is the pure essence of life that binds together the whole human family, the universe and everything in it in Divine harmony. Divine love is impersonal; it loves for the sake of loving, it is not concerned with what or who it loves nor with a return of love, love is like the sun, its joy is in shining forth its true nature. Compassion is an aspect of love and mercy that is prompted by an understanding heart. A person of compassion sees the error, but does not condemn. *"Neither do I condemn thee: go thy way; from henceforth sin no more. John 8:11*

At his touch, Michael is filled with Divine love and an awakened compassion for the fear-filled man in bat and for the woman who imagines herself a slave. He is instantly determined to find a creative way to harmonize the dualities in each of them and to create a resolution that enriches everyone involved.

The **Diamond** imparts the clarity to focus life into a cohesive whole and brings love, commitment and attracts abundance. The stone amplifies and harmonizes the energy of the dual poles of everything in form and clears and purifies emotional pain minimizing fear and creating a space for new opportunities. Diamond stimulates imagination and inventiveness and links intellect with higher mind leading to enlightenment that lets the soul light shine out showing the way to spiritual evolution and the divine light within. Diamond imparts fearlessness, invincibility and fortitude, and provides a link between the intellect and the higher mind.

The diamond is associated with the apostle **Matthew** who represents the **will** faculty in man. Matthew (originally named Levi) was a tax collector who, before becoming a disciple of Jesus was regenerated by the process of controlling, directing, teaching and disciplining the faculties of mind. To do this, Levi had to withdraw from his mercenary occupation and the material ambitions that absorbed his time and attention. Levi willingly gave up his money-getting preoccupation to devote his time and attention to following the master, Jesus. Peter, the man of faith, doubted the decision of Jesus until the master assured him by saying "Verily I say unto you, there is no man that hath left house, or brethren, or sisters or mother or father or children or his lands for my sake and for the gospel's sake, but he shall receive a hundredfold…" what he has left behind. In making this right choice, Levi entered his new self and rejoiced because in Christ, there is rejoicing for the deeper and stronger relationship, love is increased, and real world possessions are multiplied. Matthew demonstrates for all of us that the power of will *always* makes the final choice and right choice facilitates an openness to begin the schooling in truth.

Before even touching the stone, Michael senses the clarifying and aligning power of the diamond that infuses his body, mind and spirit, imparting new and refocused dedication and clarity. Smiling in anticipation of his own choice to devote himself to deepen and strengthen his personal relationship with Source, Michael strokes the stone and is infused with a multi-faceted vision of possibilities. He looks to the light in the brilliant diamond, seeing only light and perceiving the way and path to a new beginning for the man bat and for the woman who believes she is enslaved.

Michael is powerful, fearless, invincible and valiant with nothing to prove and nothing to hide. He is also wise and willfully dedicated to divine right outcomes and names and claims the true desire of his mind and heart: *I AM always the strength to hold a space for people to return to integrity – without shame or blame.* In the brilliance of the diamond facets, Michael sees possibilities and potentialities that don't serve him nor the people involved, and don't serve *Him. Useless baggage!* Deepening his inner oneness with Source, Michael is inspired by joyous possibilities in the patterns the diamond makes across the mosaic of life, sees a way that everyone heals, grows, blooms and he dances a joy jig.

Amber is not a stone but a fossilized tree resin that is strongly connected to earth serving as a grounding stone transmutes negative energies into higher outcomes that link the everyday self to spiritual reality. Amber stimulates a drive to achieve, promotes a sunny bright disposition that respects tradition, its flexibility dissolves opposition, encourages peacefulness, develops trust and brings wisdom.

Amber is associated with the apostle **Thomas** whose power is the power of **Understanding**; the ability to know, perceive, comprehend, apprehend and to ask. Ideally, understanding and will function in unity so that will is tempered and focused by understanding. Jesus modeled the relationship between these two powers of man when he did not ignore Thomas' demand for physical evidence of His identity knowing that enlightened understanding would support Thomas right use of the power of will in making his choice to believe that the dead man Jesus had indeed resurrected as he said he would. Knowing that the power of understanding has a physical component (*prove it*), Jesus required Thomas to put his hand into the spear wound to *experience* the evidence of Truth and activate man's right use of the power of understanding that open the door to the kingdom of God in the awakened mind of man. Jesus knew that will can make it happen, but cannot show the way, it is the understanding mind that finds the path to well-reasoned and joyous outcomes.

The one unenlightened stone is the **Peridot** and before touching it, Michael shifts his consciousness into the stone and receives its spring green power. Doing so, he experiences the cleansing, energizing power of the gem, feels toxins released from his body, mind and brain and the corresponding release of old baggage from the past and from current outside influences and feels an awakened communication with higher energies. He accepts the easing and release of dysfunctional and negative vibrational patterns that empower him to move forward with easy grace. Releasing separation fears, jealousy, resentment, spite, anger and stress, Michael welcomes enhanced poise, confidence and motivation for evolving on mental, emotional and spirit planes. He reviews past life lessons to experience the gifts, knowing that forgiveness of self and others for past mistakes empowers rebirth into a new awareness that activates hope, and faith in a restored unity with all of mankind, in conscious oneness of with all of life. He knows man can live on the sense plane until he becomes animal in nature and that the human has taken on the small minded self-serving sentience of a bat.

Now Michael strokes the Peridot and is filled with faith that he has the strength and courage to rise to the challenge winging toward him, and he rejoices greatly that the man in bat and the enslaved woman are already reborn into an abiding and assured awareness of Oneness as Truth. With the twelve stones of power lit Michael honors the relationship between will and understanding and calmly walks the path of power into the continuum where the horned one in bat drag speeds across the void hell-bent to flee the outcomes of unenlightened choices through one small door in space and time.

The power of Peridot flushes through him releasing negative vibrational patterns and opening new frequencies, views, destinies, and spiritual purposes. He savors the gifts of past experience. Springing on the energy of Peridot, Michael admits mistakes and moves on. Breathing easy confidence and eager composure in the face of a spiritual purpose and destiny forever forming, the Archangel is filled with clarity, confidence, assertion without aggression, and a fiery passion in the quest for spiritual truth.

The apostle **Andrew**, brother of Peter, represents the power of **strength** and **courage**. Metaphysically, Andrew is the strong man with the strength of mind to rejoice greatly when it finds the inexhaustible Source of all strength who exclaims "*We have found the Messiah.*" Reuniting with his brother Peter, Andrew bonds the power of strength with the power of faith that propels him along and through the most adverse experiences.

"Touch the **Hiddenite** stone on your helmet over your third eye and open it," comes Jacob's placid command and the angel commander obeys. At the touch Michael knows a gentle sweet softening strengthening not unlike the tender unfurling of new leaves that lengthen as they grow. The clear iridescent green of the stone seeps into him opening and linking him to the transfer of knowledge from higher energy realms, healing error thought, and sharpening focus and awareness. He knows now how it is that people who had to grow up fast can become hard, crusty, and even mean, for the early loss of innocence. He has another peep at bat and knows certain and sure that the trusting innocence of the boy abandoned within the man in bat was too soon lost, gone, and never redeemed.

As his fingers brush the white striations of the crystal he sees that the woman who thinks she is slave put on a false brave face too soon and too often for want of understanding the complex and confounding connections among the humans in her small world composed of a kitchen and a hen pen.

The hen pen had a kinder and more lucid energy about it. The wounded child now slave to the whims and wiles of people bigger and more powerful, and – to her abiding faith that she was never clever enough to know how to please others, or to be invisible to them. Interesting. Michael absorbs the rising rushing healing power of the vital green along with an infusion of infinite clarity, wisdom, and insight from the white striations crossing the heart of the Hiddenite lens. *Thank you for that, Jacob. I trust you saw and experienced all that too?*

I did. Jacob nods their one head and adds, *I'm ready, are you? Prepared and ready – have you noticed and felt the changes to my war dance? I have indeed.*

Good, aren't I? We are, Jacob grins a minor course correction. Sensing the bat's course shift before it shows Michael's body flows without thought or effort to meet the ancient adversary as joy fills and floods him until it bubbles out in lilting laughter that, if heard by a human ear might indeed sound deranged. *"When thine eye is evil, thy body also is full of darkness." Luke 12:34.* Combat ecstasy erupts from Michael in a power surge that disorients the bat, pausing it in mid-flight like a video on Pause. *I didn't know bats could stop like that. Something new every day in your service, Lord, what a great and awesome God you are.*

In a brilliant flash of surrender Michael decides and declares, *I will not destroy what you have made My Lord"* His reaper grin is back *"but in Your Name I* will *incapacitate the serpent of deceit so that the possessed human may live free again…, if he chooses.* Without visible effort, Michael *is* where the bat flies at bat-Mach speed into the upright silver sword held steadfastly in Jacob's human hand within in silver gauntlet of Michael's armor. For an instant the bat sizzles against the blade, then molasses slow slides down to plop insensate to the floor. The silver sabaton covering Archangel Michael's foot pins the stunned creature to the floor before Jacob's mind receives the signal that his body has moved.

Ben enters the room at a run, skids to a stop beside Jacob and grins eyeing what lies pinned beneath his foot, "Good man, Jacob, you captured a man in a bat suit," he congratulates, clapping a hand on Jacob's shoulder. Wincing he pulls his hand back, lamenting, "I *never* remember to *not* clap you the shoulder when you wear armor. You, my friend, are downright prickly when you go Archangel Michael on us."

Jacob's laughter reverberates within the silver helmet and carillons through the nose and eye vents, he cocks an unseen brow. "I need three pieces of silver," he orders in angelic voice, "what have you got?"

"A pair of buffalo nickels," Ben grins holding them out, "and I already know where these buffalo roam." Dropping to a knee by the bat Ben slides a buffalo coin face up between the elbow of a wing and the spine of the bat, then places other buffalo between the elbow and back of the other, and turns to rise.

"I'm in for a silver eagle quarter," Counselor raises the ante by flipping the coin to Ben who catches it on the rise and drops again to place it prudently on the breast of the beast.

"A life was once sold for *thirty* pieces of silver;" growls a voice at the door "surely a man in bat drag needs at least *four* pieces of silver to be saved – if saved he will be. He swaggers to the bat, "I have a silver Walking Liberty dollar; and, just like Ben," he elbows him aside "I know *exactly* where it goes." He stoops, rests a forefinger and thumb against the breast of the beast, then touches the head, sensing for a moment. He looks up and announces, "The bat has a heartbeat and *very* slow brainwave activity. I believe it is safe, Jacob, for you to remove your silver *sabaton* from this insensate creature while I place my guard on it." He edges Jacob's foot away, "and change into your regular clothes please."

"It's always a pleasure when you arrive, Luke...." Jacob replies stepping away and into bib overalls, chambray shirt and work boots, then bends to watch Luke.

"Counselor, I'm moving your silver eagle away to put the Walking Liberty on the bat's breast. Lady Liberty *ought* to infuse the heart of the awakened beast with the very truth that liberty's light is the innate right of every being."

That done, Luke carefully places the silver eagle in its new place and Jacob exclaims, "Oh, son..., that is *just* so wrong!" Luke giggles light bright delight as he coils up and away from his completed mission.

"Jacob, what's Luke done with my silver eagle?" Counselor queries cautiously.

"He put it *face down* on the bat's groin."

"Oh. *Ouch*! It's enough to inspire a man to compassion for the fellow when he is conscious again." Casting the sentiment indifferently aside he asks "Will he shift shape before he comes to again?"

"Probably. Usually..., and, as his body returns to the size of a man, the coins grow with him." Jacob shrugs, "it's something in the magic of Michael that I do not fathom."

"Oh....," Counselor nods knowingly, "the magic of Michael.... I should have guessed. Remind me to never give you reason to be fractious with me, Jacob." Turning a sharp eye to Luke, Counselor adds "as for you, *Light Bearer*, you have a *shockingly* dark side to you for one so young." Luke bobs a bow with an affable grin and takes a chair in the circle while Counselor bites a cheek to check a chortle.

Pain Eater

"Here come the Daughters now" Doc crows the rising light.

"Led by my lovely wife in her fine regalia," beams Counselor in obvious admiration.

"May I always cherish my Hester as you obviously do your mate, Counselor," Jacob declares.

"May you always be sane enough to give praise for, and *to*, your mate, Jacob," Counselor counsels.

"May I always be in awe of your wisdom," Jacob replies with a puckish grin as the ringing and singing of dulcet voices fills and cheers the room and stills all sidebars.

Hester neither leads nor follows as she enters the common room to see with a sweep of eyes, the silver studded prone bat, the crumpled pile of clothes, and the woman rising in round eyed recognition from a chair between Doc and Counselor. The woman bears a distinctive two-hole mark in the curve of her neck over the carotid artery. Hester swallows a cry as her world implodes into the time her untainted sense of self was assaulted, desecrated, and left abandoned without hope. Surrendering her separate sense of self she consciously expands awareness to embrace only the two of them, for she knows two are needed to forgive and two to heal the separation from Source that enables one to feed on the life force energy of another. *Two to do the sin, two to heal it*, she reflects in a final thought before yielding to a higher power to flow and heal through her. | **Michael Gott: Thy Will Be Done** |

Fixing eyes and will on the woman, Hester lifts a graceful hand to touch two fingers by the paired scars over her carotid artery in the place where enflamed punctures leach color and life from the woman. She blinks shaking her head 'no,' yet hope rises like the first dawn on the first day, and she breathes "how...?" Without thought she yields her passion to know the outcomes and contingencies before giving her unconditional yes. She let go of all of that. She *just* let go. | **Rev. Sapphire Rose: She Just Let Go** |

Hester reads the energy of the whispered question and responds by opening her heart to receive the pain shackling the spirit of the bowed being before her and time is suspended for she has slipped mortal bonds and fallen headlong into the infinite and eternal space between the formless and the formed. *Thy will be done* her heart sings as her eyes weep, *Thy will be done — through me.* Joy fills, overwhelms, uplifts and elevates her as time twists and warps and does not behave well at all and no one minds for all know that when one is healed all are whole for all are one when all is done.

Pain punches Hester with the force of a blow as the cocoa woman falls boneless to the floor. She chuffs out air, then in greedy gasps inhales, force feeding oxygen to her body, mind, and brain. She exhales a soft slow sigh, eyes lancing into those of the fallen woman willing her strength and courage and hope and hope and hope..., and tears flow and neither ever knows who first cries, who first dies, who first lives again, who first finds Lazarus fresh awake, still stiff and awkward from being too long dead to and separate from

Source. *Lazarus is not the* only *one who can be resurrected and live anew. The promise is given* through *him – even as it was given* to *him.*

The bent woman *hears* Truth Words she never before heard and, inhaling with Hester she fills her lungs gently full with oxygen and holds it there while blood delivers the breath of life powerfully throughout her body brain and mind. A tentative smile plays on her lips as she sees and her heart knows her newly resurrected self is *outrageously*, unexpectedly, and brilliantly gifted to be the amazing self she sees in the eyes of the woman lifting her up on the power of love across an infinite domain of time.

Hester pulls the breath of life powerfully filling her lungs and bronchia to capacity and holds for a rhythmic count of ten relishing the self-induced euphoria of an oxygen high. Pumping breath like a bellows through the crucible of her heart she fires the dynamic power of love resident there turning it to molten liquid life light love. Exhaling to a slow count of ten she allows the pain to flow and resolve to its level in the purifying passion of unconditional love. *Thy will be done,* she gasps another greedy gulp of air directing it to her heart center to feed and fuel the passion fire, knowing, loving, surrendering to what will come. In a distant central part of her mind she hears music…"

> **John Adorney: If a Rose Could Speak**

On inspiration Hester touches her chest above her heart and is surprised to feel the shape and texture of a felt rose with petals arrayed flat like a tea rose full open. She watches the woman's eyes go round in recognition and smiles at what cannot be yet is, while gently fingering petal edges she turns the petals knowing they reform to curve and curl into the upright shape of an American Beauty rose. She whispers "If a rose could speak, it would say: [Dear Reader – pause to feel the words the rose speaks.]

"Breathe," Doc softly coaches the woman, "inhale deep, hold, exhale slow, relax, do it again three times, breathe deep, hold, exhale slow, relax. Pant now, pant like a dog fresh from a run, pant, pant, pant," Doc chants out a new rhythm of the life song from before time began and the woman loses herself to the pant chant and surrenders to ever more present at-One-ment with the Source of all of life.

While hope springs eternal, faith is a power to be earned, learned, and won. Though no words are spoken, the woman hears Hester's gently probing asking when and why she accepted herself as slave. Initially shocked, the woman defends that she was born a slave. *As was your mother? Yes,* the woman replies in silence. *Did your mother think of herself, or behave, as a slave?* The woman blinks shock at the astute depth and fractal facets of the question and knows she cannot deny or hide her true reply. *No, she never behaved slavishly. She always had the assured dignity of one born free. If your mother did not behave slavishly but always conducted herself as one born free though owned by another, how* did *you come to deny the truth your mother knew? How did you come to believe and behave as a woman* enslaved *by another?* The woman moans under the unyielding weight of a truth she could never accept and cannot now deny. *My mother… never loved me….*

Hester laughs delight despite herself, and thus the woman sees the silliness of what she has said. Hester probes *Did you have healthy food to eat, clean clothes to wear, a warm dry place to sleep, a chance to learn things you didn't already know, a safe place to play and friends to play with?* Yes, the woman admits feeling the first soft tugs of assurance that the freedom she denied was never denied to her.

When did you begin to feel and believe you were disempowered and powerless? Hard questions, woman, why do you plague me? Why will you not face me when accusing me of tormenting you? Who can own power over you when you have denied it is yours alone to own and wield? Is your power available to anyone you can project blame on who will not defend themselves? Ouch! You are hard, woman! Facing one equally hard in her self-enforced separation behind which she hides to casts darts of blame for the consequences of her own choices. I did not choose this! The woman protests in impotent rage. Hester shrugs calmly: *Passive choice counts too. Which brings us back to the question of* when *you denied your own power and began believing, and behaving, as though someone outside you owns you and determines the fate of you. You won't let up will you?* Hester's smile is genuine, *Do you choose to be healed and whole, or do you choose to continue slavishly allowing someone else to exercise the power you freely give daily?* The woman juts her lip petulantly and Hester interjects *Jesus always asked two questions before healing anyone, what were they?* A sullen moment of silence passes before she replies: *Do you believe you can be healed, and are you willing to be healed.* Hester nods, *Faith, the power of Peter, and Will, the power of Matthew. Both men demonstrated passive, fear-based use of their power before using it rightly. Like you, Peter demonstrated faith in* human *power by denying the man he called master. He also used his power rightly by stepping from a boat into a stormy sea to walk on the water toward Jesus.*

The woman across from her frowns and says: *But then he fell in!* Hester nods wise agreement: *The storms of life often drop even faith filled people into the hard liquid reality of life in physical form. Is that what happened to you?* The woman hesitates a moment then sighs: *If I ever had that much faith, then yes, that is what happened to me.* Hester cocks a grin; *Perhaps your faith was not invested in a higher power at all, but was rather a seemingly safe dependence on the humans you believed owned you.*

The cocoa woman will not meet her eyes, and Hester continues: *Matthew was a tax collector and that worked very well for him by physical world measures, yet he willingly chose to give that up to follow the Master, and that right use of will led him to riches on the spiritual and the material plane. Are you willing to give up security of dependence on physical world sources, release yourself to a higher power and to trust in the rewards of that?*

What security have I? Someone else to be responsible, someone else to blame, the false sense of security of dependency. What do you know, you white face judge? Thinking you can put me down because you are whiter than me. Hester studies the woman a moment then opts to answer her question rather than to defend her charge: *You have the word of the Most High God, the same security Peter and Matthew had when facing the choice of reality bites, or taking a leap of faith.* Extending a hand and smile Hester invites: *Come, step out of the boat you have built to keep yourself adrift and isolated, leave the security of the wild wiles you relied on; and step into the promise of a better forever future — even if you don't know what it will look or feel like to be free or to be full to overflowing with peace and joy abiding.*

The woman discharges the pains, slights and assaults of a life no longer a part of who she is and wills herself to stand firm and tall. "You have been very kind and I thank you, but you must stop now."

"Stop?" Hester blinks, refocusing her eyes to see the woman in her physical form again.

"Yes, stop. I tried to stop the flow of pain you took from me by blocking it, I even sent mean thoughts to and about you…." She huffs indignantly "that did as much good as dropping a rock in a river; the pain flowed right around it. You – you are a *Pain Eater*," her face crumples for being freely given more than she is capable of receiving.

Hester smiles serenely "I Am that, I Am." Then she frowns puzzled, "but why do you weep?"

"What you eat you *become!*" The woman cries, "You *must not* do this, you must stop *now!*"

Hester nooses a giggle into a small smile, folds her hands over her heart, and says "watch this." Gently opening her hands like wings around her heart she invites "follow the flow of your pain, and see what becomes of it here," she taps her chest springing with a replenishing abundance of heart center energy.

Many in the room know what the woman facing Hester will see and watch her instead, charting her reactions to the implausible sight of an enflamed and joyous heart encompassed in a nimbus of gem light, willing to freely give any essential assist. The woman's instincts are true and guided, she gasps, then pants like a dog fresh from a run. She does not look away nor take reprieve from the terrible tender flow consuming her anguish but inhales a sweet breath of longing as purified liquid pain pours into Hester's heart and shapes and forms into dazzling crystals of astonishing color, cut, clarity and size. Seeing the jewels formed from pain in Hester's heart, the woman receives and sanctions her own cauterizing agony and intuitively allows and eases the pain of the man in bat craving only the freedom to enslave. *How small, how powerless, how cowardly, how helpless, angry and hopeless, he must be, to sink as low as he has gone. Thank you God that his has not been* my *fate for all my failings, fears, faults and frailty. Use me. Use me — as you will, use me.*

After an epoch and eternity of healing the woman sighs "*I want to do that…,*" her words are a longing for a surrender and return, for a dropping of arms and defenses, for a willing submission to a higher and purer power that is seldom known on the physical plane in the body, brain, or mind of man. "Will you teach me…?" she prays pleas into Hester's eyes.

Hester laughs surprise delight. "You already know how to be a Pain Eater, you are one. You have not accepted that truth yet, that is all that is lacking."

"*I* am a Pain Eater?"

"You are that," Hester nods an assuring smile. "Touch the mark on your neck."

The woman obeys, blinks doubt jerking her fingers away to see the tips not red wet but only clean dry skin. She touches again softly exploring the healed dry scars like those on Hester's neck. Tears sting her eyes, "Does that mean *I* can eat pain and it turns into jewels in my heart, like happened in yours?"

Hester nods, "I'm sure of it. Would you like to try then?" The woman kicks a fear habit doubt and nods confidently. "Ben," Hester smiles the name "will you come to me please?" Ben obliges warily wary. She continues as he approaches, "As you see from his uniform, Ben is our peace keeper." She tucks a hand in his elbow. "Keeping the peace is surprisingly more challenging than enforcing the law. Keeping peace means Ben eats a *great* deal of pain in the course of doing his work effectively." She smiles fondly up at him, "I think Ben is mostly unaware of the hurt he eats to find and forge peaceful outcomes. If Ben agrees, are you willing to try your hand…, and your heart, at absorbing the pain of another?" The woman looks at Ben who grins, shrugs, and nods with anxious ambiguity and a nervous *heh, heh, heh.*

The woman grins at Ben, shrugs and confesses, "I don't know what I'm doing either, Sheriff, if that's any comfort to you." Ben nods. She hesitates, bites her lip, and casts a quick look and plea to Hester. "Will you stand by me? …To support me?" Smiling, Hester quickly moves to stand by the woman facing Ben.

Ben chuckles uneasily "I'm feeling a *little* alone here right now.…"

"I'll stand by you, Ben" calls a sweet voice borne on the quick nimble step of a natural dancer gliding to Ben's side to slip a hand under his elbow, smile up at him, and say "I'll be right here by your side."

Tipping back his head, Ben chortles, "I don't know if I'm more comforted, or more challenged by that."

The dancer grins, "It'll be fun finding out won't it? Pay attention now, I want you to tell me later *exactly* what it feels like to have your pain eaten." Ben cocks a dubious brow at the dancer, then turns to face the woman preparing to eat his pain.

Hester steps behind the woman placing her left hand on her spine at the level of the heart, her right hand on the woman's right shoulder. Inhaling fully, she slips to a meditative trance to guide and to feel the woman follow her there. As one the two inhale and exhale to ten heartbeats.

Those watching see the woman raise upright in her power, trusting Source to lead and guide her in its correct use, and as she exhales, they see her heart open to reveal its true passion and give it a homecoming welcome. As one, they feel pain release, ease and flow, and as one, experience resolution and restoration in the crucible of love, each holding fast to the essential truth of wholeness in body mind and spirit.

The dancer feels and yields to Ben's surrender and the melting closure that weeps from him, with him she accepts the reviving breath, the measured treasured exhale, and the fresh uprightness of body with the next breath of air. He bows chin to chest and surrenders will, trusting and yielding to Spirit to find and release his burdens while time stands still to watch the silent prayer play with vital vigilance.

In Ben's experience, each pain tormenting him is at once alien and as familiar as a twin, as fully known as an alternate self, as true his own breath and the body that breathes it. At times pain racks and rocks him until he thinks his body must break and rip to sundered shreds no more repairable than Humpty's shattered shell. And all the infinite while a guardian voice chants *"breathe…, breathe…, breathe…, breathe…, all is well, all is worthy, all is whole, breathe…, only inhale and exhale, breathe.…"*

In the way a coming storm changes temperature by tens of degrees in seconds, Ben's pain cools and calms to become a strong element in his blood and body as health returns and repossesses every cell and atom of his body/ mind/brain. Ben finds that only whole health remains and he respires in the giddy glad gratitude of irrational joy. He opens dewed eyes and smiles thanks into the ones across the circle.

The woman blinks "I did it," she whispers amazed. "I ate his pain…." The statement raises at the end like a question, "and I am *stronger* than I was before," she crows out her joy. I *am* a healer!" she sings in sweet surrender, "I didn't know that about me before;" she smiles serenely, "now I know who I Am."

"Part of it, dear heart, only part of it, there is more for you to learn, accept, master and know," Hester assures stepping around to embrace her with a motherly sisterly smile. *I'm a pain eater!* The woman mouths into Hester's ear and the two of them share a coming home joy laugh.

Fight Dance

"Well, bat man is a dud for entertainment value," grumbles a dancer toeing the slight static form on the floor. "You *sure* he isn't dead, Luke?" Luke bobs his head in affirmation brows arched in petulant pique. The dancer shrugs, "Let's *do* something then; let's make something happen while we wait for the dead to arise…, or not," she says with innocent indifference.

"What do you want to do?" Luke asks giving her the attention she craves.

"Fight dance!" She shouts with an infectious cheerleader jump and smile. Some see crepe paper pom-poms fluttering though none are there at all.

"*Fight* dance?" Ben and Luke harmonize the puzzlement of all.

"Is that anything like the Schottische?" someone asks playing silly, and some chuckle, while all lean back to see the theatre of the weird that is certain to follow.

The dancer grins, pleased with the spontaneously evolving entertainment. "Not much like the Schottische at all;" she contradicts, then gives an impish grin "but it *could* be part of the fight dance if someone put Schottische steps and moves into it," she demonstrates as she speaks, improvising fight dance steps as she twirls around the circle slapping toes and palms where a shoe might stamp a Schottische step. "Who wants to learn the fight dance? It's no *fun* dancing alone," she whines

"You're making this up as you go aren't' you?" Ben asks circling opposite her matching her sure step and form as she moves. Eying and matching him she clacks imaginary castanets casting them as weapon nets nearly snaring him in her web. Ben shreds the web and she snarls exploding into a back flip to snap upright before him reaching behind with a shapely calf to slap the backs of his knees throwing him off balance, and with a grin nimbly back flips away.

"Okay, I'm getting the hang of this, I see how it works," Ben chuckles his signature *heh, heh, heh,* "All I have to do is stay on the other side of the room from you and I'll be fine."

"Will that work for you" She coos from behind him light-fingering his handcuffs from his belt clip, "do you think?" she grins jingling the cuffs in his face.

"How do you *do* that?" He growls.

"The first, and perhaps the *only*, rule of Fight Dance is always keeping them guessing, unsuspecting, surprised and off guard. Do you want to participate in this dance; or is complaining enough for you?"

"Sure," Ben snaps, snatching his cuffs away, "I'm teachable," he shrugs, "and I got some time." She twirls around him slapping the bottom of his baton with the sole of a foot so it leaps from its holder at his waist to arch over his shoulder where he catches it in astonishment."

You won't be needing that," the dancer smiles, pushing him toward his chair. "Leave the gun, the handcuffs, the knife, *and* the shoes under your chair; and *everyone*, make this circle bigger so the ladies can sit too, or," she entices, "can join the dance."

"If you show me how to get Ben out of his weapons," the dancer's young sister coos as she glides into the ring, "you can teach me *anything* else you want, Sister dear.

Luke clears his throat stepping lightly between the sisters "Start with what makes it a *fight* dance since no *weapons* are allowed, except, it seems, your fast feet and hasty hands." He grins a spin out of reach.

The dancer smiles demonstrating a twirl then lighting fast, extends a shapely leg to clip the backs of her sister's knees lifting and rotating her into a full body flip in the air and she lands with a solid "whoop" of joyful triumph.

"Okay, that taught *me* how to flip, now you teach me how to make someone *else* flip." Her grin is deeply wicked on such an angelic face, "oh wait...," she smirks down at her astonished sister *not* sleeping on the floor by the slumbering bat "I just did that didn't I?" Her delighted giggle is both strangely sinister and yet oddly infectious.

Luke leads with his toes as he slinks around the ring circling the sisters eyeing them with devoted intent and a disarming smile. "Tell me about the fight dance, and since it is a dance, where's the fight? If it's a fight, where's the dance? And perhaps most important of all; "who leads?" He circles and spins to, with, and around the girls whirling one into the other then watches the grace of their improvised response. Smiling the light he bears, he thinks: *what fun if we all and each of us lead and follow, and all and only for the joy of sharing with no expectation except to discover infinite opportunities for unexpected expressions of Truth that all is One Infinite and Expanding Whole, Wholly, Holy, and Here, and Now!*

It is good that I don't talk out loud much.

The sisters twin themselves to mirror or to move counterpoint with Luke and with each other and are aware as one when Ben steps back into the swirling circle, moving with and challenging all of them "if the fight dance is a competition, what is its purpose? What's the objective? What's the prize? If our only goal is to show muscle and style and form; that is *far* too easy…, we'd be bored before the hour is up.

"What we need is a challenge, a goal; an objective to stretch us and to keep us engaged…, here's what I propose." Ben circles them like a kindly interrogator, playing the drama to the audience as he engages each in his play and powerful grace, enticing them into the circle. He smiles bright delight, "By ancient Inca tradition the winner of every competition is honor bound to teach and train those he has defeated until each can stand against him as his equal. Teaching and learning would make this fight dance of yours – whatever it turns out to look like – a pastime worth the doing, and watching, and deserving of the time it takes doing it."

Jacob rises with a grin to join the circle "I admire that Inca tradition, Ben, but I'd propose a change" he tips a nod to each in the circle, "I will teach *each* of you hard and well, and one day…," his grin is a wicked challenge" you will stand *with me* as my equal."

The dancer slinks a step toward him "Next year, Jacob, next year. *This* year, I will be teaching you, and if you are attentive and practice daily, you can complete your training in a year's time and be *able* to stand against me as my equal."

"Oh ho ho, *show* me…, little girl, don't tell me, else I'll put my money on you growing up to be a skillful politician and not a collaborative Spiritual warrior." The dancer snorts crossly at Jacob's back that hides from her the mischief in his eyes and smile. He meets raised eyebrows in the circle facing him, he turns his hands palm up and feints bewilderment at the reaction.

"You are such a pot stirrer, Jacob…, what do you intend to add to this fight dance idea that makes it an entertaining pastime…, other than hot air?" a watcher asks.

Jacob shrugs a grin, "I don't know yet, I don't know the rules…, or even if there are any. My bet is on the Inca having rules, watchers, and trainers, all we got so far is words…, and some appealing dance moves."

The dancer huffs again, "then I shall be forced to teach you the toe slap dance."

"Oh, I am *so* in for that" cries the sister dashing to her side.

In that toe slap instant the bat shifts into his human form. "Oh look – the man in the bat is back," the younger observes, "and fortunately, its skinny naked body is tucked in the natal position so we can't see it." She studies the bat with a frown. "That silver eagle laid where it was before the shift, might cause a body itself to curl into that protective pose." She nudges the man with a toe as her sister had done the bat. "It's still breathing," she observes, "and that is *still* all that can be said for its entertainment value."

The wall clock strikes two chimes.

"Time's a passing," Jacob grumbles, "who's going to tell us what this fight dance looks like?" He claps his hands like a coach hustling his players to attention and focus, "what are the rules, what does it take to win, are there teams or is it every player for *her*self, are there style points…, are you making this up as you go?" He demands of the dancer.

She grins but not apologetically, and shrugs, "well…, *yeah*! Everyone's sitting around like a bump on a log and that's as entertaining as watching a bat nap. Practically *anything* would be more entertaining. I thought bats hung upside down in caves to sleep…."

Jacob winks an evil grin "I think the man didn't expect to be unconscious just now; and his long sleep is *no* reason for you to propose something just as dull to pass time until he wakes up."

"Jacob, Jacob, Jacob," Ben intervenes, "in addition to rules, every good game needs at least two teams, some good players, some fair referees, a bunch of enthusiastic fans…, and *few* critics. You obviously are not a player, nor a referee, nor even a fan, you, my friend, are a critic. You belong on the sidelines," he prods Jacob back to his chair pushing him firmly into it, "… where you can be as cantankerous as you please." The circle erupts in hoots of laughter. "Sit. Stay." Ben orders turning back to the dance.

"Okay, we had some good action going on before our resident critic gave his review; let's make this fight dance a competition worthy of watching and doing. You, dancer, what are your favorite elements of a dance competition?"

Caught off guard the dancer gapes drop-jawed. "If you've lost your tongue and can't speak, *show* us! Come over here, little sister, your elder needs some inspiration; show us what you got while she evolves beyond the mouth-breathing stage." Ben narrowly ducks a toe slap upside the head but is bumped off sides by the swinging hip of the slinking sister. *He, he, he,* he chortles triangulating himself between the girls, "Luke, you showed us some good moves before, is that all you got?" Ben grins provocatively. "If so, go lie down by the man in bat drag. You can be as dull as a lump of coal over there." He narrowly dodges Luke's jump kick to his head to spin away and catch Luke's ankle with a foot to flip him airborne again. "Woo-*hoo*! What a great *move*, Luke! What else ya got?" Ben goads.

On a silent cue the sisters' dance in to separate the men mischievously provoking their competitive routine and introducing their own gymnastic gyrations to the evolving dance.

Musicians among them improvise a driving beat, lilting tune, and sublime harmony to inspire the dance and the dancers. Wise elders watch and give points for style, originality and performance perfection.

Soon the circle is filled with leaping, weaving, thrusting, pulling, shoving, tumbling, spinning, jumping and laughing youths who break out to watch, cheer and take a breather while practicing new moves for the dance of cosmic silliness before returning to the sphere of jubilant gyration.

None have laughed so deep and so well for as long as they can remember and all cherish this time as a favorite memory for as long as they live.

The Awakening

The chirping calls of a bat rise from the unmoving man in the natal position on the floor drawing all eyes to the still form. Slowly the twittering sounds evolve into tormented moans from a human throat growing louder as the weight of the silver presses and burns.

"Anyone hungry for barbeque?" someone quips and is quickly silenced by glares from around in the room, the dancers scowl and step away, and the musicians lay aside their instruments.

"What have you done to me?" the searing man moans.

Doc leans back in his chair extending the soles of his feet to the man, "why son, we have given you one more chance to answer Jacob's question and tell all of us how one man can own another."

The man moans "we've already been through that and you took the word a slave over that of a free white man."

"Huh! You don't *look* free to me," Ben observes caustically.

"I *mean* I am not a slave, you dolt."

"'Dolt', I haven't heard *that* discouraging word since I was knee-high to a grasshopper." Grinning amiably into the face of the prone man, Ben sing-songs "sticks and stones may break my bones, but words will never hurt me."

Seeing a human face shift to the face of evil is a disquieting demonstration, the hissed words of the silvered man are more unsettling still "your laughter is a sign of your *ignorance*."

"Well *that* was just plumb unkind," Ben pulls back with a grousing grumble, "and me just trying to add a bit of levity to this *unfortunate* situation."

"There is nothing funny about this situation," the man snaps.

Eyeing the naked man livid with hardly contained rage Ben nods amiably and observes "that is a matter of perspective, son. From the angle of *my ignorance* the situation in which you find yourself, captured as a bat, allowed to shift to human form, pinned to a dusty floor by silver coins, and on top of *that* your impotent bullying, well, son, that is just plain rib-tickling ri-*dic*-ulous."

The pinned man growls "if I could get up, I'd …."

Ben's eyebrows arch expressively, "*bite me?*" he growls. The man looks away with a sullen scowl and Ben's eyes narrow to a hard line. Reaching into a shirt pocket Ben pulls out something letting it drop into his palm, "I've carried a token for most of my career thinking someday I'd find someone I'd want to give it to," nodding once he adds, "today's my day, and you're my man." He tosses the thing so it lands lightly on the prone man's shoulder.

The man shrieks and writhes away and the token rolls to the floor beside him, "a silver bullet…" he shrieks, "you insensitive *brute!*"

"*This,* from a man who enslaves and feeds on the life blood of *another?* It is plum hard to feel fairly judged by a man like you." Ben stalks resolutely toward the lying man who flinches away at his approach. "I'll have my Lone Ranger silver bullet back since you *obviously* have no appreciation for the finer things in life." Ben's grin is devilishly as he veers away to his chair.

The silver studded man eyes the faces in the circle and finds them relaxed, alert, aware, and fully present without expectation or judgment, yet with one outcome they anticipate and patiently await. The realization is chilling to the man whose foremost talents include manipulation and control. *They have no stake in this, not* one *of them, yet there is an outcome they will have, and will accept no other.*

It rankles him; these nobodies without status, entitlement or authority binding him and deciding his fate with meticulous indifference and merciless compassion. In face of the steadfast serenity of the circle, he focuses his considerable concentration on life, liberty and the pursuit of freedom. Happiness, he has never known, and discounts as having no value.

Across the room an awakening sense of self-determination shreds habitual bonds of timid submission infested into the consciousness of the cocoa woman, leaving her with a bewildering clarity that she was *always* free to choose her own fate and thus to also bear the consequences. Freedom and fate war within her as fierce as mythical dragons each bound till death to oppose the other. The winged serpents swoop, swirl and spit fire, each intent on destruction of the *other* in her, and of all she knows and believes until the space of her consciousness is too narrowly constrained to contain the conflict of the winged beasts and she feels herself hurled blind into a vast void beyond space and time.

Doc senses her absence though she sits beside him still, and reaches to assist her when suddenly she yelps and elevates on an impossible trajectory from her chair, left foot riding something unseen, arms propellering in pursuit of elusive equilibrium. All feel the jolt of balance as her right foot is swiftly and smoothly supported and she rises like a shot through the roof newly supplanted by infinity and its strikingly spirited sentient silence.

"Dragons…," comes a single awed whisper from the circle.

"*Who are you?*" The rider in another dimension asks to know.

"*Fre,*" replies the serpent beneath her left foot,

"*Edom*" says the other.

"*What's happening?*" The unsettled woman cries.

"*Perspective,*" breathe the dragons in one word thought. "*You were too close to your small human self to clearly see your options and make a wise choice and so we spirited you away.*"

"*Options?*" The woman puffs panting.

"*Yes. Fear is a human habit that practically predicts outcomes because fear always precludes options. What was the choice before you when we came for you?*"

"*Freedom…,*" she pauses pondering; "*or fate.*"

"*Which would you have chosen?*"

She groans "*Fate, I suppose…, fear habit. Doubt.*"

"*Name your doubt,*" demands one.

"*That I can be free…. To do what I choose, and to know that I can survive and even thrive on that.*"

"*Self-doubt.*" Breathes one, "*Is it possible the man you are with is possessed by the same fear?*"

The infinite thrives in timeless silence and the dragons soar, spiral and spin in endless exuberant space beyond time until the woman owns and allows the truth she has denied and the dragons return her to the chair where she began her quest. Doc lays a comforting hand on her wrist, silently reading her pulse and finding its rhythm and pace curiously more composed than before she left on her wild ride.

"Let the man free," The woman directs unexpectedly…, and expects it to be already done.

"*What?*" The circle demands as one, mouths agape.

The dark woman withdraws behind lowered lids, mourning for a moment the blamelessness of slavery and life at the mercy of a mean malicious man. She understands the margins of being owned. She knows how to resist passively, and how to win at that, and to survive. *Slavery is not for the slow, the slight, or the submissive,* she observes silently. *Only the brave survive slavery.*

Raising her eyes to the restrained man she speaks to the circle, "Look at him and see…, *truly* see. The shackles that bind him are not the searing silver coins. The man sold himself cheap before the Archangel dropped him where he lays."

The man struggles feebly to rise to her level. "Remove the coins," she snaps an order, "and give him his clothes. None deserve to suffer the shame of his nakedness…, most especially him."

"Point taken," Luke agrees gathering the worn gaudy garments, dropping beside the man. He casually takes and pockets his Walking Liberty coin and lays the jacket on the man's chest. The man gulps lungs full of air, eyes wide with relief and doubt; and something oddly akin to fear. Next Luke removes the buffalo nickels that instantly revert to their normal size and weight, and flips them to Sheriff Ben. Luke then removes the Silver Eagle quarter, and drapes the trousers over the man's groin and legs, setting the shoes nearby. That done Luke graciously returns the Silver Eagle to Counselor's palm.

Revelation and Reckoning

When he is dressed again the man looks at the woman and asks "Did – did you… ride two dragons in…, into space – like it *looked* like you did?" The woman nods and he bobs his head with her, his eyes round wide with her truth. "I was afraid you'd say that; and I hoped you wouldn't. I never saw anything like that, not even on a weekend bender, or after clearing the glasses after one of the master's shindigs."

"You *drank* the wine his guests left?" the woman asks incredulous. "Never mind," she turns away, "I really don't want to know." She grimaces, "any more than I do now."

The man shrugs indifferently, "it was that, or throw it away and that seemed a prissy waste."

The woman eyes him with new perception. "The master's car, tell me about that." He turns away nervously and she crosses her arms cupping elbows in her hands, posing the patience of Eternity.

"You changed…," he offers an alternate answer.

"The car first. *After* that…, comes your time to ask questions."

"They didn't find us." He snaps. "I *told* you they wouldn't look for a safe hole in the back of the cellar and we'd be safe there."

She frowns at the memory, "did the master or the mistress know about the safe hole?"

Shaking his head no, he adds "I found it the day the lady had me clear out the canning room and throw out the old fruit and vegetables to make room for the jars of fruit and vegetables harvested that year."

She smiles remembrance, "I'm thankful you threw the old food in the direction of the slave quarters. Even old vegetables and fruit in winter are better than none."

"And I thank you that the jars and lids were clean when you brought them back for the next canning, it saved me a caning. The mistress could be a hard woman at times."

"Civil war – was there *ever* a war that was civil? – And looters on the front porch make even generous folks tightfisted and mean. The mistress was a good and kindly woman before the war."

"She was that," the man agrees amiably.

"Could *none* of the family be saved? The girls…, the young boy?" The woman implores.

The man shakes his head quickly, "They knew how many were in the family, even the number of servants and slaves; it was dangerous business trying to save *anyone* let alone a whole family."

Her eyes narrow, "*How* did they know how many were in the family?"

"Looters. They kept their liberty by stealing and by turning in the ones they stole from. When some of master's horses came up missing from the far pasture, I knew what was coming. Men stole horses to sell to the blue coats, and then sold information about plantation owners and their families to the carpetbaggers. Hungry people *cannot* be trusted. A son who stayed behind to run the family farm was branded a Union supporter or a spy. Neither the Yanks nor the Rebs had money to feed hostages; or the medicine to treat wounded civilians."

The woman watches him thoughtfully a long while and asks "*why* was no one but me and you in the safe hole big enough for the whole family?"

"Too much risk, I told you that," the man snaps clam tight shut.

"Too much risk for whom?"

"If they'd come and found nobody in the house, they'd have searched first, taken what they wanted, then torched the place, watched while it burned, and shot anyone who ran from the fire. *Everyone* would have died then, is that what you wanted? This way at least you and I live."

"You and me…." Her eyes are clear solemn sad, "The master, his wife and children, the servants and slaves were taken away with everything of value including the contents of master's safe and the lady's jewel case. The safe hole *was big enough to keep them safe too.*"

"I'm telling you the carpetbaggers *knew* how many were in the family, how many slaves, how many horses and cows, if I'd tried to hide the family *we'd* have been at risk even in the safe hole."

"*How* did they know? Carpetbaggers had never been that far south before…. The master and his family were good people, they cared for the slaves as well as for the servants, horses and stock animals," she pauses "that's a sadly rare state in the slave owning South. Someone turned them in for money, or for their own freedom…." Her eyes narrow "someone who knew when they would come and had time to hide before they arrived." The man tucks his head and does not speak. "Someone who *didn't* tell the raiders about the Rolls Royce and the *other* slave you hid with you. Tell me why you did that."

"I did it for you," he protests peevish.

Her laugh is sour, "You never did a thing for anybody unless you got paid for it. *Why* did you hide me and no one else?"

"You're like a daughter to me," he explains shy soft serious, "a daughter I never had." He pleads into her eyes and she knows he speaks his truth and she does not understand nor believe a word of it.

"So, you think it is okay to feed off another human – a *daughter* – so long as you fancy they owe you?"

"No!" He protests, "It's not that at all, I owe *you*…."

"*Why?*" She crosses her arms, and waits.

"You were born because of me." He admits in a whisper and a hush falls over the room, even the wall clock waits without tick or tock for the remainder of the tale.

"Before you were born, the master held a posh party and all the plantation owners, their families, and a few old bachelors that couldn't keep a mate if she was deaf, dumb and blind were invited. I owed one such man a gambling debt I couldn't pay. The master refused to help me, said he would not countenance his employees gambling, let alone lend or give them money to pay a gaming debt.

"The man I owed was at the party, horny old devil...; and he fancied your mother."

The woman's mouth rounds in silent dread of what comes next. Heedless of all save himself, the oblivious orator continues "the horny wolf said he'd forgive the gambling debt on the spot *if* I arranged for him to have time alone with your mother during the gala. I said no, of course; and he threatened me, saying he'd see me in debtor's prison until I rotted unless I did what he required. When I hesitated he vowed he'd get me fired unless I made the arrangements for him *that night*.

"What's a man to do but what a man has to do? I told your ma a guest wanted to use the master's study awhile and she needed to go there and make sure the master's papers were locked away and the room well cleaned. Well, she'd cleaned the room that day, as always, and told me that the study was spotless and that the master's papers were locked away in his desk or safe as was his constant habit.

"The butler, as you know, manages the house staff so I ordered your ma to go. I told her she was to wait there until I came to get her..., which I had no intention of doing until the randy wolf returned to the party and gave back my token." Keeping his head low he murmurs "You were born nine months later."

The woman shudders with shock and whispers: "I am the child of *rape*! My mother was *raped* because of you? who had responsibility for the wellbeing of the servants and slaves? And bodily raped by a randy rooster she despised so you would be excused of a debt you owed the man?" Anger explodes in her. "How *could* you? How could you save yourself from the consequences of your own ravenous lust for ill-gotten gains by betraying *all* the house slaves to satisfy your venial vile greed? No *wonder* the other household slaves shunned her, they blamed her rather than you because they had to obey you..., just as my mother did. If you arranged for my mother's rape, they were *all* at risk of being pimped by you.... But if mother went *willingly*, they could..., and did, make her their pain eater... for she could not hurt them."

"Just *her*." The man defends dimly, "none of the other slaves was ever touched, then or later."

"*Touched*?" The woman cries, "Do you *imagine* no other slave was harmed by your betrayal of duty to the master? Do you even *imagine* the other slaves didn't know what happened? Didn't know when mother began to show that they *too* were at risk of betrayal by the man the master entrusted to care for their well-being? You are a *despicable* human being!" She spins away screeching, "Can I *kill* him?"

Counselor places a calming hand on her arm, "*he* may deserve a quick death, but you do not. Our Sheriff Ben would be duty bound to arrest you for murder; and I, bound to hear your case and sentence you to prison for *premeditated* murder." Counselor allows time for consideration of the facts and evidence; and adds "It is a hard sentence for you who have been through so much, to be content with the sharp slippery satisfaction of killing a man who wronged you and your mother."

Her eyes weep into his, "mother could never *love* me," she pleads, "She could not *be* mother to me. I was an orphan though my mother lived and breathed. The slaves shunned and punished her, believing she went willing to the covetous man. She suffered that indignity alone and mute in her shaming."

Sheriff Ben clears his throat calling all eyes to him and away from the stricken woman across the circle. "Tell us how it happened that you left your master's service."

Welcoming the topic change, the orator reclaims his place at center stage. "Well sir that is a powerful curious tale in itself, and one I'm happy to share with you. As I said before, the carpetbaggers came and looted the house taking the master and his family away. I was able to save myself and this slave girl."

"And the Rolls Royce," Ben adds.

"Yes; the car too."

"Why didn't the carpetbaggers find the master's auto?" The woman probes, regaining her composure.

His smile is self-congratulatory, "Well that's because I drove the auto to the gully back of the house and covered it with windfall and brush so they'd not find it, you see I knew those greedy bastards would take that fine auto too if they found it."

"Then you knew they were coming and took time to hide the car and prepare yourself?" Ben observes.

"Yes sir, that is a true story, and it was right clever of me too if I do say so myself."

"*How* did you know they were coming?" the woman demands.

He pauses before speaking, "You may not know this but gambling at cards always involves hard spirits that loosen men's tongues and one of the gamers said he'd heard at market that the carpetbaggers were coming South looting and killing and taking whatever they could sell or trade for liquor, so I hastened home and prepared myself for what was to come."

"You prepared yourself by hiding your master's auto?" Ben asks conversationally and the orator nods agreeably, "and by taking the car title and one slave document from the master's safe?"

"Well sir, the way you phrase that is not kindly at all. It is downright unfriendly if you ask me."

"Which I didn't. My question had to do with *intent...*, having to do with that car outside, and with this woman you brought with you and who now bears *your mark*." Ben softly hisses the last two words.

"Now see, that's just plain discourteous, and judgmental too, the way you say it."

Ben shrugs and cocks a brow indifferently, "I'm in law enforcement; I'm not paid to be polite when questioning a suspect."

"A suspect? Suspect of *what*?" the orator demands.

"Theft of an automobile; theft of a slave. Selling out your master and his family isn't against the law, at least not in this state, but such treachery is downright reprehensible to good folks everywhere."

The orator blanches and lowers his eyes but cannot hide his unease at the direction the exchange is taking. Watching closely by nature and training, Ben observes the orator casting about for an escape route, looking first toward the door by which he entered the room. The man feels more than sees Jacob's casual vigilance and winces at the memory of Michael and his upright silver sword. He casts the front door option aside looking for a back exit, and notices for the first time the burly man standing like a wooden statue with a proprietorial presence by the counter and the door leading to the back.

"You haven't met Smithy yet have you?" Ben asks tipping his chair back on two legs. "Smithy is practically a legend around here because if he hasn't got the part you need in stock, he'll forge it for you and it will fit better than the original. That Rolls need any replacement parts before you take off again?" Silence permeates the great room. "Since you have no answer to my questions, I believe the lady has a question or two still unanswered, why don't you do her the courtesy of giving your answers while you consider your available options."

"She's no lady," the visitor snaps.

"You don't treat her like one, but that's a different measure altogether; and by my lights you are a far piece from measuring up." Ben uprights his chair with a sharp crack that resounds like a shot causing the man to jump nervously.

"Let me refresh your memory then, the lady asked why you didn't save the master and his family, and what happened to them when the carpetbaggers came and took them away."

"I don't know," the orator sullen snaps.

"You don't know, or you think it's safer to ignore the question?"

Hester steps to Ben's side laying a cool hand on his shoulder, "perhaps I can be of help Ben." She says pleasantly then turns to the man. "Tell me about the master's family, were there children?"

Her soft conversational style is disarming and the man replies readily, "yes, mam, he had four children, three girls and a boy, he was right proud of those young ones he was."

She smiles "how old are they?"

"The boy was the oldest, nine or ten, I imagine, the girls were seven, five and three, fine looking youngsters they were."

"You speak of them in past tense, why is that?"

The man starts, "because they were taken away with the master and his lady, I've not seen them since."

She nods "so in your mind they won't have aged in the six months since you left with this woman?"

"Well, yes, mam, they will have aged six months since then." He snaps with a firm frown.

"What do you suppose happened to the family after they were taken away?"

"Oh, mam, those carpetbaggers are beasts of a nasty nature, they'll have sold them into slavery unless I miss my guess."

"Slavery?" The cocoa woman gasps, "You sold them into *slavery?*"

"No! I done no such thing! I ain't responsible for what lawless carpetbaggers do."

Hester rubs her chin thoughtfully and observes, "I notice when you speak to me you use proper English as I imagine a butler at a plantation house might do; but when you speak to this woman you brought here against her will, that you use common language, why is that do you suppose?"

"I – I didn't notice."

Bobbing her head she observes "Yes, I have detected that pattern before in people who only respect up, and always *dis*respect down." The woman catches Hester's eye and gives her a knowing smile. Only Hester's eyes return the smile as she turns back to the man now dressed in aged brocade. "Why do you believe the family will have been sold into slavery?"

"Because they're used to eating well when they're hungry. An army moves on its stomach. The bluecoats pay well for fresh food, the grays…, they have nothing but confederate paper," he spits the words. "Soft potatoes growing roots are worth more than a whole *box* of confederate money."

"Hum, I see you make it a point to be well informed." The man nods heartily. "You said you thought the family was sold into slavery, who would purchase a family of soft plantation owners as slaves?"

"Uh – oh, well, there are men who like fresh meat if you take my meaning, and the master's girls were pretty young things."

"Oh…, my poor sweet baby girls," she the woman wails into hands that shield her mouth but leave her eyes unmasked to clearly see the horror of the man's words and deeds.

With brutal candor, Doc eyes the man while speaking to the woman "not just the girls, dear heart, the boy too."

"No-o-o-o!" She wails a supplication and denial. "No, no, *no!*"

Doc nods his own misery "and the mother…, and the father as well."

"*No!*" The woman screams protest of the unthinkable. Springing from her chair she stamps the floor with both feet and yells "*can* – I - kill - him?"

"He's not worth it, woman," snaps Counselor taking her arm and pulling her firmly back to the chair indifferent to the tears now staining his suit coat.

"Hes," Jacob inserts from across the circle, "maybe you could let him make a break for it and then Ben can shoot him trying to escape."

Ben grins "tempting…, but that's not happening on my watch. Keep the Archangel on alert though."

"Oh like he *ever* sleeps?" Jacob grumbles.

Hester rolls her eyes, stifles a grin, and turns back to the visitor. "Tell us about the car and the one slave you saved, why did you choose to do that?"

"I needed the car, and," he winces "the girl matters to me, I care about her and her safety."

Hester cannot make her brows *not* arch sharply, "*Safety?* To have her blood sucked by the man who stole her, now claims to own her, yet calls her *daughter?* Curious kindness you offer your kin. How much money did you get for selling the family to the carpetbaggers?"

"What?" The man snaps eyes to hers.

Hester shrugs indifferently, "I'm curious by what motivates a man such as you who openly claims no integrity or morality, yet pretends to be a good and thoughtful man. Were you ever an actor?"

"Yes," the man smiles broadly "how did you know?"

Hester's brow bobs, "Mother always said I was psychic," she says dryly, "perhaps that's it."

"Could you tell my future?"

Hester replies in solemn exasperation "I don't think that's a good idea today!" A giggle arises in the circle followed by a chortle then a guffaw and soon the round is laughing and slapping thighs in glee.

"What's so damned funny" the orator demands red faced.

"You are, that's what." The elder sister growls as she rises from her chair to stand before the orator. "Any fool can tell your fortune today and safely predict that you won't like it. Hester's no fool…, *fool*."

"Well I ain't talking to you am I?"

The younger sister blasts from her chair to leap protectively before her elder. "*Don't* speak to my sister like she's a slave!" Her eyes flash menace, "or I'll *bite you* and spit your blood in your face. Maybe you can use your long bat tongue to lick it off and *drink it*." She hisses. "It may be your last supper."

The orator turns a bilious green in the face of the scalding scolding threat and searches the circle for a friendly face or even a soft pair of eyes. Finding none, and possessed of a consuming passion to be anywhere else but where he is and calls plaintive to a nameless god who, surprisingly, comes to his aid in the form of a dragon that sweeps him from his chair and into infinity beyond the roof of a local Feed and Grain store.

"Well! Whoda thunk it? *Another* dragon rider!" Settling back in his chair the man adds, "Let's give points like this is a rodeo and him a bareback rider."

"He's plainly got no experience riding bareback. I'll give him two minutes tops before he's dropped in the dirt." Ben growls, "Smithy, when *are* you going to sweep this floor again?"

"When a dang bunch of farmers quit tracking in plow dirt and grain dust, when I ain't busy all day fixing broken parts or forging new ones because your trucks are too old to have replacement parts, when…."

"Okay, okay, Smithy…, don't get your dander up, I'm just asking."

"*Smart ass*-king if you ask me," Smithy growls a surly smirk.

"I didn't…, but thanks for sharing." There is a chortle, a giggle, then a snort, and soon the circle is laughing and hooting until Smithy can do naught but join, his barrel chest raucous as a forge blast.

When the circle settles again, returns to watching the dragon flight and calling points or demerits with no one keeping score, someone asks "when you plan to have my transmission repaired so I can drive my truck again?"

"*Repaired*? Your truck is so damn old there are no parts to fix it anymore so I'm having to forge you a whole new transmission. Ya otta just get a new truck," he grumbles sotto voice.

"Hell, I'll do good to pay for the transmission rebuild let alone a new truck."

"That's what keeps me up nights worrying."

"You got a *forge*?" The woman asks short-circuiting the intermittently unvarying squabble.

Smithy looks round the circle for the voice finding it in the face and wide eager eyes of the cocoa woman. "Course I got a forge, that's why I'm called Smithy. Had a real name once but I plumb forgot it now," he complains to his beefy hands. "Why do you ask?" he looks into the eyes of the woman giving free rein to his puzzled curiosity.

"Do you think…, I mean, could I…?"

"Spit it out, woman," he says with feigned vexation.

"Do you think I could make glass in your forge?" she asks in a rush of words.

"*Glass*? Why on Gods earth would you want to make something as common as glass?"

The woman flushes lowering her eyes timidly, then inhales and raises bold eyes to meet his. "Because I want to make beautiful things out of glass, and I need a kiln to do it." Her lip juts resolutely.

Smithy's curiosity flares like a heated forge and he asks as calmly as possible, "*why*?"

The woman blinks puzzlement and has no reply. Smithy shrugs contorting his face into confusion, then rephrases his question "Okay, what is it you *do* you want to make in glass?"

"Beautiful things – I already said that."

Smithy's head bobs and his eyes go round. "What *kind* of beautiful things do you want to make?"

"Oh…," again she is without words to speak her dreams and her face wilts and her eyes well for the weight of idea that cannot be cramped into words. "Have you any shop paper?" She asks instead.

"*Shop paper*?" He repeats thrown.

"Yeah," she frowns, "like brown paper you wrap things in when you sell them."

"Of course I do, there's a roll of it behind the counter." She beams a brilliant smile, jumps from her chair and dashes behind the counter. "Did you *ask* if you could use some of my shop paper and I missed it?" He scratches the back of his beefy neck to hide a mischievous grin.

He hears the woman's hands plop on the counter. "Can I *please* use some of your paper, Smithy?"

"Sure, how much you need? And what do you need it for?"

"I don't know how much. I will use it to draw things I can't say in words."

Smithy's eyes round and his brows raise. "Oh," he says to a circle of grinning open faces. "Reckon you'll be done by the time the stranger returns from his dragon ride?" he wonders.

"Don't know. Why, does it matter? You got some charcoal?"

"*Charcoal?* I got a forge, woman, of course I got charcoal."

"Um…, would you show me where it is?"

Smithy laughs the way a father might at a difficult daughter asking too many questions without answers. Rising he passes the counter waiving a brawny hand to the woman to follow and hears her scampering feet trailing him. *"Daughter"* he thinks, *"whoda thunk it? And me without a wife."*

"I reckon you'll wants sticks of charcoal if you'll be drawing things that can't be explained." She arches a brow and tilts him a grin. "And I reckon you'll want hardwood charcoal so it don't break unless you want it to. You know how to tell hardwood charcoal from soft wood, like cottonwood?"

"I sure do," she replies studying the charcoal sticks "hardwood burns slower than soft wood and is more black than grey like soft wood is," she says fingering a grey stick that crumbles at her touch. She then touches a black stick and picks it up with a brilliant smile. "This one will do for now."

Smithy reaches into the ash pile to pick out more black sticks tucking them into a paper bag and handing her the bag. "Just in case you have a *lot* of things you can't tell but can draw."

Her smile is brilliant, "Thank you, Smithy, you're the best!" Raising to her toes she plants a soft kiss on his cheek and turns away quickly so as not to see his blush. "Ready?" she asks turning back and pulling him along in her excitement to draw imagined beautiful things. "How about chalk, you got chalk?"

I might just follow you anywhere you lead, Smithy thinks but instead laughs and says "I got chalk too."

Back inside the girl woman scampers behind the counter and begins slashing flowing curving lines on the sheet of shop paper totally losing herself in the heart and art of creation.

| **John Adorney:** <u>Always Remembering You</u> |

Curious at the focused work of the woman, the Regaliaed One rises and walks softly to the counter to see what she draws with such power and purpose. Despite herself, she sighs a soft smile disturbing the woman who stops mid stroke to look up at her. "Oh, I'm so sorry, I did not mean to interrupt or disturb you…. But that is so *utterly* beautiful I could not contain myself. Finish dear, please finish." Her face creases "may I watch…, if I promise to remain *absolutely* silent?"

Across the room Counselor chortles, "My darling wife, I have come to believe that it is utterly impossible for you to remain silent for any length of time. You even sleep out loud."

"Oh hush! Telling bedroom tales in public! Shame on you." Though her tone is severe she makes no effort to hide her smile of shared pleasure with her husband. "Wait until you see the birthday gift you will give me, Darling." Turning back to the woman she asks "you *can* make this in crystal can you not?"

The woman smiles and nods "I can…, *if* Smithy will let me use his forge to make the glass and blow the pitcher, will you Smithy?"

"That I will," Smithy agrees readily. "You *do* know how to use a forge don't you?"

"I sure do, Smithy, and before you ask, I know what I'll need to make glass, all of which is commonly available, sand, soda, and ash, the ash can come from your forge." She grins impishly "can I have some of your *ash*, Smithy?" The room erupts in glee as Smithy's face reddens and not from laughter alone.

"Let me introduce myself," the watching woman grins, "I am the Regaliaed One."

The woman blinks doubtfully and says, "Your *name* is *Regaliaed One*?"

"Yes, dear. You would have to know my dear departed mother to understand such a curious name. It's a tale not worth telling. Call me RO, like everyone else." Touching a corner of the page, RO asks "may I?"

"Not yet," the woman blocks her hand, "it isn't finished." She smiles as she caresses chalk onto the paper pulling highlights on the round bowl, the comfy curved handle, and on pouting the lip of the pitcher. When she is finished adjusting and admiring her drawing, she nods to RO who takes it and turns to walk to Counselor saying "look, darling, at the birthday gift you will give to me."

Counselor studies the charcoal and chalk drawing for a long while and the woman holds her breath through the silence. "That is utterly exquisite in its gracefully simple lines, it is no wonder you like it, my dearest RO, but could you lift and pour from a pitcher made of crystal *and* filled with liquid?"

RO rubs his cheek fondly "well, my dearest, if it is too heavy for me, then you will have to pour for me will you not?"

Counselor smiles up at her "I would walk to hell and back for you my dearest," he says. "Yes, I will pour for you, and I will pour making certain each and every guests has a clear view of your exquisite pitcher and they will be as envious of your birthday gift as they are of your luscious lemonade." Hearts soften around the circle seeing the unabashed affection shared between the two, and each silently pledges to love their own mate with more genuine warmth and good humor.

"Okay, I must see the drawing" Hester says rising from her chair to step behind Counselor and peer over his shoulder. She is soon joined by others who also do not speak but smile in silent wonder.

"Okay, pass it around so all of us can see" demands a sitter.

"No *way* is that happening!" RO replies firmly. "It's drawn in charcoal and chalk and if someone blurs even one line or shadow on it I will have their head on a platter" she grins cheekily "*just* like Salomé. I'll bring the drawing around so everyone can see."

As RO steps away, Counselor pushes up from his chair to walk softly to the counter and lean across to whisper to the woman. "What you have created with charcoal, chalk and paper is not only functional, it is art, and even though the piece is utilitarian, your work must – and *will* – command the price of art. When you have completed this piece you will make for my RO's birthday gift, I will set your expectations by paying you the price of art for this piece. Thereafter, I will teach and coach you so that *none* of your glasswork is sold for less than the value of art."

The woman stares at him openmouthed and speechless. Fatherly now, he pats her arm and smiles. "The next thing you make for RO will be even more priceless," he breathes, "it's a thing she's wanted a long time and could not find. It will be a one of a kind." His eyes follow RO with an adoring light, then turns back to the silent woman to add, "RO had no way – before today – to have her vision made manifest. You can do that for her. And as God is my witness you will be paid its worth, even if I have to work another decade to keep my word to you," he grins and pats her hand, "it is already done."

As Counselor returns to his chair, Smithy hears the woman pull another sheet of shop paper from his role and smiles a soft heartfelt smile. *Whoda thunk I'd have a probably profitable glass forge instead of a make-ends- meet metal forge? The wonders of the Lord are an unending amazement.*

Return of the Dragon Rider

In the midst of the milling circle of friends, the orator plops unceremoniously to the chair from which he was swept puffing mighty bellows of air into and out of his lungs.

"That was quite a ride you took there, fellow." Ben comments, "For a while I thought you'd fall plumb off that dragon and be lost in space forever. Catch your breath and tell us about your ride." Eagerly the milling group returns to their chairs and settles in again, expectant eyes fixed on the returned rider.

"Well, sir and ladies; that was indeed a unique experience and one I fondly hope never to again have."

"Was it bad?" the cocoa woman asks gentle concern evident in her voice.

The orator studies the one he so cruelly used and sees nothing but sincerity. He shakes his head smiling. "Only at first when I was hanging on for dear life and knew that dire dragon was doing all in its daunting power to unseat me and ditch me forever on some god forsaken planet. Which he did do, in fact.

"The first sunrise on that petite plain planet, the dragon chastised me right proper for abusing animals *so callously, his* words. I defended myself for I was the master's horse trainer, many of which won championships for him and brought extra income from stud fees. The master had an eye for spirit power in horses; that he did. I was an important part of his success.

"Well that dragon filled its lungs – I feared – to shoot flames at me and burn me to a carbon crisp, but instead, he just thundered at me. Have you any idea what a roaring dragon *sounds like* in deep space? My ears hurt now just remembering that boundless bellowing voice. My heart pains me remembering the lecture he delivered into my face at blow your hair back force and power. That daunting dragon demanded to know whether I had trained the master's horses with *equal* insensitivity to the body, *mind* and hide of the animal or if I had somehow, simply forgotten how to be sensitive to other living creatures than horses." He winces, "Singed my hair ends it did, gave me a dark leathery tan in seconds.

"The dragon required me to say honest and true if the only thing that mattered to me was the way *my training* showed up in the obedient body and mind of the animal…, and, well, it was. If something else mattered to me, the dragon demanded that I name what it was, and why it counted for me.

"Well that got my back bowed up and I informed the brute beast I was one of the *best* horse trainers the South ever produced. Thought I was bragging that dragon did, demanded me to prove it. That set me to thinking about some of the horses I'd trained and recollecting the ways I talked to a new horse while I fed, petted, admired, exercised, groomed and curried it. I'd tell the horse all the amazing and lovely things I saw in it, and when they were preening and proud and eager, I'd set them to a run or another task to test and prove the speed, grace and pace.

"I did the same with the dragon as I talked and soon enough all its scales were unruffled. I threw an arm over the dragons back while I told of doing the same to a horse to let the animal experience and practice the new and strange in a safe way. I scratched it soft where muscles connect, palming over the smooth shining hide and the long muscles of the legs; and just when I thought the dragon and me were bonding…, real snotty like, that demon dragon demands to know how I can make such claims having torn a *dozen* of his finest scales from his neck, back and shoulders.

"When he did let me on his back again I saw not one damaged or dislocated scale on that bitter beast. He'd made his point though, and I proved mine or I'd not have been allowed on his back again.

"*Fine* beast that one is; scales the color of morning sunshine and moss in a deep clear pond, with eyes of red and gold. What they say about dragons spitting fire from their mouths, I never saw that, though his eyes spit fire that burned through my heart and down into the roots of my soul. Made me weep it did.

"When the dragon saw my tears it gentled a bit and demanded I tell him *how* I could tame horses to reins, saddle and rider, yet could not ride a dragon without ruining its *fine precious* scales.

"Well you don't have a saddle, or reins that I can see," I snapped back defensive and just as snotty.

"Oh like you'd have *noticed* anything but yourself?" the dragon snarled. That took me plum aback. I was speechless for the first time in my life. *How?*, the beast demanded again, so I told him everything I did with a horse before I ever lay a blanket on its back as gentle and tender as a mother covering a sleeping babe, all the while doing the same with the dragon…, whose heart is touched, I can tell.

"Now I know that dragons have hearts just like every other living breathing thing on God's green Earth…, and on other every living planet and star beyond that too. It all made me smile, but that the wee planet was as cold as hell is hot and my cheeks was plumb froze to ice. So I talked to that dragon warm and gentle and sweet just like I did the master's horses I trained to ride and race.

"That dragon took pity on me and puffed up his chest and cheeks, and I thought I was about to be scorched as hard and brittle as a lump of coal. Instead, that gold and emerald creature puffed damp warm-hot air down on me and my wee planet until rain fell and grass sprouted and bushes and trees were full with fruit hanging ripe and heavy on its branches, and silver rivers sang and splashed and played in an atmosphere much like other planets close to the sun, all warm and balmy it was.

"But not a *trace* of game anywhere on that whole new Earth. Well, folks, I do like the taste and chew of meat so I complained to that dragon that evening. When he came back the next day, and every day thereafter, the dragon brought fresh meat of small birds and game, gutted clean as a whistle, and that marvelous monster carried them in its great mouth where they baked and broiled to succulent perfection in its juices.

"Thought I might like to stay there, but that dragon had other plans for me. I slept on that small paradise for seven nights, and every sunrise the dragon came to set me on a new errand for the day and to prove it done, I was to bring him a token. Every day at sunset the dragon came for dinner and a chat.

"You weren't gone more than 20 minutes!" Ben declares doubting.

"True as that may be, sir," the teller grins, "still I spent seven mornings and evenings on that planet."

The room silently puzzles the teller's tale against Ben's fine point of time. "It seems you know a bit about the first chapter of the Bible," Ben allows. "Continue with your tale, there's a storyteller in you – and maybe you don't know that yet." All eyes return to the teller.

"Where was I? Oh yes, my first day with – or without, actually – the dragon. We had a nice brunch, fruit, berries, tubers with grains and herbs, and we talked friendly like. Then without so much as an if you please, that brute beast grabbed me up in its claws and flew me up and away, dropping me rudely in a small round boat without sail or mast, oars or oarlocks, and no rudder – in the middle of an ocean without a horizon and only a hazy half-light to see by. Of course, there was nothing to *see*, that being the first day of creation.

"At sundown the dragon came with food, and asked me to tell about my first day and what I'd experienced and learned, so I told him about the boat – which bored him *angry* – he seemed to think I was a complaining ingrate."

"*Imagine....*" The woman says thoughtfully.

He gives her a narrow look and returns to his tale. "So I told of my day, not mentioning the feather at all; and there was little to tell without the boring boat and the endless sea in the tale." The teller grins mischievous, "So I'm making up stuff that might have happened but didn't to fill up the hours from sunup to sunset and still not mentioning the feather..., the only interesting thing that did happen. At that very moment the feather took the opportunity to poke me in the head in protest for being ignored, or worse, forgotten altogether." The man laughs remembering the squirming impatience of the dragon over the forgotten feather. "Unfortunately, I *still* don't know when to leave well enough alone," he tries but can't suppress a giggle, "and I baited that dragon until it wanted to bite my head off but there was the feather flashing fascinating contraries in delightful designs and he didn't want to damage the feather he wanted as his token of the day and my experience of it. He didn't want to bloody and gross it out.

"I live and breathe this day solely for the reason that I am to *strongly* warn everyone I meet against *ever* baiting a dragon." He shudders a shivering giggle remembering that he got away with *not* giving a required token to the dragon…, and lived to tell the tale of seven sunrises and sunsets with the dragon. "As you know, on the first day, the Creator separated heaven from the earth, and divided light from dark. Source made duality that day – that's it! And he saw that it was good *because* without opposites things don't show up in physical form; and all of creation was actually ideated on that first day.

"Including that wee boat without oars, sails or rudder in which I found myself adrift on a sea without horizon, in an infinite silence that echoed and reverberated without any sound at all. Silence… whispering eternally into the omnipresent ear of infinity…, and the dragon nowhere in sight Though alive and calm, I had an urgent hazy mindfulness of a forgotten mission needing completion before sundown and the niggling notion of a token of my day I am to give the dragon at sunset.

"Since I had nowhere to go and no way to get there, I set myself to grasping the Divine Idea behind dividing light from dark and the essential duality of energy inhabiting physical form. The very *idea* of life in form invokes duality into the creation inspired by the idea, so that must be the lesson the master dragon wants me to take from this *already stupid* game of days. As I pondered alone and adrift it occurs to me that duality is essential to the physical world but isn't to the Infinite. The infinite has polarity, but no duality.

"But what's the dragon token if duality is the message of the day?" I ask myself and fall into deep thought, so focused I take no notice of the feather dancing, spinning and weaving about and above me and my boat, one half black, one half white each with a dot of the other, one at the top, one at the tip. As the unreliably white feather danced and twirled it caught the light of day and the dark of night spinning and swirling the opposites into endlessly shaping possibilities of form, design and delight.

"*The dragon token*, I think to myself. At my very thought the feather shrinks away in a ghostly ghastly ghoul howl of black horror and fright white. I couldn't help myself, I laughed aloud…, and that further flustered the flighty feather whose India ink black part bled messy like into the white of its pattern.

"Well then," I said to the fuzzy feather, "I see you have – *costumes* to fit your mood; and the pattern changes with your thought. I'm curious, what *do* you wear when you decide that you are a simply precious one of a kind creation, you *love* that, and you think it is perfectly true and suits you *just right*?

"If I could have been in any one of a dozen different universes to see and experience thousands of new and wondrous things, I'd trade them all for watching that feather fluff her stuff in crisp quick mosaics of black and white. '*Oh* my!' Is all I can say when I catch a breath again, and she is suddenly shy.

"You are the most brilliant thing I have ever seen." I says thinking I'd found the perfect dragon token and then add, "The dragon will *love* you and will prize you as a fluid flawless emblem of the first day of creation when God separated light from darkness. You are light *and darkness* in molten motion. A worthy token for the dragon on this first day of my self-re-creation."

"It's all about you isn't it?" The feather sniffs turning away and showing mostly her dark side.

"You too," I retort. You *are* a feather after all. Nothing more than that…. *If* no one ever sees you to appreciate you… *and* your magnificent mutable manifestation."

The feather flutters into other possibilities, then poses pleasantly "where do you suppose your dragon pal might want towear me? And… do you think he will let me find my *own* place to ride his hide?"

"I imagine the dragon will let you find your own proud place *so long as* you make him look good at the same time. *This* dragon would wear you proudly and display you as art. Dragons live forever you know. It is *good* to have a way to be your most amazing self, and a forever place to show yourself proud." Well, that about settled it because the feather drifted down and corkscrewed itself into a curl of my hair. Yeah, I know my hair has no curl, but then it did, and I'm telling you what happened, nothing more."

"At sundown that day the dragon came and we drank tea and talked of the day, and all the while the dragon is studying the feather in my hair more than listening to me. Well, I commence making up words and talking like I had something to say…, until the dragon caught my eye, raised a brow, and said: "You are talking stuff and nonsense, and it offends me deeply that you think I won't notice." He sniffs his snit and thunders "What did you learn today? And where is my token? In that order, if you please."

"On the first day of creation, God called for light and saw that it was good. Then God separated the light from the darkness covering the surface of the deep and called the light day and the darkness night. It occurred to me that Spirit, First Cause is without form and is forever integrally whole and therefore *must* have little functional awareness of being separate in the way a human has a sense of being in separate skin and physical body mind brain. Spirit just is.

"And that *is* enough.

"Except it's *not*. There is no *experience* in beingness, it just is. People *need* things to do, goals to achieve, ways they can change the world into a better place. They need understanding, and the will to challenge habitual responses so that better experiences show up for them in life.

"That's why Spirit created a shadow self that is capable of facing the polarity that arises from inhabiting a mind with a consciousness of a self *very* separate from everything 'out there.' Thing is, everything 'out there' is *intrinsically* at-One with Spirit, except man who has an ego mind wholly *convinced* that it is and forever will be, separate from everything else that is, *including* The One That Is. My dear dragon, the feather is the token of the day. And, wait. Don't be grabby, *she* wants to find her own place to adorn your great scaly physique. Are you *okay* with that?" I demand, letting on I won't give it to him if not.

"It was a dumbfounded dragon that heard those words, the small skull beast could *not* comprehend a thing, anything, wanting to make it beautiful. Dragons may be magical and wise but they are *not* smart.

"Well, finally, after a flighty flirtation by the flying feather, the dragon sits on his hands to let the feather find its place, and welcome it aboard – enthusiastically when she suggests she perch on the ridge above its third eye and swing down before his great eye to show him all the options and both sides of any decision. *I will make you known as the Wise One among dragon kind for you alone shall see what I show to inspire wisdom and understanding in* every *decision, choice and change that comes. And,"* she hisses *"the one before you will see* only *a white fluttering feather..., you* cynical, skeptical *serpent.*

The dragon apologizes profusely until the feather appears appeased and takes its chosen place, then she pops a few sharp poses, cocks me a brow and asks *"How do I look?"*

"Well, folks, sore tempted I was but I didn't grin or laugh. I wrestled both grin and giggle into a sincere face with a mouth saying in earnest awe: "you look *magnificent*!"

The posing dragon freezes, cocks me a brow over a blasé eye and snaps "I *always* look magnificent. How do I look *with* the fabulous feather?"

"Even finer than before…, and I *thought* that would be impossible," I said with a sincere straight face.

"*Don't* make the same mistake again," the dragon drones dreadfully and I obey. Then and forevermore.

"The short story of day is that the dragon got his feather for a token by deciding to be simply delighted at the idea of the feather choosing its place of adorning, beautifying and flattering – yes, he liked *all* of that – such a powerful and provocative serpent. Thus day one ended in hushed peace and happiness.

"The dragon returns the second sunrise and after breakfast, sets the day's task for me, which is to understand and apply the Truth of what God did on the second day of creation, why God did that, and tell how that applies to me and my life, and, oh yes, bring back a token of my day's enlightenment. Then that sinister scaly serpent catches me up in its claws to fly far and fling me into the free floating coracle on a formless sea midway between never and forevermore.

"Well, on the second day of creation, God separated water from water and set an expanse between the water above and that below, and he called the expanse "sky" and the firmament he called heaven. I could tell the water under my boat was liquid because my boat floated on it and it made my hand wet. I knew the water above was atmosphere, air, because I could breathe it. That got me to thinking that maybe the water below represents the expressed capabilities of the subconscious mind – which can't think – but can ideate. If that be so, the subconscious mind *needs* the conscious mind to decide on the idea and then to will and declare the word of it, thereby directing the idea down to the subconscious where it evolves enough to be made manifest. Sort of like that dragon marinating meat in its maw until it is cooked to perfection for dining.

"So there I was the afternoon of day two and with the idea and again, no clue of a dragon token. So, I let that puzzle stew in my mind just like the first day while I had a wee nap in the boat and dreamed that a single drop of water coalesced from the sky above and fell into my boat at my feet. I sat looking down at that drop of water and I saw an ocean in the drop. That surprised and delighted me and I spent a minor eternity lost and contentedly adrift in that ocean in a drop…, until that danged dingbat bird came, cross and cussing, something about feather she lost the day before.

"Real calm like I asked the bird to describe her lost feather thinking it's a white feather because every feather on her body is solid white. Sure enough that dim fowl said it was a white feather just like her other ones. I knew she told a lie but played along to see where she'd lead, so I told her true and sincere that I had not seen a pure white feather before she arrived brilliantly full feathered with the very ones she sought after. Then I added that if she was missing even one feather I certainly couldn't tell because she looked *perfect* and perfectly handsome to me.

"Well that set her to preening, but I could tell something wasn't right with that batty bird and it wasn't physical either, she was *lying* sure and clear. *Why* though? I decided to play her out and I asked about her missing feather, to describe it in detail, and then, as a kindness to me I asked her to tell me why she would even want one missing feather back since she was perfectly, stunningly beautiful just as she stood. One more feather, I said, would be *redundant*, would spoil her peerless perfection.

"She pouted anyway, silly bird, so I asked her again to describe the missing feather in detail, so I could tell the dragon all about it when I saw him and state why she wanted that one feather back so much. Which she did do, in *dreary* detail; and never saying a word about *anything* but a white feather.

"I was *really* wary now. Enough that I completely forgot about the dragons daily token and peeled my newly narrowed eyes away from the gift potential of an ocean in the drop, and fixed 'em the cawing bird flying stationary before me. "First, you must describe the feather to me in *complete* detail. Then you will explain to me *why* you are being *simply rude to me* who never did you one single harm in all the moments you have known me!" Well I may as well have hit the bird upside the head with a two by four because she commenced to gasping, flapping her wings and squeaky cawing screeching until she plumb run out of wind, and fell like a stone into my wee round boat squashing that ocean in a drop the way eons of heat, weight and time will do, into a flawless diamond of faultless cut, clarity and brilliance.

"Then I laugh because apparently that transformation of substance let off enough heat to blast that bird off it and into the sky with such force that the hot rock dropped from her thigh and into the sea sinking into the infinite blue below. My dragon token of the day was gone beyond reach or recovery.

"The dragon didn't forget. Dragons don't forget, plus they have no functional grasp of time whatsoever. When he arrived at sunset and heard the mean bird's complaint the dragon cocked brow and set a cold gold eye on her and asked why one missing feather was so significant to her that she'd *beard a dragon in its den* for a solution. The sly snake knew that she'd lie, or if not lie, at least fail to tell the whole truth, nor drop a hint or clue that she knew about the changeable nature of the missing feather.

"The – the feather is – um - white, all white." The white bird titters nervous and shakes a wingtip at the feather suspended over dragon's third eye. "Like the one in the middle of your head!" She tries not to snap her beak closed but snap she does.

Dragon eyes up at feather, gives it a private grin and thought whispers *good job!*, then turns his wicked eye and a grim grin on the plump white foul saying with a sad shake of his head "I'm afraid I can't help you, I have seen no pure white feather such as the one you describe.

"There's one on your *head,* you doltish dragon!" the hot hen retorts, losing her mind, and jeopardizing her head in the boot.

Dragon's eyes narrow, he purrs in a way that sounds disturbingly like hissing "*why* do you want *my* feather? Which you *sorely* abused by dumping all your dark angry thoughts and feelings into this *one tiny little feather* – and now you say you want it *back*?" The dragon snaps, "So you can abuse it *again,* even more, and maybe even *better* than before?"

The bird blinks owlishly three times in a futile attempt to process what the dragon said and the upshot of it. It doesn't compute. "Oh!" she flaps her wings in exasperation, "you just don't get it do you, you myopic monster. What you see as abuse was me *honoring* her among all my feathers by preparing her to live well and prosper in the physical world where she will go, but I will not. Have you *any idea* how long it takes pure-as-the-driven-snow *me* to gather and collect enough negative energy to make even one small dot of black on a feather? Oh, that won't have occurred to *you* will it, your wee small head on so gigantic a body *can't* hold much brain can it?" The bird is teetering on the edge of insanity lost in the *story* behind the rage of her tight grip on anger and gaga giddy with the power of *finally* having a place, *and* an occasion, to speak her pique.

Sounding miffed the dragon snaps "there's no need to be cruel or to say offensive things about someone you never ever met before!" Leaning an elbow on a knee the dragon rests his chin on a paw and invites, "Tell me *why* you'd go to all this effort to collect *dark energy?* What will you do with it…, if you ever get *enough?*"

"Easy for you to ask! You have enough darkness in one small claw to create massive black holes housing *dozens of* eternities." She peeps at the dragon whose jaw still rests in a paw, his maw set in an amused but bored smile, waiting for a hen's reason while eyeing her lost feather flashing mostly black into his third eye. The bird takes another rarely used tack – confession. Truth.

"You see," she says, "That one feather of all my brood has a dream of living on a place called Earth that she says God will create on the fifth day but I'm just a mother I don't know these things. My fine feather wants to be a bird God will create that day to fly above the earth and to sing joy songs every morning and evening.

"Well *that's* a noble cause," the dragon notes, "perhaps I can help."

"Help? *You? How?*"

"You can have some of my darkness." His grin is a torrid tease, "As you keenly observed, I've more than enough for one *infinite* dragon lifetime, to feed your – oh wait…, it's *my* feather now – *my* forward looking feather that may *already* have enough darkness to live long and prosper on the Earth that God will make. What is an *Earth*, does anyone know?"

"Read Genesis. You'll get the whole story there." The bad bird barks.

"Acting superior *always* makes me cross;" the dragon rumbles, "and I'm *already* annoyed enough with you for abusing your feather, to broil you whole and eat you for dinner." The white bird goes a ghostly shade of pale and shivers in her pins while the dragon lounges into a more comfortable position, then orders: "Tell me *everything* you know about this Genesis story, especially the fifth day of it, and I will *forgive* that you were unkind to me. Dragons never forget…." He shrugs, "And *rarely* forgive…."

The bird swallows hard – three times – to finally get what she *really* wants to say back down her craw. She takes a deep breath and hits the high points of the first four days of creation and then tells our now enchanted dragon about the Great One creating hoofed, clawed, and winged things on the fifth day. On that day *her* fine feather would descend to Earth and become a bird. She sighs a motherly satisfied smile as she ends her tale in uncommon peace and silence.

"The dragon's eyes narrow in thought and the dim bulb bird thinks it's all about her like she's the center of the universe and everything in it and so the narrow eyes *must* signal the beast's irritation with *her* story and shivers in her simple silliness. The dragon rumbles his inspiration "Why don't *you* become a bird that goes to earth on the fifth day of creation?"

The staggered bird needs an instant of eternity to process that she is no longer on the dragon menu before she can process the idea the dragon offered. "Me?" she peeps, "me go to Earth… as a bird?"

"Why not you? If not you then who?"

"Oh…. Well then, what sort of bird would I be?"

"A patio pigeon?" offers the droll dragon.

"What's a patio?"

"I think you should be a parrot!" I interject before the dragon can answer the patio question.

"What's a parrot?" the bird asks squinting in an effort to imagine one.

"I smile because I can't help it, then I reply: "a parrot is a magnificent bird with feathers in every color you can imagine and long bright plumes on its tail and head." Seeing her uncertainty I add: "Better than being entirely insipid snow white like you are now."

"I'm a beautiful white!" she protests petulant.

"Until the dragon puffs hotly *"who put all her* own *darkness* into this one small feather!" He inhales to cool down and adds sweetly to the bird, "If you'd kept it all yourself, you'd already be a *fine* pigeon!"

"Don't ask," I order the pigeon. "You don't want to know," I assure her before she can put her foot in the dragon's mouth. I see her bird brain process the vision of a mostly grey bird with bits of black and white, which she promptly discards, along with the impetuous idea of perplexing a petulant dragon.

"That was the end of that, and the dragon took the white bird as his token for the second day giving her the position of helping him mother *his* feather and receiving some of its duality wisdom while she prepares for the fifth day of creation, and her debut on Earth stage. That day ended well except the petulant wannabe parrot would do naught but complain about the burdens of tending a feather she couldn't even *reach* without going perilously proximate to the jaws of a dire dragon.

"On the third morning the dragon came with broiled game and we had our breakfast feast with fruit and grains I'd gathered the evening before and when we'd had our fill, the dragon asked me to tell him all about the third day of creation and so I told about the Divine One dividing the water from dry land and causing it to produce vegetation, seed bearing plants and trees each seed according to its kind. The dragon nods agreeably and then clutches me up in its claws and wings me back to that coracle adrift on a sea now separate from land and drops me there. Well, that fine boat charts its own course and soon lands me on a beach where honeymooners will one day go to begin their together lives in idyllic bliss and beauty. Before I set foot on the sandy beach I was already convinced that green must be God's favorite color because every bush, tree, herb and fern was alive with iridescent greens of every shade and hue. Seeds were the Divine gift of the third day, and the dragon's gift on this third day of creation.

The utter abundance and variety of seed bearing things stopped me in my tracks. *How do I know and learn the seed for each seeding thing since some are in pods – easy enough – some in tassels of grasses, some cloaked in plump fine fruit, and some nested deep in the earth among the roots of that green and seeding thing? How do I collect and carry them?*

As thought staged this way, a woman gowned in green rises effortlessly and steps from a moss lined pool to move on a scented breeze to where I stand. She smiles and whispers, "You ask the plant to reveal itself and its power and vitality to you in a way that you will clearly understand, know, and remember forever, the truth that each plant willingly teaches when you learn to hear and speak its unique language of love.

Do not be concerned over how you, in your puny mortal mind, will remember all the Wisdom I teach you. For the only way I teach is by entering into willing oneness with you, and you with me so that all my wisdom is already your wisdom. Your training is only – and vitally – to guide you in finding and loving the relationships of your life, to help you remember again with the truth of why you chose *them for this time in which you live and for the problems you came to discover and heal in your walk of life on earth.*

Look around you, choose a plant that appeals to you, first with your eyes to see its shape and drape and the quality of its colors and the way it catches sunlight and rainwater, what it smells like when you're close and far. When you are surely in love with the plant and honor its gifts and values, only then ask about her seed. When you love and value her seed much as she does, she will gift you with her seed.

As is true with first love, in an abiding way, it is always first and for forever even though you will love another one plant and her seed, and then another. Each love is always first and forever for a plant and its seeds. You will easily and quickly collect the seeds you need for the dragons cache, and don't worry, plants have very *short memories, lots of abundance consciousness, and an excess of love. Each mother will give you the perfect carrying pouch for her finest seed. All you do is ask and receive with gratitude.*

And I did give praise to every seed and root, and to the mother plant that gave it; and gratitude because the third day gift was one I, or any man in his right mind, would receive with humble and effusive gratitude from his sister wife on their marriage day. So it was that the dragon token for the third day of creation was prepared, packaged and given by earth mother herself. When the dragon received and then explored his third day token he was squirmy pleased as a puppy being praised and given treats. When he left as the sun sank sanguine into the sea, I imagined that our acquisitive dragon would spend his time visiting and seeding distant planets with his fabulous mother gift. The tale teller smiles reliving that sunset and imagining the dragon creating and attentively seeding lover's beaches with their scented sensuous scenery and delighting in his humble gratitude to the judiciously generous Earth Mother.

Into the celebrating silence the young dancer softly says with an infectious grin "I saw the dragon seeding those beaches and raising and planting mountains to gather and share life water with the Eden gardens he imagines and makes real." She adds with a shy smile "I spent some time on one dragon beach, and a cabana boy brought me a lounging beach chair and then fruit drinks whenever my glass went empty. I want to spend time on *another* dragon seeded island with maybe the same cabana boy."

"Daughter!" Counselor cautions shocked, "you do understand that your mother and I will go with you do you not?"

"Me too!" Says the elder dancing sister in a rush to gush with her giggling sib, "and I *will* want my own cabana boy."

"Daughter! Counselor reiterates, now to the elder dancer daughter. "*Why* did we have children, RO? Remind me again for I have forgotten and cannot name even one persuasive reason to have…"

"*Don't* say it father." The girls command as one each clapping a hand over his mouth. "You *mustn't* say the words you were thinking, even in exasperation with us for…" she smiles a wise innocent smile "imagining something wholly new and pampering – o-o-o-h, I haven't been pampered properly since I was a *baby*, daddy." She grins wicked, "Besides, you would have to buy the tickets anyway."

Counselor chortles daughter delight and notes "The power of the purse, I still hold that…, for now."

"We *love* your generosity, Dad, we delight in all the ways you please yourself by pleasing us – *after* mother, of course!" They roll their eyes, smiling all the while. "We wouldn't trade you for any other dad." The girls lean down to plant a kiss on each cheek. "Look, he blushes, that is *so* cute." Giggles one, and then the other; thus enticing everyone in the circle to join the fun, including Counselor. Returning to their seats, the dancer prompts, "Day four, tale teller…, hit it."

Grinning, the orator returns to his tale, "On the fourth day of creation God created the greater gold orb and the lesser silver one and placed them in the sky along with all the firmament of stars, and then God divided light from darkness. He did that so he had a place to put the sun and its bright light, and a different space to put the moon whose silver light reflects the sun's spiritual light into the night…, here, where humans abide…, where the ghosts and goblins of our fear come in, or out, to play.

"You see, the great gold orb of the sun is a symbol of spiritual light. Mother moon represents personal human intelligence, the intellect of man that can only reflect the light of the sun, or the son, either word and meaning works here. The pure silver light of the moon most intimately discloses Truth to us mortals in our darkest hour, for only there, can the bright light and truth of Spirit be safely revealed to man.

"The star now, represents the first awakening of man when he apprehends and expresses the wisdom and power of the indwelling Christ Spirit. Just as the morning star heralds the light of the rising sun, so does the star of the mind first reveal the way to the wisdom and glory indwelling the son of man son of God. I got silver a star for mastering that fourth day lesson. It was dropped into my boat when the evening star first appeared, and it would be the dragon token for the fourth day of creation.

That dear daft doofus dragon was by then *so* ornamented with bling things, feathers and trailing plants that he went into a wardrobe tizzy trying to decide where to sport the star token. That goofy lizard was beginning to look *disturbingly* like a boy scout wearing all his merit badges.

"The Dragon returned at sunrise on the fifth day wearing all his tokens (except that batty bird, which I *sincerely* hoped he'd basted and we ate together, but I dare not say so) and when our repast was done he set me to my task for the day, and, as unceremoniously as ever, dropped me with a plop into my wee coracle that promptly spun about and headed for a distant speck of land so tiny I wasn't sure it was land at all, but maybe one of those mirages you see over water, or ghost dancing over land so flat you can see the curvature of the earth.

"Well on the fifth day of creation the Creator made the water teem with living creatures and created birds of every feather to wing and sing the sky and the trees, and to my absolute delight my coracle delivered itself with a soft thump up on a beach and I was washed out by a wave raised by a giant dolphin that caught me before I fell and dove deep with me in its fins, and I breathing water as easy as I breathed air above the waves.

"Meanwhile, I was in utter panic that grew apace with each fathom that whale dove with me until we reached the deep floor of the ocean and it dropped me to walk about with the same ease as walking on land while breathing water, and *not* air. The ocean is a rich fertile place teeming with food of the sea that lives in a circle of life knowing that the one who eats is at one with what is eaten for what is eaten is assimilated and eliminated as the perfect food for *another* thing living in the sea. Assuming I needed a picture, Sea Mother spun her wheel of life reeling a moving picture of all the wondrous ways she lives and thrives by manifesting abundance.

"It probably helps that Sea Mother can just as easily raise hard harsh energies that roil through and above her waters while she clears away a clutter of overly exuberant life forces accosting Earth Mother, and wresting from her what she willingly and must give, freely and of her own accord. Mother knows a man who cannot receive cannot give and is forever destined to take, and in some measure, to take by force and with anger. Guiding man through the polarized dualities of the physical plane and teaching and revealing the symbiotic balance of the Divine Law of polarity is a passion purpose of Sea Mother.

"More than anything Sea Mother wants to teach humans the high heart art – and key – of *receiving* generously from a heart teeming confidence and forever full with delight. She wishes more passionately than anything else, for man to find within himself her own abiding consciousness of abundance and to know beyond doubt that all giving and receiving is meant to be equally sweet and joyful.

"It was Sea Mother who introduced me to the Dragon's token for the fifth day of creation when she dropped me into a deep crab hole where I not only got my toes snapped but also found a hermit crab…, in my hand…, looking up at me with round blue eyes (I didn't know they had blue eyes), like it knew me, like it knew I was the one meant to receive and to deliver its message. *Interesting!*

"Before I could get proud for being a chosen one, the suddenly not-so-retiring crab informed me I was its *delivery boy, not* its messenger. Let me just tell you now…, you cannot out-crab a crab. After a mini infinity with the contrary crustacean I finally got it! *My* job, the bossy hermit told me, the one and *only* thing I was to do, was to take that confounding cross crab to the doubting dubious dragon and give it as my token for the fifth day of creation.

"Faced with no alternatives, I opened a vest pocket invitingly and held it for the retiring one until it tucked itself securely in a corner at the very instant I was whisked up and out of the water, into the coracle and slapped into a seat just as the boat rotated ninety degrees and zipped away toward a wee speck against a pulsating sunset with light rays shot like a great golden fan across the horizon.

"Much to my surprise the dragon was not pleased with my daily token and bellowed full blow at me: *Were am I supposed to put* another *fine ornament on my already exquisitely jewel encrusted, feathered and ornamented body?* The dragon leans down until its eyes are level with mine and hisses: *Did you ever think about me? About how time consuming it is to* deal *with all these gewgaws and gems you bring me every* blessed *day of creation?*

"Well, ladies and gents, you will be proud to know I kept a straight face…, biting the inside of my cheeks bloody so they wouldn't move to betray me. I kept my eyes lowered like I was properly chastised so he wouldn't see my mirth. I was doing fine until my chest began heaving under the force of bubbling bottled laughter and the dragon asked "Are you *cry*ing?" all duly anxious and unsettled. That did it, I giggled, I chortled, I cawed and croaked my glee so he would not see. He did see – and hear.

"He was not amused. Demanded I explain myself, which, in itself, is a *very* demanding role, even for an experienced actor and orator such as myself." He catches and returns grins around the circle, then, with a palm up and shoulders shrug,

"I commenced to tell that dubious dragon precisely what I thought of him and his navel gazing addiction. Intimidated the daunting dragon it did. It *is* unlikely that anyone before ever had the heroic *hutzpah* to take him by the whiskers, look him in the eyes, and demand and hold his gaze and attention. And lived.

"What if…," I snap soft, "you began doing *everything* you did, you beastly beast, with a keen awareness of how it would *and might*, affect others, *including* the trees, and the crops, and the streams, around you before you did it? *One* day they'll call a space formed by a consciousness very much like your own slash and burn habit, ground zero; and survivors will measure it by the number of deaths that occurred there. You, my dragon friend, are *not* here to create a ground zero. You *need* a shift in perspective," I cock my brow and fix him with stern stare, "Like what *if* you just stopped being totally controlling and let the token of the day choose where *it* would like to lodge in your commodious hide and armor?

"Let me tell you what's in it for you, *witless wyvern*. That will help you decide that you really do *want* to let the hermit crab choose its own place to hide. Hermit crabs *like* not being seen. You have no room to display a hermit crab properly." The dragon is dubious so I add the *piece d'resistance*, "They eat fleas."

"Crabs live on sand, what fleas…?"

"Sand fleas." I snap, "Hermit crabs love them. Dragon fleas are probably not *that* much evolved over sand fleas… although you *totally* deserve bigger, hungrier, and meaner fleas than other land animals. Now shut up and watch." I hold the hermit crab on my palm moving it slow and close to the dragon's chest, pausing as it moves to my fingertips. When they are level with the dragon's heart the sand crab jumps off to wiggle and tickle below a dragon scale over its heart, and there it finds a momentary fill of its favorite fulsome fat fleas. The dragon is purring like a kitten and obviously approving his choice to let the shy crab pick and choose the then current location of her Movable Feast.

"I love this crab," the dragon announces, "It's the best gift you have yet chosen and given me.

"What if – you offered that same compassion to yourself? What might change if you could say with equal sincerity that you love yourself? How would those attitude changes show up in your world?

"The dim dragon didn't get it so I shouted at him like a *very* disappointed dragon rider and I might *never* again ride a dim bulb beast that could not stop navel gazing long enough to connect some dots that go *beyond* his navel and his crusty hide. I demanded to know *why* a *real* dragon never applied the power of Imagination, or the gifts and powers of the Divine Feminine to see, share, invite and inspire *her* evolving vision into the Divine Masculine. How *else* do you expect to excite the masculine aspects of you to choose and will to evolve and give birth to *one* beloved and inspired new outcome?

"The light still didn't come on in the dragons loft so I said preacher-teacher like, "It is a simple choice. Would you rather keep on being an uncommitted, know-nothing toothless dragon, or be a dragon who has, and does, choose and serve its rider at the need?"

The dragon blinks a long silent while then says "I never thought of it that way. So how does this work, who teaches who what?

I frown fierce and fiery "We teach each other. And we do it spontaneously and respectfully, or it doesn't happen. You can go back to whatever pit you hole up in…, just *take me home first.*"

The dragon leers a grin "where's home?" Then he frowns, "W*hy* do you want to run away before the sun sets on the last day of creation? It's all the time we have left to learn and master ways to ride the wind as one being in two bodies."

"Home is here the heart is…. If I ask you to be my wing-man, do you know what that means?"

"That I am your eyes, ears, and senses for what you cannot see, that I guide guard and protect you when we go where you cannot safely go without me. Do you know what it means to be a dragon rider?"

"That I am your eyes, ears and senses for what you cannot see, that I go where you cannot go, and that I do for us all the things I can do but you cannot do. And, I do *not* live with you.

"Deal," the dragon slaps his hand on a rock narrowly missing the sand crab, "oh there you are my little hungry one. I didn't mean to scare you like that, I didn't know you'd jumped off me, here let me give you a lift, you tell me where you want to stop and burrow awhile." When the crab has settled in, the dragon yawns and stretches "guess me and the little one will be off for the night. Sleep well, I'll see you at dawn's early light.

"At dawn the dragon returned, and after we ate and chatted, he sidles up to a boulder, settles his great self, and tells me to climb up on the rock. I do that, and I'm standing high enough to step over and onto the dragon's massive shoulders where the wings connect. I do that, and see my boots that are new, with soft leather soles and uppers to my knees. I really hoped the dragon would let me keep those boots…, I'm still wearing my butler shoes. Disappointing. "Where do I step aboard?" I ask the dragon.

"Watch." The dragon replies commencing to raise and lower the elbows of its wings until I see the foot sized hollow spots on either side of its spine. The dragon looks up at me with a full scale smile – *disturbing* – and invites me aboard. I step on and get the feet feel of his muscles as he raises and lowers wings, and rotates his head. Without him telling me to, I drop my hips and ride his moves on my thighs just like a jockey crouching in the saddle to ride balanced over the stride of the beast. The dragon steps away from the rock and I can feel and ride the muscles that move him over land. When that great beast began to raise, lower, tip and tilt its wings like it was flying I whooped a glee giggle; provoking the dragon to run, flapping its wings and he leapt into the air and waggled his cheeks to raise his two black whiskers and slap them into my hands. Soon we were at a comfy cruising speed. At least that is what I believed until the dragon informed me conversationally that a *true* dragon rider would use his feet to let the dragon *feel* what the rider wants to do, where he wants to go, and how high and how fast.

"Oh," I say with a grin and gently heel my right foot into the right wing control panel, leaning right, lifting the right rein and the winged wonder takes to sky and stratosphere. Curving my right shoulder back and up, I suck rarified air into my lungs, let out a whoop of wonder, and in that instant the dragon joins me. I feel the rumble of his laughter through the soles of my boots.

"On the morning of the sixth day I got see my options for the day, and I heart select what turns out to be the precise place the big butt bird shaped a diamond and dropped it into the sea. My feet tell the dragon where I'd go, and when we arrive the beast shrugs me off and I fall headlong into the sea.

"Where a laughing dolphin catches me on its back, turns me a wise eye, and plunges us into the depths below clicking, clattering and chattering me into a calm state of wondrous wonder at the bounty and the teeming beauty of Mother Earth in her role as Water Keeper. I thank Water Keeper for her kindness in letting me breathe liquid air, and for the wise guiding company of her dolphin during my fathom fall through a lavish extravagance of fluid hue, shape, form, and motion.

"The dolphin glides me into a cavern shaped like an open clamshell where, in the distant depths of the grotto, a pearl glows. Except it wasn't a pearl. It was actually an open mouthed clam holding the pearl radiant from core to outer nacre sheen with a luminous brilliance.

"Before that moment my *hand* never wanted a thing but now my palms *ached* to cup that pearl inside them. I raise my eyes from the pearl to the eyes of the clam…, old, wise eyes that spoke to me in feelings and thoughts reading me through and through. *Why this pearl? Why you?* Mother Clam posed and for a time I knew no answer. She knew it too. She swept me up into her eyes so I could see me clear from behind them, from *her* mind. *Disturbing.* And just the disturbance I have needed for forever and a day of my life. I have always thought of myself as not measuring up, not being enough, *always* lacking, always a day late and a dollar short. *That* man I thought I was, had absolutely no *right* nor worth to even want or to dare touch this Pearl of Great Price and know the true value of it. Humbling. It seems the son of man must always follow the path of the Son of man, and must *willingly* meet the death of all he holds dear to create a space where he *can* lose his EGO life, and win free to redeem and regain *true* Life again.

"The man I'd become returned the deep gaze of the Elder Mother clam and asked *what makes the pearl so brilliantly clear and iridescent?*

"A diamond," she sighs, *"that fell into our sea on the second day of creation and I took it up and swallowed it. It didn't suit me…, irritated me cruelly. I did what clams do against irritants; I sheathed it in nacre layer by layer day by day, every day of my long life.*

"Uh – it's the *sixth* day of creation – you ate the diamond no more than four days ago." Her wise eyes are wise to me and do not value what she sees." He winces, "Even the *dolphin* turned away like he never knew me and had nothing at all to do with my being in The Grotto of the Clam Queen.

"That *is* assuming the seven days of creation were 24-hour days." I amend quickly. Her gold eyes are withering and I whimper like a chastised puppy. "Please, continue your tale, I clearly see no less than a *quantum* of layers of luminous nacre on your pearl of great price.

"The clam leers a withering grin, and probes "what will you *pay* to take my pearl?"

"I – I – I – have nothing," I say turning my pockets inside out.

"What makes you believe that *things* can purchase a pearl of great price?" The Mother Clam drifts into Dreamtime where time does not matter nor measure, and I go wait there too. There I intimately and indellibly learn that the true worth and purpose of time lies in *not* putting linear limits on it.

"When I'd served my time and otherwise proved myself worthy of receiving, I told Mother clam that if she chose me, I would receive and deliver the pearl of great price to the dragon. Turns out Mother Clam knew the dragon and spewed the pearl into my hands in her dying exhale. Humbling. I had my sixth day token for the dragon, and all I had to do was get back to that far island where the dragon would meet me at sundown. The cheerfully devoted dolphin chattered a traveling chant, lifted me on its spine, and wave rode me back to my wee lush island to await the dragon and present my sixth day token.

The Tale Teller bows his head in profound silence awhile, "The dragon didn't come at sundown that day. I sat by my small fire in the solitary dark, dispirited, bewildered and bereft. A Dragon Rider with new purpose and drive, but no dragon to ride to its fulfillment. I rage and wail and moan; and in my angry tears I meet my father again yelling telling me I'd never amount to a damn, and that as lily livered as I am, I am no child of his…. And I am small and powerless and alone again with all my inadequacies.

What is *the* function *of a dragon rider without a dragon to ride?* I wail bereft into the eternal still silent empty void of who I think I am, and as I sit abandoned and alone watching puddling stars, they lean close and sing me a song: | **John Adorney: Always Remembering You** |

"As the stars sing and I re-member, I *forget* who I think I am. I plumb forget, and have not a memory thread left. Maybe who I think I am didn't matter anymore, or maybe that all my data points of self were no longer connected to a scenario where I kept on being the person I always was. Whatever the source, I *had* to start living like I want to be and express *I AM*. With stars listening close and playing a healing air, I commence thinking how I'd *like to be*, who I'd *admire* being, and *why* I'd admire being such a man. With no prelude at all, I *am* that man, and I *do* admire him. On the Holy Instant of *getting* that *functionally*, I decide, I will; that if I am being given a chance to re-vision and reinvent who I think I am, I *am taking* it."

"At sunrise on the seventh day a spot crosses the face of the rising sun, and with no data points to apply and nothing else to do, I wait to see what comes of this odd spot on the sun. Soon I see wings of the serpent sweeping emerging from the sun-shadow-spot, riding rising ray waves of light on its trajectory to me on my once again idyllic island.

"At the call of the dragon I respond, but not from my head this time. I leap up on a nearby sunbeam, dance along it awhile, then quick step left to an adjacent ray of dawn and stride confidently from shaft to shaft until I meet the dragon in the heart of the sun on a new day of creation. We were One for the first time all over again." Tale teller smiles a soft glow, "We spoke long and long of feats and deeds and dramas of the sundry paths and detours we see, choose, and walk in each and every One Holy Instant of time. The dragon asks *Who do you think you are?*

"I am breathless as a newborn and remain so until my body is wholly bereft of air. The physical body itself must inhale to live and so it does and I do; over and again. That gives me a kick start of oxygen to ride on, and I *choose* again, wisely and responsibly now. I follow the Code of the Dragon Rider – which I somehow know by heart – to do with faultless faith in the One Source of All Life, everything that comes before me to do *this day*; even those acts and deeds that are *preposterously* beyond my ability. In the authority of that truth I know the answer and I reply with calm confidence. 'I AM a dragon rider. *Your* dragon rider. I came to change the world. I cannot do that without you because without you I cannot return to the world to be *able* to change it. Will you carry me back to the Feed and Grain?

"Sure thing." The dragon agrees, "Seventh day breakfast first. I brought a special treat for you today. You will be so pleased…, it's something you *cannot* live without." The dragon pulls from his mouth a small crystal goblet without a stem that catches and arrays rays from the rising sun. Turning away, he pours liquid into the cup, turns back with a '*Ta-da! Your favorite treat,*' and hands me the crystal chalice.

I smile at the deep red richness of the wine and my gratitude, raise the cup to my lips already pursed for the first sip, and I gag, I retch, I puke, I spew, I hack and cough until my nose spouts like Spindletop before it was capped…, until there is nothing liquid left in me. With seeping red eyes I take a gallant look at the piquant liquid and retch again until I cannot breathe and fall boneless to the sand. There I unleash and release all the tears of my life that I never cried before. I crawl to the surf wanting the puke washed away and there I collapse and heave some more until I am gulping as much sea water as I'm spewing bile. Before I drown the watchful wyvern hooks a claw into the waist of my pants and drags me bodily from the surf to sand still wet with my tears. When I can breathe again, I bawl and blubber over the EGO lies I believed and lived over my span of years. The agony of my sins of omission and commission, my persistent fall from grace, my error thoughts and their outcomes become ghosts of the undead that rise to dance with me, while the dragon watches.

"When I recovered and healed from boogying with my boogeyman bad guys, I lumber up, shake off the sand, and sit to talk with the dragon about the song of the stars and what I'd learned from it. After I confess my sins, the serpent of power gave me the penance of practicing atONEment *with* my *sins,* and informed me that *sin* is an ancient archery term meaning to miss the mark, in this case, Oneness with the Source of my Truth.

"*AtONEment?*" I sputter and the serpent launches into actually, a *rather good* lecture on the evil men do under the influence of accepting as true that they actually did, or ever could, fall from grace and, will never recover. *Grace,* He explains, *is an eternal gift eternally given and forever actuated by the asking. There is no qualification…, not one, of deserving, winning, or earning it. We exist and have our being in grace. Yet we are more truly innocents unaware…, held twisted tight in the hands of an angry god.*

"Did I say this all happened at sunrise on the seventh day?" Several in the circle nod. "Well, the sun tarried a time to watch what follows, and that is that I had to tell the dragon how every one of those mean petty nasty small thoughts came to serve me. "*Serve me?*" I shriek.

"Indeed they do. How?" The beast settles serenely into an easy slouch, lays its head on a paw and commences to wait and watch until I solve his puzzle.

"Well folks, dragons may live forever, but people don't. That is a vital thing to remember when working with a dragon. Particularly one who is possibly a *Sensei* master warrior dragon or an ascended master, with no *concept* of space or time. I set myself to the dragon's task and a trivial eternity later I parse out all the *good* things about everything I once thought was bad about me, my life and the whole world as I knew it. The dragon then set me to the task of making all the things I named bad come out of me and take a form so I could see and talk with them. And they *did* that!

"Real stern like I ask each of my bad actors to tell me exactly how they have served me. The short story is that *every one* of them said they came to protect me from the things *I feared* might, could, would, should, and ever *had* hurt *me.* They came to *protect me* from what I believed was true about me that I had denied and repressed. I ponder the mission for a brief eternity, then I thank my inner actors for their wisdom and their service. For that loyalty, I give each of them their freedom as a parting gift.

"They protest that they do not want to leave because there is nowhere else for them to go, they were formed from *my mind,* my beliefs and my fears.

They are mine. They live in. Always have done. I pretend to consider this new evidence and soon I feel their anxiety, for it is *their* fate of freedom or protective service I'm deciding. I rub my chin and I say *if* I let you stay you must tell me *how* you will serve me in future. They huddle awhile, then ask me if I'm willing to experiment, to try thinking of them like dials and gauges on the dashboard of an auto, which are *not* there to alarm the driver, but to give *alert* to what should be done to keep all things under the hood working silent and smooth."

"Well *done*," the dragon professor approves. Sitting erect now he asks: "Where's my sixth day token?"

"I give the dragon the glowing orb, and this time the besotted beast does not complain about excessive adornment but sets about placing the pearl on various parts on his body, head and paws, and liking *all* of them. With wisdom in my journey kit and no time for a navel gazing dragon, I hop on it back like I always knew how to mount a dragon, and I ride that mythical worm like I always *was* a dragon rider. And *this* darling dragon is, and becomes, part of *my own self*."

In the profound silence that follows the dragon rider tale, the cocoa woman murmurs timidly, "What… was in the crystal cup the dragon gave you to drink?"

Tale teller emits a bilious burp "blood. Human blood." They a share look of horror and without thought, the healing woman eats his pain, tasting the weight and hate of the daily dramas of his history, his story. She knows why, and how, he came to feed off the blood energy of others. Silently she asks to know why and how he came to see himself so needy of what lies outside of him that he blinded himself to the wealth that lies within. He is blinkered. His first semi-sane thought is *I am a dragon rider! And you are dead on to my habit of quick offence and instant defense. Retaliation in small doses,* he scowls tasting the gall of his bitter bile, *administered with a hard heart, fast fingers, and deniability.* He knows she heard, and that nothing changed. Except one…, *the pain is gone…, almost as though she ate it.* "You *did* my pain!" The woman nods a wee wise smile. "Teach me…," he whispers, "I *really* want to do that."

The woman starts back protesting "you didn't ask me to stop, or to know what happens to me when I eat your pain. It's all about you. You have no spare thought for any other being, man nor beast."

He eyes her silently, cocks a brow and replies, "If you taught me to eat pain, I would *gladly* eat your hard habit of thinking of yourself last and projecting that forever-last judgment on to others. *Then* this conversation never happens because you have no pain left. You'd hold only sweet and joyful memories that you tale tell into your own mythic story that only you can tell." He shrugs, "That is my *only* hope when I'm back home fessing up to my Truth Ghosts, while you stay here doing good, right and beautiful things. Yours is a better story to tell, all in all. A wise and aware teller would make her journey and the work she will do here, a mythic tale." He grins a lopsided challenge, "You up for that?"

Her smile is thoughtful and slow as she says "Maybe I *did* teach you to eat pain…, because I have none left. I am free as a bird and high as a kite. It's *all* good!" She eyes him long and asks "What changed?"

Tale teller wells with emotion, sighs, and replies, "It was the star's song, *Always remembering…*, I could *not* feel alone, nor even imagine being separate from anyone or anything while the stars sang. It felt so good, so right, so true, and so very real, that I *chose* to believe that, and on my own will, I changed." Into the silence that follows, Time says, "I'm supposed to give you something…, from the dragon." He places a fist sized pouch in her hand, from which she draws a crystal goblet with no stem. The newly confirmed woman releases the anger reserved for the Great Deceiver that housed in the small hard heart of the man who would be Time. "Thank you," he says softly. You should know that the dragon requires, and I will, go back to recover the family and their possessions, and to return the Rolls Royce."

Across the circle the dancing daughters huddle and whisper, both sets of eyes fixed on the tale teller, "let's go see what's there.…" They nod as one, rise, and walk to bend over the man, who squirms under their focused inspection. "I told you there was something there." "I told *you*," the other replies.

"*What's* there?" he asks covering his nose reflexively until a dancer slaps his hand away.

"It's a star, wee, pale and indistinct – until you remembered again with the saving grace of that sixth night when the star shone, twinkled and glowed like the first star, the leading star, the way shower star. Anyone aware of your star brand will *clearly* know when you fake truth or fiddle with facts or figures. I suspect the star looks like a mole then…, a cancerous one." She gives him a pointed petite pout.

"Or," the elder options, "you can obviate that whole cancer scare thing by deciding to just let go of the script for your mean little self, stop investing your bright mind and light energy in *more* separation; and choose instead to just be and become a better man who is *worthy* of a living a better life. That will mean amending for the rapacious greed that led you to us in this place and time." She grins brightly, "Do apologize to the dragon so he doesn't singe your tail feathers when next he sees you."

The eyes of the slapper sister narrow on his, "think again about telling us the star song and the dire dragon drilling you with questions, and your responses to the wise wyvern…," she grins wryly, "*Think* about the feelings you were having then and everything you were remembering and telling us. See, there it is again. Oh, how sweet! What a *divine* tattoo, and how telling too…, for an *aware* tale teller."

"Oh," Jacob's head pops up, "Until now I forgot to give you Michael's message. He left his master's mark on you, on the place where your bat body first made contact with his upright silver sword, and that by this mark every man with eyes to see will know you and the truth of you." Jacob scratches his chin, "It occurs that the way people *see* and *know* Michael's truth proof might be helpful in producing better outcomes for your life, depending on *you*, and your choices right now. So, tale teller, will Michael's mark be an insignia of you, and who you are, or an ugly abiding warning to be cautious in your company?"

The tale teller masks his nose and mouth below high arched brows, slides his hand slow down his face and chin, remembers the man to whom the stars sang sad and soulful and sure, then turns smiling eyes on Jacob and replies, "Well, sir, I do hope to meet that dragon again…, as friend and master rider, not as piteous penitent; and I've a road ahead to travel that's littered with wrongs to make right; and some rights to be won and celebrated. None of that can be done by the man I was. I'll be choosing to *show* Michael's Mark to best do, and to undo, and all of that and make it better."

Into the still silence that follows a voice calls: "I'll buy the master's slave," Smithy tips his head to where the woman stands, "and then the tale teller can take *that* money to the master too." He turns to Counselor "I reckon you can make the purchase legal?" Counselor nods, "and then, can you prepare her *man-u-mission* document, did I say that right?"

"You did, I can, and I will do all that is needful to make her free as the good Lord meant her to be."

"Well, *former* slaver," Ben peaceably teases, "I can help you with the dragon's requirement that you see your master and his family restored to their home and their life. I've been talking with the local law in Mississippi, they tell me the plantation house and barns weren't burned, some horses already came back, some slaves came back home and keep care of the house, farm and animals. When you go back with the gold and jewels you took and stowed in the boot of the Rolls…, *of course* I looked, it's my *job* - you get to play the returning hero role, *and* get your old job back.

"It is my *personal* wish, and I will take it as a personal favor, that you do everything you can to persuade the master to legally free plantation slaves to leave, or to stay and be paid fairly for their work."

"I'll remember your kindness Sheriff." The tale teller tips back his head and laughs at the curious turns life takes while you imagine you're managing it. "I'll call the master's horses along my way. See I taught them to untie themselves from tie lines, to free themselves from stalls, and to come to my call. Never knew why I did that, but now I feel downright visionary. I take it as my personal mission to win back the family's freedom and to see them safely back home again."

"On that note," Ben informs, "I will give you an escort out of town and set you on your route to Mississippi. I've lined up my mates along the way to keep watch over you, and give you good speed."

"Thank you, sir, that's mighty fine help you give. In return, I will tell your mates along the way all the good news I find, and when I'm home I'll pass the good news to the locals and ask them relay it to you."

"Deal." After they shake on the bargain, Ben asks, "What is the name that dragon gave you?"

"Time Turner. Curious name; and I aim to live up to it."

"Good deal!" Jacob rubs his palms briskly, "As you left on your seven day dragon cruise Smithy's clock chimed two bells." He nods to the clock, "While you were out gallivanting around galaxies, we learned at least a dozen new dance steps, discovered an artist, saw her work, commissioned some of her art glass, *and* Smithy agreed, though not out loud, that the artist could turn his metal forge into a glass kiln. Despite all those *time consuming* pastimes, Smithy's clock *still* says it's two o'clock. The sun still casts a two o'clock shadow, and I, for one, am six o'clock hungry. Would you *kindly* demonstrate for us what a Time Turner might do in an unlikely situation such as this?"

Time studies the unassertive face of Smithy's Big Ben on the wall, shakes his head and says *"that's* not the clock in need of righting." He turns to long-leg across a nearly nearby galaxy to stand before a clock so towering tall it curves back on its spine to admire an infinite celestial blue sky puffed with cotton candy clouds and peppered with plump birds twittering and tweeting. The hands of the cosmic clock show two hours, same as Smithy's Big Ben. *Interesting,* Time thinks, stepping to the cabinet while pulling a key from a pocket. He fits the key in the lock, turns it, hears the click, and watches as the drawer slides open with a whispery whoosh, and out steps a crane. The kind with wings and feathers. *Disturbing!* "What floor please?" the crane asks. "All the way to the top," he replies, but I doesn't know why.

Arriving at the heart of the mechanism he sees that it is broken in shatters and shards, and he does not know why. He asks. The heart of Time responds: "I am Time," she whimpers. "I am infinite, everywhere present, even in the void where *nothing* is, there *I am*. Yet, I am *required by man's* small concept of me to *only* move forward!" Time hisses, "I am nothing but a grandmother who lives too long in her estate while heirs and relatives impatiently wait – or perfidiously plot - her untimely death. I am the temporal equivalent of *white noise!*" Time whines through her chimes. "I am used, scheduled, clocked and *measured…*. But I *will not* be proven! I am *Time!*" she shouts, "I am *eternal, without* boundary, form or dimension; my essence *cannot* be held in thought nor confined within any concept.

"Ideas, now, ideas are formed by the brain firing neurons that have no shape or mass and so have no functional use of time. Ideas turn my key, they transport me, inspire me, give me utility, character, and cause. I can work with that. *But*," she glares, "I – will – *not* – *d*ie!

"Nor will I become man size small! I took a work stoppage instead. It's an idea that will catch on. Until then, *Time is functionally dead*."

"Houston…, we have a problem and it's bigger than eternities of neglected grandmothers. It won't be fixed by a crew of space techs, and while some ascended masters might help, there's nary a one in sight. That's when I remember my dragon rider name and I ask myself, what *would* a Time Turner *do* in a case like this? I imagine such a man might just sweeten the bitter tea Time's prepared for her solitary confinement, so I start talking about all the things I admire about clocks and timepieces, the fine wheels and gears made of copper and other shiny stuff, and how all hers need is a bit of cleaning and a nice calming oil rub; and all the while, I'm doing what I'm telling her about, so when she sighs a smile I ask "*doesn't that* feel better?

"If you take a quick peek inside you'll see how magnificent you look now. Why in no time at all you'll be humming, whirring, and tolling like a brand new clock. Listen to you…, already purring like a contented cat. When I'm done inside, I'll polish your beautiful case and all its fittings until you shine pretty as sunrise over water."

When the clock of Time eternal chimes her next interval, she sings, intones, resonates and rings like a divine diva. Oh, look now, Smithy's clock tick tocks too at two past two.

A Naming Convention

"You got a name, but I didn't…," the cocoa woman praises and pouts in one expression.

"You got a name!" come encouraging words springing on Luke's light feet.

"I did?"

"You did. But it's not a christening name. It's the name of who you *are*, your secret name known only to you and to the One who gave it. Even though you don't remember it, you do know it."

"I do?"

Luke wears an assured smile for his dance around the one who does not know her name. "The dragons you rode spoke your name, do you remember it?" The woman shakes her head solemn slow as he light toes round her. "What are the names the dragons gave you?"

She scowls, squinting, "They told me *their* names…, not mine."

Stopping his dance with a toe slap before her, Luke eyes her down, "*Stop thinking of a name suitable for a christening. Tell me the name of *who you are!* What name tells *anyone* with ears to hear what you came to life to do?" The woman blinks thrice, and Luke enlightens, "Tell us the names of your dragons."

"Fre, and Edom," she scowls.

"Say it as one word," Luke coaches.

"Fre…, Freedom!"

Luke's smile is brilliant, "What did you do on that dragon pair?"

"I rode them."

"So you are…?" She eyes him silent. "Think *role* here," he jabs a finger at her, "*not* baptismal name."

"Freedom… *Rider*?" she measures for fit and beams, "my name is Freedom Rider. I *love* that name!"

"It is a name that will go down in history," foresees Counselor. "Let's make history today. Time, you too have a new name, one you have already proven, one that speaks well of you. Now that we have both names, we have documents to prepare and for you to sign."

"You're going to write these documents with a *pencil*?" Time asks aghast.

"It's a step up from charcoal," Counselor grumbles beneath a scowl. "What would you have me use?"

"You got ink?"

Counselor shrugs "Yes, and Smithy's probably got some, why?"

"Well, sir, if I can talk the owner of the fine geese keeping the sidewalks clean out of a feather, I'll cut and drill a quill pen for you to use preparing those *very* important papers you'll write today."

"No." Snaps RO firmly. "You will not have *one* quill from my birds. You will need at least two. And one for me, of course. Will you trade me a quill pen for three feathers?" Time nods. "Come then, time's a wasting, let's go pick quills, I'll introduce you to my girls." Time's eyes go saucer size as he mouths "*girls?*" then sprints after RO to pull quill.

"I gotta *see* this," Freedom says scurrying to the door, "it could be more fun than a calf scramble and a horse race in one fair." Gleeful voices trail her outside where RO and Time collect quill. When three are chosen they politely ask permission of the bearer birds to have the feather, and RO deftly plucks them from the air as they feather to her, one tucking in one hand, another in the other, the third twining itself in a curl to waft and wave stylishly as she moves.

Time smiles stepping lively with her and asks "the large sturdy goose feather, that's the quill I will cut for Counselor, correct?" RO nods. "The peacock feather would be to make a quill pen for you; am I right?" RO and her feather nod again, both grinning now. "The third feather…; who is that for?"

"Freedom Rider," RO replies. "*Any* great artist needs finer tools than chalk and charcoal, although they have a place among fine art media. She'll need at least one good brush too. Can you also make brushes by chance?" Time nods, and RO smiles "what would you use for brush handles?"

"I saw some bamboo growing in the back yard of big house and if you know the owner, and she agrees, I'll come at the lady's convenience and collect a stalk or two for pen handles."

RO chuckles, clapping Time on the shoulder, "Somehow I imagine you know the bamboo is in *my* back yard…," she grins, "and the lady agrees. Shall we cut it now? It needs time to dry a bit before the bristles are set in. Shouldn't the bristles be sable, do you think?" Time nods. "Good," she grins. My fur has been *years* in need of redesign, and now my dear conservative husband has good reasons to spend the money." Time tips his head back in glad glee as a regaliaed woman guides him safe along his giddy grace.

With ink loaded quill pen in hand, Counselor proudly prepares to prepare identification papers for the ones with new names. *Freedom first*, he thinks, collecting from Smithy the money to purchase a healthy slave, he prepares the ownership transfer to Smithy, then prepares Freedom's manumission document for Smithy to sign. "What a fine pen to work with," Counselor praises.

"And what fine work to do with it." Time Turner, you're next; and you need only identification documents right?"

Time nods, clears his throat, "That's right, sir; but I got to thinking about all the games of chance the master and me both admire; and that some of them have time limits so the keeper calls "time!" and rings a bell. Awkward.

"It *also* occurs to me that the master won't know me as Time Turner and," he grins "he does value and manages his time so well that I know he would *not* admire learning a new name for me.

"I will take the name my master gave me, James Butler." Counselor smiles and sets quill to parchment.

"Well, dang…," Ben grouses. Can we call you Time *while you're here?* We just got *used* to the name."

Time grins, "That would please me well, Sheriff."

The Scrying Bowl

"Well, *energy sucker*, Smithy *said* the forge would operate exactly the same way it does when he's forging metal, it just has to be fired at the right temperature to melt sand soda and ash into a cohesive molten liquid. And, Smithy said the tools used for shaping a crystal bowl would *not* need to be different nor even used differently than for forming a bowl out of metal.

"Why you talking small-self talk to me? Like you're trying to make me feel small and powerless so you can bully and push me around like before. I think you pulled a fast one on that dense dragon pretending you no longer *can* feed off the life force energy of others, all the while swearing off only the blood form of it. Why are you coming at me like my whole internal committee of doubting ghosts trying to scare me out of being strong and whole and powerfully *truly* me? Why you bullying me, new born into a new life, with ghosts of an old life and *your* abiding faith in what I *don't* know and how small and powerless *I am*? Why you feeding off my life energy *this* way acting like you're not getting high on it same as drinking my blood? You pulled a fast one on that dragon but I am *not* fooled. You are an energy *vampire.* Curled up like a pill bug with your hard scaly side out, looking at your butt hole, and telling me it's mine you see."

The former Time titters, chortles, snickers, and admits, "You're right. I spent a lifetime hiding behind the role of butler and doing everything right so I couldn't be corrected…, even when my motive was wrong." He tips a lopsided grin, "and, it's also true, Freedom, that when the Mistress had a broken glass or bowl, she'd ask me to repair it and if it couldn't be fixed, to melt it down and reform the crystal into a new bowl, glass or vase." He looks to RO, "I never did put gemstones into the molten crystal of a thing I formed, and never stroked jewels like wet paint into the design of the bowl…, I want to *see* that done, I want to *help* do that, I want to be part of making that real. And, if you'll allow, I'd also prize having one good peek into your finished bowl to see what I scry. Can I please help make your bowl, can I? I won't stop talking until you say I can help...." RO's silent stare stops him mid breath for he knows she masters greater power than he, she uses her power more compassionately; and, she does not suffer fools.

"I take your point, *Ms.* Rider. It is ROs bowl, her gemstones, her money that pays for making it, it's hers to decide if and how I can help, and if I get paid." He turns to go and pauses, "Thanks for letting me figure that out for myself, Freedom, and for the kindness of not telling me what I *should* do..., like I'd have done." Freedom smiles and waives him away.

"It seems you have had some experience in forming crystal objects and in heating and firing a kiln to the proper temperature to achieve the desired result." RO's voice turns him back, "Perhaps you *can* be of some help – and, there is a condition you will agree to before I accept you as one of my helpers. The condition is this: Freedom is a free and independent woman, trained and gifted with skills you do not have; and she is a woman. *If* you assist in this art I will do with *my* assistants, you will be obedient wholly and solely to the call and to the command of Freedom. Know this: you *will* be required to amend and atone for the persistent and pervasive domination of women by men, the utter submission of self often required by men, and for the physical, mental and emotional abuse inflicted on women by men. Furthermore, you will knowingly and willingly submit to this requirement as personal atonement for the abuse you ruthlessly inflicted on Freedom. You will serve only at her request, you will perform ably, willingly, well, and *always* obedient to her direction..., to the smallest detail. Do I make myself clear?"

"Yes, abundantly clear..., and *that* changes the proposition doesn't it? Freedom could be hard on me and justly so. She might punish me and give me paid for what I have done to her; and righteously so." He studies her and her look of patient observation, feeling her energy of waiting without expectation, just to see what comes next. *Powerful*, he thinks, smiling at who he sees from behind Freedom's clear tolerant eyes. He searches for the word, *indifferent... to outcomes..., but* not *to the process.*

Holding smiling eyes on Freedom, Time inclines his head toward RO, "I freely submit to Freedom's orders for they will come from her heart first, and *then* from her head... where vengeance, and passion for perfection, dwells. I promise you, Mistress RO, that I will do all Freedom asks the way she wants it done and with every best thing I have to give." Time chuckles, "Freedom should have been the one giving orders all the while I knew her. I'd have been a better man for it. But then, perhaps I wouldn't have met the dragon and learned how, *and why*, to consciously co-create a better world. And then" he frowns, "I'd have missed the song of the stars, and the heartbreak of knowing the truth of what kept me separate and mean; and I'd have been less the man I am today."

"Well, that's settled then." RO says, "Smithy, will you turn your forge into a glass kiln heated to properly fire and form crystal while there's still enough daylight to get the job done?"

"Yes, I can, *Mistress* RO," he grins mischief, and gets an arched brow in exchange.

"I will want the help of our resident Crystal Master," RO continues, "and *she* will require support from her assistant, Time, and, Time, please do what is needful to engage the Eternal Mistress of Time so every step in this creative process is completed in order and my bowl is ready to receive pure water before the moon rises this night. Come, Smithy, show the way to your forge and make it *hot, hot, hot.*"

The man once called Time falls in by Freedom and whispers, "she didn't even *ask* if it could be done, or if the Mistress of Time *would* even cooperate."

Freedom rings true delight, "in part that is because you already met and charmed the Mistress of Time, but even more so because RO could always manage time to a tock and a tick. I suspect there is a Magi under that fine regalia she wears, and," she backhands him on a shoulder, "I bet you the Lady RO was a time turner before you even met the Infinite Clock, found the broken Heart of Time, shined, timed and tuned the box and clock and everything in it until the Heart of Time was a thing of beauty and restored her joy in the multitude of ways her theatre of infinite multidimensional time is *mystically magical.*"

Time is mute at the elbow of the wise Master and willingly follows on her path to whatever it is she, as Crystal Master, will do to produce a stunningly magnificent and mystical Scrying Bowl for a woman who *doubtlessly* passed more lifetimes as Magi than as mere mortal.

The next man to tell me it is right and proper for a woman to be meek, and subject herself to her man, I am going to hog-tie him and drag into Smithy's to meet Mistress RO and the Lady Freedom. If a tea time with our pair of mad hatters doesn't set his mind to right, he's not worth spit. Meantime, we got a magical bowl to make and I'm not missing one fleeting infinite moment of the making.

Smithy's forge is a magically enchanted place when the Crystal Master and her helper step out and into a radiant, jubilant and transmuted space emergent with an energy potent in power, transformation and translucent wholeness. Smithy, as Forge Master of mythic fire and power directs by thought and eye, the shape, height, width, color and heat of each tongue of flame licking the caldron red gold in its fiery fervor to *be* a place of regeneration and transformation.

Fire of the Sun, Father Sky, bless and receive this offering prepared for you to thank you for entering into our work to transform common elements of Earth Mother into crystal pure, clear, translucent, true and through with the wholesome passion of your love for Earth Mother.

Earth Mother, mother of wind, water, fire and earth, we bless and thank you for giving of yourself to enable us to transform a vision into a thing of weight, shape, form, function, and great beauty and grace. We thank you for the gift of your vision and for your inspiration of Father Sky to lend us his volcanic heat to make flow that which is fixed in elemental form. Bless us richly, deeply of your graceful eye, and guide our hands as we shape this transparent liquid of you into a crystal bowl of power, beauty and grace.

We thank you already for guiding each of us and your Lady RO in flowing and forming the twelve stones of power into a crystal flower of twelve petals each of different hue. Lady Earth, use us — to create a bowl of far-sight, beauty and power worthy of your own hand and eye. Thank you Mother. I feel you here…. I see you flow slow stir the glass, see the dross ebb away like water into sand, see the crystal clarity of you settling into the infinite indefinite space between water and sky. My heart is full with your grace.

"And my forge never looked, smelled or sounded better. Thanks for that too, from me to you, Lady Mother.

His invocation complete, Smithy steps to the right, extends a hand to Freedom inviting the Crystal Master to step into and be her role in the creation. She gazes into the pot luminous with liquid light in a color with no pigment, yet holding all shades and hues. Inhaling long and being in joy with the moment and those to come, Freedom exhales sub-audibly slower still, and when empty of air, extends a hand to Time to join them at the forge. She smiles at RO facing them to her left across the forge and feels the flow of strength and confidence coming through her. *It is already done,* she thinks, *and it is beautiful.*

Those working the forge act and flow as three minds in one with six hands devoted to one mission and purpose, and one vividly evolving vision of the art of glass. As one they know when the shaping is complete and they step back to gape and smile giddy like parents of a new babe and it the only one.

"Mistress RO," says Time, "if the bowl shape meets your approval, it is ready to receive and embody your twelve stones of power."

"Oh – I don't know if I can do this…, I've never done anything *remotely* like this before, oh…!"

"Mother! *Stop dithering* and just do it. Or you will never have a thing you *always* wanted and now have within your grasp. You're playing small doesn't *become us*! We – and you – are *worthy* of better."

Ellen Rogers: I Am Worthy

RO pulls herself erect, "Thank you, Dear. You're right, of course, how silly of me." Reconsidering, she amends, "How utterly *human* of me. I rather *like* being silly.

"First, my team, Smithy, you are my forge master who has found the perfect heat to shape and form my bowl." She pats his arm, "you will find and hold the temperature of the glass so it's pliable yet firm while we spell gems to feather fluid along the center ridge of each petal. Thank you my dear friend, for being the rock you are for me, and for all of us.

"Freedom, you are my artisan, my art glass master in the making, you will be my other self, outside and apart from who I am and from the role I play in the life of our town. Will you join the energy of your art with Smithy's fiery power and then fuse it with the art of mine as together we do this thing that's never been done before?" Freedom nods her willing will.

"Time, we, Freedom and I, need you to keep the wheel rotating at the precise speed that best support the flow of our work over time…, be at one with us as we meld this act of creation into form." Time nods willingly into the bow of a knight submitting to an oath by sword in support of a higher cause.

"Counselor, dear, you have the pave diamonds?" He nods, pats a vest pocket, and smiles at her artful application of order and process to create the space for new possibilities and outcomes to appear as a virtual firmament within a bowl of crystal painted with the colors of power and light.

The bowl, resplendent with twelve succulent curves of petal each color etched to catch, reflect and reveal the power of each other stone, is then masterfully strewn with spiral galaxies of pave diamonds. When the basin of far-sight is complete, alive, poised atop the placid dais of Smithy's kiln and filled with rainwater, the full moon rises. The moon beams on her refection dancing patterns of pure silver light across the bowl that reveal only sights and scenes evoking soft sighs and smiles from the watchers.

Perhaps most blessed of all, the bowl of truth foretells only mythic futures where even the bad is good and the only outcomes perceived and seen are holy and whole for the sole body of One. The One Master smiles well pleased; and lovingly caresses His Master's Mark into the heart of every one.